Praise for *Along a Storied Trail*

"Gabhart's skillful use of period details and the Appalachian landscape lend plenty of atmosphere to accompany the lessons of hope, compassion, and fortitude amid hardship. This is her best historical inspirational yet."

Publishers Weekly, starred review

"Gabhart crafts an absorbing story that deeply explores the rich tradition of storytelling."

Booklist

"Fabulous! This beautifully written book brings a little-known part of American history to life with characters so real they leap off the pages into readers' hearts and linger there long after the last page is turned. *Along a Storied Trail* is a story to savor, to ponder, and to read again and again."

Amanda Cabot, bestselling author of *Dreams Rekindled*

"Ann Gabhart has woven a tale of a feisty, endearing, and thoroughly memorable character, Tansy Calhoun, as she settles into her route as a WPA packhorse librarian in Depression-era Appalachia. Adventure, a romantic triangle (or two!), plus an unexpected natural disaster roil up, spilling into a dramatic, heart-pounding conclusion. *Along a Storied Trail* might be Gabhart's best book yet."

Suzanne Woods Fisher, author of *The Moonlight School*

"From the very first sentence of *Along a Storied Trail*, Ann H. Gabhart has hand-delivered a tale that will make readers feel right at home. With a voice that is every bit as distinct and special as Gabhart herself, the reader feels as though she's riding along with her new friend Tansy, seeing the beauty of Appalachia even amidst the hard times of the Great Depression, through loss and adversity. This is a story of resilience that is not only representative of the 1930s, but a story of resilience that we so deeply need in our times."

Susie Finkbeiner, author of *The Nature of Small Birds* and *Stories That Bind Us*

Praise for *An Appalachian Summer*

"Gabhart takes readers to the majestic Kentucky mountains during the Great Depression in this enjoyable inspirational romance."

Publishers Weekly

"Another compellingly crafted romance from the pen of Ann H. Gabhart, *An Appalachian Summer* deftly reveals what can happen when a young woman musters the courage to leave behind a restrictive past for a wide-open future of true love."

Midwest Book Reviews

"*An Appalachian Summer* by Ann H. Gabhart is one adventurous historical romance. . . . Ann H. Gabhart knows how to grab my attention and keep me inside the story."

Urban Lit Magazine

when the
MEADOW
BLOOMS

Books by Ann H. Gabhart

Along a Storied Trail
An Appalachian Summer
River to Redemption
These Healing Hills
Words Spoken True
The Outsider
The Believer
The Seeker
The Blessed
The Gifted
Christmas at Harmony Hill
The Innocent
The Refuge

Heart of Hollyhill

Scent of Lilacs
Orchard of Hope
Summer of Joy

Rosey Corner

Angel Sister
Small Town Girl
Love Comes Home

Hidden Springs Mystery as A. H. Gabhart

Murder at the Courthouse
Murder Comes by Mail
Murder Is No Accident

when the MEADOW BLOOMS

ANN H. GABHART

Revell

a division of Baker Publishing Group
Grand Rapids, Michigan

© 2022 by Ann H. Gabhart

Published by Revell
a division of Baker Publishing Group
PO Box 6287, Grand Rapids, MI 49516-6287
www.revellbooks.com

Printed in the United States of America

Library of Congress Cataloging-in-Publication Data
Names: Gabhart, Ann H., 1947– author.
Title: When the meadow blooms / Ann H. Gabhart.
Description: Grand Rapids, MI : Revell, a division of Baker Publishing Group, [2022]
Identifiers: LCCN 2021041429 | ISBN 9780800737221 (paperback) | ISBN 9780800741471 (casebound) | ISBN 9781493436200 (ebook)
Classification: LCC PS3607.A23 W48 2022 | DDC 813/.6—dc23
LC record available at https://lccn.loc.gov/2021041429

Scripture used in this book, whether quoted or paraphrased by the characters, is taken from the King James Version of the Bible.

This book is a work of fiction. Names, characters, places, and incidents are the product of the author's imagination or are used fictitiously. Any resemblance to actual events, locales, or persons, living or dead, is coincidental.

Baker Publishing Group publications use paper produced from sustainable forestry practices and post-consumer waste whenever possible.

22 23 24 25 26 27 28   7 6 5 4 3 2 1

In memory of my father, J. H. Houchin,
who passed along his love of the land to me,
and of my mother, Olga Elizabeth Houchin,
who loved her girls beyond measure.

1

"You will never be completely well. Tuberculosis leaves its mark on your lungs."

"I know, Doctor." Rose Meadows looked at Dr. Bess Halvechs across the desk from her. "But I am so much better. I've been walking about the grounds and manage the stairs to the dining room instead of eating in my room."

"Yes." Dr. Bess's forehead wrinkled in a frown. The doctor was devoted to her patients at Rest Haven Sanitarium and worked tirelessly to help them keep breathing. "You have made progress, Rose. Excellent progress, but as you know from your time here, relapses do occur. Even if that doesn't happen, you will continually struggle with some aspects of the disease."

Rose didn't argue with the truth of the doctor's words, but she didn't have to be cured. She merely had to be well enough to leave the sanitarium and go get her daughters. "I have accepted that, but with care, I can manage."

"With care." The doctor fingered the stethoscope that hung around her neck as though she might get up and come around the desk to check Rose's lungs right then. Dr. Bess was older than Rose, one of the first women to be accepted into a medical school. "Those are the words we must consider. With care. Do you have someone willing to give you that care?"

Rose met the doctor's eyes. "My oldest daughter will be fifteen next month. Old enough to help." Her care wasn't something she wanted to thrust on Calla, but the need to be with her two girls again burned a hole in her heart. She hadn't seen them for almost two years.

"But how will you survive, dear Rose? Do you plan to hire your daughter out to bring in money?"

"Hire her out?" Rose shrank from the thought. She couldn't imagine sending Calla off to a factory job or to be a maid. "No, no. She can help me fashion hats. And there's my husband's army pension."

"A paltry amount, I fear. Not enough for rent and food, and while you can still practice your milliner skills, you won't have the strength to work steadily as you did in the past. Do you have family who might help you?"

"No." Rose's heart sank. "As I told you, my husband died during the influenza epidemic. My parents passed on years ago."

"No sisters or brothers?"

"None living. A sister and brother died at a young age."

"So many troubles in this day." Dr. Bess clucked her tongue. "But, Rose, I cannot in good conscience release you unless you can give me some assurance that you will have a proper place to stay. You can't live on the street or in some hovel where you would be exposed to the damp and not have the proper clean air and sunshine."

"I'm well enough that my girls wouldn't be at risk if I am with them. Isn't that right?"

"Your sputum is negative, but that doesn't mean you aren't prone to a relapse." She paused and studied Rose before she went on. "Stay with us a bit longer. Get stronger for those girls of yours."

"But I think they need me now. I got a letter from Sienna. Something about it didn't sound right."

The letter was only a few lines. *I am fine. My teacher is nice. I get enough to eat. I am learning to listen.* It read like a school assignment, with sentences dictated by the teacher. The only part that seemed truly like Sienna was the tiny sketch of a bird for the dot above the *i* in her name and a drawing of a long-tailed mouse on the bottom of the page.

Sienna had been entranced by anything in nature since her first baby giggle at the sight of a butterfly. But it didn't have to be something pretty to catch her eye. She liked spiders and once picked up a garter snake. When it bit her, she hadn't cried. Instead, she gently put down the snake and apologized for scaring it.

"Sienna is the younger one, right? How old is she?" Dr. Bess asked.

"Nine," Rose said.

Dr. Bess looked sympathetic. "At that age, she surely lacks letter-writing skills, don't you think?" She waited for Rose's nod and then went on. "Has your older daughter written to you about any problems?"

"No, but she might not if she thought it would upset me." Calla's last letter had only been a couple of paragraphs, the words stiff somehow, as though she had nothing good to write. "I just have the feeling something is wrong. Mothers have an innate sense about their children."

"Of course they do. You do." Dr. Bess stood up and came

around the desk to touch Rose's shoulder. "But your children need you well. Not sick. And worry will only make you worse. Your girls are being cared for at the orphanage. They will surely be fine for another month or so."

"It's been so long already." The doctor being right didn't make it any easier to accept.

"I know, but it's best not to rush things. Let's see how you're doing in a few weeks." Dr. Bess patted her shoulder. "Now run along and find a chair outside on the sun porch. Fresh air and sunshine are the best medicine we have."

Rose did as she was told, even though every inch of her screamed to go pack her few belongings to leave. But reality kept poking her, bursting her balloon of hope. She had no car, no house, no way. When she'd left the girls at the Home for Girls, she'd thought it would be for a few weeks, no more than a couple of months, but the months had piled one on top of another.

She hadn't gotten well. She'd gotten worse in spite of the bed rest and hours in the sun. The doctor warned her it would take time, but Rose hadn't expected it to be a slow slog through mud. That was how it had felt. As if each movement was an effort she could barely make. For a while, she thought she wouldn't fight through it, that the mud of tuberculosis in her lungs would swallow her. At one time, she was so worried she'd never see Calla and Sienna again that she wrote them each a final letter about how very much she loved them. The letters were still in the envelopes in her suitcase, ready if the need arose.

But now she was finally better. Still weak. Still with a cough but no streaks of blood in her sputum. Her hands trembled so that piecing together the hats she'd made for some of her fellow patients was a struggle, but she had finished the work.

She lengthened her stride as she went down the corridor toward the door that led out onto the porch. Her breath stayed even, surely a sign she was in remission. She was so pleased she wasn't getting short of breath that she forgot to look away before she caught sight of herself in the mirror at the end of the hall. Why they left it there to mock the patients, or guests as they preferred to call them, she had no idea.

She hated that mirror. In her room a quick peek in the small wall mirror above the washstand was all that was needed to be sure her hair was combed. But this mirror blasted her whole reflection back at her. The first time she'd passed the mirror, she had looked behind her to see whose reflection it might be. As if some strange woman was beside her and her own image wasn't there.

Since then, she always quickly turned away from the mirror, but today she stopped and stared at the frail woman staring back at her. Her cheeks were hollow and dark smudges circled her eyes. Gray streaked her honey-brown hair.

Could she really persuade Dr. Bess that she was ready to leave, ready to care for her daughters?

She sent up a prayer. Could she persuade herself that she was?

2

$\mathcal{S}$ ienna was in trouble again.

"Annie Meadows."

Calla Meadows's heart sank when the head of the orphanage called out her little sister's name. Not Sienna's real name but what those in control had decided to use when Sienna was considered an unfit name. A flower name, Calla's mother said, the same as hers, but not common flowers. Daisy or Lily would have been fine. Even Iris was acceptable, but Sienna and Calla were too different.

The names made them stand out. They needed to fit in at the home. Conform. Sienna was changed to Annie and Calla to Callie. Calla didn't care what they called her. Sienna didn't either. That wasn't why she didn't answer.

"Annie Meadows." Miss Warfield repeated in the tone that was not to be ignored. Her face was so stiff that moving her mouth enough to speak appeared ready to crack her cheeks.

Sienna didn't respond.

Calla looked across at her sister. In the assembly room, the girls lined up by age. Calla, at fourteen, was with the older girls. Sienna, nine, stood with the middle group. She did not appear to hear the name she was expected to answer. Sienna wouldn't be ignoring Miss Warfield on purpose. Instead, her

14

mind had no doubt drifted off. She saw things no one else did. Cracks in the plaster might make her imagine a bird or perhaps an actual bug was climbing the wall. Any creature of nature could capture her full attention.

Sienna was slight, delicately slim. She often neglected to eat in the time allotted for their meals. Her white-blond hair curled around her face, and while Calla wasn't near enough to see, she knew her light blue eyes would be calm as a still pool of water. That was what worried Calla most—that Sienna didn't seem to care whether she was punished or not. She endured whatever they did to her.

She wouldn't even know what she'd done to bring down Miss Warfield's wrath on her. Most probably she had failed to pay attention to her teacher, Miss Agnes. In charge of the middle age group, the woman was not slow to report infractions to the headmistress.

Rules meant nothing to Sienna. Calla felt the same about the rules at Louisville's West Side Home for Girls, but she followed them anyway. It was only for a little while until their mother came back for them. But the little while kept stretching into another week, another month, until now it had been almost two years. Her mother would come back for them. She'd promised and nothing would make her break that promise.

A finger of fear poked Calla's heart. What if the treatment at the sanitarium didn't cure her mother's tuberculosis? Two other girls in her group were at the orphanage because their parents had died from that disease. Calla tamped down that fear. She'd gotten a letter from her mother a week ago. She said she was better. Improving. Not dying.

A little girl in the youngest group began crying. Calla

wanted to wail along with her. Instead, a single tear slid out of her left eye down the side of her cheek. She dared not wipe it away to let anyone see. Miss Warfield had already given Calla a warning look. Not that Calla wouldn't scream and disrupt the whole room if she thought that would shield her little sister from whatever was about to happen. But it wouldn't. She'd tried in the past and ended up making things worse for Sienna.

Miss Gertrude, the one in charge of the older girls, must have noted the tear because she slipped over to Calla's side and touched her arm. Not a warning tap, but a sympathetic one. Miss Gertrude did care about the girls under her care. If only Miss Agnes was as kind.

Miss Gertrude's fingers trembled against Calla's skin. Poor woman seemed every bit as terrified of Miss Warfield as the girls lined up around the room. The headmistress's stare could make anyone's blood run cold.

The woman took a menacing step toward Sienna, which must have pulled her away from her dreamy reverie. When she saw Miss Warfield towering over her, she smiled. Sincerely. But that may have been the worst thing she could have done at that moment.

Color rose on Miss Warfield's neck. A sign every girl in the room knew was reason to beg for mercy. Every girl except Sienna, who continued to smile in the face of the storm descending on her.

"Were you calling me? I fear I forgot to listen as I should." Sienna's voice was musical, as if she might break into song.

The red spread into Miss Warfield's cheeks. Her eyes had to be flashing sparks. The girls standing on either side of Sienna scooted away from her.

"Are you fey, child?" Miss Warfield's voice whipped through the air.

Sienna's smile faded. Then instead of being silent, which was the only response Miss Warfield expected, she said, "Is that the same as tetched in the head?" She didn't seem concerned if it was. Nor did she wait for an answer from the headmistress. "If so, I don't think I am. My mother told me I wasn't and not to pay mind to anyone who said I was."

"Your mother was wrong." Miss Warfield spoke quietly, but that just made her sound more threatening.

The girls around Calla pulled in their breaths even though they were across the room from Miss Warfield. Miss Gertrude tightened her fingers on Calla's arm.

Sienna didn't back away from Miss Warfield. "My mama was not wrong."

The woman held up her hand to stop her from saying more. "Your mother was no doubt glad to be shed of a strange child like you who doesn't listen."

"Fey sounds better than strange." Sienna calmly stared up at Miss Warfield. "Are you going to hit me?" She sounded more curious than afraid.

"Rebellion cannot go unpunished."

Calla jerked away from Miss Gertrude and stepped out of line. She couldn't help it. No matter the cost, she couldn't simply stand there without doing something. She ran across the room.

Miss Warfield didn't look around at the sound of her approach. "You are not to interfere, Callie Meadows. Go back to your place."

Calla didn't obey. "Let me take the punishment for her. She is so small and she didn't intend to not listen. She can't help it." She could almost feel the strap hitting her, but she could bear it.

Miss Warfield turned cold eyes on Calla. "You both seem too eager for the strap. Perhaps a different punishment will be more effective. Some alone time to think."

"No!" Sienna spoke up, her eyes wide as she looked concerned for the first time. "Not the closet. Please not that, Miss Warfield."

Calla shivered at the thought of being closed in the space under one of the stairways in the old building. She had endured that punishment once for speaking out of turn. Darkness unbroken by any light of the moon or candle terrified her. Locked in that small dark space with things one couldn't see had made her ready to claw her way through the door.

"Yes, the punishment closet will be the perfect thing for the two of you." Miss Warfield peered at Calla, and even though Calla tried to hide her dismay, the woman noted it. The corners of her lips lifted a bit. "The isolation will give you both time to consider the necessity of changing your ways."

"How long?" Calla's voice was faint. She was sorry for her words as soon as they sounded in her ears. Asking not only revealed weakness but showed Miss Warfield she had picked the most taxing punishment for Calla. Sienna must feel the same, since she started whimpering like a lost pup.

"As much time as you need to convince your sister to pay mind to the rules while you think on correcting your own willful behavior."

Sienna kept up the pitiful sounds as she started toward the door that led out of the large room to the hallway. But Calla noted no drag to the girl's feet the way her own feet wanted to refuse to move. As if Sienna knew her reluctance, she wrapped her fingers around Calla's and stepped closer to keep their hands hidden in Calla's skirt. Even as she made another sound of misery, a bit of a smile curled her lips now that her back was to Miss Warfield.

Calla had no smile. The evening meal had not yet been served. Hours stretched out before her in the dark closet. She pulled in a breath to calm herself. She wouldn't think of the darkness ready to steal her air. Better to think of how being in the closet with Sienna would give them time together.

She had scant time with her sister without breaking rules, which she had done in the first months they were at the home. After the lights were out at night, she would slip from her bed in the dead of night to find her sister's bed to comfort her. She had never been sure which she feared most—being caught or how the night shadows reached for her.

"Go and be sure the door is locked, Miss Gertrude." Miss Warfield must have noted Miss Gertrude's gesture of sympathy toward Calla and used this duty to chastise her lack of sternness.

Miss Gertrude hated punishing any of the girls, so Calla wasn't surprised to see her eyes filling with tears as she hurried past Calla and Sienna to lead the way.

Miss Gertrude was softly rounded in the middle and lacked inches being as tall as Calla, who had her mother's willowy height. One of the girls told Calla that Miss Gertrude had grown up in the orphanage and never left. The woman had a youthful look and lacked any gray in the brown hair that peeked out around the cap she wore.

At least the girls weren't made to wear head coverings in the home, although Calla's red hair often got disapproving glares from Miss Warfield. She had the freckles to go with her hair, but while they had once worried her tremendously, the red spots decorating her skin didn't bother her at all now. She liked the familiar look of them. Something the same.

"I am sorry," Miss Gertrude whispered as she opened the closet door. "But you really do need to listen, Annie."

"I know, but my mind has a way of straying." Sienna sighed softly. Her whimpering had stopped the minute she was out of ear range of Miss Warfield. Now she patted Miss Gertrude's arm as if she were the one who needed comfort instead of them. "Don't worry. We'll be fine until someone comes to unlock the door."

"But that might not be allowed until morning. You'll have to go without supper."

"We will eat tomorrow." Sienna again sounded ready to sing, and not a song of sadness either.

Calla, on the other hand, stared into the small space in front of them. Once the heavy door was closed, the dark would be complete. Her heart began pounding.

Sienna grasped Calla's hand tighter, stepped into the closet, and pulled Calla after her. "You may close the door, Miss Gertrude."

Calla held her breath to keep from making the same pitiful whimpers Sienna had made earlier. She wanted to jerk away from Sienna, push past Miss Gertrude, and run from the darkness waiting for her. Instead, she forced herself to stand still. There was no escape.

"Wait." Miss Gertrude stepped into the doorway, blocking the view of anyone who might be in the hallway. She pulled two small apples from a skirt pocket and handed them to Calla. "Here."

When Calla started to thank her, Miss Gertrude gave her head a warning shake and lowered her voice until her words were bare whispers in the air. "You must eat it all. If you leave so much as a seed, we will all pay the price."

Then she stepped back quickly, shut the door, and turned the key in the lock. Calla bit her lip to keep from screaming as all went black.

"I like her." Sienna's voice was calm. "Do you think she is an angel?"

Calla tried to answer, but her throat was too tight to let out more than a squeak.

"Oh, dear sister," Sienna said. "Are you scared?"

"You're not?" Calla managed to say.

"No. I like being here with you." She snaked slim arms around Calla. "Feels like a gift to me."

"But it's so dark."

"It's dark every night." Sienna sounded puzzled. "Are you afraid of night?"

"Aren't you?"

"Oh no. I love it when the light fades and night surrounds me. I think about how Mama would sing to me. To us."

"But she sang because she knew we were afraid." Calla tried to swallow down the fear rising in her.

"Afraid? I don't remember being afraid."

"But I was."

Sienna lifted her head away from Calla, and even though Calla couldn't see her, she knew she peered up at her. "Why?"

"Because Papa was gone and we were alone."

Things were bad after her father left for the Great War. Calla was seven, but Sienna at only two wouldn't remember that sad time that got even sadder after Calla's father died

21

of influenza at an army recruitment camp in Massachusetts. Every night Mama held Calla and Sienna close and sang hymns. The sound of her mother's sweet voice singing about the Lord's love helped Calla feel safe as she drifted off to sleep. If only she could hear her mother singing now. Then maybe the dark in this closet wouldn't press in on her from every side to steal her breath.

3

"What a friend we have in Jesus," Sienna sang softly. The words of the hymn whispered through the darkness. That was one of their mother's favorites.

Instead of going on to the next line, Sienna sang the first line over before she said, "Help me, Calla. I can't remember the words."

"All right." Calla pulled in a shaky breath. "But keep your voice low. If Miss Warfield hears us, no telling what she might do."

Calla could hear the smile in Sienna's voice when she answered. "You are right. She would decide to use the strap after all if she knew how happy I am in here with you."

A giggle tripped through the dark to Calla's ears, and in spite of the way her heart pounded in her ears, a smile started as she whisper-sang the next line of the hymn. "All our sins and griefs to bear."

"I know. Let's say fears to bear instead of griefs." Sienna squeezed Calla's hand.

Calla sang the line with the word changed while she imagined throwing those fears up into the air where the Lord would make them disappear like smoke on the wind.

Again Sienna giggled as she hugged Calla. "I love you, Calla. Do you love me even if I did get us in trouble?"

Calla leaned down close to Sienna's ear. "Not trouble. A gift, remember? But even if I did count it trouble, nothing could make me not love you, my sweet little sister. Nothing. And don't you ever forget that."

"Mama said the same when she left us here." Sienna's voice changed. "Do you think we will ever see Mama again? It's been so long, and sometimes at night when I try to see her face before I go to sleep, I can't."

"But you remember how she loved you. Loved us."

"Yes." The stiffness in Sienna's shoulders relaxed. She stepped back from Calla and pulled her deeper into the closet. "We can sit back here. But don't bump your head on the stairs."

"I might trip over something." Calla scooted her feet timidly.

"Nothing in here to trip over except maybe a mouse," Sienna said.

"A mouse?" Calla opened her eyes wide, but all she could see was grainy darkness.

"I keep hoping one will come out of its hole to keep me company. But it never has." Her voice went from sad to hopeful. "Maybe it will tonight." She lifted Calla's hand and pushed it against the wall. "This is the best place to sit."

"How do you know? Have you been in here a lot?"

"Oh yes. I'm always getting sent to the punishment closet. I pretend to hate it so they think it's worse than hitting me, but I really like it. Of course, it would be better if a mouse would come out to see me."

"But you couldn't see it. It's too dark."

"It might crawl up into my hand."

"That would make me shriek."

"Silly Calla. A mouse is too small to hurt you."

"Not if it bites me." Calla touched the wall and scooted down to sit on the floor. She pulled her knees up close to her chest.

"I would tell it not to."

"So you know mouse language?"

"Maybe. I can't be sure until I get to talk to one nose to nose."

"The mouse might bite your nose." Calla reached over in the direction of Sienna's voice to tap her nose. She brushed her eyelashes instead and the giggle came again. Somehow the sound helped Calla bear the dark.

"Can we eat the apples now?" Sienna scooted closer to Calla.

"If you're hungry." Calla handed her one of the apples.

"I'm not that hungry, but it would make me sorry if someone came to let us out before we ate them and Miss Gertrude got into trouble for being kind to us."

"As it would me as well. We have to do as she said and eat every bit. Even the stems and seeds."

"I'll chew up the stem first and save one of the seeds for the mouse if he comes out. But don't worry. I'll swallow the seed if I still have it when they open the door."

The apple, withered since it was a leftover from the fall, still moistened Calla's dry mouth.

"If I swallow the seed whole, will an apple tree grow in my stomach with the branches coming out my nose and ears?"

"Now who's being silly?" Calla laughed.

"Mama used to say being silly was fun." Sienna leaned

her head against Calla's arm. "Do you remember when she taught me to whistle?"

"Yes, then you copied the bird songs."

"Miss Agnes won't let me whistle now." Her sigh whispered through the dark. "Do you know why?"

"They have rules," Calla said.

"So many rules. I can't remember them all. Maybe because I'm fey like Miss Warfield says."

"You're not fey. She just didn't like it because you weren't listening." Calla put her arm around Sienna.

"I was listening. Just not to her."

"What were you hearing?"

"A bird I heard outside the window this morning. It sounded so pretty that I kept its song in my head." Another sigh. "Mama would have let me whistle its song."

"She would," Calla agreed.

"Calla?" Sienna's voice sounded very small.

"Yes?"

"You would never lie to me, would you?"

"No, of course not. Why would you ask me such a thing?" Calla tightened her arm around Sienna.

"Because there's something I need to know."

Sienna felt stiff against her. "What do you need to know?" Calla hoped she would have a good answer for Sienna.

"Is Mama ever coming back?"

"She said she would."

"But it's been so long. Do you think she's too sick to come?"

Calla breathed in and out while she tried to think of what to say. She did believe her mother would come back. If she could. But her father had promised to come back. And he hadn't. "We got a letter. She said she was better," she finally said.

"But she didn't say she was coming."

"No."

Silence wrapped around them for a moment before Sienna asked, "How long have we been here?"

"Only a little while. Why don't you lay your head in my lap and try to sleep?" Calla straightened her legs out to make a place for Sienna.

"I don't mean in this closet. I mean how long have we been here at this place?"

"Oh. We came in April 1923 and now it's February 1925. So almost two years."

"It seems so long."

"Yes." Sometimes it felt like half her life, even though that was far from true.

"I can't stay here forever, the way they say Miss Gertrude has."

"Two years isn't forever."

"It feels like forever." Sienna shifted against Calla as though the floor had suddenly gotten too hard. "Do you ever think about just walking away?" She went on before Calla could say anything. "I do. Every time I pass a door. I could go out it and not listen to anyone telling me to come back. I'm good at not listening."

The thought of her sister alone on the streets of Louisville froze Calla's heart. "Where would you go?"

"I could live in the park where Mama used to take us."

"You couldn't live in the park, Sienna. You wouldn't have anything to eat."

"I don't care." Sienna sounded determined.

"They would find you and make you come back."

"I would hide."

Calla started to say something else, but Sienna put her fingers over Calla's mouth. "You can't talk me out of it. If I die because I don't have anything to eat, I'll go to heaven and see our father. I don't remember him, but in heaven I think I'll know him right away, don't you?"

"Maybe. But you can't leave." Calla searched for the right words. "What if Mama came for us and you were gone? That would make her cry."

Sienna was quiet a moment before she said, "It might."

"Then promise me."

"All right." Sienna blew out a long breath. "I will wait. I do want to see Mama again."

Calla kissed the top of Sienna's head. "You will. We will. I know it."

"How do you know?"

"I've been praying. Mama said the Lord answers prayers." Calla wouldn't think about how her mother had prayed for healing so she wouldn't have to go to the sanitarium and how that prayer wasn't answered.

"I will pray too."

"Good. Now put your head in my lap and try to sleep." When Sienna did as she said, Calla stroked her hair. The light, almost white color was visible in the dark.

"Have you ever seen a meadow, Calla? A real meadow."

"Only in pictures."

"I think about meadows a lot because of our name. In stories the meadows always have flowers and bees and butterflies. I know there would be mice, and birds would fly everywhere."

28

"That sounds beautiful." Calla pictured it in her mind.

"I want to lie down in a meadow like that," Sienna said. "Do you think I can ever do that?"

"Maybe someday." A meadow sounded full of light. "If you go to sleep, you might dream about a meadow in bloom with daisies."

"Oh, I hope so." Sienna was quiet for so long, Calla thought she might be asleep. But then she said, "If the mouse comes out, you have to wake me up. Promise."

"If it tickles my toes, my squeal will wake you."

Sienna patted Calla's leg. "Don't worry. I'm sure he will be a sweet mouse who will wish he was in that meadow with us."

"Hush, little meadow girl, and go to sleep."

Calla leaned back against the wall after Sienna's breath evened out. She kept her eyes shut as she tried to come up with a way for them to leave this Home for Girls even if her mother wasn't well enough to come for them.

If only they had a relative who would take them in.

"Please, Lord. Show me what to do," she whispered. Suddenly a memory popped into her mind of her mother sending a telegram to a man named Dirk Meadows after Calla's father died. Her father's only brother, her mother said.

For weeks, Calla had pestered her mother with questions about this uncle she hadn't known she had until then. Her mother couldn't tell her much. She'd met Dirk Meadows once when Calla's father had taken her to Meadowland, the family farm, to meet his mother. When the poor woman died the next year, Calla's mother never went back to the farm.

"Your father went for her funeral," Mama told her. "But

I was well along carrying you, and such a trip would have been difficult for me and perhaps dangerous for you."

"But didn't Papa want to go back later? After I was born."

"He didn't ever want to go back to Meadowland. He said his brother wanted to be left alone and so did he."

"Why?"

"I can't say for sure. Your father refused to talk about it. Your uncle, poor man, was tragically burned in a fire when he was a young man. Left him with dreadful scars on his face and arm. Perhaps that was why he liked to stay in the shadows away from people. To keep his scars hidden."

"Was he scary to look at?" Calla asked. "Like a monster?"

"No, of course not. He merely had scars like that one on your arm from when you fell against the stove several years ago." Her mother pointed toward Calla's inner wrist. "That scar is small and of little notice, but your uncle's scars cover much of the side of his face and head."

"Oh." Calla had stared at her small diamond-shaped scar and tried to imagine a face covered with something like that.

Calla rubbed the burn scar on her arm now. Perhaps the Lord had put that memory in her mind to answer her prayer. If only she knew how to contact this uncle to see if they could go live with him. Sienna would like being at a place called Meadowland.

Calla leaned her head back against the wall and thought about a flower-filled meadow with butterflies and bees until she finally dozed off.

4

Rose didn't know why she continued to stare at her piteous image in the mirror instead of turning away. No longer was she the bonny woman, barely past girlhood, who had married Frank Meadows. He had been almost as young and so handsome her heart fluttered every time he looked at her.

She blinked and tried to recall that girl so in love and eager to make her husband happy. But her love never seemed to be enough for Frank. He would say it was, but then he would leave her alone to go seek out something more in the city's nightlife. When the baby came along, Rose hoped that would change Frank, but it didn't. He loved Calla. How could he not? But he couldn't bear it when she cried and Rose struggled to quiet her. Colic, the doctor said. The baby's constant crying stoked the anger Frank couldn't seem to shake after he came back from his mother's funeral, claiming his brother had stolen his inheritance. He'd hated his job working on the city roads. He wanted to go west. But she'd gotten with child again.

When she lost that baby and then another, she sank into a dreary, sad place with no energy left to buoy her own spirits, much less his. She trudged through the days, doing what had to be done with no joy. Calla, past the colic, was still prone to tears, and no wonder with a mother struggling with melancholy and a father angry over his lot in life.

But then Miss Wilma from their church had taken Rose and Calla under her wing. Miss Wilma, widowed without the gift of children, treated Rose like a daughter and taught her how to make hats. She baked cookies for Calla and delighted in making the child smile. While they weaved ribbons around hats and chose feathers to decorate them, Miss Wilma would share favorite Scriptures from memory.

Trust in the Lord with all thine heart; and lean not unto thine own understanding. In all thy ways acknowledge him, and he shall direct thy paths.

Those verses from Proverbs took root in Rose's heart and changed her life. She faced the truth there were things she couldn't change and others that she could. Being happier for her child was one she could. Making her husband happier with his life was one she couldn't. He wanted adventure, not stability. So, even after she carried another baby to term, sweet Sienna, he still wasn't ready to settle into family life. Instead he had gone to the army. That imagined adventure sadly hadn't turned out as he expected.

With a sigh, Rose closed her eyes a moment before opening them again. This time she stared into the mirror, not flinching from the truth of the image reflecting back to her. Sickness had aged her, but it hadn't killed her. She wasn't old. Not really. On her birthday in a couple of months, she would turn thirty-four, but that wasn't so many years. She could get stronger. She had to. Her girls needed her. Even more, she needed them.

She turned away from the mirror and went outside to find

her assigned chair on the veranda of the three-story building that had been converted into a sanitarium. The sun was shining, but the February air was cool. Rose wrapped the white blanket around her legs. She looked down the line of chairs with other patients wrapped in the blankets too, like so many cocoons waiting for a transformation. She thought of how lovely it would be to peel back the blankets and seize wings of health, to start a new chapter in her life.

Sunshine and fresh air were considered the best treatment for *lungers*, those suffering from tuberculosis. In the nearly two years she'd been at the sanitarium, she had been chilled more than she'd been warm. Even when inside, winter or summer, the windows were often left open to allow the air to flow through freely. The fresh-air treatment was more pleasurable when the sun was shining, as it was on this day even if it lacked much warmth.

In a few days it would be March fifth, Calla's birthday. She had so hoped to be with her to celebrate the beginning of her fifteenth year, but unless something miraculous happened, that was not to be. She thought ahead to the summer and Sienna's tenth birthday in June. If only she could find a way to be with her girls by then.

Dr. Bess was right. She wouldn't be able to work enough hours as a milliner to keep a roof over their heads and food on the table. Even before she was sick, they were often one hat away from going hungry. The army pension did help, but as Dr. Bess pointed out, it wasn't enough when rent had to be paid. She'd had to give over the pension money to the sanitarium while she was there, so she hadn't been able to save anything for when she could leave the treatment center.

Dr. Bess said the girls were being cared for. Rose supposed

they were. An orphanage might not be the best place to spend a childhood, but the girls had shelter and food. Rose wished that thought made her feel better. Sometimes life gave a person few choices. Then, one had to make the best of whatever happened.

She knew about bucking up and making do. After her parents died, she spent an unhappy year with an aunt before she ran away and found a place as a kitchen maid. Not long after that, she met Frank.

Life with Frank had not always been easy, but she had loved him and been blessed with two beautiful daughters. A sad ending didn't change that.

She was determined to give her girls more than a sad ending. She simply had to find a way to care for them. Find someone willing to help and not fear being near her. Those with rooms to rent would look at her and know she had TB. That could mean doors shut in her face. She'd heard of some lungers going west to live in tent cities where they hoped the warmer sunshine would keep them well.

What a turn that would be after she had been unwilling to go west with Frank. Then, she had worried about the unknown, but perhaps if she had gone with him to whatever future he dreamed for them there, the western sunshine would have kept her from getting sick. Kept Frank from the army and away from the influenza. They might, even now, be living somewhere in California or Arizona with their own house. People wore hats there the same as in Louisville.

But a person couldn't go back in time and change what had already happened. Frank said that was what his brother wanted to do. Dwelling on the past had made him a recluse. That wasn't Frank. He was always searching for something new, something more. Now Frank was gone and she was here in an invalid bed soaking up the afternoon sunshine.

Nobody was in the chair to her left and the woman on the other side appeared to be sleeping. Some of the people on down the row were chatting, but she couldn't tell what they were saying. Their voices were like the sound of birds in distant trees.

She shut her eyes and imagined being in a place with no sick people around her. A place where birds sang as they flew over fields of flowers.

Rose pictured Sienna and Calla running through a field like that. Calla would be picking daisies while Sienna chased butterflies or let a worm crawl across her hand. While they had never lived in a place like that, they had gone to a park near their rooms whenever they could. The park was small, but it was green and brightened up the town's dreariness.

The only time she'd seen an open field of flowers was when Frank had taken her to Meadowland to meet his mother. What a beautiful place. She had walked with Frank down a hill and through flat bottomland to the river that ran along the back of the farm. A flock of bluebirds had lifted out of the grasses and fluttered away. Bees buzzed past her head, but when she swatted at them, Frank laughed and promised the bees were hunting flowers, not her. While Frank fished in the river, she wandered through the fields with each new sight and sound a gift put there by the Lord especially for her.

She'd been startled when she came across Frank's brother, sitting still as stone and staring at a bush. When she met him at the house the day before, he had stayed back in the shadows of the room and then hadn't joined them for dinner. Mrs. Meadows said he was busy writing. Frank said more likely Dirk was hiding out, too self-conscious of his scars to sit with her at the table.

His mother had given Frank a look as a pool of silence settled around them. Rose waded into that silence with compliments about the dinner, especially the homemade bread. She'd been surprised when Mrs. Meadows said Dirk made the bread.

"That's my brother. Baker. Writer. Scientist. Farmer." Frank reached for another slice. "No telling what he could do if he wasn't afraid to be around people."

In the field that afternoon, Dirk had worn a broad-brimmed straw hat, but it didn't hide the burn scars that ravaged one side of his face. She flinched at the sight of them, but fortunately, even though he had to know she was there, Dirk kept staring at whatever he saw in or under the bush.

She narrowed her eyes in an attempt to discover what had him so engrossed, but all she saw were tiny pinkish blooms among the leaves. Surely something more than that held his complete attention. With her voice barely above a whisper, she asked, "What are you looking at?"

When he gave no sign of hearing her, she wondered if she should just back away slowly or wait for him to answer her. She was still frozen with indecision when he finally spoke.

"A mouse. It's gone now." His voice was rough, as though those words might be the first he'd spoken all day. The look he shot her over his shoulder left no doubt he not only blamed her for the mouse's departure but that he also preferred the mouse's company to hers.

"I'm sorry," she said.

"People are always sorry." He stood up and walked away without a backward look.

Somehow, she knew he was no longer talking about a mouse.

When she told Frank about it later, he laughed and told her not to worry. "Poor Dirk. He doesn't know how to be normal anymore. Too ready to think people can't handle the way he looks. So he hides out here at Meadowland. I've never been sure if he wants to disappear or simply hopes everyone else will."

"He surely doesn't want you to disappear from his life. Or your mother."

"Well, not Mother. But me, that might be a different matter."

"Weren't you ever close?" Rose thought of how she often wished the brother and sister she never knew had lived.

"Oh, yes. Dirk was a wonderful big brother. After our father died, he went out of his way to take care of me."

"What happened?"

"The fire. Things were never the same after the fire. And now, if he wants to be left alone, I can do that for him. Respect his wishes. You will have to do the same."

She did as Frank said and avoided Dirk for the rest of their visit. Then, after Mrs. Meadows died, Frank wouldn't even talk about Meadowland or his brother. Said Dirk was stuck in the past and he refused to be the same. They had to live for the future. But now her future was threatened by disease. A step back into the past sounded like the only step left to take.

Dirk Meadows was family, her children's uncle, whether he wanted to be or not. She remembered the farm's address from writing Frank's mother to let her know Calla was on the way. She still had the letter Mrs. Meadows had written back to her safely tucked in her Bible. The woman's joy at the prospect of a grandchild had warmed Rose's heart, but then the next word they received from Meadowland had been about her funeral arrangements. A stroke, Dirk had said in the telegram he sent.

She stared at the blue sky dotted with fluffy white clouds floating past and remembered the porch that wrapped around three sides of the spacious farmhouse. Maples grew in the yard, but sunshine would sneak through somewhere for her to continue the advised treatment. Country sunshine would abound, with summer on the way.

Unless Dirk Meadows had married and had children, the house had plenty of room where she and the girls could be quiet little mice and not disturb him.

She shook her head. While that sounded wonderful, a place at Meadowland was too much to ask of a man she not only scarcely knew, but a man who wanted to be left alone.

Instead, she would do as Dr. Bess suggested and wait a little while as she continued to get stronger. Then she would write to Dirk. Not to beg for a place at Meadowland, but for money to tide them over until she could make a few hats. He would surely give his brother's widow a loan.

5

*M*arch. Calla had always loved March. Not only was it her birthday month, but before the Home for Girls found a way to rub all the joy out of every day no matter the season, March was flowers poking up out of the winter snow to promise spring. Not callas that bloomed later, but crocuses and daffodils.

Calla smiled, remembering how she had once asked her mother why she didn't name her Daffodil. People would know what a daffodil was. Nobody knew what a calla flower looked like.

She didn't herself until her mother found a picture of one in a plant book at the library. Her mother had stroked the picture and said, "I picked Calla for your name as a way to remember my mother, who loved calla lilies. She had bulbs she planted every spring."

"I wish you still had your mother's calla lilies."

"Oh, so do I." Her mother's face looked sad. "But I dug up the bulbs and planted them on her grave."

"Did you ever go see if the callas still grow there?" Calla wanted to imagine them blooming each year.

"Once when you were a baby. You cried the whole way, and

your father was ready to give up on finding the graveyard out in the country where my mother had grown up."

"Poor Papa. He never liked crying, did he?" Calla felt sorry that she had cried so much.

"No, perhaps because he couldn't find a way to make things better." Her mother paused in threading a ribbon through the hat she was making and stared at the wall, as if seeing something there Calla couldn't.

"I don't cry now," Calla said.

"I should say not." Her mother looked back at her. "If you cried, Sienna might cry and then I would cry and things would be awful." Her mother made a face as she rubbed her cheeks as if wiping away tears.

Even though her mother was pretending, Calla knew she sometimes did cry because Calla's father had gone to the war and would never come home again.

"Sienna doesn't cry," Calla said. And she didn't, even though she wasn't quite three. Instead, she studied things with her light blue eyes as if she understood more than Calla did.

"Not much anyway, but I do wish she laughed more." Her mother sounded tired as she went on. "I wish we all laughed more."

Calla wished that too. "But were the calla flowers blooming when we went?"

"No, sweetheart. Calla bulbs have to be dug up every fall and replanted in the spring. But some daffodils grew along the fence beside the graves. They were bright and cheery."

"I might be bright and cheery if you had named me Daffodil."

"You are bright and cheery with your beautiful red curls." Her mother had ruffled Calla's hair. "And it could be you

40

wouldn't have been so happy with that name if everyone started calling you Daffy."

Sienna surprised them by scooting out from under the table to hug Calla's knees as she giggled and said, "Daffy."

Then they all laughed, and their mother grabbed up Sienna in one arm and held Calla's hand as they danced around the room. Calla smiled now, remembering that golden moment. If only their mother could come take them away from this place so they could share more moments like that.

Since their night in the punishment closet, Calla had done her best to stay out of trouble and was relieved each time she caught sight of Sienna in line with the other girls as she was supposed to be. She continually worried Sienna would walk out the door of the Home for Girls and be lost to her forever.

Calla desperately needed a plan for a way to leave here before that happened. She had so hoped remembering about her father's brother had been an answer to her prayer. But she had no idea how to contact him or if he'd come if she did. Her mother had obviously not appealed to him for help before she brought Calla and Sienna to the orphanage. Then again, perhaps she had and he had refused.

Calla pushed that thought away. She wanted to think he would be ready to take them in if he knew how awful this place was. Her mother would surely know his address, but Calla hesitated to write and ask her for fear her mother would forbid her to write to Meadowland at all.

Meadowland. The very name sounded like heaven. Calla had dreamed of meadows every night since the dreadful dark time in the punishment closet. Miss Gertrude had been especially kind to her since then. She even gave Calla an extra cookie on her birthday.

Fifteen. Miss Gertrude had given her a worried look. "Miss Warfield doesn't like to keep girls your age here. Two to thirteen is written in our admission rules. You've already had a year over that."

"I don't have anywhere to go."

"Nor did I when I got to your age. That was why Miss Warfield said I could stay if I found ways to make myself useful."

"And you did."

"I did." Her mouth twisted as though she'd eaten something sour. "But worry not. Miss Warfield doesn't push girls out in the street without some placement. Perhaps as a live-in maid or some other position. You could probably serve as a tutor. You're very bright, but Miss Warfield thinks your red hair might give employers concerns because of the reputation redheads have of being quick-tempered. I don't know why she can't see how you aren't like that at all."

"Is she looking for something for me?" That was a new worry. Instead of Sienna leaving her, she might have to leave Sienna. "I don't want to be separated from Sienna."

Miss Gertrude looked puzzled for a moment before her face brightened. "Oh, you mean Annie." She patted Calla's arm. "Don't worry. Things will work out for the best."

"Did they for you?" Calla had asked.

"Yes, I'm sure," she said, even though she hadn't looked at all sure.

But fifteen was old enough to do something. Calla could offer to clean her uncle's house or work on the farm if he would let them stay there until her mother was well. She prayed every night that somehow she would find out where Meadowland was.

The day after her birthday, Calla caught a cold and was

sneezing and coughing so much that Miss Gertrude told her to go lie down instead of coming to class.

"You'll have us all sick," Miss Gertrude said. "I will inform Miss Warfield. It will be fine." She only had a slight tremble in her voice as she went on. "I'll bring you some soup later. Now go on along with you." Miss Gertrude shooed her toward the door.

"May I take a magazine to look at in case I can't sleep?" They occasionally received old magazines from donors.

"I suppose, but there's no time for you to be dillydallying over which to pick." She reached behind her and grabbed a magazine. She glanced at it as she handed it to Calla. "This one looks boring enough to put you right to sleep. *A Journal of Science*. But there is a pretty lily on the front."

Calla took the magazine, thanked Miss Gertrude, and headed up to lie down. She did feel bad. Her head hurt and her sides were sore from coughing. Calla slipped off her shoes and precisely lined them up under her bed as she was told to do every night. Being alone in the room with the neatly made beds felt odd. Actually, being alone felt odd, as if she were breaking rules and might get caught any moment. Muffled voices rose up to her as the girls marched past the stairs to the dining area.

She was tempted to go peek over the banister for a glimpse of Sienna, but she stayed where she was and imagined Sienna watching and listening as she walked silently along with the other girls. The voices faded, and Calla heard the faint sound of chairs scooted out from the tables and the clatter of forks on plates.

They weren't allowed to talk except in soft whispers while they ate. Rows of girls in plain blue cotton dresses with hair bobbed just below their ears, eating the same food to be ready to move on to the next task like ducks all in a row. Should one get out of line, someone was there to squawk and peck them back into the proper formation. And here she was a lone duck with no one watching to be sure she moved along as she should.

Out of habit, she dropped to her knees beside her bed as she was instructed to do each night to say her prayers before the lights went out. They repeated the Lord's Prayer aloud and then were told to ask for blessings on everyone in the Home for Girls. Calla always added silent prayers for her mother.

She whispered the familiar words that started the Lord's Prayer. "Our Father who art in heaven." She stopped and let the prayer of her heart rise up in her. This time she only mouthed the words and didn't speak them aloud in case someone was listening besides the Lord. He didn't need aloud words, only sincere ones.

Help us, Lord. Show me a way to write to my uncle and let him want to come get us and Mama too. Please. She skipped down in the Lord's Prayer to finish, whispering again. "Lead us not into temptation but deliver us from evil."

She did so want to be delivered from this place and Sienna delivered with her. Not that the home was evil. Miss Warfield was very strict but not evil. Calla could bear life here, but she worried Sienna couldn't. Again she mouthed her prayer silently. *We need a meadow and sunlight. Sienna needs flowers and bugs, birds and love.*

Then she whispered the end of the prayer. "For thine is the kingdom, the power, and the glory, forever and ever. Amen."

Before she stood up, she pulled the box that held her

mother's letters from under the bed. She took out a sheet of paper, a pencil, and an envelope, and then after she sneezed and wiped her nose, she sat on the bed with her back propped against the wall. The magazine against her knees would give her a surface to write on.

She stared at the blank page as words flitted through her mind. *We need you. Please be well. Come get us before we lose Sienna.* Calla sighed. She couldn't write that. Her mother knew they needed her, but if she wasn't well enough, she couldn't come. She might not understand about Sienna, or if she did, she might leave the sanitarium too soon. She might get sicker. She might die because Calla had asked too much.

Calla's heart was beating too fast. Her head hurt. Her throat tightened and she started coughing so hard she had to sit up straighter to hold her side. When at last the coughing fit was through, she collapsed back against the wall again and breathed in and out slowly. The magazine slid from her lap onto the bed and the paper flew off on the floor. She needed to rest a minute before climbing out of the bed to retrieve it. So she picked up the magazine and flipped it open. Maybe more pictures of lilies would be on the pages. Maybe even a calla lily.

Miss Gertrude was right. The articles did look to be the kind to put her to sleep. The one about lilies didn't have a single picture, just long scientific names and advice on where they grew best. If she'd had any lily bulbs to plant and a yard to plant them in, that might have been good. Plus, when she scanned through the flower names, she didn't see the first mention of calla lilies.

She flipped through a few more pages, and there jumping

out at her was the name Dirk Meadows. She blinked, not sure she could believe her eyes. Maybe she was imagining it or dreaming, but no, she traced over the name with her finger. Dirk Meadows.

She read the title of the article out loud. "A Comprehensive Study of Fireflies."

She loved watching lightning bugs in the park in the summertime. She and Sienna ran in circles, not to catch the bugs, but to simply let them light on their hands. To rest a moment, Sienna would say. Then when they took wing again and lit up, she claimed they were wishing she could fly with them.

Calla shook away the memory and let her gaze rest on the words beneath the title. "By Dirk Meadows." There couldn't be more than one Dirk Meadows, could there? And when she was asking all those questions about the uncle she didn't know, hadn't her mother said he studied nature?

She let her eyes race through the writing, skipping over the scientific terms, not knowing what half the words meant, but feeling excited that her uncle had written them. The uncle she wanted to find. She could scarcely believe her eyes when she saw these lines at the end of the article.

Dirk Meadows, an expert on flora and fauna, conducts his extensive research at his Meadowland Farm in Glenville, Kentucky.

Calla got off the bed to retrieve the paper and envelope. Her hands were shaking so much she had to stop and take a deep breath before she sat back down on the bed. She carefully printed *Mr. Dirk Meadows, Meadowland Farm,*

Glenville, Kentucky on the envelope. His name looked a little shaky, but the postman could read it.

She chewed on her pencil as she tried to think what to write to this Dirk Meadows. She considered *Dear Mr. Meadows*, but that sounded so formal. Finally, she settled on *Dear Uncle Dirk*. That seemed right. He was her uncle even if they had never met.

After that, she wrote swiftly, worried that Miss Gertrude would remember to bring her soup and insist on seeing what she was writing. Calla let the words spill out about how they needed rescuing. She put in about her mother being better too. Calla did hope that was still true.

Will you please come get us? She added another "please" and underlined it, then promised to help him on the farm or clean his house.

She stared at her words a moment before adding two more lines.

We will be very quiet and not do anything to disturb you. And please, if my mother can leave the sanitarium, can she come sit in the sun at Meadowland?

She signed her full name, Calla Harte Meadows. After she folded the letter and tucked it into the envelope, she laid her hand on it and silently prayed. *Dear Lord. You made Miss Gertrude hand me this magazine. Please let this letter get to my uncle. Amen.*

She got one of the stamps her mother had sent in her last letter so that Calla could write to her. Calla licked it and stuck it to the envelope. Then because she wasn't sure whether Miss Warfield would allow her to send a letter to her uncle, she put her shoes on, straightened the bedcovers, and tiptoed downstairs through the front hall while all the girls and teachers were in classes. She moved as silently as possible to the front door and hoped it wouldn't be locked or make any noise as she pulled it open to slip outside. A metal mailbox sat on the corner a block from the home. She'd seen it from the upstairs windows.

But the Lord wasn't through blessing her. The mailman was coming up the walkway right to their door.

He smiled when he saw the letter in her hand. "Looks as though I'm right on time." His smile got bigger as he raised his eyebrows at her. "Writing your fellow, maybe, and don't want them in charge to see the hearts you drew on it?"

She blushed. "No, my uncle. Hard to have a fellow living here."

His smile faded as he looked at the brick building. "I guess so. But love can conquer some mighty obstacles." His smile came back as he took her letter and tucked it in his mailbag. "You better get back inside before you're missed, hadn't you? Wouldn't want you to get in trouble sending out a letter to your uncle." He winked at her to show he still thought she was slipping a letter to a boyfriend that would get her in trouble with Miss Warfield.

He might be right about getting in trouble, even if not for the reason he thought. She was very glad the letter was safely in his mailbag. Now she simply had to keep praying it would find its way to Meadowland. And that she wouldn't get caught when she went back inside.

The mailman helped with that too, sharply rapping the door knocker against the plate at the very same time that Calla opened the door enough to slide through, closing it behind her. Her breath caught when she heard Miss Warfield's determined steps on the tiled floor coming toward the front. Calla did her best to make no noise at all as she turned down a different hallway at the last possible second to keep from being seen.

Behind her, she heard the door open again and the mailman started whistling a tune.

"You appear to be very happy this day, Mr. Roberts," Miss Warfield said.

"Oh yes, ma'am. The sun is shining, and I think love is in the air."

She made a dismissive sound. "We don't need any of that nonsense around here."

"I guess not." His voice was still cheerful. "Here's your mail and a good day to you and your girls."

Calla heard the door close as she tiptoed up the staircase back to the sleeping room. Her heart was banging around in her chest. She had no idea what Miss Warfield would have done if she'd caught her outside. But the mailman had saved her.

"Thank you, Mr. Roberts," she whispered.

Once more sitting on her bed, she picked up the magazine and read every word her uncle had written about fireflies over again, even the long scientific words. If the Lord could send a mailman to help her, then maybe he would also put it in her uncle's heart to help them.

6

*D*irk Meadows never knew what he might find when he made the walk down his long lane to the mailbox. Maybe a magazine with one of his articles in it. Maybe a check for those articles or a request for something new. Sometimes even a letter from someone who had read what he wrote and had more questions to ask. A few times an embarrassing note from some misguided woman who thought he needed a wife.

That was the last thing he needed or wanted. He liked the silence of his solitary life. But then, it wasn't really silent. All around him were the sounds of nature that showed spring awakening at Meadowland. A cardinal sang a courting song in the tree by the lane. A bee circled his head, mistaking his hair tonic for a flower.

He didn't know why he bothered with tamping down his remaining wiry red curls. He couldn't do anything to make his appearance better. No hair grew on the scarred left side of his head above what was barely recognizable as an ear. It looked hideous, but he could still hear. That was what he had learned to dwell on. What still worked. He could breathe. He could talk in spite of the way the corner of his mouth was twisted down by the ridged, scarred skin of his cheek.

Except on his face, his scars could be hidden with long sleeves and a high collar. He had even learned ways to lessen the impact of his face on others by wearing floppy-brimmed hats and keeping the scarred side of his face turned to the shadows. But things were easier here on his farm where it didn't matter how he looked, because no one but his dog saw him. Maisy didn't care about his scars. She was happy as long as he scratched her behind the ears now and again.

With her ancestry mix of shepherd, hound, and who knew what else, the dog lacked some being a showstopper as well. Her yellow fur was dotted with darker spots that could be mistaken for mud but weren't. Maisy didn't like mud and tiptoed through unavoidable puddles with obvious disdain. Then she would sit down and clean her paws like a cat. Sometimes he wondered if her DNA had gotten mixed with a feline in some weird, impossible way.

But how she looked didn't matter any more than how he did. She was loyal and knew to stay still whenever he gave her the sign while he studied this or that bird or animal. That surely went against all her canine instincts, but she wasn't completely lost to dog ways. She did like digging up moles to deposit at his feet. He'd watched her in action, stalking up to the mole tunnel, her head flicking first one way and then another to listen before pouncing all in one motion to come up victoriously with a very surprised mole.

He supposed he could have made her not dig up the moles, but while most creatures got his full sympathy, the moles did have a way of burrowing in the most inconvenient places. So Maisy was free to be a dog on the hunt.

Nature could be harsh. Rabbits ended up food for foxes and hawks. Spiders wove beautiful webs to capture insects.

Birds pulled worms out of the ground. Cats caught mice for their supper, and every creature had to worry about man. Including his fellow man. Or woman.

He didn't push away his wandering thoughts soon enough. Anneliese bloomed in his mind like a spring flower. This time of year, her memory continually played through his mind, because spring was when they had made forever promises to one another and planned to marry in the summer. Anneliese wanted to wait for the meadow to bloom. She loved the daisies and Queen Anne's lace and said they had no need of a church building. Only a preacher.

But spring was also when their promises and plans went up in flames. When he lost his Anneliese. If he only knew why or, even more, where she went.

Dirk pulled in a deep breath and let it out slowly. It had been too many years. Over twenty now. No need dwelling on what couldn't be known or understood. Better to think on the day now, with the March sunshine on his shoulders, his good dog beside him, and something awaiting him in the mailbox.

He'd seen the mailman stop and heard the tin mailbox lid clanking closed while he was out in the front field turning over rocks to find some beetles. A man had to admire the staying power of the beetle. So after he studied those he disturbed from their hiding places, he headed for the road to check the mail. Even if it was no more than an advertisement, the walk did him good. The sameness of it was a pleasure. Every day except Sunday at four o'clock, a walk to the mailbox. He thrived on routine.

Nature had routine. Seasons followed one after another. A man could know the precise time the sun would rise and set. The moon went through the same phases month after month. Birds built nests, hatched eggs, and then fed their nestlings when the spring sun warmed the earth.

Not that storms didn't upset the routine at times, or then, perhaps the storms were part of nature's routine as well. A way to keep man from becoming too complacent and expecting nothing but sunshine and gentle showers. Still, even with storms, a man could trust nature to stick to ways that went back through time. The preacher wrote that truth in Ecclesiastes. *A time to plant and a time to pluck up what is planted. A time to love. A time to hate.*

He'd had that time to love and had conquered the time to hate, although bitterness had lived in his heart long after the fire. He might have died in the fire if not for Frank, who had braved the flames and smoke to pull him out. Frank had been so young then. Fourteen.

Dirk supposed he'd been young too. Only twenty-one. Too young to die. He'd heard his mother plead that with the Lord while he wandered in a dark haze of pain only partly relieved by the doctor's tonics. The man's words pierced his consciousness too, although the doctor clearly thought they wouldn't as he tried to prepare Dirk's mother for what he thought inevitable.

For in truth, no one was ever too young to die. Babies died without a chance to smile. Fevers took youngsters who, the week before, ran and played. And death could take a young man on the brink of happiness with his one love.

He might have given in to the pain, turned to the comfort of the hereafter, if not for the hope that had flowered in his heart when those who came to help Frank rake away the debris of the barn found no sign that Anneliese perished in the flames. Her body could not have been completely consumed by the fire. That meant she still lived and she would come back to him, no matter what her father wanted of her.

But weeks passed, then months that added up into years. Someone had surely told her how the fire damaged him, turned him into a sideshow freak with a drooping eyelid and twisted lips and no hair to hide his damaged ear. Perhaps her brother.

Dirk had cornered Jerome alone in his field once to make him tell where Anneliese had gone. Dirk couldn't go to their house. Not then. Anneliese's father had threatened to shoot him once. He had no doubt he'd carry out the threat if Dirk confronted him again. A long-standing disagreement over a piece of land.

But Jerome had always been civil enough if they happened to meet in town. That day out in the field, he had looked uneasy. People often were when they saw Dirk after the fire. The sight of his damaged face caused them to shrink away from him. Dirk caught Jerome's arm. Didn't let him run away. Made him listen.

Jerome had no good answers to Dirk's questions. He kept his eyes turned to the ground or the sky and said Anneliese had gone away. He didn't know where, but he was sure she would never return. Not even to see their mother.

Gone away. Deserted him.

Now Dirk rubbed his fingers over the rough ridges on his face.

He couldn't blame her. For a long time after the fire, he'd had to summon up courage to look at his reflection in a mirror. The sight of his scarred face made him flinch. He'd once been handsome enough. Not as dashing as Frank, but no one ever doubted they were brothers in spite of how differing in personality they were. Frank's smile had ever been easy on his face. He was always ready for fun, for something different. He had no patience for farmwork. He continually wanted a fast return for any labor instead of a harvest that took a season of planting and tilling.

More than once, Dirk had taken care of Frank's gambling debts. After all, he owed Frank his life. But perhaps he had done his brother no favors by making life easier for him. Dirk had hoped and prayed that marriage and children would settle Frank into a steadier life. Perhaps it had. Dirk wouldn't know. He never saw his brother again after their mother died.

Another hard memory that he needed to turn from. His brother was dead. Buried out in the graveyard on the hill beside their mother and father and the little sister who never drew breath, born in the years between him and Frank.

Dirk shook his head. This day of sunshine shouldn't be wasted on dark thoughts and memories. Maisy, sensing his mood, whined and licked his hand as they reached the gate.

"Good girl, Maisy." Dirk ruffled the dog's ears, then slipped the fastening chain off the nail on the post and pulled the gate open. "Let's see if the mail brought us some wherewithal to buy provisions. One of those new cameras would be a fine thing if surprises are found in the box, don't you think?"

The thing about Maisy was that she listened as though his every word was not only true but important as well. He smiled as he pulled out the bundle of mail and stepped back through the gate before he fingered through it. He didn't want anyone to pass on the road while he searched through his mail as though looking for a love letter.

He'd given up on getting that letter years ago, or so he told himself. Still, his heart nearly always clunked around a little differently in his chest each time he got mail. As if, even now, he might still hear from Anneliese.

Two magazines were in the bunch. One with an article of his inside and the other a scientific journal he would read later by lamplight. Towns had wires strung everywhere to bring electricity to the houses, but who knew when the lines would make it this far out in the country. Not that he cared. He glanced out at his fields. Poles with strung wire would spoil the view across his land.

Lamplight wasn't so bad. He didn't need modern innovations.

An advertisement for the sale of farm supplies. Another thing to peruse later. Four envelopes. He shuffled through them as he made his way back toward his house. Two from magazines, so perhaps a check for that camera or needed farm supplies. Not that he farmed all that much. Only a few cows. Some chickens for eggs. A garden and a field of corn.

He didn't need to farm to keep things going. His articles managed that easily, with some to save away for a time when readers might not want to know about the world of nature here on his farm or his hand got too shaky to write.

His name written on the third envelope did look as though a trembling hand had penned it. In spite of himself, his heart gave a lurch. It wasn't Anneliese. He well remembered her script, but could she have had a daughter and told her of Meadowland? He shook away the foolish thought. She would have no reason to share their secret history with any new family she had found. No doubt some schoolgirl requesting information for a biology paper.

Still, his fingers trembled as he moved that envelope aside to look at the last one. No mystery here. His name was written in bold feminine strokes and the sender's name and address notated on the upper left corner of the envelope. *Mrs. Frank Meadows, Rest Haven Sanitarium, Maryville, Kentucky.*

Sanitarium. Guilt shot through him. He should have kept in touch with her after Frank died. Before Frank died, as far as that went. Their one contact since she had visited Meadowland after marrying Frank had been the telegram informing him of Frank's death. In the army. What had the man meant? To leave his family for the army when his age and the fact that he had two children would have exempted him from service. But that was Frank. Always ready to take chances and gamble away his future.

Now Frank's wife was sick and obviously in need if she was writing to him after all these years. How many years had that been now? Seven. He had given little thought to Frank's family since he had heard nothing from her after he collected Frank's body and brought him home to be buried at Meadowland.

He had not even considered arranging for her and her daughters to come to the burial service. Later, when he read her oddly impersonal note of thanks, he did wonder if that upset her. Her words had been the sort one might write to a stranger, but then Dirk supposed that was what they were after only one meeting. Now she must need some sort of assistance. Monetary, no doubt. He could think of no other reason for her letter. He thought of his savings and how much he could spare to send her way.

But he didn't have to wonder what might be in the letter. He used to be amused when his mother did a guessing game about any letter she received instead of simply opening it to see what was written to her. Here he was doing the same.

All at once, a memory flooded back of his mother's happiness when she'd received a letter from Frank's wife telling her about the baby on the way. Then a stroke had felled his mother to cheat her of the chance to ever see that grandchild or even hear of the child's birth.

Frank had not bothered to let him know the child had been born. They had not parted on good terms after their mother's death. Frank had wanted him to sell Meadowland. Said he had debts that needed to be paid. But their mother must have known Frank better than Dirk thought. She had left the family farm to Dirk and an inheritance from her father that had been untouched in the bank for years to Frank. Not untouched for long then, as Frank cleaned out the account before he left town. Dirk wanted to believe he would use it to make a better home for his wife and the baby on the way, but he heard later Frank had gone from Meadowland to a racetrack.

Dirk had no way of knowing, but he doubted Frank made it home with more than change in his pocket. What made one brother too responsible and the other not responsible enough? Frank, as the youngest and the one who comforted his mother's heart after the loss of her baby girl, was ever able to smile and cajole his way out of trouble. Even more so after their father died.

His mother never stopped loving Dirk—he knew that was true—but his scars had injured her almost as much as they did him. His emotional scars might have separated them even more. He was relieved but surprised she left Meadowland to him. Here he could live without continually shrinking from the pitying stares of others.

At the house, he steeped a cup of tea while Frank's wife's letter seemed to glare at him. He had thought she might have remarried by now. Hoped she would. She had been a lovely young woman. But her name on the envelope showed that was not true. Whatever she asked he would have to give if he had it in his means.

With a sigh, he slit open the envelope and pulled out the letter.

Dear Mr. Meadows,

That greeting showed their division. No family feeling there. Were she to be sitting across the table from him, he might call her Mrs. Meadows. He read on.

I hope this finds you well. As you may deduce from my return address, I have not been well. For almost two years I have been treated here at the Rest Haven Sanitarium. My doctor said it might be my only recourse if I cared to live long enough to see my children to adulthood. You may remember I was with child when your mother died. Calla just turned fifteen. A second daughter, Sienna Rose, will be ten this summer.

If you haven't married to have children of your own, you may not understand my dreadful sorrow at being separated from my girls. But I had no choice but to take them to an orphanage before I entered the sanitarium.

No choice? Had she not remembered he was family? But no, this wasn't her fault. It was his for not keeping in touch with her after Frank's death. Guilt gathered in his heart as he thought about Frank's girls abandoned to an orphanage. He pulled in a long breath and began reading again. She had yet to say why she was writing him after so many years.

At the time I thought it would be for a few weeks and no more than a few months, but tuberculosis is a hard taskmaster. Although still weak, I have finally recovered enough to leave the sanitarium. My doctor doubts I will be able to make enough hats as I did after Frank's death to house and feed my daughters.

I know I have no claim on you or reason to expect help, but I am desperate to see my girls and rescue them from the orphanage. Perhaps rescue is not the right word, but it is the one my heart feels when I read the letters they write to me. If you could find it in your heart to loan me enough to pay a room's rent for a few months, I am sure I will regain more strength. As much as I hate the thought of it, Calla is old enough to find a position somewhere to be able to help as well.

I prayed for an answer and the Lord put your name in my thoughts. However, I do understand if you cannot help, but I would appreciate a response to let me know. If you say no, which is your right, I need to explore other options.

Your sister by marriage,
Rose

What did the woman expect of him? Sick with tuberculosis. Even if he sent her money, she might find no one willing to rent her a room if they knew of her illness. He remembered the pretty young woman who had visited Meadowland those years ago. She had done her best not to stare at his scars, but he sensed her aversion. Now she might carry different sorts of scars that would reveal her plight. Those with tuberculosis sometimes simply wasted away, pale and listless.

But not every person died of the disease. Some found healing at the sanitariums with their sunshine and fresh-air treatments. The late afternoon sun slid through his window to light up the letter he had dropped back on the table. He had sunshine and fresh air. But she hadn't asked to come to Meadowland.

He sipped his tea, cool now, and stared down at the other letters. Maisy pushed her nose against his thigh and whined. She knew when it was eating time. He filled her bowl with scraps and sat back down to go through the rest of his mail.

He didn't have to answer the woman's letter right away. He needed time to think about what was best. Money would be easy to send. He should have made sure she had resources already. Perhaps he could even go and rent the rooms for her. Her daughter at fifteen would be old enough to care for her if such was needed. With the proper precautions the girl could surely avoid contracting the disease. He certainly had no desire to be exposed himself.

He leafed through the magazine to find his article about bees. He scanned it quickly. They hadn't changed anything. That was always a relief, since some magazines cut out the most important parts of what he wrote to make his piece fit into their available space. He put down the journal and opened the envelope with the check. A goodly amount. He could set it all aside for Frank's widow.

Last, he picked up the envelope with girlish writing. He no longer had any illusions it had anything to do with Anneliese. That was foolish thinking. This would be a young schoolgirl with a dozen questions. With a sigh, he slit open the envelope, prepared to spend entirely too much time writing out answers the girl could have found for herself by looking in an encyclopedia. He kept asking the magazines not to put information about him with his articles, but they continued to do so without compunction.

Dear Uncle Dirk,

Uncle? His eyes flew to the bottom of the letter.

> *Sincerely,*
> *Your niece,*
> *Calla Harte Meadows*

The girl's entire name. Frank's daughter. Had she and her mother intended the letters to arrive in his mailbox in concert? But that would be difficult to plan, even if they had been together, instead of the mother at a sanitarium and the girl at an orphanage. Mail delivery here in the country was often unreliable.

He let his gaze go back to the beginning of the letter.

Dear Uncle Dirk,
    We have never met, but my mother told me about you when you took my father to be buried at Meadowland. She said you wanted to be left alone. So she told

me I couldn't write to you then. I think she would tell me the same now, but I am desperate.

You see, my mother is in a sanitarium. She has tuberculosis, and since we had no place to go while she got treatment, we are in an orphanage, the West Side Home for Girls in Louisville. She hoped to come back for us right away, but almost two years have passed since then. My sister, Sienna, and I have been fed and sheltered here, but it is not a happy place. I adjusted to the situation and could stay on without complaint, but now that I am fifteen, they will soon turn me out to find my own way. I dread having to leave my sister behind. Sienna is only nine and has always been something of a dreamer. Because of that, she often is punished severely for forgetting to follow the home's rules.

I must hurry to finish this before my teacher finds me writing to you, but it is my hope that you will see our desperate need. I cannot bear the thought of being separated completely from Sienna. And she speaks of running away and living in the park. As I said, she is a dreamer and lacks knowledge of the world. But if you could find it in your heart to rescue us, we would only need a small space. I could clean and cook for you or work on the farm. We would take care not to disturb your peace.

I have been praying for a way to help Sienna, and my teacher randomly handed me a magazine with your article about fireflies. There was your address, or at least enough of your address that I hope you receive this letter. Meadowland sounds like heaven to me, and I

dream at night about Sienna running through meadows
of daisies and butterflies.
   I pray to hear from you soon.

> *Sincerely,*
> *Your niece,*
> *Calla Harte Meadows*

He stared at the letter, not seeing the words now, but imagining the girl. Places in the writing were smudged as if tears might have fallen on it before she folded it to place in the envelope. He had to wonder how she posted it without the help of those in charge at the orphanage. Was the shaky writing of his name on the envelope because of her hurry or her fear of being caught writing to him?

He stared out the window toward the pleasant field in front of his house. His quiet, peaceful house. The silence gathered around him only broken by Maisy's breathing as she slept at his feet. He didn't need a cook or a housekeeper. He liked his solitary life.

But "punished severely." What did that mean? Spare the rod. Spoil the child. But what could a little girl, a little dreamer of a girl, do that was so bad? He blew out a slow breath and read through both letters again.

The mother and the daughter had both mentioned the need for the girls to be rescued. They had prayed and he had been their answer. The one who might rescue this child, Sienna. And in spite of his reluctance, he, too, could see the child running through a meadow. His meadow.

7

*D*irk started to write to his niece and her mother a dozen times, but he couldn't seem to get past the Dear Calla or Dear Mrs. Meadows. It wasn't that he didn't want to help Frank's family. He did. He simply couldn't decide the best way to do so.

Each time he sat down to write an answer, he would stare at the blank paper with no idea of what to promise. Then he would abandon the letter writing and wander through his house. He had rooms enough. He didn't need much other than a bed, a place for his writing desk and books, and use of the kitchen. Most of what he needed was outdoors.

His mother's bedroom was the same as the day she died. Her clothes were in the wardrobe. Her brooches and necklaces spilled out of a jewelry box on the dresser as if she'd just chosen the one to wear for the day. He should have packed up her clothes and given them away years ago, but it was easier to keep the door closed and leave it for later.

Upstairs, the door to Frank's boyhood room stayed closed as well. It, at least, had long ago been stripped of memories. Nothing there now but the bed and an old dresser with empty drawers. The bed didn't even have a counterpane or sheets.

Just a black-and-gray-striped ticked featherbed and pillows his mother had probably made before Dirk was born.

Even Dirk's once upon a time bedroom beside Frank's was unused except for storing some boxes of magazines and books. After his mother died, Dirk had moved his bed and desk down to the glassed-in porch beside the kitchen. He needed extra blankets in the winter, but a few shivers were a small price to pay for waking to sunlight, rain, or snow every morning. Outside his windows, the tree limbs danced in the wind and the birds sang in season. He knew before he got out of bed what the day would be like. And at night he could see the stars.

He couldn't deny that he had the rooms necessary to house Frank's family, but inviting three females into his home would upend his life at Meadowland. Besides, the woman, Frank's widow, hadn't asked him to take them in. She might not even want to come to Meadowland. The child had asked that. The girl was the one who had written of her sister's need to escape the orphanage. To be rescued. A child in need. Children in need. The mother had also written that she desired to rescue her daughters. The word "rescue" buried itself in his thoughts.

After yet another failed attempt at letter writing, Dirk left the house behind and walked across the fields with Maisy following along. He ended up at the river that flowed along the border of his land. The narrow river was never very full of water along here except in times of downpours that could cause it to jump its banks.

Without thinking about where his feet were taking him, he ended up in a favorite place where a spring-fed creek wound down the hill to slide over rocks smoothed by centuries of flowing water. Rocky bluffs were on either side of the small cascading waterfall, but the creek made an easy way to slip into the river. Farther down the river, through the bottom-land, the banks leveled off and the stream spread out wider. Back before better roads were built, the folks around took advantage of the shallow crossing place there to take a shortcut to town across Meadowland. But one neighbor never used the crossing. Herbert Rainsley drove his team of horses miles out of the way to keep from setting foot on Meadowland. Dirk's father said their dispute over a piece of land went back to his grandfather's time, with more hard feelings popping up through the years. A lack of fences. Cattle crossing the river to destroy a corn crop. A favorite hound killed by the other's dogs. All before Dirk was old enough to know any of the happenings, so he was never sure whose dogs killed whose dog or which side owned the cows or the corn.

His father waved off any questions. "No need banging on that hornets' nest. Wouldn't do nothing but stir up new trouble," he'd say.

And that was fine. Until he caught sight of Anneliese Rainsley wading in the river and nothing was ever the same again.

Dirk sank down on a rock on top of the bluff beside the waterfall and leaned back against a tree. Maisy gave him a look with a slow wag of her tail and then stretched out beside him in the sun sifting down through the branches. Dirk stared at the water flowing past while his thoughts went back to that day so long ago.

He had stood on this very same spot looking down at her. She had pretended not to know he was there, but she had. He could tell by the way she kept her head turned away from his side of the river.

Every detail of that moment was seared into his memory. Damp ends of her dark brown hair curled down on her shoulders. Her white top was soaked and clung to her breasts in a way that made his pulse speed up. Her blue-and-white-striped skirt swirled out around her as she trailed her hands in the water and spun around as if she'd never done anything she enjoyed more.

She was acting for him, wanting him to note her beauty. He did. He stood spellbound by the sight of her, afraid if he spoke she'd climb out of the water and run back to the house he could see across the field on the other side of the river. He didn't want her to disappear. He wanted to hold her there in front of his eyes as long as possible.

He knew the Rainsleys had a daughter. He'd seen her at a distance in the fields with her father, but he'd never actually met her. They knew all the other neighbors, but the Rainsleys and the Meadows did not speak. The longtime feud.

Dirk asked his father why they didn't let bygones be bygones. His father said there wasn't any way to talk to a Rainsley. Especially Herbert Rainsley, who wanted to claim half their best bottomland field as if the river wasn't a natural property boundary. That field was part of Meadowland and did not belong to the man across the river no matter what he said.

Now there in front of him on that beautiful June day was a Rainsley who had him ready to give up that bottomland field for the chance to get to know her.

She didn't move on up the river or back toward her farm. Instead, she stepped closer to his side of the river and whipped her hands through the water in a vain attempt to splash him on the rock ten feet above her. He had to laugh.

That made her stand up straight with her hands balled into fists and propped on her hips. She glared at him with no hint of a smile. "Are you one of those dreadful Meadows men who have lizard eyes and horns growing under their hair?"

"Lizard eyes?" He rubbed his hands through his hair. "And horns? I don't feel any horns, but I am one of those dreadful Meadows men. And you? Are you the beautiful Rainsley girl who lives across the river?"

A smile touched her lips then. "Why don't you come down here and find out?"

"So you can see my lizard eyes?" he asked, even as he was slipping off his shoes.

"I don't like lizards. I run the other direction when I see one of those." She gave a little shudder.

"But lizards are lovely creatures. They catch flies and such and never do anybody any harm." He stayed where he was and stared down at her.

"Other than the flies, I suppose."

"There is that."

"If I am going to see those lizard eyes, you best come on down off your perch, Mr. Meadows. My ma will want me home soon to help with supper."

"The sun's still high in the sky." Dirk scrambled off the rock and slid down the waterfall rocks into the river, not at all worried about any damage to his trousers. The water was colder than he expected. When he gasped, she laughed and sent a spray of water toward him.

"That's really why you wanted me to come down here, isn't it?" Dirk wiped his eyes. "To splash me." He stayed at the edge of the river, fearing he might scare her away if he stepped toward her.

But she seemed to have no fear at all as she moved through the water until she could have touched him if she wanted to. "A little splash never hurt anyone. It can wake up a person. Make them pay attention."

"And what did you want me to pay attention to?" His heart was beating extra fast.

"Me, of course."

"You can splash me again if you want, but you already have my full attention." His breath came a little faster as he felt as though he was being swallowed by her green eyes. He surprised himself again by saying, "Your eyes are luminous."

"Luminous?" She lowered her gaze and then gave him a flirtatious look up through her eyelashes. Her lovely eyelashes. "You must be the Meadows son who has been wasting his time off in that college in Louisville learning words like that. Luminous. Lightning bugs have luminous tails. The moon is luminous."

"And a beautiful girl's eyes are luminous," he said.

She stepped even closer to him then, until the river water pushed her skirt against his legs. She didn't bother corralling it as she stared up at him. "And your eyes don't look much like a lizard's. A rather ordinary blue. The color of a summer sky. Of course I've never looked that closely at a lizard's eyes to note the color, and there is that red hair."

"Lizards don't have red hair." He was glad his voice came out sounding at least almost normal.

"I've seen some with a blue tail."

"The blue-tailed skinks."

"Is that what they teach you at that fancy school? About lizards and skinks? Along with how to come up with pretty words to try to turn a girl's head. I bet you tell all the girls they have luminous eyes."

"Only the ones who do. But the fact is that until today, I have never met a girl with luminous eyes." It was all he could do to keep his hands down in the water instead of reaching up to smooth a lock of her hair away from those luminous eyes.

As if she guessed his thoughts, she hooked the stray strand behind her ear as she kept staring at him. "And I never met a man with curly red hair."

"So, what do you think?" He lifted his eyebrows at her. "Like it?"

"Like it or not, my mother says to be wary of redheaded men. She claims they have the temper of a mean tomcat." She paused a moment before she went on. "And my father says he's never met a Meadows worth exchanging the time of day with."

"He's never met me," Dirk said. "And I'm more like a friendly old hound dog than a mean tomcat."

"Pa has two old hound dogs. I'm not particularly fond of either one." She whirled away from him with a swish of her skirt through the water.

"Poor dogs," Dirk said. "And I don't know what time of day it is to exchange with you."

That made her laugh and turn back toward him. "It's an hour past too late."

"I hope not." He fastened his gaze on her eyes. They were practically exploding with sparks. "What say you just forget I'm a Meadows and we can be friends?"

"Friends?" Her coy look was back. "Wading friends?"

"I'd be glad to wade a few rivers with you."

"Would you now?" She ran her hands under the water to send a spray up at his face.

He didn't hesitate and splashed her in return. Then the war was on, with both of them splashing as furiously as they could to make a water storm. Between sputters, she kept laughing until she slipped and fell backward, sliding all the way under the water.

His smile froze as he grabbed her hands to pull her back to her feet. She came up out of the river with water streaming off her. For a minute he thought she might be choking from swallowing the river water, but then he realized she was still laughing.

He turned loose of one of her hands so he could yank out his handkerchief for her. "Here. Maybe this will help."

She pulled her other hand free and dried her eyes and blew the water out of her nose. She stopped laughing but a smile continued to play around her lips as she stared up at him. "Kind of you to keep me from drowning."

"I doubt you would have drowned."

"You never know." She twisted her lips to try to hide her smile. "I might have bumped my head on the rocky bottom and knocked myself silly."

"There is that," he agreed. This time he didn't resist as he gently smoothed her wet hair back from her face. "You're beautiful."

"Come now, Mr. Meadows." She didn't shy away from his touch. "You've already said that. Twice, I think. Can't you come up with something better? Something luminous?"

"Your beauty has stolen my words, Miss Rainsley." He dropped his hand away from her face.

"I doubt that. Do you know my name?"

"Ann Louise?" He thought that was what his mother had called her once.

Again she laughed, the sound tinkling through the air like tiny bubbles. "That might have been a more sensible name for me, but no, not Ann Louise."

"Then I fear I don't know. Should I guess again?"

"Perhaps we should leave it a mystery. You could probably guess all week and not discover my name."

"Is this a Rumpelstiltskin game we play, my lady?"

"I can assure you that my name is not Rumpelstiltskin. And I am fairly certain that yours is not Dirt, as I've heard my father say."

"He is not far wrong," Dirk said.

"Nor are you far wrong with Ann Louise. But wrong, nevertheless." She turned away from him and moved toward the far bank. She looked over her shoulder to say, "Now, I must go back over to my side of the river and you must return to yours."

He stood still in the middle of the river with the water flowing around him. "Will I ever see you again?" The thought that he might not jabbed him with sorrow.

"Whisper my name on the breeze and I might appear once again."

"But I don't know your name."

At the edge of the river, she stopped and looked at him for a long moment. "Nor do I know yours."

"Dirk," he said. "Much like your father said, only with a *k* and not a *t*."

"Dirk. What a short, angry-sounding name. Fits a man with curly red hair, I suppose."

"And what name fits a radiant girl like you?"

"I should make you wonder." Her smile was secretive as she turned and deftly climbed the bluff out of the river. Once at the top, she took pity on him still standing down in the water. "Anneliese." Then with a whirl of skirts, she disappeared from sight.

He scrambled up the same rocky path she'd taken and at the top called her name. "Anneliese." The name slid off his tongue like music.

Although he didn't say it loudly, she must have heard him. She looked over her shoulder as she ran barefoot across the field and the tinkle of her laughter drifted back to him.

Now these many years later, he watched the river water flow past as he sat on the very rock where he'd stood when he first saw Anneliese.

He spoke her name aloud. "Anneliese."

The sound was sad and futile in the air. He had long ago given up ever getting an answer. Her family no longer even owned the property across the river. After her parents died, her brother had sold the farm to a family named Williamson. Nice people. He'd met them a few times. They had no knowledge of the disputes his father and grandfather had once had with the Rainsleys. Dirk saw no reason to tell them, although others in the community might have done so.

Maisy raised her head to see if he was asking anything of her. When he stayed silent, she huffed out a breath and put her dog chin back on her paws to wait until he was ready to move.

The river water continued to roll past with energy fed into it by a spring rain the day before. He imagined his voice speaking Anneliese's name rolling along with the water. That was what he should have done years ago. Dropped it all in the river and let the current carry his hopes and sorrows away. Anneliese was never going to come when he said her name as she had done so often that year when she was seventeen and he was nineteen.

He was turning forty this year. Time to forget lost loves and tend to the family he had, even if he didn't know them.

"Come on, Maisy." He stood up and headed back across the river bottom and then the meadow field to the house, without even noting the bugs that flew up around him. He stopped in the garage to pull some cardboard boxes off a shelf.

It was past time to clean out his mother's room. Now he had a reason.

8

*C*alla didn't start watching for a reply from her uncle right away. She calculated how long it might take her letter to reach Meadowland by how long it took her mother's letters to reach her. Of course, she had no idea how far away Meadowland was or how far away her mother's sanitarium was either. All she knew was the confining space of the Home for Girls.

As yet, Miss Warfield had not put her out on the street, although she was no longer allowed to attend school classes. The Monday after her birthday, Miss Warfield had informed Calla she could choose to leave or she could stay and work in the kitchen.

"Not forever, mind you." Miss Warfield had settled her stern gaze on Calla. "A few months if you prove a capable helper to Mrs. Jenkins."

Before Calla could dare to ask what she'd be paid for her work, Miss Warfield's eyes tightened in a frown as though she guessed Calla's thoughts. She went on. "This is not a position here at the Home for Girls, but merely an offer from the goodness of our hearts to enable you to continue to have food and shelter. You best keep that in mind in the days ahead. Our admission rules don't allow us to take in girls over thirteen. And what are you now?"

She didn't pause to let Calla answer. Instead, she tapped the file open on the desk in front of her. "Fifteen, I see. Already you have had a year beyond the normal age allowed."

"Yes, ma'am." Calla couldn't deny the truth of her words. She did have reason to be grateful, but she still had to force out the words admitting it. "Thank you for your kindness."

That brought Miss Warfield's tight-lipped smile as she waved her out of the office to start helping Mrs. Jenkins.

Calla didn't mind the work. She'd already been helping in the kitchen during some meals, but now she started early in the morning and worked until the last kitchen chore was done at night. She missed the chance to read, but even if Miss Gertrude had been willing to loan her books, she was too exhausted to do anything but fall into bed and sleep.

She took her meals with Mrs. Jenkins instead of with the other girls. The cook was as nice as Miss Warfield was not. Mrs. Jenkins didn't slack on giving her work to do. Calla peeled buckets of potatoes and washed stacks of dishes, but she also learned about putting ingredients together to make something that tasted good.

"Knowing how to cook is a skill that will serve you well, Callie. Folks that say the way to a man's heart is through his stomach know what they're talking about. Make a good soup or cake and you'll be a leg up on finding a husband."

The cook made the last swipes of caramel frosting across a cake half the size of their worktable. "My Harvey did love my spice cake." She handed Calla her spoon with a wink. "Here, you can sample the caramel before you wash up the dishes."

Some of the other girls took turns working in the kitchen too, but they did things like setting the tables, pouring drinks, or bringing in more dishes for Calla to wash. In spite of the way her hands were chapped from the hot water and strong soap, Calla was happy working with the cook. Mrs. Jenkins made sure Calla had the opportunity to carry a pitcher of water out to fill glasses while Sienna's group was in the dining room, and she always asked afterward how that little sister of hers was doing.

"I had four sisters," she told Calla. "The three older ones were by my pap's first wife. Never took to me nor did I take to them. But that little sister, she had my heart from the first time I saw her in my mother's arms. I weren't but six at the time, but I took more care of her than my mam ever did, I'm thinking. Of course, she had to see to all the others, my brothers and those other girls she took on when she married, so she was glad enough to hand over the watching of Helen to me. Your little Annie puts me in mind to my Helen."

"Did she have blond hair?" Calla asked as she stacked another plate in the drying rack. The plates weren't so hard to wash, but the cooking pans took plenty of scrubbing.

"She didn't look like your Annie. Her hair was brown and she wasn't skinny like your little sis. But what brings the thought to mind is more the way she is. Your Annie, I mean. That was how Helen was too. Always ready to dream away her day. I reckon I did spoil her some. Didn't never want to see her shedding tears."

"My sister . . ." Calla hesitated on the name, but then used the one Mrs. Jenkins had. "Annie hardly ever cries, but I haven't been able to keep away reason for tears whether she sheds them or not. Were you able to do that for your sister?"

"Till she was older. But things were different for the two of us. My mam and pap were kindly souls, and once those hateful older sisters married and were gone, our house was a fine place with food enough and even more laughter."

Calla washed another plate. "That sounds wonderful."

"I guess you'uns haven't had much reason for smiles lately with your mam sick and all. But I'm praying things get some better for the two of you. Poor little Annie seems to have a way of getting on the wrong side of the teachers."

"She's trying harder to pay attention to the rules."

Mrs. Jenkins sighed. "Them rules can be a problem, but it ain't a bad thing to learn to do what one oughta."

"How about your sister? Are you still close?"

"We will be one day. When I move on up to heaven where she's there waiting."

"I'm sorry. What happened to her?"

"Walked that hard baby-birthing road and didn't make it through. I took the baby in to raise, even though I already had five of my own by then. Helen's no-good husband weren't fit to raise no baby girl. Barbara Lou weren't much like her mam. Took back after her father instead, but I did my best for her. She found a fellow and went out west some years ago. I ain't heard from her since."

"I'm sorry," Calla said.

"Nothing to be sorry about. That's just how life is. 'Twas the same with my natural-born children. They had to be on about their own lives. That's when I started here at the home where I could make sure you poor little waifs had good food to eat."

Waifs. Calla knew what that meant. Abandoned children. She and Sienna hadn't been abandoned.

"Our mother is coming back for us." Calla started scrubbing a big pot with more fervor than needed.

"Of course she is." Mrs. Jenkins didn't sound as though she believed it.

Calla didn't bother to argue. The only proof would be her mother showing up to take them off to a new home.

Each night when she went to bed, she closed her eyes and imagined her uncle making his way through a beautiful meadow. Butterflies and birds flew up around him while flowers nodded in the spring breeze. In his hand he had a letter for his mailbox. A letter to her, saying he had a place for them at Meadowland.

With no idea of how he really looked, she imagined him something like her memories of her father, except her uncle's face was always shadowed. She couldn't picture how his scars might look.

However he looked, she wouldn't care as long as he answered her letter and promised to come get them. Sometimes she paused when she carried out the garbage to let the sun touch her face. What a wonder it would be to live in a place where she could go out into the sunshine anytime she wanted. In the time between when she finished washing the lunch dishes and Mrs. Jenkins was ready for her help preparing the evening meal, Miss Warfield gave Calla the task of sweeping the hallways.

"Idle hands are the devil's workshop." Miss Warfield had shoved a broom into Calla's hands the first time she'd caught her sitting down while waiting for Mrs. Jenkins to give her a new task. "You can sweep the front hallway every day."

Mrs. Jenkins peered up from making a list of needed supplies to give Calla a sympathetic look, but Miss Warfield's word was law in the Home for Girls. Calla didn't mind doing the sweeping, especially since that meant she was cleaning the hallway when the mailman came with his packet of letters.

He remembered her, and each day he pulled a sad face to let her know no likely letter was in the stack he handed Miss Warfield. Sometimes he would start singing some silly song about young love. While the letter she hoped for was nothing like the mailman imagined, at least when he shook his head, she knew Miss Warfield hadn't found a letter from her uncle and kept it from her.

Her uncle would write her. Surely he would. But she had no idea what his answer might be. She prayed while she swept the hallway. She prayed while she washed dishes. She prayed at night until she was too exhausted to hold the words in her mind.

The days passed, one after another with no word from him. Perhaps he'd never gotten the letter. Perhaps she had written the wrong words. Most likely he didn't want to be saddled with two waifs. While she had resisted that description when Mrs. Jenkins had used it, the word haunted her thoughts now. Waifs. Abandoned girls. Whether by choice or not, they were abandoned and lost in this gray building.

Calla feared every morning when she rose before dawn to hurry to the kitchen that this might be the day Miss Warfield pushed her out on the street. Then how would she ever know if her uncle did answer her letter? Worse, she would have no way to know Sienna was all right.

She wasn't all right. Calla knew that each time she saw Sienna. She was so very pale and moved the way Calla remembered her mother's unsteady steps before she had to go to the sanitarium. Sienna wasn't coughing. Calla held on to that thought and to the hope that if they could leave the orphanage, Sienna's face would light up and she'd smile again.

Even Mrs. Jenkins noticed Sienna's listlessness. One day she looked up at Calla from chopping carrots. "That little sister of yours is looking some droopy lately. I don't like it."

Calla wasn't sure how to answer so she just nodded a little.

"I've seen other youngsters here with the sad, dragging feet. They tend to get sick with something or other straightaway."

"Do you think Sienna is sick?"

"Sienna?" Mrs. Jenkins seemed puzzled for a minute before she went on. "Oh, that's Annie's born-to name. Sienna." She said the name slowly, letting the syllables roll off her tongue. "Pretty name but too fancy for those here at the home, I'm guessing."

"I suppose. The name they picked for me, Callie, is more like my real name. Calla."

"Your mam must have hunted through some name books to come up with those." She shook her head and chopped up a few more carrots before she scraped them into the soup pot.

Calla shrugged. "They're flower names. Mama said her mother had calla lilies she planted every year. That's why she named me Calla. Then Mama's name is Rose and she said she'd heard of sienna roses. That's Sienna's whole name. Sienna Rose."

"My mam named me plain. Iva after her grandmother. Told me to be careful about who I married though, or my name would have people laughing. Like Iva Bird or Iva Payne." Mrs. Jenkins laughed. "My mam was a funny one sometimes. Every boy who came around she'd check out his name even when I didn't have the first thought of attaching his name to mine. But when Harvey showed up on our doorstep, she said Jenkins was fine. She did think my Harvey was a prince."

"That would have been a fun name. Iva Prince." Calla smiled as she picked up another potato to peel.

"I reckon so." Mrs. Jenkins smiled too.

"In fairy tales a prince always comes to the rescue." No prince was going to show up to rescue her and Sienna, but an uncle would be just as good.

"A prince?" Mrs. Jenkins shook her head. "Scrubbing pots and peeling potatoes must have you feeling like that Cinderella in the fairy tale."

"You're not a wicked stepmother."

"Some others might fit the stepmother role better." Mrs. Jenkins gave her a look through her eyebrows. "Best forget I said that or I might see the street before you do. But I am some worried about that little sister of yours, fancy name or not." She clucked her tongue and shook her head. "Poor child."

Calla dropped the peeled potato into the pot of water. "I don't know what to do to help her."

Mrs. Jenkins sighed. "Not sure there's a thing you can do so long as you're here. The world can load down a heap of trouble on some mighty young shoulders in this here place."

Surely there was something. Maybe they should both run away. To her uncle's farm. If only she knew how to get there. She picked up another potato and stared at it as though she didn't know what to do with it.

Mrs. Jenkins stepped over to put her hand on Calla's shoulder. "I didn't aim to get you bothered about her. Could be I shouldn't ought to have said anything, but seeing as how I did speak my worries out loud, the two of us can promise to pray for your little sister. The Lord will listen."

That Calla could do, and it was good to think of Mrs. Jenkins praying the same.

A few days later, Miss Warfield sent one of the girls to summon Calla to her office. Calla's heart jumped up in her throat as she set down the pan she was drying and looked at Mrs. Jenkins. She'd been working in the kitchen almost a month.

"Worry not, child," Mrs. Jenkins said. "If she's aiming to send you on your way, I'll tell her I can't do without you. And there is some truth to that."

"Another girl could do what I've been doing."

Mrs. Jenkins squeezed her shoulder. "No need thinking the worst. Could be the Lord sending that prince you've been praying for."

Calla had no hope of that as she walked along the empty hallways. Her footsteps sounded loud on the floors she'd just swept a few hours ago when once again the mailman had given her that sad shake of his head. No letter. No rescue.

If it was only her, she might be glad for a chance to make her own way in the town. But there was Sienna. She couldn't leave Sienna alone in this place.

9

irk should have written that letter to Frank's widow. He hadn't expected resistance to what he had decided was the right thing to do. He thought he could show up at the orphanage and claim his nieces with no problems. He was family. They had expressed the wish for him to come for them. He had the girl's letter in his pocket.

That meant nothing to this unsmiling woman staring at him across her wooden desk. Miss Warfield—a name he thought fit her very well—hadn't shied away from his scars as many did when they first met him. Instead, she narrowed her eyes on him as if assessing what wrong he'd done to suffer such wounds before she twisted in her chair to lift a file out of a cabinet behind her. She didn't bother to invite him to pull up one of the chairs pushed against the wall nor did he ask. She placed the file precisely in front of her and then took paper and a pencil out of a desk drawer that groaned when she opened it, as though reluctant to give up anything inside it.

"What is your name again?" She held the pencil poised over a small tablet.

He'd already told her his name. Twice. But he repeated it

again. "Would you like me to spell it for you?" He kept his voice calm although his irritation was growing.

"That won't be necessary, Mr. Meadows."

He watched her print his name in perfectly shaped letters on the blank page. He stood silent, not shifting back and forth as he imagined many youngsters had at times before this stern-faced woman.

"And what brings you to the West Side Home for Girls this day?" She peered up at him as if he hadn't already told her he was the uncle of two girls named Meadows here under her care.

"I have come to take my nieces, Calla and Sienna Meadows, home with me."

She looked down at her file. "We have a Callie and Annie here by the name of Meadows. No Calla and Sienna."

He could see the names on the top line of the file. "I believe if you will take another look at your file, you will see their names clearly written there."

Perhaps not the best thing to say to get on the woman's good side. If she had a good side.

She didn't look down at the file. "Yes, well, here they are Callie and Annie."

"Very well. I have come to take Callie and Annie home."

"I don't think they have a home. At least none besides this one we are generously providing for them while their mother is in a sanitarium."

"They have a home now. Mine."

She tilted up her chin and stared at him through the bottom halves of her spectacles. "I'm sure you can understand, Mr. Meadows, that we can't allow just anyone to come into our home and spirit away our girls. We know nothing about you. We can't be sure you are even the uncle you say you are. You might want to carry these girls away for nefarious reasons. Their mother left them in our care, and unless she comes for them, I fear we cannot in good conscience allow them to leave."

As much as he hated to admit she was right, she was. Still, he did have Calla's letter and Frank's widow's letter. That was proof of him being family. "I have their mother's letter asking me for help with the girls." He pulled it out of his pocket and handed it to her, even though he doubted if Rose Meadows would want her to read the words she'd written.

She took the letter from him as if it might be tainted by his touch and held it gingerly while reading it. Then instead of handing it back, she dropped it on her desk. "Yes, well, this does seem to confirm you are the uncle of these girls." She looked from the letter up at him. "But it also shows you and your brother's family have had little intercourse with one another."

"Family is still family." He leaned forward and took the letter from her desk. He folded it carefully and tucked it back in his pocket.

"It appears Mrs. Meadows asked you for monetary help and not to take custody of her children."

"I plan to take her to my home for her continued recovery."

"You would expose these children to her illness." She raised her eyebrows and didn't bother hiding her disapproval. "I don't think that would be advisable."

Dirk stared at the woman. She stared back, an immovable roadblock to his plans. He would have to go get Frank's widow and then come back to claim the children. That was what he should have done initially, but he had to pass through

87

Louisville to get to the sanitarium. He'd thought it would be a pleasant surprise for their mother to have the children with her as she made the decision as to whether to accept his offer of shelter.

Perhaps, he thought she would be more likely to agree if the girls were there to encourage her to come to his farm. But was that what he even wanted to happen? Surely it would be easier to hand over a sum of money and go back to his undisturbed life at Meadowland. Oddly enough, that idea lacked the appeal he thought it should have.

He gave in to the inevitable result of Miss Warfield's firm and reasonable stand. The mother was the one to say where the children went or didn't go. "Her doctor has said Mrs. Meadows has recovered enough to leave the sanitarium, but I suppose you are right. She does need to be the one to collect her children."

The woman looked smugly victorious. "Yes."

"But I want to see my nieces before I leave."

"I'm not sure that would be wise."

"Wise or not, I insist." He locked his gaze on her and made no move for the door.

Again her eyes narrowed as she stared at the dreadful misshapen skin on the left side of his face. He had not removed his hat, a breach of gentlemanly rules, but a courtesy to those who found the sight of his face unsettling.

Miss Warfield not only didn't seem bothered by his burn scars, she also lacked any polite kindness. "I'm not sure I can allow that. The sight of you could be frightening to the children."

He considered jumping toward her and shouting boo to see how frightened she might be, but he restrained the urge.

Instead he merely smiled. "Most people have some life scars, Miss Warfield. Sometimes they show. Sometimes they do not."

She was unmoved by his words. "Yours do and children the age of Callie and Annie are very impressionable."

"I don't doubt the truth of that, but I'm not leaving until I see my nieces."

They continued to stare at one another for a long moment. Finally Miss Warfield reached toward the phone on her desk. "Don't make me call the police to have you forcibly removed."

"Go ahead. Call the police," Dirk said agreeably. "But I doubt they would deny me the privilege of seeing my nieces after I've driven nearly two hours to check on their welfare. Instead, they might wonder why you would deny a family member a visit with one of your charges."

She pulled her hand back from the phone and let out an exaggerated sigh. "Very well. If you intend to be difficult, I will summon the two girls. But if they are traumatized, it will be to your blame and to our sorrow when we have to help them overcome it."

"I have scars, madam, but I'm an ordinary man. Not a monster."

"I daresay I have made no such accusation, Mr. Meadows." She stood up and skirted around the desk to her office door where she summoned someone to go for the girls. She waved a hand toward a chair along the wall. "Feel free to take a seat while we wait. Once the girls are here, you have fifteen minutes. I will not allow you to disrupt our schedules."

"Very well." He did as she said and sat down.

She returned to her desk where she pulled another file

out of the cabinet to pretend to work, but she continually looked over at him as if he might disappear. Or perhaps wishing he would.

He hadn't gotten his intended result of taking the two girls out of here with him, but he would. He wouldn't leave Frank's daughters in this cold, gray place. As the child Calla had said, they needed meadows and sunshine.

He did hope he hadn't made a mistake insisting on seeing them. The stern woman might be right. An impressionable child could be frightened by how he looked. The young woman who had opened the door when he knocked had shrunk back from him as she pointed toward the director's office. That could be because of the stone-faced Miss Warfield and have nothing at all to do with him. Or it could be because he did indeed look somewhat monstrous.

—————

Janet, the girl who had fetched Calla from the kitchen, hadn't waited while Calla washed her hands and hung up her apron. But now, she stopped Calla in the hallway before she could go into Miss Warfield's office.

"Wait," she said softly as though she feared Miss Warfield might hear her through the door.

Janet was a couple of years younger than Calla and never seemed to get in trouble with Miss Warfield or any of the staff. Some of the other girls didn't like her since they thought she received preferential treatment, and she did. Calla didn't fault her for that. Each of them had to do whatever she could to survive in the home. The other girls might think Calla was getting favored treatment by Mrs. Jenkins, and they'd be right.

Janet took Calla's arm and pulled her away from the door before she said, "Miss Warfield sent for Annie too. So you should wait until she gets here before you go in."

Calla frowned. "Why did she send for both of us? Is Annie in trouble?"

"Isn't she always?" Janet gave her head a little shake. "I'm sorry. That wasn't nice of me to say."

Calla sighed. "But unfortunately true." Something really bad must be wrong if Miss Warfield had sent for both her and Sienna.

"I know. Poor thing," Janet said. "But no. You have a visitor."

"A visitor?" Calla's heart jumped up with excitement. "Our mother?"

Janet put her hand on Calla's arm. "Not your mother. A man. He says he's your uncle."

Calla's heart kept beating too fast. "Uncle Dirk?"

"I don't know. When I let him in the front door, he merely said he was Mr. Meadows to see the director. So I showed him to Miss Warfield's office. She didn't look happy to see him."

"Why not?" Calla asked.

Janet shrugged. "She doesn't like seeing anyone unless they make an appointment. I guess he didn't have that. Anyway, in the afternoons, I am to wait outside her office in case she needs me to run errands for her. So after I told her he was here, her face got all tight the way it does when she's cross, but she had me tell him to go in. He didn't push the door completely closed, so I heard them talking. She threatened to call the police." Janet's eyes got wider.

"What did he do to make her say that?"

"He wanted to take you home with him."

Calla shut her eyes and let a thanksgiving prayer circle in her mind.

Then Janet went on. "But she said he couldn't. When he said he wouldn't leave without seeing you and Annie, she told him she would call the police to make him leave."

"Did she?"

"I don't know. I guess not since she had me go for you and Annie. I didn't hear what else they said. I got worried she might come out in the hall to tell me to go get someone to help her. I didn't want her to catch me listening." Janet's eyes narrowed on Calla. "And you better not tell her I told you this."

"I don't want to tell her anything."

"Good. Then I won't have to tell her anything about you either."

"There's nothing to tell." Calla frowned.

"There's always something." Janet gave her a knowing smile.

Calla stared at her without saying anything. Maybe what some of the girls said about Janet carrying tales to Miss Warfield was true.

"But about your uncle." Janet's smile disappeared as she made a face. "He's creepy looking."

"He got burned in a fire years ago," Calla said.

"So you know how he looks. I guess if he's your uncle you're used to it, but I thought he might have stepped out of a monster book." Janet gave a little shudder.

Calla didn't bother to tell Janet that, no, she didn't know how her uncle looked. She didn't care how he looked. He was here. He wanted them to go with him. Miss Warfield would have to let them. He was family.

"Here comes Annie," Janet said.

Sienna was dragging her feet as she walked toward Miss Warfield's office. Her head was down and her shoulders slumped.

"Poor thing. She must think she's headed for another strapping." Janet looked sad for Sienna. "I would have told her not, but Miss Agnes wouldn't let me talk to her."

The little girl glanced over her shoulder in the direction of the front door, and Calla had the sudden fear she might make a break for the street. Just when things could be turning in their favor.

"Sienna," Calla called quietly. "I'm here."

A smile lit up Sienna's face as she turned to see Calla. Then worried confusion mixed with it as she had to be wondering if they were both headed for punishment. Calla smiled to let her know things weren't bad as she held a hand out toward her. Sienna ran the rest of the way on tiptoes to keep her shoes from clacking on the tile floor.

"Calla!" The confused look got darker. "Are we in trouble?"

"No, no. Someone is here to see us."

Happiness exploded from her. "Mama!" She didn't bother to soften her voice.

"Shh!" Calla shook her head. "Not Mother. Our uncle."

"Uncle?"

"Uncle Dirk." She started to whisper a warning about their uncle's appearance, but the door suddenly swung open behind them.

Miss Warfield loomed over them. Janet scooted away down the hallway.

"Dear girls." Miss Warfield's lips turned up in what must have been meant for a smile but looked more like a grimace. "Don't stand there chatting. Do come in. You have a visitor."

Pleasant words coming out of Miss Warfield's mouth sounded so foreign that they struck more fear in Calla than her usual stern orders. The director put her hand on Sienna's shoulder and pulled her past Calla into the room.

The man stood to the side of the room, his face turned a bit away from them. He wore a wide-brimmed hat with a silk scarf around his neck and tucked into his jacket collar. At first Calla couldn't see why Janet said he looked creepy, but then he turned his head and the damage to his face was obvious. Red and purple ridges crumpled the skin on his cheek and pulled down the side of his mouth to make his smile oddly crooked.

A flicker of uncertainty showed in his eyes when he saw them, but that didn't dim Calla's smile. She could feel Miss Warfield's disapproval, but that didn't matter either. Her uncle had gotten her letter. He had answered in the best way possible by standing here in this room with them.

If only she'd had a few more seconds to tell Sienna about his scarred face so she wouldn't shrink away from him and spoil their chance for a new home. One with a meadow of flowers.

She needn't have worried. Sienna took one look at the man and rushed toward him. "Uncle Dirk!"

Surprise flashed across his face as she wrapped her arms around his waist. He held up his arms for a moment as if he wasn't sure what to do with them, but then he touched her head with one hand and gingerly patted her back with the other. Calla sneaked a look over at Miss Warfield, who did not appear to be pleased as she watched Sienna hug the man.

The man looked from Sienna at Calla. "Hello, Calla."

That was all the invitation Calla needed to move past Miss Warfield over to stand in front of him. She didn't hug him. At Sienna's age, a hug was fine, better than fine to show Miss Warfield they were family. But at fifteen, a girl had to be more reserved, although seeing him there made her want to jump up and down and clap her hands. Janet said he came to take them home with him.

"Thank you for coming, Uncle Dirk," she said.

10

irk couldn't remember the last time someone had hugged him. Maybe not since that final hug from Anneliese before the fire. His mother might have wanted to hug him while he was recovering from the burns, but any touch was painful then. His skin had been tender for months after the burns healed, and by the time the soreness had gone away on the outside, the inner pain had worsened. He hadn't been open to any kind of affectionate touches.

He would have thought that still the same, but the small girl's arms around his waist felt good, even if he wasn't sure how to respond. Across the room, Miss Warfield watched with hawk eyes, waiting for him to do something wrong. The trouble was, he had no idea what was right to do as this child burrowed her head into his middle.

The older girl, the one who had written him, looked something like he felt, as if she wasn't sure what to do. While the other child ran straight to him, she stood back and studied his face. He had purposely turned to let her see his scars, thinking it best not to try to hide them from her.

She hadn't averted her eyes the way the girl who had answered his knock had done. His scars didn't seem to concern her. Instead, she looked very glad to see him when she thanked him for coming.

He smiled at her, even though he knew the smile would be crooked. That didn't bother her either as a smile lit up her face. She had the same red hair he did. Frank's hair had been red as well, but more a brownish red, not the true red the girl and Dirk shared.

Finally, the scene must have been too much for the director. "Annie, turn him loose," the woman said. "Your behavior is unseemly, and it is time for Mr. Meadows to leave."

The child kept her arms tight around him as she raised her head to look up at him. "Please don't leave."

"Annie." The woman's voice was harsh.

"Yes, ma'am." The child trembled as she slid her arms away from him and stepped back.

The older girl moved closer until the child could lean against her. Calla kept her gaze locked on Dirk's face and ignored the woman. Dirk wasn't sure if she spoke to him or the director as she asked, "Have you come for us?"

They both looked at him with such hope-filled eyes that he wanted to grab their hands and run for the door. But of course, he couldn't do that. Not without this dragon of a woman having the right to call the police and perhaps spoil any chance of them ever being able to leave with him.

He tried to sound as kind as possible. "I did come for you, but Miss Warfield has rightly pointed out that I must have your mother's consent for you to leave here."

"She would want us to go with you," Calla said.

"Oh yes. Please." The little one begged.

"Girls," the woman spoke up again. "None of that. Mr. Meadows has already told you he does not have the authority to take custody of you. That is not going to change, and I won't hear any foolish requests from the two of you, or you will suffer the consequences."

When the child flinched, the older one wrapped her arms around her before she said, "Yes, madam. We will do whatever you say."

She dropped her gaze away from Dirk's face, but not before he saw the worry in her eyes. He looked closer then and noted bruises on the younger girl's arms. She seemed so small and lost as she bent her head to stare at the floor, as if she'd known all along she shouldn't have dared hope for rescue.

Rescue. Both letters in his pocket had included that word and now he knew it was not written without cause. This child needed rescuing from this place that was draining away her life.

He squatted down in front of her and put his finger under her chin to tip up her face until she had to look at him. "I will be back. Soon you will be at Meadowland."

She blinked and he could tell she wasn't sure she could believe him. Too much had gone wrong in her young life. He knew that emptiness of hope, since he had the same hole inside him.

He leaned close to her ear to whisper for only her to hear. "I promise."

She stared straight into his eyes then, as though assessing if she could trust him. He couldn't tell what she decided as she moved her head away from his hand and squared her thin shoulders as if preparing for battle. He thought she might have stepped away from him if the older sister hadn't blocked her.

He stood up and looked at Calla as he repeated, "I will be

back." She at least looked readier to trust his word. Should he have made that promise? Who knew what tomorrow held? Hadn't he and Anneliese once promised to be together on the morrow?

Miss Warfield's voice cut through the room like a whip. "Back to your duties, girls."

"Yes, madam." Calla gently turned her little sister toward the door. She did dare to look back at him to repeat her earlier words. "Thank you for coming, Uncle Dirk."

"Goodbye, Uncle," the younger child said barely above a whisper.

She did not seem ready to embrace any hope he would ever return in spite of what he said. He wanted to rush after her and find a way to prove he could be trusted. Instead, he stood silent as they left the director's office and the sound of their footsteps grew fainter.

Miss Warfield went to the door and held it all the way open. "And good day to you, Mr. Meadows."

"I will be back," he said as he passed her.

"So you keep saying."

He ignored her words. "And when I come, I don't want to see more bruises on that child."

She stared at him with cold defiance. "The girl is clumsy. And badly behaved. If there are bruises, she's earned them all."

"I suggest she not earn any new ones."

"Your implied threats are unwelcome, Mr. Meadows. These girls are under my charge, and it is my duty to make sure they learn proper behavior. You have no right to insinuate I am not discharging my responsibilities in a proper way."

"I am fairly accomplished with my pen, madam. A few

letters to newspapers or prominent donors to this home and you might find your responsibilities and duties changed."

"You have overstayed your welcome, sir."

Perhaps he had and spoken too plainly. He tipped his hat to her and left without another word. The girl who had let him in earlier watched with wide eyes as he passed her.

It was good to be out in the sunshine again. Out of that gray house that had sucked the hope out of Frank's youngest daughter. The child definitely needed rescuing. He wasn't sure he was the right person to do it, but it appeared he was the only person she had.

Once he made it to the sanitarium, Dirk found himself in another office confronted by another administrator. At least here he'd been offered a seat, and this one, a doctor, seemed genuinely concerned with the welfare of her charge and patient, Rose Meadows.

"Dr. Halvechs, I assure you I have only the welfare of my sister-in-law in mind." He met the woman's eyes across the desk. That she'd said "doctor" instead of "nurse" had surprised him, but perhaps being female would make her more sympathetic to the plight of Rose Meadows being separated from her daughters.

"As do I, Mr. Meadows." The doctor leaned toward him over her desk. "Rose has made much improvement in her health, but I can't say she is completely cured. It could be if she leaves here too soon, she'll simply have to turn around and come back for more intensive treatment once again."

"I understand that your treatment here is fresh air and sunshine."

"Indeed. But that is not the only treatment we supply. We also do a procedure where we collapse the diseased lung to give it augmented opportunity to heal without the work of breathing for the patient."

"And is that always successful?"

"Not always." Dr. Halvechs sat back.

She made a steeple with her fingers and studied him. Her gray hair was chopped off short, as though she had no time for feminine vanities. He guessed her older than his forty years. Definitely a pioneer in the medical profession.

He waited for her to say more, but when she didn't, he said, "Then Rose . . ." He stumbled a little over her name since he didn't feel he knew Rose Meadows well enough to call her by her given name. Even so, if he was to claim her as a sister-in-law, he needed to act as though he knew her. "She might be as well off in the country sunshine at Meadowland. And with her children again. With her permission, I plan to take them from the orphanage."

"Yes, she does greatly miss her children. But there is the risk of infecting them." She dropped her hands down to the desktop and leaned forward again. "And you."

He had thought of that. He certainly did not want to come down with a disease that would make walking in his fields difficult were he unable to breathe normally. The doctors had warned him after the fire that his lungs were sure to be damaged from the smoke he had inhaled, but he had built up his strength little by little until he noticed no inability to climb hills or rock cliffs and do whatever he wanted.

Would this feeling of family obligation change that and turn him into an invalid again? He mentally shook his head. He needed to keep his focus on what was best for Frank's daughters. He looked directly at the doctor. "Is that a sure thing? That the children will be infected? Even if Rose is in a state of healing?"

This time calling her Rose was easier. It was simply a matter of being used to saying her name after so many years of not giving her even a passing thought. If this doctor could be convinced to release her patient and said patient agreed to come to Meadowland, he would have plenty of other things to get used to about having a family.

"Not a sure thing," she admitted. "As long as you take sanitary precautions. A clean living environment is very important."

"I will see to that, and my older niece is anxious to help her mother however she can." He didn't know that the girl had actually written those words to him, but it was implied. He considered pulling out the girl's letter to show the doctor, but before he could, Dr. Halvechs put her hands flat on the desk and stood up.

"Very well. Come. It is time to let Rose be aware of your offer since you say you did not write to let her know of your visit. Once the two of you talk, then she can weigh the options and make a decision."

He stood up too. "Will you try to discourage her leaving?"

The doctor smiled. "No. I have already told her in past consultations that I'm not sure she is ready to leave, but I will leave the choice to her." Her smile faded as she looked over at Dirk. "I think you should do the same."

"Of course. I have no reason to pressure her if she does not want to come with me to Meadowland." Instead, he might be relieved if she did turn down his offer of a home. But then he remembered the stricken look of the child named Sienna.

He held in a sigh. Life was easier when he was in the fields at home with Maisy by his side and nothing to consider except which insect, bird, or plant to study next.

"Meadowland. The name of your farm does make it sound like a paradise."

"It has always been a refuge for me."

"A private one?" As if Dr. Halvechs realized she had asked something he might not wish to answer, she quickly went on. "Many of us feel that way about our homes, but if you have valued privacy, then it might prove difficult for you to welcome your brother's family into your home."

He wanted to ask how she knew he didn't already have a houseful of children, but he kept quiet and merely nodded. She had instinctively hit on a concern troubling his thoughts. He pushed that away. He was committed now. No turning back unless Frank's widow refused his offer. And then, even if she did, his solitary peace might be broken by thoughts of that little girl's face lighting up at the sight of him and coming straight across the room to hug him.

Dr. Halvechs summoned Rose to a small sunroom with windows thrown open to the outside air. She often met with patients there instead of in her office. But once Rose came into the room, the doctor told her she had a visitor, opened the door to let Dirk Meadows enter, and slipped back out to leave them alone. Rose was surprised to see Frank's brother in front of her. Then, before she could even sit down, he blurted out his reason for being there. To take her to Meadowland. Her and her girls.

She had prayed he would help her with the resources to

rent a room somewhere, but now he was offering rooms at Meadowland. That thought had played through her mind before she wrote to him, but she had pushed it aside as too much to ask. Frank said his brother so desired solitude that he chased people away. Had even chased him away.

When Rose married, she had hoped to embrace Frank's family as her own, but then Frank would not so much as mention Dirk's name after he refused to sell the family farm. While Rose never admitted it to Frank, she was glad the land hadn't been sold. Even if they never returned there, the beauty of the place lived in her memory.

Now Frank's brother was offering a way to return to that beautiful place. She leveled her gaze on Dirk Meadows. He didn't shy away from her stare, but it was difficult to read his face in the shadow of his broad-brimmed hat.

"I wasn't expecting this, Mr. Meadows." Rose dropped down in one of the chairs, feeling short of breath as she considered his words. She waved at one of the other chairs.

"No, I suppose not." He sat across from her and removed his hat to balance it on his knee.

The scars had not changed much over the years. Gray streaked his red hair over his right temple. The color and the way it curled were so much like Calla's that her heart ached for sight of her daughter.

She pulled in a slow breath and stared at him. "I don't know what to say."

"The answer seems plain to me." His voice was brisk as though her hesitation upset him. "Meadowland has an abundance of fresh air and sunshine, the very treatment advised for you here. And your girls will be out of that institution."

"What do you know about my girls?" She narrowed her eyes on him.

"I went there first. To the orphanage, but the administrator wouldn't allow the girls to leave with me." He clenched his fists, but then appeared to purposely open up his fingers to let his hands relax on his thighs. "Which I suppose was only right, but I had hoped to bring them with me when I came for you. I thought that would please you."

"That would have been wonderful. You have no idea how anxious I am to see them again. To be with them. But I don't have money enough to rent a place. That's why I hoped for your help. For a loan. I would attempt to repay you in time."

"I can give you funds to rent a room if that is what you prefer. If you can find a boardinghouse that will allow you in. Those with tuberculosis are often denied housing. I've heard in some places the poor people live in tent cities." His voice was void of feeling as if reciting something he had read in a book. "I do not think you would wish your daughters to live in such circumstances when they can have a home on their family farm."

"How did you know where to find my daughters?" She peered across at him. "I don't think I mentioned the West Side Home for Girls in my letter."

"Yours was not the only letter I received, Mrs. Meadows." He pulled a folded sheet of paper from his pocket and leaned forward to hand it to her. "Your daughter's letter came the same day as yours."

Rose read Calla's words quickly. She closed her eyes as she pictured Calla writing this plea for help. She pulled in a shaky breath and fought for composure before she opened her eyes and looked at him. "Did you see the girls?"

"I did." Something changed about his face. "I insisted the old dragon let me see them or I wouldn't leave. The older one, Calla." He pointed at the letter. "The one who wrote me seemed sturdy enough. But the little one." He paused. "The child does need to be rescued from that place."

Rose lowered her eyes to read through Calla's words again. She swallowed hard and dabbed her eyes with her handkerchief. "Is she sick?" She bit back the words, *like me*.

"She's very thin, but I couldn't see signs of illness." The man stared straight at Rose. "I promised her I would return to take her away from that place. Please give me that ability."

"But we would disrupt your life."

"Yes."

They were both silent for a moment as if imagining that disruption. He spoke first. "I am outside most of the time. I don't need much room in the house. It can be yours except for my sleeping room and some use of the kitchen." He stopped as though for her to speak, but when she did not, he went on. "If you are concerned about your reputation, we can marry."

"Marry?" She put her hand against her chest when her heart began thumping.

"In name only," he said.

"My name is already Meadows."

"So it is." A smile twisted up the unscarred side of his mouth. "I only offered that in case you were concerned about appearances."

"What others think is surely the least of my worries," she said.

"Good. As it is, we are already family."

"Family." She stared down at the letter as once again the

106

silence built between them. She truly didn't know what she should do.

Suddenly he leaned toward her again and put his hand on her arm. "Mrs. Meadows, you can see my scars. They are very visible to the eye, but sometimes scars don't show, as you well know after fighting this disease here. And after losing Frank. Trust me now when I tell you that place is wounding your daughter. Wounds that will leave scars. Please agree to come with them to Meadowland. At least for the summer to allow her to heal."

She slowly raised her head to meet his gaze straight on. He might sound brisk, but she saw kindness in his eyes. "Yes."

He blew out a breath and leaned back. "Thank you." Then he looked toward the window. "It is late today. I'll come back for you tomorrow morning. It's a good ways from here to Louisville, but if you are ready to leave early, we can be at the orphanage around noon, barring travel difficulties."

Without another word, he stood and left the sunroom. Through the window, she saw him pause to study a forsythia bush blooming beside the walkway. When a bird began singing, he looked up toward the sound.

As though he knew she watched him, he looked back at the window. "A mockingbird."

Then he walked out of sight. She stayed where she was, hoping she'd made the right decision as she listened to the bird fill the air with song.

11

ill he really come back?"

The question Sienna had whispered to her before they parted in the hallway repeated in Calla's mind over and over as she went back to the kitchen and put on her apron. She had told Sienna yes and tried to sound as sure as she could, but she had no way of being sure.

Their uncle had seemed ready to take them out of this place with him today if Miss Warfield hadn't forbidden it, but he might have second thoughts. He might decide rescuing them was too much trouble. Her mother might not be well enough to come back with him to get them. Miss Warfield might not believe a letter her mother would write, giving them permission to leave with him. She could call the police and make her uncle leave.

So many things could happen.

When Calla told Mrs. Jenkins why she'd been called to Miss Warfield's office, a worried frown chased across the cook's face.

"I see." She picked up a spoon and began stirring the pot of soup on the stove.

Calla waited for her to say more. When she didn't, Calla said, "You have been so good to me, and I know you need help here in the kitchen, but if he comes back, we'll go with him."

"Of course you will. You can't pass up a chance for family. Someone else will help me here, though you've been a bright spot in my days." Mrs. Jenkins smiled over her shoulder at Calla, then turned back to stir the soup with even more vigor.

Calla didn't say more. Mrs. Jenkins would tell her what was bothering her when she was ready. The kitchen was silent except for the clang of the spoon against the metal pot.

Finally, Mrs. Jenkins blew out a long breath and laid down her spoon to turn toward Calla. "I might as well be out with it. Could be good for you to consider what might happen before that uncle has time to get to your mam and then back here. You need to think about what to do if it does."

"If what does?"

Mrs. Jenkins stepped away from the stove closer to the table where Calla was cutting a pan of corn bread into squares. She was almost whispering when she started speaking again. "She won't like him coming. She could blame you."

"I did write to him." Calla kept her voice low too. "I've been whipped before." She clenched a little at the thought, but she could stand whatever Miss Warfield did. As long as she didn't punish Sienna.

Mrs. Jenkins pulled her into a hug. The woman smelled like onions and spices. Such an odd mixture that Calla almost smiled.

"You are the dearest child," the cook said. "But the strap might not be the worst of it. She could put you out. Send you off to work somewhere."

"Oh." Calla's throat felt tight. What would she do if that happened?

"If she just turns you out, that won't be no worry, Callie." Mrs. Jenkins pushed her back to look at her face. "If it comes to that, you can sneak around to the back door to hide out in my room until your uncle shows up."

"But what if she sends me off to work somewhere?"

"That might take her a few days. Your uncle will be back before then."

"But what if he isn't?"

"He will be." Mrs. Jenkins hugged her again. "Didn't you tell me he said he would?"

Calla nodded.

"Then believe. I'm thinking that man is the answer the Lord sent us for all them prayers we've been throwing up to him about your Annie."

After the evening meal, Calla was washing up the last of the pots when Miss Warfield came into the kitchen. Calla knew she was there, but she didn't look around until the woman cleared her throat and spoke. "Callie Meadows."

"Yes, ma'am." Callie turned toward her, but after she saw the woman's face, she stared down at the floor.

Mrs. Jenkins, who was putting away the stirring spoons, dropped one on the floor where it clattered, bounced up, and clattered again before she grabbed it to wipe it off on the towel over her arm.

Miss Warfield frowned. "Good sakes, Mrs. Jenkins. You'll wake the whole house."

"I am sorry, Miss Warfield. The rheumatism in my thumb gives me trouble and goes numb now and then. That's why it's so good to have Callie here helping me. She's been a blessing out here in the kitchen."

"Yes, I am sure. But we have a houseful of girls."

"But they aren't the workers this one is." Mrs. Jenkins motioned toward Calla.

"Your comments have been noted." Miss Warfield looked around the kitchen. "It appears you are through for the day. So good evening to you."

"But she has been a fine help to me."

Calla peeked up at Mrs. Jenkins and then at Miss Warfield, whose eyes had gone cold on the other woman.

Miss Warfield spoke very distinctly. "Good night, Mrs. Jenkins."

Calla stared back down at the floor as Mrs. Jenkins said, "Yes, ma'am." She took off her apron and hung it on the hook beside the door out of the kitchen. Her footsteps sounded slow as she shuffled down the hallway.

The silence practically throbbed against Calla's ears as she waited for whatever Miss Warfield had come to say.

The woman tapped her fingers on the worktable in the middle of the kitchen. "I gave you this chance, Callie. It appears that you don't have the proper gratitude for my kindness."

"I am grateful, ma'am. I like working with Mrs. Jenkins."

"So that is why you wrote your mother that you needed rescuing from this place?"

"I don't know what you mean. It's to my shame that I have neglected to write my mother at all for several weeks." She couldn't believe her uncle had shown Miss Warfield the letter she'd written him, speaking of the need to rescue Sienna. But how else had she come up with that exact word?

"Now you're compounding that shame by lying to me."

"No, ma'am. I haven't written anything to my mother, but I should have written to tell her how nice you were to let me stay. You can ask Miss Gertrude. She handles all the letters." Calla kept her eyes downcast. While what she said was true, she had slipped that one letter to the postman without involving Miss Gertrude. She had no doubt Miss Warfield would note the subterfuge in her face.

"Yes, but be that as it may, you still seemed very pleased at the idea of leaving us." Again she drummed her fingertips on the worktable. "You do know that after you pass the age of thirteen, we no longer can count your presence in order to collect funds to keep the home operating to help unfortunate orphan girls. Those who donate to our good cause go by the number of girls we are serving. I have overlooked you being past the acceptable age for far too long. I can no longer rightfully receive funds for you, but I was willing to allow you to earn your keep by working here in the kitchen."

"Yes, ma'am. I have done my best to help Mrs. Jenkins." Calla did look up at Miss Warfield then. No lack of truthfulness in those words.

Miss Warfield wasn't impressed. Her eyes bore into Calla. "So you say. You also seem very ready to leave our house, and so that wish is granted. As of now, you have no place here."

"Yes, ma'am." What else was there to say? "Can I gather my things before I leave? And say goodbye to my sister, please?"

"I wouldn't turn a girl out at night, but in the morning, you must be gone before breakfast. And no, you cannot speak to your sister. She would cause entirely too many problems. She will adjust better with no last-minute histrionics. Do you understand?"

Calla's voice was faint. "Yes, ma'am."

"Look at me," the woman demanded. After Calla raised

her head to look directly at her, she went on. "If I find out you slipped around me to see her before you leave, she will be the one to receive punishment. Again, do you understand?"

"I understand."

"Very well." The woman almost smiled. "I do hope you will find your way out on the street. Normally, I would find you a position, but you seem to be in such a hurry to leave, I do not want to delay you."

She started toward the door but then paused to look back at Calla. "If you do end up going with that strange-looking man who says he's your uncle, I can only pray for your sake that he is not as wicked as he looks."

"Wicked?" Calla frowned.

"Indeed. Just the sight of him gave me shivers. Trust me." Her eyes narrowed on Calla. "No one is marked like that without deserving such from the Lord."

Calla stood still until she could no longer hear the woman's determined steps going away from the kitchen. Only then did she speak up for her uncle. "Scars aren't a sign of wickedness. Mistreating children is a sign of wickedness."

The words hung in the air, doing no good at all. Calla sighed and took off her apron and hung it on the hook for the last time. She listened to see if maybe Mrs. Jenkins might come back to the kitchen, but she wouldn't know Calla had been ordered to leave before breakfast. That didn't mean Calla couldn't come to tell her goodbye. Miss Warfield hadn't forbidden that. Only forbidden her to speak to Sienna.

But how could she leave without at least telling Sienna she would be watching for their uncle to return? And how would she do that without a place to be?

She tried to picture the sidewalk outside the home. Could

she simply walk back and forth, watching and praying for her uncle to drive up? With her mother. What an answer to prayer that would be. How long could she do that without food or shelter? A day? Two? Mrs. Jenkins would help her, but if Miss Warfield found out, then she would take out her anger on the poor woman and perhaps on Sienna as well.

Calla straightened her shoulders and headed toward the stairs to her bed. She would find a way to keep watching. She wouldn't lose hope. Her uncle had not looked wicked, even if he hadn't seemed to know what to do when Sienna hugged him. That had nothing to do with wickedness any more than his scars did. It just meant he hadn't been hugged for a long time. Somehow Sienna must have sensed that.

The other girls in the room were asleep or at least pretending to be. Calla did the same until after Miss Gertrude walked down the middle of the floor between the rows of beds to check to be sure each girl was lying on her side with her hands folded by her cheek above the blanket. She stopped by Calla's bed for a long moment, but then moved on.

Once her footsteps faded away, Calla pushed back the cover and quietly got up. She still wore her dress that smelled of grease and dish soap. As quietly as she could, she pulled the box with her few belongings out from under the bed. She was grateful for the moonlight that slipped through the windows as she lifted the contents from the box and spread them on her bed.

Folded at the bottom was the cotton sack that had held the few things she'd brought with her to the home, along with the dress and sweater she'd been wearing that day. Calla was glad she'd been allowed to keep them. She took off the blue orphanage dress but didn't put on the white nightgown.

Instead, she unfolded the old dress and ignored its musty odor as she pulled it over her head.

The bodice was too small. Her body had changed from a girl's to a young woman's in the last two years. Determined to get the dress on, she tugged and yanked on it so hard a side seam ripped open. That let her pull the dress down over her chest. The sweater would cover the tear. The waistline was big enough and the full skirt slipped over her hips with no problem but hit above her knees.

She turned up the bottom of the skirt to see a deep hem. After Calla painstakingly picked loose the threads holding the hem, the skirt lapped over her knees. It looked a little ragged, but it was decent enough. She would have to wear the orphanage underwear, stockings, and shoes, but she would never again have to pull on the orphanage dress.

She hoped it wouldn't be cold outside tomorrow. Coats were kept in a cloakroom on the first floor. None of the girls had their own coat. They just grabbed one that fit before going outside, since only a few girls went on outings at one time.

No reason to worry about that. It was spring. She wouldn't need a coat. Trees were budding out. Birds were singing. At her uncle's farm, the flowers would be beginning to bloom in the meadows. She did hope she and Sienna would soon see those flowers.

She peeked over at the girls in the beds next to hers. Their breathing was soft and easy as they slept. She should try to sleep too, but instead she sat on the bed and silently mouthed the Lord's Prayer. *Lead us not into temptation, but deliver us from evil.*

After she said amen for that prayer, another one circled

in her head. *Please let him come back tomorrow.* She hoped Mrs. Jenkins was praying the same thing for her and Sienna.

She packed her mother's letters in the cloth bag. When she felt around in the box to see if she'd missed anything, her fingers touched the handkerchief her mother had given her the day she'd brought them to the orphanage. Sienna had hugged their mother without weeping, but Calla could not hold back her tears.

"Shh, sweet child. It won't be for long. A few weeks and I'll be better." Her mother had looked ready to cry herself as she pulled a handkerchief from her pocket to wipe Calla's cheeks. She pressed the hankie into Calla's hand before she found another one for Sienna.

"I'm not crying," Sienna said.

"I know, but this one has pansies on it. Pansies can survive in the chilliest weather and keep on blooming."

Sienna studied the embroidered purple and yellow flowers on the handkerchief before she asked, "What does Calla's have on it?"

"Tiny daisies all around the edges. Daisies always make me smile, and I hope any time you feel sad you'll both pull out these and know I'll be back soon."

With those memories fresh in her mind, Calla lay down and pulled the covers up to her chin to wait for morning. She kept the handkerchief next to her nose, as she had done often in her first weeks there.

Even after months passed, Calla could still catch the scent of her mother's perfume, lily of the valley. Her father had bought her mother a small bottle of that fragrance before he left for the war. He said she could remember him each time she dabbed the perfume behind her ears. So the scent not only brought up thoughts of her mother but also the image of her mother and father embracing.

She'd watched them a moment before she pushed in between them to be part of the hug. Then her father had picked up Sienna and held her high in the air as he had once done Calla before she grew too big. Sienna didn't squeal the way Calla always had. Instead, she had giggled as she stared at him with wide eyes. Sienna was only two at the time, but she claimed to remember that moment, the only memory she had of their father.

Calla had other memories of angry words filling the air whenever her father came home from work after somehow losing his pay. Calla never understood why, but she remembered the fear of not having anything to eat. In truth, if not for Miss Wilma, they might have often gone hungry.

So that sweet embrace, even though sad because her father was leaving, was a treasured memory.

At the first hint of gray dawn, Calla got out of bed, straightened the covers, and spread the orphanage dress neatly on top. She picked up the cloth bag and her shoes. A couple of girls raised their heads to look at her but didn't speak as she tiptoed past them out of the sleeping room. They had no way of knowing she was leaving for good.

She felt a little like a ghost as she slipped silently down the stairway and through the dining area to the kitchen. Mrs. Jenkins was coming in the back door at the same time and clicked on the overhead light since the sun hadn't made an appearance as yet.

The cook's face lit up at the sight of Calla. "So you've come to work with me." Then she noticed the dress Calla wore and her smile disappeared.

"I'm sorry I can't help you with breakfast. I have to leave." Calla blinked back tears. "But Miss Warfield didn't say I couldn't tell you goodbye."

Mrs. Jenkins held out her arms and Calla walked into her hug. The woman hadn't pulled on her apron as yet, so she smelled like soap and comfort. "You're gonna be all right, Callie. The good Lord will take care of you and give you strength to do whatever has to be done."

Calla stepped back from her. "I know." She said that only because it was what Mrs. Jenkins expected. She really didn't know anything. "But I can't tell Sienna I'm leaving. It doesn't feel right to not tell her."

"Could be that uncle of yours will be here before she knows you're gone out of the house."

"I hope so. I will stay close to watch for him. But if he doesn't come . . ." Calla let her voice die away. She had no idea what she would do if he didn't show up.

"Don't be borrowing trouble. If he don't come today, you come on around to the back and I'll sneak you in. Then you can write that sister of yours a letter explaining things if you want to. I'll find a way to get it to her."

"I don't want you to be turned out on the street too."

"That isn't likely to happen without some warning since there are a pile of girls here needing three meals a day." She smiled. "But were it to happen, I've got a daughter who'd take me in. Might take you in too if'n I asked her to. Leastways till you found a place to work."

Calla lifted her chin and tried to sound sure as she said, "Thank you, but I think he will come. Maybe with my mother. That's what I'm praying."

"I was praying the same right along with you, but in case

there's delays, you take care out on the street. Don't you be going off with no man no matter how nice he might seem. None other than that uncle of yours anyhow. Much as I hate to say it, there's people a girl like you can't trust. So you stay back in the shadows and try to look like you got a place to be. Pretend to be heading that way if anybody is noticing. Best pay attention to a store open along the street you can go in if the need arises."

"All right." A tremble went through Calla. She'd never been totally alone on the streets of Louisville.

"I'm not aiming to scare you, but best to be forewarned so you can avoid bad things happening." She moved over to the cabinet and pulled out some bread and cheese to wrap in brown paper. She filled a jar with water and handed it to Calla to put in her cloth bag. Then she reached up on the very top of the cabinet and pulled down a jar with coins in it. She poured out several into Calla's hand. "That will tide you over a little while. If you're feared to come back in here tonight and need a place, a friend of mine, Mrs. Hawkins, has a boardinghouse two blocks over. You tell her I sent you and that if she needs kitchen help, I said she should take you in."

"Thank you, Mrs. Jenkins. I'll never forget how kind you've been to me."

"The Lord intends us to do good for one another." She reached back in a tin box and pulled out a biscuit. She found a piece of leftover bacon to add to it. "A girl needs breakfast no matter what anybody says."

The way Calla's stomach felt, she didn't know if she could eat a thing without it coming right back up, but she took the biscuit and bacon with another thank-you.

119

Mrs. Jenkins pushed her toward the back entrance. "Now, you better be on out of here before trouble starts brewing. Me and you, the two of us, can keep on praying that uncle shows up to rescue you."

Calla stepped out the back door into whatever happened next. She stood still and watched the first rays of sunshine push up into the sky over the buildings. *Please, Lord, let that next thing be Meadowland.*

12

"nneliese!"

Her cries came back to him from the burning barn. He ran through the flames climbing the timbers around the door. He had to get to her. He called her name again, but he couldn't see anything through the smoke rolling down from the hay in the loft. He put his arm up in front of his face to protect his eyes. Where was she?

A rafter fell behind him, scattering the flames. The scorching heat stole his breath. He would die if he didn't get out of the barn, but he couldn't leave without Anneliese. His shirt caught fire.

"Dirk!" Someone yelled his name. It wasn't Anneliese. Then hands were beating out flames on his head.

"You can't save her." His brother jerked him back toward air.

Dirk tried to fight him, but his strength was gone as he struggled for breath. The flames from his shirt flashed higher. Frank knocked him to the ground and lay on top of him to smother the fire.

"Anneliese." The name echoed in his head. Anneliese.

Dirk woke with a start, disoriented and unsure where he

was. Not his windowed sleeping room at Meadowland. Only one small window here to grudgingly let in the gray light of dawn. He pushed back the blanket and sat up to stare around the room. As the images in his dream receded, the events of the day before swooshed back at him. He was in a seedy hotel in the town of Maryville, a couple of miles from the Rest Haven Sanitarium where Frank's widow awaited his return.

He shook his head to shed the last traces of the dream. The nightmares had once come nearly every night, but time had pushed the terror of the fire deeper in his mind. He hoped he hadn't screamed Anneliese's name loud enough to wake others in the hotel. His breath was still raspy as he got up to stare out the window. Morning light was creeping along the town's empty street. He raised the window and breathed in the outside air to clear his head of the memory of smoke. A truck stopped in front of the hotel. The clank of the milk bottles the driver carried to the door signaled the beginning of the day. A normal day.

Not that anything about this day would be normal for Dirk. As soon as the sun came up, he would go back to the sanitarium to get Frank's widow. Then the two of them would rescue her children from the orphanage before he drove back to Meadowland. With them still in his car.

That seemed almost as much of a fantasy as the dream had been. But was it a nightmare? Sharing his home with three females was going to upend his life, but good or bad, he intended to take them to Meadowland. He had that in mind when he drove his Model T away from the farm toward the orphanage yesterday morning. He might have still found a way to sidestep the situation until that little girl had wrapped her thin arms around him. Nothing could shake his resolve now.

The milkman's truck pulled away from the curb, on to his next delivery. Across the street, a man stopped in front of a barbershop to unlock the door. Dirk ran his hand through his hair that could use a trim. At least the hair he still had.

His mother had wanted him to get a wig to hide the damage to his scalp, but what would hide the damage to his face? A mask? When he had asked her that, she had stood silent as if mulling over such a course. She had wanted him to consider many things after he recovered. Prayer for one. Forgiveness for another.

He was never sure exactly who or what she thought he should forgive. When he asked her, she had gone back to how he should pray. She'd asked the preacher to come pray over him while no one expected him to live. Later, once he was well enough to talk again, he'd sent the preacher on his way. Prayers were simply empty words after he lost Anneliese. What could prayer do for him? Or for his mother once she was felled by a stroke?

He'd come in for supper to find her on the kitchen floor. Perfectly fine when he'd gone out on the farm after lunch and unable to speak when he knelt over her. He had wanted to weep at the way her face was twisted. Something the same as his, without the scars. He hadn't prayed for her, even though he imagined her eyes begged him to do so.

He did fetch the doctor and sent for the preacher. The doctor had sadly shaken his head, but the preacher had prayed over her more than once in the three days she had lingered. Perhaps the man's words gave her an easier passing. Dirk would not have denied her that, no matter how false the prayers sounded to his ears.

Dirk sighed, wondering if the dream had brought these other sad thoughts to mind. As he stepped back from the window, he looked at the rumpled bed, but no need trying to get any more sleep. Morning was here. Time to face whatever lay ahead. He couldn't go back but only forward. It had always been that way, even on the days when he had wanted to walk back in time and reshape the present.

After he slipped on the shirt that he'd draped over the back of the one chair in the room, his eyes landed on the Bible that lay on the wobbly table beside the bed. His mother had pushed the Bible at him. She printed out verses and laid them on his breakfast plate every morning. If he wouldn't pick up a Bible himself, she was determined to take the Scripture to him however she could. At times she left a Bible open on the table by his bed. He always closed it without reading whatever she hoped would bring him back from his unbelieving ways.

As he stared at the Bible on the table beside him, he smiled at the thought that her ghost must have slipped the book in here. If so, she'd picked a good time, with him having nothing else to read.

Shaking his head at his foolishness, he picked it up. Gideons had placed it there. He knew about them. He'd once gotten a letter asking him to join a Gideon group in Glenville. The letter writer, a Mr. Wallace, had gone into great detail about the blessing of businessmen like himself putting Bibles in hotels and other places to reach those who were spiritually bereft.

Spiritually bereft. The man hadn't realized he had written

to the very kind of man he thought needed the Bibles instead of a man ready to share them.

Dirk sank down in the chair and flipped through the whisper-thin pages. Psalms. His mother had loved the psalms. He stopped on Psalm 23. That had been a favorite of hers. She often printed out the whole chapter to leave on his plate. *Yea, though I walk through the valley of the shadow of death.* She told him he'd been in that valley with the shadow of death over him and the Lord had brought him through.

He didn't argue that truth, but if he gave the Lord credit for getting him through the valley and out the other side, wouldn't he also have to give him the blame for Anneliese being gone from him? She hadn't been in the fire. Instead, she'd deserted him. No prayer could fix that pain.

He slammed the Bible closed to get away from that psalm. No goodness and mercy in his life. He was setting it back on the table when he noticed a few pages doubled over wrong. Whether the Bible spoke to him or not, he couldn't leave it damaged. Opening it once more, he smoothed out the crumpled pages with his hand. Psalms again, and another verse jumped out at him. Psalm 118:24. *This is the day which the Lord hath made; we will rejoice and be glad in it.*

Anneliese had sometimes quoted that one to him whenever they met at the river. Her voice would sing out joyfully as she looked from him up at the sky. She always laughed when he told her he was glad the Lord had made her so beautiful.

He shut the Bible again, this time gently to keep from crumpling any more pages, and laid it back on the table. He thought again of the men who had placed Bibles in these hotel rooms with the hope of ministering to strangers. Perhaps others would find joy in the psalms rather than the memory of sorrow.

He put on his boots, stood up, and gathered his belongings to leave the room and the Bible behind. He wondered if Frank's widow had found comfort in Scripture after Frank died. Rose Meadows looked like a woman who would believe in prayer and the Bible. If that was so, he would let her know at the first word that he would not abide her preaching at him.

They would each have to walk their own paths in regard to the Lord. He didn't doubt the existence of God. He saw the wonder of creation in the nature he studied, but that didn't mean he believed the Lord had a speck of personal interest in him.

In front of the small mirror over the chest in the room, he smoothed down his hair and jammed his hat down on his head. He arranged the scarf to hide as much of the scarring on his neck and cheek as he could. Then he stared at himself in the wavy mirror.

If things proved difficult for him with Frank's family taking over the house, he could always build a small cabin down by the river where he could watch its waters flow past. That way he would have a place if solitude wasn't possible at the house. A man like him needed solitude.

On the way to the sanitarium, he stopped at a little store to fill the gas tank and buy a sandwich for his breakfast, along with some crackers and cheese to take with him. Frank's widow might be hungry, although she would surely have eaten by the time he got there to pick her up.

He shook his head a little. He needed to stop thinking of her only as Frank's widow. She had a perfectly nice name.

Rose. It suited her. He'd thought so when he first met her after she and Frank got married. The one time he'd met her. A beauty then with the freshness of youth. Even now, in spite of how her illness had taken the bloom from her cheeks, she was a beautiful woman.

He wondered again why she hadn't remarried. His face warmed a little as he thought about offering her a marriage of convenience if she was concerned about her reputation. The offer had surprised her. It had surprised him. The words had spilled out before he thought, but he had no reason to be embarrassed about it. He was simply trying to put her at ease.

Still, he shouldn't have been so frank in speaking to her. She barely knew him. He barely knew her. He finished off the sandwich and started up his car to continue on to the sanitarium.

He caught a glimpse of his face in the car's rear mirror as he adjusted it. He had to laugh at himself. Even the thought of marriage to someone who looked like him, whether in name only or not, was surely reason enough for the way she shrank back in her chair after his foolish offer. She would not want to close the door on finding a proper match if she regained her health.

As she should. He had never entertained the idea of marriage after his Anneliese disappeared from his life. He had lost the chance for love when he lost her.

His hope of getting back to the orphanage before noon was lost amid the sanitarium paperwork and the last-minute consultations the doctor insisted she had to have with Rose. There was nothing for it but to pretend patience and wait in the visitors' room. More than once, he had to willfully stop the nervous bobbing up and down of his right leg.

A few magazines were scattered on a side table but none that could claim his interest. Some had silly romantic stories. Others, unbelievable stories of the Wild West. He almost wished the Gideons had left a Bible in this place. Almost.

He had not set out on this trip prepared. He should have brought a notebook with him to jot down ideas for a new magazine article or at least bought one when he realized it wasn't going to be the one-day trip he'd imagined it would be.

Mental notes. He could make those or might have been able to if his thoughts weren't so disjointed. He kept thinking about Frank's daughters, who by now might be wondering if his promise had meant nothing and he was not coming back to rescue them. A few hours one way or another, even a few days wouldn't matter. He would keep his word to that child whatever it took. He stared at the wall across from him in the small room and hoped the doctor didn't talk Rose into staying.

Rose. There, he had thought of her by her name instead of as Frank's widow. That had to be an improvement. She had smiled and looked happy when she saw him that morning before he was ushered to this small room and told to wait. No one else was waiting. He got up and paced back and forth, but it was barely two steps one way and two steps back. If he tried to go in a circle, he'd end up dizzy. He should have insisted on waiting outside or in his car. Was the doctor hoping he would leave without Rose?

He shook his head. That might be true of the battle-ax at the orphanage, but not Dr. Halvechs. She appeared to truly have the welfare of her patient in mind. Perhaps he was wrong to take that patient to Meadowland, but he couldn't keep his word to the daughters without their mother.

At last someone told him to bring his Model T to the front door. After another wait, thankfully shorter this time, Dr. Halvechs came out with Rose. A young man followed them with Rose's suitcase and a box of what looked like feathers and ribbons. He handed Dirk the box and set the suitcase down before telling Rose goodbye and going back inside.

When Rose noticed Dirk frowning at the box, she said, "My milliner supplies, but I can leave them here if there isn't room. Or perhaps hold it in my lap."

"That won't be necessary. We'll make room."

He had never been particularly happy with anything but the price when he bought the touring car from a lawyer in Glenville. Now, however, it appeared he had just what he needed to transport Rose and her daughters to Meadowland. His mother would say that was the Lord knowing what lay ahead for him. He pushed the thought away. Handling that Bible this morning had opened doors on thoughts he hadn't had for years.

"If you're sure." The poor woman looked pale and uncertain.

The morning appeared to have already drained her energy even before the long drive ahead of them. He should have come on the train and hired a car to the sanitarium and the orphanage. That would have made for a faster trip, or perhaps not if the train schedule didn't match theirs. His car wasn't new, but it was reliable. It would get them home, and home he aimed to be before the day was over.

He did not want to spend another night away from Meadowland. At least he had arranged with Lincoln Rainsley, the boy who helped him with farm chores, to come feed the animals, milk the cow, and see to Maisy. Dirk had intended to be home last night, but Lincoln knew to check to be sure, since travel glitches could happen. Maisy and the cow would be fine. Dirk was the one not feeling fine with all the delays. He did like things to stay on schedule.

"It will fit. The girls won't need that much room." He balanced the box on one arm while he pulled open the car door to shove the hat-making supplies onto the back seat. Then he stowed the suitcase in the space behind the seat.

"The girls." Rose whispered the words like a prayer as a smile lit up her face. She turned to the doctor to say her goodbyes.

"Remember to rest, Rose dear." Dr. Halvechs looked past her to Dirk. "You must see that she does, Mr. Meadows."

"Yes, ma'am," Dirk said. "She will have sunshine, fresh air, and as much rest as she wants or needs."

The women hugged. Then the doctor stepped back and swiped a tear off her cheek. "It is always good to see someone well enough to leave here. Do take care. I will pray for you." She touched Rose's cheek and then gestured toward Dirk. "And for you too, sir."

"Me?" Dirk frowned at the doctor. "I'm not in need of prayer."

Dr. Halvechs shook her head with a small smile. "My dear sir, we are all in need of prayer each and every day."

"I'm sure your patients keep you on your knees enough, Doctor, without adding me to your prayers."

"You speak the truth there, Mr. Meadows, but I also pray for my patients' families."

He wanted to tell her to save her prayers, but he feared that might bring on a lengthy sermon. They did need to get on the road. So instead, he merely nodded as he helped Rose into the front seat.

At last they left the sanitarium behind.

13

ose leaned out the window to wave and then coughed as she sank back into the seat. While she hated to admit it, she was exhausted. Dr. Bess had warned her fatigue would continue to bedevil her, but she kept thinking she could conquer it. Sadly, some things took more than simple willpower.

After a couple of slow breaths to ease her wheezing, she glanced over at Dirk gripping the wheel of his car. "I do hope you won't be offended if I nod off. I didn't sleep well last night. Too excited, I suppose."

He kept his eyes on the road. "If you can sleep, that would be fine. You need to conserve your energy for when we get to the orphanage."

"I can't wait to hug my daughters." Rose shut her eyes and pulled up the image of Calla and Sienna when she'd left them. She tried to imagine how much they would have changed in the two years since. "For a while, when my tuberculosis continued to be active, I feared I might never see them again." She opened her eyes and smiled over at Dirk. "Thank you, Mr. Meadows. This is so much more than I expected when I wrote you."

"But not more than your daughter asked." After a quick

glance at her, he stared back at the road. "And please, let us be friends enough to not be so formal. Call me Dirk."

"Yes, of course." She hesitated, but he was Frank's brother, the same as family. There was no wrong in calling him by his given name. "Dirk. Is that a family name?"

"No. My father knew a boy named Dirk once and the name had always stuck in his head. He thought it sounded manly." He shrugged a little. "Hoped it would make me strong, I guess. But both Frank and I were also named after him, Samuel Franklin Meadows. My mother tacked Samuel onto my name and gave Frank his middle name and her maiden name Franklin Barton."

"Frank never told me his name was Franklin." Funny that she had loved Frank without ever knowing his birth name.

"I doubt anybody knew except family. He didn't like Franklin. Said Franklin Barton Meadows was more name than any man might need. Just plain Frank Meadows suited him better."

"That does sound like Frank." Rose smiled. "He liked being direct."

"Yes."

Rose thought directness might be a trait he'd shared with his brother. Dirk Meadows had been very direct when he'd offered to marry her to protect her reputation. An offer made with kindness, she was sure. It could be that she and the girls moving into his house would cause talk. Perhaps he was concerned about his own reputation. He appeared to be a man of honor who would want to do the right thing, but what was the right thing?

Silence fell over them. She was glad the Model T wasn't open to the air. The sun coming through the window beside her felt good. She so often felt chilled. She should have asked Dr. Bess for a lap blanket for the trip.

The car sputtered along at what seemed a fair speed, bouncing over rough stretches of road here and there, although Dirk appeared to slow the car to avoid the worst bumps. He kept his eyes on the road and did nothing to initiate conversation. Perhaps driving needed that much concentration. She didn't know, since she'd never been behind a wheel to drive anything. She'd rarely even ridden in a motorcar.

She had said she might sleep, and the chugging rattle of the car motor could make talking difficult. Not the same as riding along in a buggy. Still, if she was going to live in this man's house, she should try to get to know him better and the ride to Louisville seemed a good time to do that.

With his right side toward her, she couldn't see any scars. He had a strong profile, a nice-looking man. His nose reminded her of Frank, but nothing else did. The way Frank's eyes lit up when he smiled had always been his best feature. This man, his brother, didn't look as though smiles ever set easily on his face. No smile crinkles spread out from the corner of his eye, but surely he did smile sometimes, even if he did want to close out the world.

How would her girls manage with such a solemn man? Rose shook away the worry. They wouldn't need his smiles. They would have plenty of their own. Not that Frank had always worn a smile when he was home. She had never been able to make him as happy as she wished she could. But then, as Miss Wilma had told her, one couldn't be totally responsible for another's happiness. Contentment came from inside a person when they were right with the Lord and ready to dwell on the things of life that mattered.

Dear Miss Wilma. If only she had still been living, she would have taken in the girls and loved them without measure. So many ifs in life. If Frank had been happier with her. If he hadn't hated his job working on the city streets. If she had supported his idea of going west. If he hadn't gone to the army. If any of those things had or hadn't happened, Frank might have never caught the influenza. They might have lived in a better place, a warmer place, and she might not have gotten so sick that she had to spend time at a sanitarium.

Again she thought of Miss Wilma. She always looked on the positive side. She would advise Rose to think of more positive ifs. If not for her years with Frank, she wouldn't have two daughters to love. If not for her time in the sanitarium, she might not be alive to love them more. If not for this solemn man beside her, she might not be on the way to get those daughters and have a place to live. A place in the sunshine.

Be thankful for each and every blessing, Miss Wilma was always telling her. Things like how sunshine through the car window felt so nice. How she was able to pull a breath into her lungs. The blessing of this man willing to help his brother's family. For the steady noise of the car taking her ever closer to her daughters.

When they bounced over a bump, Rose braced herself with a hand on the dash. The jostle brought on a new burst of coughs she covered with her handkerchief.

"Sorry." Dirk glanced over at her. "Are you all right? Do we need to stop?" He eased off the gas.

She shook her head as she wiped her mouth. When she could talk, she said, "No, no. I'm fine. I hope the coughing doesn't worry you. Dr. Bess said I would continue to cough and be short of breath at times, but that as long as I was careful, no one should catch anything from me."

"I wasn't concerned about that," he said.

"You should be. It's a debilitating disease that is often deadly. I worry about Calla and Sienna." She did worry that she might be endangering them simply because she had such a need to be with them again.

"I'll be fine and they will be too." He gave the car more gas to continue down the road.

"I don't think we can be sure of that, but we can hope," she said and then remembered Miss Wilma again. "And pray."

"Sounds like my mother. She was always ready to pray about something or anything."

"I'm sure she said many prayers for you."

"Oh yes. And for Frank as well." He didn't sound happy about her prayers.

"I suppose all mothers pray for their children," Rose said softly.

"That could be true," Dirk said. "Whether their prayers help anything is another matter."

"Do you not believe in prayer?" Rose couldn't keep the surprise out of her voice.

"Oh, I believe people pray. At one time, I threw a few prayers up toward the sky. Never had much luck with any of them. So I stopped."

"I don't think prayer has anything to do with luck. Faith is what matters when you pray."

"Faith. Another interesting concept. Did you pray that Frank would come home from the war? What happened to your faith when he didn't? Or when you had to leave your children at an orphanage. What kind of answer to prayer was that?"

"I did pray the war would end and Frank would come home. And no mother would want to leave her children at an orphanage."

"Then it sounds like a few of your prayers bounced off clouds and brought nothing but sad rain. Do you still have faith that prayers are answered?" His grip on the steering wheel tightened before he seemed to purposely loosen his hold, finger by finger.

"Yes." She said the word flatly, then added, "The Bible says we'll all have troubles, but the Lord will never desert us."

"He deserted me."

"How sad that you think that, but—"

He interrupted her. "We might as well get one thing straight right away." He didn't look toward her, but it was easy to hear the frown in his voice. "I know you mean well, but I won't be preached at."

She clutched her hands in her lap as she searched for what to say. Prayer had always meant so much to her, especially when things were difficult. She couldn't imagine life without the assurance of the Lord's love. At the same time, she was dependent on Dirk's charity and she would have to abide with his wishes. She sent up a prayer for the right words.

"Please forgive me if I spoke out of turn. I didn't intend to preach at you." She paused to gather more courage for her next words. "I will be more careful to not intrude on your beliefs, or lack of belief, but I do request you not try to turn my daughters from the Lord."

"I wouldn't do that," Dirk said. "I'm aware of the comfort some get from religion. If your daughters have managed to not feel the Lord has turned his back on them while in that orphanage, I won't be the one to convince them of the futility of prayer."

"Even as you are the answer to theirs. And mine."

"That is close to preaching again."

"Not preaching. Merely truth." Some things needed to be said.

He made no comment to that as an uncomfortable silence fell between them. She leaned back and closed her eyes in an attempt to ignore the tension inside the car, but the ride was too bumpy for sleep. She stared out the window at the occasional farmhouse they passed. The day was nice. Sunshine and blue skies. That should have settled peace over her, but it didn't.

Dr. Bess had warned her that upsets and worry could not only slow her recovery but make her symptoms worsen. She turned her hands palms up in her lap in a gesture to receive whatever the Lord might send to calm her spirit.

A passage from Romans played through her mind. *For I am persuaded, that neither death, nor life, nor angels, nor principalities, nor powers, nor things present, nor things to come, nor height, nor depth, nor any other creature, shall be able to separate us from the love of God.*

Nothing could separate her and her daughters from the love of God. Not things present or things to come. Or those things that had already happened. Not losing Frank or being in the sanitarium. Certainly not the unhappy past of this man next to her who seemed to be holding the Lord to blame for the sorrows in his life. The visible scars from the fire must be matched by invisible scars on the inside. She would determine not to be the cause of further scars.

Another verse came to mind from the Beatitudes. *Blessed are the peacemakers for they shall be called the children of God.* She could be a peacemaker or at least try to be. She searched her mind for something to say that might lead to an easier feeling between them.

Before she could come up with anything, the car bounced over another rough stretch of road, and he spoke first. "These roads need some work."

"Frank did that before he went to the army. Worked on the city streets."

"That surprises me. Doesn't sound like something he would want to do."

"He didn't like it, but it was a job. What would you have thought he would do?" Rose was curious. This brother knew things about Frank that she didn't.

"Not breaking rock for roads." He was quiet a moment before he went on. "Something with horses maybe. Or a salesman. He was always a good talker." He glanced over at her. "Or with your influence, he might have made a preacher."

She pretended not to note the jab in his words. "He did make friends easily, but he was rarely satisfied at any job he found. He wanted to go west."

"And do what? I can't imagine him homesteading. He never liked farming."

"I don't know. But I do now regret I was too timid to encourage his dreams of finding a fresh start, but the girls were so young. I wanted to be settled. I guess I didn't have his adventuresome spirit."

"Understandable enough."

"He would have liked having a car like this one, but he never had enough money."

"He should have saved the money he got when my mother died."

She wanted to ask what money, but she bit back the words. If there had been money, it was gone now. Frank had a way of letting money slide through his fingers with no thought of saving for the future. Or even the present.

"Cars were more expensive then." She wouldn't admit to Frank's brother that she knew nothing about any inheritance from his mother. Or mention Frank's anger over his brother not selling Meadowland.

"So they were," Dirk said. "And less reliable." He pulled his pocket watch out and glanced at it. "Three o'clock. We should be in Louisville in a half hour." He stuffed the time-piece back in his pocket. "You best rest to have energy to face down Miss Warfield at the orphanage."

"She wouldn't try to keep my children from me."

"We can hope not. In your case, perhaps even pray not."

Rose leaned back and closed her eyes. This time she kept them closed and welcomed the silence that fell over them. Talking with Frank's brother was stressful. In time, she might know him better and they could share easy words. Right now, no words seemed best.

He was right. She could pray. A thanksgiving prayer that in less than an hour her children would be with her again. She could forgive a lot from Dirk Meadows for making that come true.

14

Calla was tired after her sleepless night and hours of pacing back and forth on the street in front of the orphanage. She tried to walk with purpose as though she had a destination in mind. She did have a destination in mind. Meadowland. But as the morning hours passed, she began to lose hope. And to worry. What would she do if night came without her uncle coming back? If two nights came?

He would come, she told herself over and over as she walked. And then new worries popped up. He had gone to get her mother. What if she was still too sick to come? If he came back anyway, she could go with him, but she couldn't go without Sienna. She almost wished the door would open and Sienna would slip out to the street as she had threatened to do when they were closed in the closet.

Calla shook away the thought. If that happened, then they would both be vagrants on the street. Vagrants. They arrested vagrants. Her uncle would never find her in jail. No one would ever find her in jail. She looked around, hoping not to see a policeman bearing down on her.

No policemen were in sight, but there was that man again. He had already walked past Calla twice in the last hour. The last time he stopped and stared as she passed him. Something about the way he looked at her made her wish she was back inside the orphanage. Anywhere out of sight.

A car honked at her as she stepped off the sidewalk to cross the street to a drugstore. Mrs. Jenkins had said to go in a store if she got worried about something out on the street. Something like a strange man watching her.

When she went inside, the bell rang over the door, and the man behind a soda fountain counter frowned at her. He must be remembering the three times she'd already been in the store without buying anything.

Two women sat on the stools in front of the counter. Glass dishes piled high with ice cream covered in chocolate sat in front of them. Calla's mother had once bought ice cream for them from a street vendor. The cold sweetness of it was delicious.

Calla fingered the coins Mrs. Jenkins had given her that morning, but she couldn't waste it on ice cream, no matter how good it looked. She'd eaten the food the cook had given her a while ago, but she wasn't starving yet. Better to save what little she had in case her uncle didn't show up. She tried to remember how far Mrs. Jenkins had said it was to her friend's boardinghouse.

The large clock over the counter said it was already past three. With each hour that passed, Calla's spirits drooped a little more. She started back toward the door but stopped. Through the shop's big window, she could see the man across the street, leaning against a light pole and watching the drugstore door. Tears pushed at her eyes. She would have never believed she wanted to be back inside the orphanage, but she felt so alone.

She took a breath to slow down the way her heart was

pounding. The man might be nice. He could be a preacher who wanted to help her. But Mrs. Jenkins had warned her not to trust anybody, and Calla hadn't liked the way he'd looked at her earlier. She turned away from the window to stare at the big jars of candy on one of the counters.

"Can I help you with something, miss?" The soda fountain man came over to the candy counter.

"Yes. I'd like a peppermint, please." She could spare a penny. She didn't want this man to tell her she couldn't come back into his store.

The two women spun around on their stools to look at Calla. The younger woman turned back to her ice cream, but the older woman stood up and came over to the candy counter while the man dipped out two peppermints for Calla.

"Two pieces for a penny," he said.

Calla scooted the penny over to him, picked up the candy, and headed for the door. The woman lightly touched her shoulder. "Wait a minute, dear. Are you in need of some help?"

"No," Calla said quickly. She didn't see the man out on the street now and she needed to go back outside. She couldn't see the door of the orphanage from in here. With no idea what kind of car her uncle might have or even if he had come by car, she had to watch for him to walk up to the door. What if she'd missed him already?

"But thank you, ma'am," she added politely.

"You look a little lost. And cold. The wind out there lacks springtime warmth." The woman took off her jacket and draped it around Calla's shoulders.

The velvet jacket felt soft and warm. She had been cold out on the street. But she couldn't keep the woman's coat. She shrugged it off. "I'm fine. I have my sweater."

"No, no, you keep it." She put it around Calla's shoulders again. "I insist. I have another wrap over there." She nodded toward the purse and shawl on the stool beside where she'd been sitting. "Have you come from the orphanage across the street?"

Calla started to lie, but her mother said truth was always best. "I'm not a runaway. I'm too old to be there anymore. They made me leave this morning."

The woman's eyes widened a bit. "They put you out with nowhere to go? That's reprehensible."

"I'm waiting for my uncle. He's coming to get me." She tried to sound sure of that.

"Surely Miss Warfield would let you wait inside."

"Do you know her?" Calla was suddenly curious.

"I do. I give my support to help the Home for Girls."

"Oh." Calla looked toward the counter at the glass dish of ice cream there. "Your ice cream is melting."

"She's right, Mother," the younger woman still at the counter said.

"I've had enough." The woman waved her hand to dismiss the ice cream while keeping her eyes on Calla.

When Calla started toward the door again, the woman caught her arm in a firm grip. "Come sit down with us and we'll figure out what is best to do."

Calla stood still as her heart began pounding again. She was sure the woman meant well, but Calla had to be where she could see the orphanage's door. "I must be outside to watch for my uncle."

When she tried to step away, the woman kept her hold on Calla and moved with her. "Are you certain he's coming?"

"Yes." If only she were sure that was true. "He promised."

"Mother, let her go. She doesn't want your help." The younger woman came over to her mother.

The woman reluctantly let go of Calla's arm. "We'll be here a little longer if you need help, dear. The streets can be dangerous for one your age."

"Yes, ma'am. I'll be careful, but my uncle will be here soon." Calla slipped off the jacket again and this time handed it to the daughter, who took it without comment, although she held it away from her as though it had been soiled by touching Calla those few minutes. Calla wished she could keep it, but what if someone thought she stole it? That might give a policeman an extra reason to haul her off to jail.

Back outside, Calla blew out a breath of relief. That relief was short-lived when she spotted the man across the street, not by the light pole anymore but beside a tree next to the orphanage. He didn't even try to pretend he wasn't looking at her. Maybe she should go back inside the drugstore to ask the woman to wait outside with her. But no, that wouldn't work. The woman might get impatient if Uncle Dirk didn't come soon and insist on Calla going with her. Calla moved away from the drugstore's window until she had a clear view of the orphanage's steps across the street. No one was on them.

———

The sidewalks were almost empty as Dirk hurried back to the orphanage after letting Rose out and then finding a parking spot. A woman moved as far as possible to the inside edge of the sidewalk as she passed him. Halfway up the block, a man leaned against a lamppost, perhaps watching for a bus or taxi.

Rose had already climbed the steps to wait for him at the entrance. Her face was pale and her hands visibly trembling.

"You should have waited to let me help you up the steps," he said.

"I'm fine." She sounded short of breath.

"Maybe you should rest a moment before we go in."

"No, please go ahead and knock. I don't want to wait another second before I see my daughters."

The same girl who had let him in the day before opened the door. Her gaze flew from him to Rose and back to him. For a few seconds she looked as though she might slam the door in their faces.

Dirk stuck his foot against the bottom of the door to keep it open. "We're here to see Miss Warfield." Even to his ears, his voice sounded harsh. He started to smile but decided against it. With half his smiling muscles frozen by his scars, his smile could look scarier than a frown.

Rose did smile, brightly enough for both of them, as she reached toward the girl. "Hello, dear. I'm Rose Meadows, Calla's and Sienna's mother. I've come for them."

Instead of her gentle tone putting the girl at ease, she seemed even more agitated. Finally she nodded slightly. "I'll let Miss Warfield know you're here."

She left them standing outside on the steps as she scurried down the hallway that led to the administrator's office.

"Well," Rose said.

"Don't concern yourself. Unfortunately, my appearance can be upsetting to some as it was to this girl yesterday. Then, no doubt she overheard the unfortunate exchange I had with Miss Warfield to make her uneasy about having to tell the woman I'm here again." Dirk put his hand under Rose's elbow to escort her through the door. He shut it behind them. "We'll wait here a moment to see if she comes back for us. If not, we'll make our own way to the office."

"Do you hear that?" She cocked her head a little to the side to listen.

"What?"

"A child crying."

He did hear some wailing, but the sound was muffled. "I'm sure someone is always crying in this place."

"I suppose you're right, with so many girls here bereft of family." Her eyes looked moist with tears. "They are bound to be sad."

"Yes."

"This may sound foolish, but I have the worst feeling that the child crying is my Sienna." She held her breath and tilted her head as she obviously concentrated on the cries drifting down to them.

"If it is, her tears will turn to smiles when she sees you."

The girl came back down the hall toward them. She looked even more nervous than before as she stopped several feet away from them. "I'm sorry, but Miss Warfield is busy. She suggests you come back in an hour when she will be able to see you."

"That won't do," Dirk said. "We are here now, and if Miss Warfield can't see us, I'm sure there is someone else we can speak to in order to collect Calla and Sienna Meadows."

"Yes, please," Rose added.

The girl licked her lips and looked to the side and then behind her. She lowered her voice to not much above a whisper. "I'm sorry, but I can't help you. I have to do what she says."

"I know." Dirk kept his voice gentle. "Just go tell Calla

we're here. She can collect Sienna and we'll be gone without a problem."

"I can't," she said again.

"Has she forbidden it?" Dirk had more trouble keeping his voice calm.

When the girl flinched, Rose put her hand on his arm before she spoke softly to the girl. "What is your name, dear?"

"Janet."

"Mr. Meadows isn't angry at you. Nor am I. We simply want to see my daughters. If you'll just point me in the right direction, I'll go find Calla and Sienna. Mr. Meadows can wait here so that the other girls won't be upset by a strange man in their hallways."

"Calla's not here."

Rose's face turned pale.

Dirk spoke up again. "She was here yesterday."

Again the girl looked over her shoulder. "Miss Warfield said she was too old to be here any longer. She left this morning."

"For where?"

The girl shrugged. "She was gone before I got up."

Rose took a deep breath as her fingers dug into Dirk's arm. "And Sienna?"

"You mean Annie?" the girl asked.

When Rose looked confused, Dirk said, "That's what they call Sienna here."

"Then, yes, Annie," Rose said.

Again the worried look over her shoulder before she whispered, "She's here." She looked up, as from somewhere above them the wailing of the child got louder.

"That's her, isn't it?" Dirk said.

"Yes."

Rose let her hand slide off his arm, and Dirk, worried she might faint, put an arm around her. The poor woman was so thin he feared hurting her.

"What is wrong with her?" Rose whispered.

"She tried to run away and so they put her in the closet."

"The closet," Rose echoed her words.

The girl's eyes popped open wide. "Don't tell anyone I told you that. Please."

Dirk took a breath to try to control his anger, but he was ready to tear the building apart. "Where is it?"

"I can't." The girl put her hand over her mouth, spun away from them, and ran off down the hallway.

15

*D*irk stared after the girl, not sure if he should confront Miss Warfield and demand Sienna be brought to them or if he should simply find the child himself.

Rose trembled as she leaned against him and looked up. "What have they done to her?"

Her face convinced Dirk. "I'll find her. But first you need to sit down before you fall."

"No, no. I'm fine." She moved away from him but was still visibly trembling.

"It doesn't help to pretend something you're not. You're not fine." He put his arm around her waist to support her again. She didn't try to pull away. "Once we find you a place to sit, I'll get the child."

"But what about Calla?" Despair sounded in her voice.

"First Sienna." He ushered Rose away from the door down an adjoining hallway instead of toward the administrator's office. It might be better for him not to see that woman right now with the way anger boiled through him.

When they found a stairway, Rose sank down on one of the steps and leaned against the railing. "Please bring her to me."

Dirk took the stairs two at a time. A woman peeked out of

a room at him and then slammed the door shut. Suddenly the whole place was too quiet. The child was no longer crying, or at least not loudly enough for him to hear. But the woman in that room would know where she was. He pounded on her door, but the only answer was some shrieks from children inside the room.

He had to control his temper. Storming the place was doing nothing but frightening the orphans. Miss Warfield had probably already put in a call to the police. If he got himself arrested, then what would Rose and the girls do?

He moved out into the middle of the hallway, stood still, and held his breath for a moment to listen. No sounds at all. He spoke then in a normal voice. "I've come for Annie Meadows. Will someone help me find her?" He raised his voice a little. "Sienna, do you hear me?"

"Uncle." The voice was muffled but very excited. "I'm here."

He followed the sound down to the end of the hall where another stairway went up to a third floor. Under it was a closet. "Are you in there, Sienna?"

"I am. Have you come for me?"

"Yes. Your mother is waiting downstairs."

"Mama!" The child squealed and kicked against the door.

"Wait." He tried the knob, but it wouldn't turn. He looked for a key hanging nearby but nothing. "The door is locked."

"Oh, please. You must get it open," she said. "Please."

He jerked the doorknob, but the door was sturdy. He might have forced it open from the inside, but not from the outside. "I'll get a key."

"They won't let you have it." She sounded sad again.

"I'll make them."

He started toward the stairs to confront Miss Warfield when a door along the hallway opened. A pudgy little woman stepped out and closed the door firmly behind her. "Wait," she said. "I have a key."

She looked frightened as she came toward him, but her steps didn't falter. Her gaze swept across his face and he detected a shiver.

"I promise I won't harm you. I'm only here to get Sienna. Her mother is with me."

"Yes." She licked her lips. "I am not frightened of you." She shot a look toward the stairs. "Miss Warfield won't be happy with me."

"I see," Dirk said. "I will tell her I forced you to unlock the door."

"Better for her to think someone left the key hanging on the nail." She pointed toward a nail on the wall near the top of the door. "I'm too short to reach it." She stepped in front of him and turned the key in the lock.

Sienna exploded out of the closet as soon as the door cracked open. She shot a smile at Dirk, but grabbed the little woman in a hug. "Thank you so much, Miss Gertrude. I will never forget you. Never."

The woman stroked Sienna's head as she blinked back tears. "I am sorry I wasn't able to help you more."

"Do you know where Calla is?" Sienna asked.

"No, child, I don't. I'll pray you find her." Suddenly the little woman went stiff when she heard a voice downstairs. She kissed the top of Sienna's head and thrust the key into Dirk's hand. "Put it on the nail." Without another word, she scurried back into the room she'd come from.

Sienna watched her and then turned to Dirk. "I feared you weren't coming."

"I promised." He hooked the string on the key around the nail.

"And Mama is really here?"

"She is." He stooped down in front of her and gently rubbed off the remnants of her tears with his fingers. "We're going to Meadowland."

She looked sad. "I can't go without Calla."

"We will find her." He stood up and held out his hand toward her. "Come. Your mother is anxious to see you."

She took his hand and began pulling him down the hallway. "Oh, yes. I do want to see her too."

At the foot of the stairs, Rose stood beside Miss Warfield, but when she heard them, she looked up with a radiant smile. She held out her arms. "Sienna."

The child let go of Dirk's hand and practically floated off the steps and into her arms. Dirk's heart softened at the sight, even as he worried Rose might fall.

Miss Warfield did not seem moved by the reunion of mother and child as she glared at him. "How dare you go upstairs without permission and frighten our children. I should phone the authorities."

"Why don't you do that?" He gave her a hard look. "When they get here, you can explain why you locked this child in a closet and why you turned her sister out on the street."

The woman's eyes narrowed. "You have no right to question how I run this home. Discipline is necessary when a child refuses to follow rules and bend to instruction." She pointed at Sienna. "And her sister appeared extremely anxious to leave our care. I merely allowed her to do as she wished. At fifteen, she was no longer of an age to be in our institution."

"But you knew I was going to return for them." Dirk continued to glare at her.

"I only knew that was what you said. I had no surety you would carry through on your word."

"Or that I wouldn't."

"Please," Rose spoke up. "It does no good for us to exchange angry words." She appealed to Miss Warfield. "If you can only tell us where Calla might be now."

"I couldn't say. Once they leave this home, I am no longer responsible for them." She lifted her chin as though daring them to question her.

Dirk bit his lip to keep more angry words from spilling out. Rose was right. Anger wasn't accomplishing anything. A plump older woman wearing a stained apron shuffled up the hall toward them.

She smiled and nodded at them as she stopped beside them. "I wonder if I might speak to you a moment, Miss Warfield."

Miss Warfield looked ready to explode as she stared at the woman. "This is not a good time, Mrs. Jenkins."

"I do beg your forgiveness for that." The older woman glanced around at them all again. "But I was hoping you could send someone to help me in the kitchen. Since you sent Callie away, I'm feared I won't get the evening meal ready on time."

"Then perhaps you should have stayed in the kitchen to do your duty," Miss Warfield snapped.

"Yes, ma'am. But I'd been counting on Callie's help and I got some behind on my dishwashing and such. With an extra pair of hands, I'll get things done. I know how you like to keep everything on schedule and all."

Before Miss Warfield could say anything, Mrs. Jenkins looked at Dirk. "You must be the uncle Callie talked about yesterday." Her gaze shifted to Rose. "And you are surely Mrs. Meadows. It is a blessing to see you back from the sanitarium to get your girls." She beamed at Sienna. "I know Annie is as happy as a bluebird in a strawberry patch."

"I would be if Calla was here." Sienna's shoulders slumped.

"I wouldn't worry a minute about that. Your sister was expecting your uncle here and so I'm sure she's waiting outside for you." Mrs. Jenkins looked back at Dirk. "I'd give a good look around for her out there if'n I was you."

"I do think you should return to the kitchen, Mrs. Jenkins, and not be meddling in matters that have nothing to do with you," Miss Warfield said.

"I expect you're right, ma'am. I shouldn't ought to be interfering here where I've got no business." She pulled a long face, but when she turned away from Miss Warfield, she winked at Dirk before she headed back down the hallway, her step lighter.

"I think we have what we came for." Dirk looked from Rose to Miss Warfield. "We will be on our way unless you need Mrs. Meadows to sign something that shows she has reclaimed her children."

"That won't be necessary," the woman said. "I can do the necessary paperwork."

Rose showed more kindness than Dirk felt. "Thank you for taking in my children when we had such a desperate need."

"Of course," Miss Warfield sniffed. "It's my sworn duty to care for children in need."

Dirk held in all the things he wanted to say to the woman. Right then, they simply needed to get outside and find Calla. They started for the door, but Sienna stopped and gave the woman a very serious look. "Goodbye, Miss Warfield. I will pray for you."

"You better save your prayers for yourself, child. I fear you will be in more need of them than anyone here."

"No, I don't think so. You are the one who needs them." She turned away from her and continued on to the door, tugging on her mother's hand. "Hurry. We have to find Calla."

None of them looked back as they went out the door.

16

Calla hoped every car that came up or down the street would stop in front of the orphanage and her uncle would get out. She hadn't crossed back over the street but stayed near the drugstore. She didn't want to go back inside, but if the man came toward her, she would. After another quick peek over at him, she didn't look directly at him again.

Ignoring him was surely best. But simply knowing he was there was a worrisome poke. She tried to shake it away. Being alone out on the street had made her nervous. That and Mrs. Jenkins's warnings. She could be only imagining the man was watching her. He might be merely waiting for a ride the same as she was. What reason would he have to be watching her? She pulled in a deep breath and let it out slowly.

Her hand was sticky from clutching the peppermint candy. The clerk hadn't given her a sack since he probably thought she'd eat it right away. She could, but she wanted to share it with Sienna after her uncle came. Thinking that felt like a promise he had to come. She slipped the candy in her sweater pocket. A little lint on it would be better than the candy melting in her hand. She licked the peppermint taste off her fingers.

The daylight dimmed a bit as the sun slipped behind a big brick building up the street from the orphanage. That didn't mean it was near sundown. The building was tall. Even so, Calla's heart sped up a little. She couldn't stay out here on the street all night. She'd have to go find the boardinghouse Mrs. Jenkins mentioned. Calla watched the passing cars with more urgency.

A bus rumbled by, blocking her view of the orphanage's entry and of the man across the street. After it passed, the doorstep of the orphanage was still empty and the man was no longer there against the tree. Other people moved along the sidewalk, but none of them paid any attention to her.

One prayer answered. Now if the other would be answered. *Please, Lord, let the next car be my uncle's. And let Mama be with him.*

If the Lord would answer those prayers and let them all go to Meadowland, she wouldn't ask for anything else. Maybe ever.

She waited for a break in the traffic and ran across the street to be closer to the orphanage if her uncle came. Not if. When. She had to believe it was going to happen. It had to happen.

The cars continued to roll past, some rattling so loudly that she could hardly hear anything else. Others purred past, but none of them stopped. Across the street, the lady came out of the drugstore. She stared over at Calla while her daughter put her hand under the woman's elbow to urge her on up the street. The lady went a few steps before she stopped and pulled away from her daughter. She did seem determined to help Calla.

But even if she meant well, Calla couldn't go with her.

Not when Uncle Dirk would be there at any minute. He had to be. Calla walked determinedly toward the orphanage and then past it. When she turned to come back the other way, the woman was still there. Calla stepped off the sidewalk onto the bricked area in front of the orphanage's steps. She could slip around to the side of the building into the shadows until the woman gave in to her daughter's urging and moved away.

She was looking over her shoulder at the street to see if the woman had left when someone spoke in front of her.

"Hello, dear. I'm guessing you're in need of a place to stay." The man, who must have been watching her after all, pushed away from the side of the building.

Calla's heart bounded up in her throat.

"Don't be frightened. I simply want to help you." He smiled, but something about the look in his eyes was all wrong.

Calla shivered and backed away from him. "I don't need any help."

"But you are so alone. I'm guessing they put you out of the orphanage and you have nowhere to go. I can fix that for you."

"No. My uncle is coming for me."

"Are you sure he knew when to come? Maybe he forgot." The man's voice was low, insistent, frightening. "I can be your uncle." He reached out and grabbed her arm.

"No." Calla jerked away from him and ran toward the street.

He caught her before she got out of the shadow of the building and back to the sidewalk.

"You don't have to be afraid of me." He twisted her

around to look at him. "You're a pretty girl. I can make sure you never want for anything. As long as you do what I say."

Calla went very still as she stared at him. "Let me go or I'll scream."

"Merely a waste of breath, my dear. It's so noisy I doubt anyone will hear." His smile never changed as his hands tightened on her arms. "And even if they did, they'd pay it no mind. Screams around this building aren't uncommon."

"Help," she yelled as loudly as she could. The noise of the cars passing by swallowed up the sound just as he said it would.

"Poor dear. I'm your help. Come now, be good and I won't have to hurt you. My friend is pulling up in a car right over there. I've just been waiting for him to get here."

She chocked her feet against the bricks and screamed as he half carried, half dragged her along with him.

"You are making this more difficult than it needs to be." His voice lost its silken tone and became gruff.

Then the woman from the drugstore was in front of them. "Unhand that girl," she demanded.

"Beg your pardon, madam, but this is none of your business." The man sounded very sure of his words. "I'm this girl's uncle and this is merely a family issue."

The woman looked unsure of what to believe.

"He's not my uncle," Calla said.

"Poor misguided girl." The man smiled at the lady. "She's caused her mother nothing but worry since the poor woman lost her husband a year ago." The man shook Calla. "This one—"

"No, he's lying." Calla talked over his words.

He raised his voice to drown out her protests as he tightened his grip on her upper arms until it hurt. "This one is always wanting to chase after trouble. She ran away to meet a boy. You know how girls this age can be. So sure they are in love and then end up ruined. As her mother's brother, I can't allow that now, can I?"

"I suppose not," the woman said.

"He's lying," Calla said again. "I am waiting for my uncle, but he's not my uncle." She was frantic. "Please, you have to believe me."

The woman pressed her lips into a determined line as she eyed the man. "I think I saw a policeman heading this way. We'll wait and let him sort this out."

The man's smile disappeared. "I don't think so." He grasped Calla tighter, lifted her off her feet, and rammed his shoulder into the woman. She stumbled back and fell.

Calla kicked and screamed, but nobody else stepped up to help her. The man paid no attention as he moved on toward a car pulled up to the sidewalk. The woman's daughter rushed to her mother. Up the street, Calla did see a policeman. When she screamed again, he blew his whistle and started running, but he was too far away.

The man yanked open the car door. The driver yelled at him. "Leave the girl and get in before we both end up in jail."

"She's too good a prize to let go," the man said. "She's mine."

The man behind the wheel swore as he reached toward Calla to pull her into the car as the man on the sidewalk attempted to shove her in the seat. Calla kept her legs and arms stiff and refused to bend them even though she thought her arm might break.

All of a sudden, somebody grabbed the man and spun

him around. Calla broke free and fell to her knees. The man in the car sped away from the sidewalk with the open door flapping. Horns blew as he cut into the traffic.

Dirk! Calla could hardly believe her uncle had come from nowhere to grab the man and knock him down with one blow. The man scrambled up and took off. The policeman ordered him to stop, but the man paid no attention and raced past him. The policeman blew his whistle and started after him, but the man ducked down a side street and was out of sight.

Uncle Dirk had lost his hat so his entire scarred face and head were visible. That didn't give Calla pause as she wrapped her arms around him and buried her face against his chest. His heart was pounding under his jacket. Hers was doing the same.

"Thank you," she whispered and began to sob.

He gently stroked her head. "Shh, Calla. You're safe now. I'm here. And so is your mother."

Calla looked up at him. "Mother?"

His sideways smile lifted one side of his face as he nodded toward the orphanage. And there coming down the steps was her mother with Sienna. "Are we going to Meadowland?"

"Yes, indeed."

Relief whooshed through Rose as she watched Calla hugging Dirk. She sank down onto the steps, still holding the railing with one hand and Sienna's hand with the other. Thank the Lord Dirk was with her. He might not believe in prayer, but he continued to be an answer to hers.

"Are you all right, Mama?" Sienna looked scared.

"I'm fine. Now that your uncle has Calla. I'm just a little out of breath."

"Was that man trying to steal Calla?" Sienna frowned as she looked from Rose to Calla.

"It did look that way."

"Why?"

Rose couldn't explain her fears about the man's intentions to one as young as Sienna. She moistened her lips and said, "For no good reasons."

"Was he going to hurt Calla?"

"Yes, I think he was."

"Then I'm glad Uncle hit him." She pulled away from Rose and curled both her hands into fists. "I hate being too small to do anything when somebody is being mean."

Rose put her arm around Sienna and pulled her close. "And I hate being too weak to do anything when somebody is hurting my girls."

"I'm glad we have Uncle now to be strong for us," Sienna said.

"So am I, sweetheart. So am I."

Down on the sidewalk things were getting crazy. A young woman was bending over an older woman who sat on the sidewalk. Rose had no idea why. A policeman frantically blew his whistle as he chased after the man who had tried to kidnap Calla. Another policeman, also blowing his whistle, ran across the street. Alerted by the policemen's whistles, people streamed out of the shops. Traffic slowed to a crawl as drivers looked to see what was happening.

Miss Warfield stepped out of the door behind Rose.

"What in the world is going on out here?" she demanded.

Sienna edged even closer to Rose. A tremble ran through her.

"I'm not exactly sure," Rose said. "Perhaps you should ask the policeman."

"It's that man with you. He's a troublemaker," she said.

Sienna went stiff, and Rose tightened her arm around her. The child was nothing but skin and bones. Rose whispered to her. "Shh. It's going to be all right."

"Oh, my word," the woman said suddenly. "That is Mrs. Abrams. What has he done to her?" She pushed past Rose and Sienna down the steps and along the sidewalk to where the woman, now on her feet, straightened her hat while the younger woman brushed off her skirt.

"I wanted to stick out my foot and trip her," Sienna said.

"I'm glad you didn't."

"I'm not glad I didn't."

"Then I'll be glad for both of us." Rose smiled. "Now help me up so we can go to Calla. And you need to get your uncle's hat. I think he'll feel better if he can put it back on." Rose's legs were still shaky, but she no longer felt as if she might swoon.

"I don't care if he doesn't have hair on part of his head," Sienna said.

"Nor do I, but I think maybe he does. So fetch his hat for him."

Sienna snatched up the hat and ran to give it to Dirk where he stood with one of the policemen. Dirk took the hat and shoved it down on his head. Sienna hugged Calla and then slipped her hand in Dirk's and leaned against his leg while he talked to the policeman.

Rose couldn't hear what they were saying. She couldn't

hear Miss Warfield talking to the woman who had fallen either, but the woman didn't look at all happy. Rose waited at the bottom of the steps for Calla running toward her.

"Mama!" Joy warred with tears on her face.

Rose opened her arms and Calla stepped into them. "Thank the Lord we came outside in time."

Calla's words spilled out. "I was so scared. I was afraid I'd never see you or Sienna again." Her lips trembled.

Rose stroked her hair and held her gently. "But now here we are. You're safe and your uncle is opening his home to us."

"I prayed that he would come."

"And your prayers and mine were answered." Rose pushed Calla away to see her better. "Look at you. I left a youngster here and now I'm collecting a young lady."

"It's been so long." Calla pulled a handkerchief out of her sweater pocket to rub the last of the tears off her cheeks. A handkerchief embroidered with daisies.

The handkerchief brought back the unspeakable sorrow of leaving her daughters at this place. While she couldn't do anything about getting sick, she had still felt like such a failure as a mother. Rose shut away the memory. Today was a new beginning for her and the girls. "Too long."

"You look pale. Are you still sick?"

"I'm getting better, and being with you and Sienna will help me get even stronger." She pulled her close again.

After a moment, Calla moved back from her and looked over at the women on the sidewalk. "I hope she's not hurt. That lady talking with Miss Warfield tried to help me and the man knocked her down."

"We must go thank her and make sure she's all right."

As they got closer, Rose heard Miss Warfield. "I don't

think you understand the difficulty of dealing with so many youngsters. You can be sure we do our very best to care for those who come into the home, Mrs. Abrams. But when they are of a certain age, they must find their way on their own. Our resources are, as you know, extremely limited. We don't get funds for girls over age thirteen. We allowed Callie to stay well beyond that age. She recently turned fifteen."

"But a child of fourteen or fifteen should not be put out on the street." The woman was glaring at Miss Warfield. "Not until a safe place can be found for her to go. I shudder to think what might have happened to that girl if someone hadn't come to her aid."

"Her uncle was coming for her," Miss Warfield said.

"If that was so, what would the harm have been to allow her to stay within the safety of your building until he got here?" The woman shook her head. "I must say I find it totally unacceptable you didn't allow her to do so. I'm sure our church's committee will as well. We give our support with the expectation that these children will be treated kindly."

"As they are." Miss Warfield appeared to be struggling to hang on to her pleasant expression. When she noticed Calla and Rose coming up behind her, she lost it completely for a moment before she managed a little smile. "Mrs. Meadows, I'm happy you were able to find Callie all right."

"Thankfully we came outside in time." Rose squeezed Calla's hand. She looked at the other woman. "Calla says you tried to help her."

"With little effect, I regret to say." After another quick glance at Rose, she turned her full attention on Calla, ignoring Miss Warfield beside her and the younger woman fidgeting impatiently behind her. With a concerned look, she reached to touch Calla's arm. "My dear child. That had to be dreadfully frightening. Are you all right?"

"I'm okay," Calla said. "I'm glad you didn't believe that man when he said he was my uncle."

"I almost did. He told a convincing story." The woman glanced at Rose again. "So, is this your aunt?"

Calla smiled with a shake of her head. "The man over there with the policemen is the uncle I told you about, but he brought my mother."

"Your mother? How lovely!" The woman beamed at Rose. "I'm so glad your circumstances have improved so that you can have your daughter with you again. Daughters are such a cheer to a mother's heart." She gestured toward the younger woman behind them. "I don't know what I'd do without Deborah, although she does lose patience with me at times." She shot a smile over toward her daughter.

"Now, Mother, that's not true." The young woman shook her head a little. "I simply try to look out for you. If you are all right for the moment, I'll go for our car so you won't have to walk so far. I worry you may have hurt your back."

Miss Warfield looked concerned. "Are you injured, Mrs. Abrams?"

The lady grimaced and touched her hip. "When that man pushed me aside, I did fall hard, but I'm sure I'll be fine. No problem at all. As long as our girl here is safe." She smiled at Calla.

"Thank you for helping me, Mrs. Abrams," Calla said.

"Oh, you noted my name." That seemed to please the lady. "And you are Callie Meadows, I presume."

"No, my name is Calla. Miss Warfield just thought it

would be easier if I didn't have such an odd name and so she called me Callie."

"It simplifies things." Miss Warfield sniffed. "We have so many girls in our care."

"I didn't mind," Calla said. "It was very like my name, but Sienna never liked being called Annie. She did not do well here."

"Sienna?" the woman said.

"My other daughter," Rose said. "She's over there with my brother-in-law."

Miss Warfield's eyes narrowed. "Is he the one who caused you to fall, Mrs. Abrams? He has been nothing but trouble since he showed up here yesterday."

"I rather feel you must be wrong on that count, Miss Warfield." Mrs. Abrams eyed her for a moment. "If you ask me, he seems to be the hero of the piece. Saving this young lady from danger you could have prevented her facing. That would have kept me out of harm's way as well."

"I would never harm you, madam," Miss Warfield said.

"Are you familiar with the Bible passage in Matthew about not harming a little one? 'But whoso shall offend one of these little ones which believe in me, it were better for him that a millstone were hanged about his neck, and that he were drowned in the depth of the sea.'"

"I do know that Scripture." Miss Warfield sounded less than pleased.

"Good. Then I suggest you spend much time in the days ahead considering that verse." Mrs. Abrams turned her attention back to Calla. "And now I would like to meet your sister and your uncle before Deborah brings the car to pick me up."

17

*D*irk had to repeat his reason for slugging the man three times before the policeman put away his handcuffs. Once satisfied with Dirk's account of the happenings, he wrote down Calla's description of the man and talked to Mrs. Abrams, the woman who tried to help Calla and ended up knocked to the ground for her trouble. Then Dirk had to do more talking to convince him Rose and the girls were too exhausted to go to the station to repeat their statements for the record. At last, the policeman said they could leave.

Mrs. Abrams sped away in her daughter's roadster. After a last withering look at Dirk, Miss Warfield disappeared back into the orphanage. The two girls scrambled happily into Dirk's car, but Rose needed his help to get in the front seat. She obviously was far from well.

Dirk was relieved when the car started on the first crank. He was even more relieved to leave Louisville behind and head toward Meadowland. He longed for the solitude of the place, but then he was carrying home an end to his solitude. What had he gotten himself into? That thought kept running through his head.

He had no answers. Behind him, the girls talked in low

voices, but the car was too noisy for him to make out their words. They didn't try to talk to their mother, as if they realized she was too tired to converse. He glanced over at her. She had her eyes closed, but he didn't think she was sleeping. More that it took all her energy just to pull in breaths. At least she wasn't coughing.

Again, what had he gotten himself into? What if the woman died? He was far from ready to take over the care and moral upbringing of two young girls. And would Rose even want a man who had turned his back on the world and the Lord to be the guardian of her daughters?

He wondered if Frank had sometimes been overwhelmed by the enormity of being responsible for these three females. Dirk doubted the young one even remembered her father. But the older girl would. Calla.

Dirk had been ready to explode when he saw that man trying to shove the girl into his car. He'd wanted to stomp him into the sidewalk and might have, if the man hadn't been so nimble on his feet and escaped.

His hands tightened on the steering wheel as he stared out at the road. Daylight was ebbing. It would be full dark when they finally reached Meadowland, still more than an hour's drive away.

How in the world was he going to do this?

He had thought it would be easy. He'd let his brother's family live in some spare rooms at his house. They would occupy their space. He would occupy his. He would keep food in the cupboard and make sure Rose had sunshine and fresh air to continue her cure. The girls would have books and could go to school. He really didn't know when school was in session, but he could find out. He'd even drive them to church on Sundays if they expressed a desire to attend. That didn't mean he would have to attend. He could wait in the car. Watch and wait.

Wasn't that what he'd always done? Watch and wait.

He stared out at the road and remembered.

He'd gone back to the river every day after that first meeting with Anneliese. He carried his fishing pole with him and pretended a new interest in catching their supper. He didn't neglect the farmwork. Getting things done was up to him since his father had passed away in March. His mother had written about his father having some sick spells, but nothing she'd written had prepared him for his father's death. He supposed she wasn't prepared either.

Somehow his mother and Frank kept things going at the farm until his college classes were over. But then, he'd come home, taken off his student clothes, and put on his overalls to get the corn planted and the hay cut. At fourteen, Frank was plenty old enough to help, but he was a reluctant worker. He hated farming and continually pestered their mother to sell Meadowland. For once, his mother stood up to him. She loved the farm as much as Dirk's father had. As much as Dirk did.

Some days Frank would leave in the morning and not drag home until after dark. Their mother made excuses for him, claimed he needed time to work through his grief over the loss of their father. Maybe he did, but Dirk thought he could come to terms with his grief out tending the corn in the fields better than off somewhere getting in trouble.

Then Dirk came across Anneliese on that beautiful day in June, and he started making daily treks to the river to watch for her to come again. She had to come again. Sometimes he felt as if his very breath depended on it.

171

He watched and waited through the last weeks of June. A few times he thought he saw her in the distance near her house across the river. If so, she never moved closer so he could be sure. He could imagine her spotting him there by the river and smiling. She would know his fishing was nothing more than a ruse in hopes of seeing her.

She'd said to call her name, and sometimes he did. Loudly with his hands cupped around his mouth in an attempt to make the sound go farther, but if she heard him, she never came the way she'd promised.

At least he wanted it to be a promise. By July, the first crop of hay was in the barn, the corn too high to plow anymore and months to go before harvesttime. In past summers, his father found plenty for them to do, but Dirk ignored the needed repairs on the barn roof and the fencerows he could clean out. Instead, he went fishing. And waited. Eventually, she would come.

She did. On the sixth day of July, she came across the field to the river as though she owned the world. And he knew this was the girl he would love forever. She wore a white blouse tucked into a red flowered skirt that swirled about her legs as she walked. Her dark hair was caught in a ponytail at the nape of her neck. She was beautiful, and his heart banged around in his chest while he waited for her to wade into the river.

She didn't. She stopped on her side of the river and looked over at him with the slightest of smiles on her lips. "Well, if it isn't the college boy again." She pointed toward his fishing pole. "You've been doing a lot of fishing lately."

"I have."

"Have you caught anything?"

"Not what I wanted to catch." He reeled in his line and laid the pole aside.

"And what were you wanting to catch? A channel cat?"

"Something a lot better than that." He stepped down beside the little waterfall closer to the river's edge.

"What could be better than a big ol' catfish?"

On her side, she, too, moved a little closer to the edge of the river cliff. The water barely made any noise as it flowed past them. The river was at a summertime low, and here the riverbed was smooth, with no rocks jutting up to stir the current. They didn't even have to raise their voices to be heard across the river.

"I'm looking at her."

She laughed then, the way she had the first day they met. "Are you comparing me to a catfish?"

"Never. You're incomparable."

"Another of your big words, college boy?"

"Maybe." He knew he had a silly smile on his face, but he couldn't help it. "You wouldn't have any idea what kind of bait a fellow might use to fish for an incomparable girl, would you?"

"My father would say a Meadows boy wouldn't have any kind of bait that would work on a Rainsley girl." She paused a second and then went on. "If it's a Rainsley girl you are wondering how to catch."

"And what would a Rainsley girl say?"

"Already more than my pa would want me to say to a Meadows boy." She took a quick look over her shoulder as if suddenly worried her father might be heading across the field and see her talking to Dirk. But then she was looking back across the river. "But Pa's not here and we are."

"We are," he echoed her words.

"But we seem to have a river between us."

"It's not all that deep and the day is warm."

"True enough, but"—she flounced her skirt—"I can't take a chance on ruining my skirt. It's new, you know. First time I've worn it. My mother wanted to know if I thought I was going dancing when I came out of the house a little bit ago and who was I expecting to see." She smoothed down her skirt. "I didn't bother telling her."

"And who was that? The one you were expecting to see."

She looked straight across the river at him. "Who else but you?"

He didn't think his heart could beat any faster, but it did. "How did you know I would be here?"

"Don't start pretending, college boy. You've been here every day for weeks, just waiting for me to come."

"I have," he admitted. "Why didn't you come sooner?"

"Alas, my father forbade me. And worse than that, he set my brother to watching me." She stared down at the river a moment before she went on. "He was not pleased about our chance meeting in the middle of the river last month."

"And yet here you are," Dirk said.

"I didn't say I was not pleased, only that he was not."

"And where is your brother now?"

"He and my father are off to town. But the day is passing." She gave him a long look. "Your pants do not look all that new, and as you noted some time ago, the river is low."

He didn't have to be asked twice. He left his shoes on the rock beside the waterfall and slid into the river. Once he climbed out on the other side, he said, "I would swim through floodwaters for you."

174

"Would you?" Her green eyes sparkled like the sun on the river water. She looked over her shoulder toward her house across the field. "You're trespassing, you know."

"So are you." He stepped as close to her as he could without dripping water on her new skirt.

"Am I? How is that?" She raised her eyebrows at him. "My father owns to the middle of the river and some beyond, to hear him tell it. Are you claiming this side while he claims that?"

"No." He could drown in those eyes of hers. "You are trespassing on my heart."

"Oh? I didn't see any no trespassing signs." She reached and took his hand in hers. "I thought it said welcome and come on in."

"And so it did." He took her other hand and they stood there like two children ready to play a game.

What a game it turned out to be all through the rest of the summer! She found ways to slip away from her father's eyes and convinced her brother to cover for her. He was a couple of years younger than Anneliese and was easy to talk into doing whatever she wanted. Besides, she told Dirk, she had her brother believing she was merely plotting to get the field back that her father claimed had been stolen from his father by Dirk's grandfather.

"Is that why you keep coming to the river?" Dirk asked.

She smiled in that secretive way she had and shrugged. "My mother says a wise woman can always find a way to get what she wants."

By the end of summer, he would have done almost anything to keep her slipping her hand into his. He could still almost feel her lips on his from the first time they'd kissed.

A horn jolted him away from his memories. He jerked the wheel to the right, barely in time to miss the truck coming toward them. Rose gasped as the car bounced sideways. The girls in the back let out a couple of chirps of alarm.

"Sorry," he muttered. He didn't look at Rose or over his shoulder at the girls, although he could hear them trying to right the box that must have slid off the seat. "I must have dozed off."

That wasn't much of a falsehood. He had been walking through dreams of the past. But now he was awake. He wasn't sure why he kept letting Anneliese slide into his memories these last few weeks. He'd practiced shutting her out, just as she must have shut him out after she disappeared without a word. He never again wanted to feel the kind of sorrow and pain losing Anneliese had caused him. Better to close down his heart and shut everyone out.

"It's all right, Sienna. Uncle Dirk will take care of us."

Calla's words climbed through the air to Dirk's ears. But could he do what she said? When he saw that man trying to force Calla into his car, rage had filled him. And then once she was safe, he'd held Calla while she cried. He cared. Too much.

Frank's family needed a place to stay. He had plenty of room at Meadowland. In his house. But he didn't want to make room in his heart. He would see to their needs as much as he was able, but they had their mother.

They didn't need him. He didn't need them. He had the farm and his scientific studies. And Maisy. A man could depend on a dog to stay with him.

Night had fallen when he finally turned into his lane. He started to check his mailbox, but Lincoln would have gotten the mail when he came to take care of Maisy and the other animals.

A calm settled over Dirk as he opened the gate, then pulled the car through. He took his time when he got back out to close the gate. The practically full moon was shedding silver light down on the field. He was on his land, where he could close away the world and its sorrow. He would find a way to keep doing that in spite of the three in his car.

"Uncle Dirk." Sienna had her head out the car's window. "Is this a meadow?"

"I suppose you could call it that."

"Is that your house?" She pointed down the lane toward the house visible in the moonlight.

"Yes." He fastened the chain on the gate and walked back to the car.

"Can I walk the rest of the way to the house?"

Dirk frowned a little. "Why would you want to do that? It's a good ways, even though you can see the house from here."

"I want to be in a meadow. With butterflies and bees. Mice and rabbits."

"No butterflies or bees this time of day."

"But a mouse might tickle my toes and I might see a flower. Please," she begged. "Calla will come with me."

Dirk looked out at the field. He had done plenty of walking through moonlit fields to study night insects. No cows were in this field. They would be safe.

"All right. If your mother says you can."

"She does." Sienna scrambled out of the car. "Oh thank you, Uncle Dirk."

With a laugh, Calla climbed out after her. "I'm okay with

picking a flower or two, Sienna, but we aren't going to chase after any mice even if one does tickle your toes."

"I know. Mama says we can't dally. We have to run. But I want to be in a meadow."

She gave Dirk a quick hug, then took off through the field. Her giggles drifted back to him as Calla chased after her.

That child was going to be hard to shut out of his heart.

18

The moonlight felt like magic dust falling around her as Calla ran through the cool night air across the field after Sienna. She couldn't remember the last time she had felt so free. And safe. They were home.

In the middle of the field, Sienna suddenly stopped and began twirling around and around. Her white-blond hair practically sparkled in the moonlight.

Calla caught up with her and laughed. "You're going to be dizzy."

"I like being dizzy." Sienna wobbled a few steps and plopped down in the damp grass. "I'm glad we were right about meadows."

"It might be even better in the sunlight."

"I don't think it could be better." Sienna looked up at her. "But it is night. Does that make you afraid?"

"It's not dark here. It's so light I can see our shadows." She dropped down beside Sienna. She shivered at the thought of the darkness that might have been waiting for her if Uncle Dirk hadn't shown up in time.

As if Sienna read her mind, she asked, "Were you very afraid?"

"I was. More afraid than I've ever been."

"I was very afraid for you." Sienna's voice was so soft Calla had to lean closer to hear her. "Mama was too. I thought she was going to fall down."

"You mean faint?"

"I guess so." Sienna plucked at the grass between them. "Mama's really sick, isn't she?"

"Yes, but with rest she will get better." Calla did hope that was true. "We will have to make sure she gets that rest by doing whatever has to be done at Uncle Dirk's house."

"I'll do whatever you tell me to do, but I never want to go back to that place." Sienna didn't have to name the place for Calla to know where she meant.

"You won't." Calla was certain of that. She'd do whatever was necessary to make sure Sienna never had to return to the Home for Girls. "I'm older now. Even if Mama does need to be in the sanitarium again and Uncle Dirk won't let us stay here, I can find a job and take care of you."

"But I like it here in this meadow." She looked up at the sky. "I like seeing stars."

"So do I." Even with the moon full, some stars still twinkled brightly above them. "We're here now. Miss Wilma used to tell Mama not to borrow trouble. You remember Miss Wilma, don't you?"

"I loved Miss Wilma." Sienna hugged herself. "She made cookies with pink sugar sprinkles."

"She did." Calla gazed up at the stars again. "I used to think about her in heaven watching over us after she died."

"I wish I had one of her cookies now. I'm hungry."

"Oh, wait a minute." Calla dug down in her pocket for

the peppermints. "Here. I forgot these peppermints I bought for us before Mama and Uncle Dirk came."

Sienna popped the candy in her mouth. "It feels funny, but it tastes good."

"Just a little sweater fuzz from my pocket. It won't hurt us." Calla put the other piece of candy in her mouth.

Sienna leaned over to hug Calla. "I'm so glad you're my sister and that we're here in a meadow."

Calla put her arms around Sienna. They were quiet for a moment, but it was far from silent. A steady peeping noise filled the air around them, and somewhere in the distance was a screech.

Sienna raised her head. "What's that?"

"I don't know. Maybe a bird."

"A bird might make that screechy noise, but not this other." Sienna cocked her head to listen better. "Birds stop between chirps. Or screeches."

"I guess, but we're in the country now where there could be different birds. Does it scare you?"

"No. I just want to know what it is. I want to know what everything out here is."

Calla laughed. "And you will, but you can't know it all tonight. We better run on to the house so we can help Mama."

"Do you think Uncle Dirk will know what is singing in the night?" Sienna stood up and brushed off the back of her skirt.

"I'm sure he will, but I don't think we should pester him with too many questions at first. Mama told me he has been a recluse for years."

"What's a recluse?"

"Someone who wants to be alone and away from people."

"Oh." Sienna was silent for a minute. "Then we are messing that up for him."

"Yes."

"Girls, come on," Uncle Dirk yelled at them across the field.

"He sounds mad," Sienna said.

"No, just loud. He wanted us to hear him."

"He was cross in the car."

"How do you know? He never said anything." Calla took Sienna's hand as they walked toward the house.

"I just know when somebody is cross." Sienna looked up at Calla. "Do you think he will get mad like Miss Warfield if I forget to listen?"

"No." Calla tightened her hold on Sienna's hand. "Uncle Dirk won't hurt you."

"How do you know?"

Calla smiled a little. "I just know when somebody is nice."

Sienna giggled. "That's better to know, isn't it?" She yanked on Calla's hand. "Hurry. Let's run the rest of the way."

Uncle Dirk waited for them beside the car. "Your shoes will be wet," he said when they stopped in front of him. He did sound cross.

"We're sorry," Calla said quickly.

"We are," Sienna echoed.

"The moonlight was beautiful," Calla added.

He looked past them toward the field. His face changed. Looked sad almost, before he gave his head a shake as if to get rid of his thoughts.

"Shoes will dry. Come. Your mother is already inside." He took the box out of the car and started toward the house.

"Uncle Dirk, sir," Sienna said in a hesitant voice. "What is singing out there?" Her curiosity must have conquered her worry about him being cross.

"Singing?" He stopped to listen. "No one is singing." He sounded sad. "Not now."

Calla, still grasping Sienna's hand, stopped too. The constant sound hadn't changed.

"I know it's not people." Sienna stepped closer to Calla as if worried about Uncle Dirk being cross, but she still pushed for an answer. "But something must be making that noise."

When he laughed, Calla thought the moonlight glowed even brighter. It was going to be all right.

"You must mean the spring peepers," he said.

"Peepers?" Sienna seemed to forget her worry as she peppered Uncle Dirk with more questions. "What are peepers? Birds that sing at night?"

"No, little frogs that live in the woods," he said.

"Oh, can I see one?" Sienna asked.

"Probably not tonight, but I'm sure you will eventually."

When Uncle Dirk started up the walkway of large, flat rocks sunk into the ground, Sienna pulled her hand away from Calla and hurried after him. "And that screechy sound. Was that a frog too?"

"Screechy?" he said. "No, that couldn't have been a frog. Frogs down at the pond can croak and bullfrogs can bellow, but never screech. You must have heard an owl."

"A real owl?" Sienna sounded amazed. "I've never heard an owl before." She looked back at Calla. "Have you, Calla?"

"Not until tonight." Calla had to smile at the excitement

in Sienna's voice, but she would have to remind her not to be a pest with her questions. They would have time. Oh please, Lord, let them have time to embrace everything about Meadowland.

Calla let out a surprised shriek as something furry brushed against her leg. She breathed easier when she saw it was a dog.

Uncle Dirk looked over his shoulder at Calla. "Maisy won't hurt you, Calla. She's a fine dog."

The dog danced around him, jumping completely off the ground while it let out excited yips. Uncle Dirk set the box down on the ground and knelt to rub the dog. It licked his face and wagged its tail in such a flurry it was a blur in the moonlight.

The man lowered his head until his forehead was resting on the top of the dog's head. For a few seconds they were both almost totally still except for the dog's tail twitching slightly at the tip. Some of the dog's fur was almost as blond as Sienna's hair.

"Where have you been, Maisy?" He talked to the dog as if he expected an answer. "Chasing raccoons down in the woods?"

"Does she eat them?" Sienna had scooted back to lean against Calla again.

"No. She's not fierce enough for that, but she does sometimes chase them up into a tree where they sit all smug on their high branches and make faces at her." Uncle Dirk picked up the box again. "Come on. I'm sure she's hungry."

"I'm hungry too," Sienna said.

"Shh," Calla whispered. "It's too late for supper. We can wait until morning."

"I hear your stomach growling too." Sienna lifted her chin a bit defiantly.

"It's never too late to eat if you're hungry." Uncle Dirk led the way up the walk and waited while Calla opened the door for him to carry the box inside.

Without hesitation, the dog slipped in beside him. That made Sienna giggle again and Calla shrugged. Moonlight flowed through a wall of windows into the small room that had a coat hanging on a hook and boots and shoes lined up under the coat. A couch that looked more like something that might be on a porch instead of in the house took up most of the room. When Sienna bumped into it, the couch swayed a little. She jumped back as if worried she might have broken it.

"It's a glider." Uncle Dirk set the box down on the floor. "My mother always called this the mudroom. A place to take off your boots to keep dirt out of the house."

"Do you want us to take off our shoes?" Calla liked the room with all the windows. It would be light except on the darkest of nights.

"Best keep them on. The house might be chilly." He looked at their feet. "Not that those wet shoes will be warm. Set them out somewhere to dry when you take them off."

"All right," Calla said. "Where's Mama?"

"In the sitting room. You can take her some crackers and cheese in a minute."

"Oh, I do love crackers," Sienna said.

"Then you shall have some too." He lit a lamp and went through another door into a room with a big oak table surrounded by chairs. "Come along. I'll show you the kitchen.

That way, in the morning, if I'm not here, you can fix your breakfast."

"Where are you going, Uncle Dirk?" Sienna's voice sounded very small again.

"I have work out on the farm. You will be responsible for taking care of your own meals and such."

"We can help with your chores on the farm too," Calla said.

"We'll work all that out. Maybe you can feed the chickens and gather the eggs."

"Oh, please, can I do that?" Sienna said. "Will they let me pet them?"

"They might peck your toes instead," Uncle Dirk said.

"I don't care." Sienna didn't sound worried. "I'll wear my shoes until they like me better."

Uncle Dirk made a sound that could have been another laugh.

The narrow kitchen had an iron cooking stove on one side and cabinets on the other. A sink with a pump handle was at the end of the cabinets. One chair sat beside a small table in the corner next to an outside door.

"Where's the light switch?" Sienna asked.

"No electric lights. Only lamps and candles. You must be very careful with both to keep from catching the house on fire."

"We'll be careful," Calla said.

He reached up into a cabinet hanging on the wall and handed her four glasses. A bucket of milk sat on the cabinet next to the sink. "Lincoln must have come to milk the cow. Good. A cow can spoil if she's not milked."

"How does a cow get spoiled?"

He glanced around at Sienna. "You are full of questions."

"I can tell her to stop asking you things," Calla said.

"I don't mind questions." He poured the milk through a cloth pinned to the edges of a big pitcher. "If a cow isn't milked a couple of times a day and doesn't have a calf sucking her, her bag gets too full of milk and that causes problems."

Calla wanted to ask who Lincoln was and if he lived here too, but she wasn't convinced her uncle really didn't mind questions. Sienna looked ready to ask something else, but when Calla gave her a look, she stayed quiet.

Uncle Dirk poured what was left in the bucket into a pan on the floor for the dog to lap up. Then the dog settled down in front of a door on the far end of the kitchen. Uncle Dirk pointed toward it. "That's my room. I expect you both to stay out of there at all times."

His voice was gruff and Sienna stepped closer to Calla again. He didn't seem to notice as he picked up the pitcher of milk and filled four glasses. Then he cut thick slices of cheese with a butcher knife and told Calla where to find a tin of crackers.

Without another word, he got out some plates and put crackers and cheese on one of them. He picked up the plate and a glass before he pushed open the door to his room with his foot. The dog went in ahead of him and Uncle Dirk kicked the door shut.

Sienna stared at the door a few seconds before she quietly said, "Good night, Uncle Dirk."

Calla gave her a hug. "He's not used to people in his house. He probably didn't think to say good night."

"Even Miss Agnes sometimes said good night."

"Well, I am very glad you don't have to hear her say that tonight. Come on. Help me fix our plates." Calla found a tray at the back of the counter. "We can take our supper to eat where Mama is."

When Calla carried the tray to the sitting room, her mother smiled and motioned her to set it on the large square table beside her winged chair. "That looks good."

Light flickered from an oil lamp on the table and made Calla remember the lamp they'd left in the kitchen. She hurried back to blow it out, but the counter was empty. Uncle Dirk must have taken the lamp into his room. Calla stared at his closed door for a moment before she shrugged and went through the dim dining room to join her mother and Sienna. She was glad the full moon pushed light into the house.

In the sitting room, the lamp's warm glow surrounded her mother. Sienna, on the floor in front of the chair, leaned against Mama's leg. Calla found a place on the floor on her other side. It was good being close enough to touch her mother.

"Let's give thanks for our food and for being here at Meadowland." Mama shut her eyes and bowed her head. "Dear Lord, thank you for blessing us with a way to be together. Bless this food you have provided and use it to the nourishment of our bodies. Thank you for this home Dirk is sharing with us. And thank you for these two precious daughters you have given me. Amen."

"Bless Mama and Calla. Thank you for keeping Calla safe," Sienna added.

"And bless Sienna and Uncle Dirk," Calla said. "Amen."

Sienna picked up a piece of cheese and nibbled on it.

After a minute, she said, "Does Uncle Dirk not want us to be here?"

Mama put down her glass and looked at Sienna. "Why would you ask that? Did he fuss at you for something?"

"No."

Calla spoke up. "He was very patient with us and answered your questions, Sienna."

"But you thought he didn't want to."

"No, he said he didn't mind questions. I merely thought we shouldn't worry him with too many tonight while we are all tired," Calla said.

"That sounds reasonable. And we should be very thankful he's allowed us to come to Meadowland and that he was there to help Calla today," Mama said.

"I know." Sienna hugged Mama's knee.

"But don't be afraid to tell me if something is worrying you, Sienna." Mama looked from Sienna to Calla. "That goes for you too. I want to know everything about you and our time apart."

Calla thought of plenty she could tell her mother about the Home for Girls, but she didn't want to think about that now. Tonight was for being glad they were together again.

Sienna didn't say anything about the orphanage either. Instead, she still seemed worried about Uncle Dirk. "I don't think he wants me to like him."

"Who? Your uncle?" Mama frowned. "Why would you think that?"

"I don't know. I can just feel things."

Calla looked over at Sienna. "Because he didn't say good night doesn't mean he doesn't want us here."

"I wanted to say good night to him," Sienna said.

Calla started to say more but her mother held up a hand to stop her.

"Shh, both of you." Mama pulled in a deep breath and was quiet a moment before she went on. "Your uncle is doing what he thinks is his duty, but he has lived alone for many years. By choice. He hasn't wanted to have people in his life. We can't expect that to change overnight, no matter what we want. He might never open his heart to us. And if that's so, then we must respect his wishes."

"But I want to love him, Mama," Sienna said.

Mama smiled and put her hand on Sienna's head. "That you can do. Love him but don't insist he love you back. In time, he might change. But right now, I think he would rather we take care of ourselves and leave him be to do whatever he is accustomed to doing. Can you do that?"

"If that means we can stay," Sienna said.

"I don't want you to worry about that. Either of you." Mama smoothed down Sienna's hair, then touched Calla's shoulder. "He has already said we can stay."

"Oh, I do love it here already." Sienna's smile came back. "I can't wait for the sun to come up so I can look for bees and mice in the meadow."

"Then we'd best finish eating so we can go to bed. Your uncle says there is a room down here for me and one upstairs that you two can share."

"We don't have any nightclothes or any other clothes at all," Calla said.

"You can sleep in your underclothes tonight and we'll see what we can figure out tomorrow. Today let's just be glad we're together." She drank her milk and then sank back in the chair as if that took the last of her energy.

"We can wear the same dresses tomorrow," Calla said.

"Yes." She smiled. "We will take it one day at a time. That's what the Bible says to do. Tomorrow I will look up that passage and we'll read it together."

One day at a time. That Calla could do now that they were all safe at Meadowland.

19

unlight streamed through a window to wake Calla the next morning. She had to be dreaming. The featherbed was so soft. The light was so bright. She had never before opened her eyes to this kind of morning. She wanted to just lie there and wrap the good feel of it around her.

The bed bounced to pull her away from her dreamy feelings.

"Oh good. Your eyes are open." Sienna sat on her knees in the bed beside her. "Mama said I couldn't wake you up. At least not until the clock downstairs chimed eight."

Calla yawned. "Has it chimed eight?"

"No, but I counted seven chimes forever ago."

"Where is Mama?" Calla pushed up to a sitting position.

"She slept in the room downstairs. Don't you remember? We wanted to sleep with her, but she said we might get sick like her if we did that." Sienna's lips trembled a little. "I don't want her to be sick."

"You should have woke me up so I could get Mama breakfast."

"She said she could wait. That she wasn't that hungry. But

192

I am. So can you hurry and get dressed?" Sienna already had her orphanage home dress on.

Calla pulled on her dress. The side seam had torn more when she was fighting to get away from the man. She needed to hunt for a needle and thread. She pulled on her sweater to cover the tear and then slipped on her shoes. They were still damp from their run through the field the night before. She ran her fingers through her hair.

"There's a comb on the dresser," Sienna said. "The mirror makes your face look all wavy. It made me laugh. I think everything will make me laugh today."

"Even a sister who sleeps late?" Calla found the comb and looked in the mirror as she attempted to tame her curls.

"Especially a sister, whether she's sleeping or awake."

Calla looked down at the drawers in the dresser. "Anything in here?"

"All empty except the bottom one that has sheets. The drawers groaned when I opened them." Sienna pulled open the top drawer. "See? I thought that would wake you up and it wouldn't be like poking you, but it didn't."

"You silly goose. I'm awake now. Mama wasn't trying to fix breakfast herself, was she?"

Sienna shook her head. "She said it would be better if you did. That getting-sick trouble again. Besides, she looks really tired."

"What about Uncle Dirk?"

"He went out early this morning before the clock sounded six chimes."

"Did you sleep at all?"

"Oh yes. Plenty. But not after daylight. I was always awake before Miss Agnes told us to wake up. I wanted time to think about what I wanted to think about before they told me what I had to be thinking about."

"So, what do you want to think about today?"

"Butterflies and birds and mice and owls and—"

Calla laughed as she held up a hand to stop her. "Okay. You can think about all those while I see what we can find to eat." It felt so good to laugh.

"We have milk. Uncle brought a bucket of milk to the kitchen before he left again. He went off across the meadow."

"How do you know?"

"I saw him."

"You didn't bother him, did you?" Calla led the way down the stairs.

"No, you and Mama said I shouldn't. But he didn't want me to anyway."

"How do you know?" Calla looked around at her.

"I just do." Sienna shrugged a little. "I can know things when I remember to watch. I always forgot to watch at the home."

"So, are you watching me? Do you know what I'm thinking?"

"That's easy," Sienna said. "Your feet want to dance because we are at Meadowland, but you're not sure what you need to do. And you wish there was a restroom, but there isn't. Mama has a potty in her bedroom, but we have to go to the outhouse outside. You can go out the back door." Sienna pointed when they got to the bottom of the stairs.

"Have you already been?"

"Mama told me where it was. Did you know Uncle has cats? At least three. And I saw some chickens and all kinds of birds are singing, but I still haven't seen a mouse."

"No mice in the outhouse is good. Go tell Mama I'm up and I'll be right back."

"Okay. A sweet little spider is up in the corner." Sienna giggled and ran toward the room where their mother had slept.

"There are no sweet spiders." Calla shivered. Sienna might love every creature, but Calla knew some she would rather not see. Spiders were in that number, right along with those mice. Meadowland probably was home to some snakes too, but Calla hoped they were still sleeping under rocks on this April morning and not hiding in an outhouse.

She survived the outhouse trip and didn't even see Sienna's spider friend. In the kitchen, the pitcher of milk was beside a wire basket of eggs, a loaf of bread, and a jar of blackberry jam. The milk bucket had been washed and left upside down by the sink. The glasses and plates they'd used the night before had been washed too.

A note peeked out from under the basket of eggs. The handwriting was neat, almost elegant, with every letter formed perfectly.

Calla, there will be coals in the stove. You can add a few pieces of wood from the box outside the back door to cook your eggs. After you pour out however much milk you want, lay a tea towel over the top of the pitcher and carry it down to the cellar to keep it cool. You can put it on the table there. The door to the cellar is beside the pantry. I left some bacon in the warming oven at the top of the stove. Fry the eggs in the bacon grease in the skillet. Your mother can tell you how if you don't know, but make sure she rests.

You do the work. Tell Sienna to feed the chickens this afternoon about 5 or 6. Corn is in a barrel in the shed behind the house. You better help her gather the eggs out of the henhouse.

Don't worry if you don't see me. I am very busy.

Very busy. She suddenly felt a little like Sienna in that she knew he didn't want to sit down and eat with them. But he had left food she could cook.

Calla fetched a few sticks of wood to feed the fire in the stove. It wouldn't take much to cook eggs. Six pieces of cooked bacon beckoned from the plate she took out of the warming oven, but she resisted. She'd eat when the others ate.

Light spilled in on the table by the door, but there was only the one chair. The dining room table was surrounded by chairs. Eight at least. While she waited for the fire to heat up, she went to get one of them. The room wasn't much lighter than it had been the night before since the windows were covered with dark curtains. She pulled back the curtain on one of them. More curtains covered the other side of the window. That had to be Uncle Dirk's room. Where she and Sienna had been forbidden to go. Odd how simply being forbidden something made it feel that much more enticing. But she would do as he said.

She scooted one of the chairs back to the kitchen. A wooden stool sat by the cabinets. She could sit there while Sienna and Mama sat at the table. After pouring milk into the glasses, she covered the pitcher and opened the door to the cellar. Cool damp air floated up the stone steps. Her heart pounded as she stared at the lurking darkness at the bottom of the steps. No light in a cellar.

Sienna wouldn't be afraid. She could take the milk down there, but the pitcher was heavy. She might drop it. Calla pulled in a breath and ordered herself to stop being such a coward. The open door let in enough light for the steps. She could be down and back up in a minute. Less than a minute. Mere seconds.

She crept down the steps, staring at the partially open wooden cellar door. She shoved it with her foot and mustered up her courage to step into the cellar. Jars sat in bunches around the rounded stone walls. Some tall baskets sat in the middle of the cellar, but she didn't look to see what was in them. She placed the milk pitcher on the table near to the door, raced back up the steps, and slammed the kitchen door shut. She tried not to think about going back down to get the milk.

On the stove, the skillet was smoking. She grabbed the handle to scoot it off the hotter part of the stovetop. She let it go with a clatter. It was hot.

"Did you burn yourself, Calla?" Her mother was in the doorway.

"A little." Calla blew on her hand.

"Use a potholder." She pointed toward some hanging on hooks beside the stove. "I heard a door slam too, didn't I?" She sat down in the chair from the dining room.

"I had to take the milk to the cellar." Calla grabbed a potholder to move the skillet back over the stove's hot burner.

"What's a cellar?" Sienna came into the room.

"A place dug into the ground with concrete or rocks around it to keep things cool," Mama said. "When you go outside, you'll see a wall of rocks surrounding a domed bit of ground. That's the cellar top."

"Where is it?"

"Through that door." Calla broke eggs into the skillet.

Sienna opened the door and peered down toward the cellar. "Oh, do you think a mouse lives down there?"

"You and your mouse." Calla picked a piece of shell out of the eggs. Mrs. Jenkins would have shaken her head at the mess Calla was making. "But we don't want any mice in here or down there."

"It's dark down there." Sienna looked over at Mama. "Poor Calla. She doesn't like the dark. She didn't like it when they put us in the closet, but I didn't mind. I dreamed up stories."

"But you were crying when your uncle found you yesterday," Mama said.

"Not because it was dark. They told me Calla was gone. I wanted to be gone with her, but they caught me before I could get out the door."

"I'm so sorry, girls." Mama dabbed her eyes with a handkerchief. "I had no idea things would be so bad there."

"Don't cry, Mama. It's all happy now." Sienna shut the door to the cellar and did a spin.

Mama's tears changed to smiles as she reached to steady Sienna before she banged into the table. "Careful."

After Mama thanked the Lord for the eggs and bacon Calla dished up for them, they dug into the food. Calla hadn't enjoyed a breakfast so much since she'd eaten Miss Wilma's waffles years ago.

Sienna looked up from spreading jam on a piece of bread. "I like being happy."

"So do I," Calla said. Yesterday's worries seemed to slide away in the sunshine that slipped through the window to warm them.

"Did you know 'blessed' is a word for happy in the Bible? That's how I'm feeling. Very blessed that we're together again." Mama reached to touch Sienna's arm as she smiled over at Calla.

"I wish Uncle could be happy too." Sienna took a bite of the jam sandwich she made.

"How do you know he isn't happy?" Mama asked.

"He doesn't smile. Even at the home, I sometimes smiled." Sienna licked jam off her fingers as she looked over at Calla. "When I saw Calla."

"Maybe he doesn't have someone like that to make him smile," Mama said softly.

"Is he unhappy just because he got scarred in the fire?" Calla asked.

"There's more to it than that. Your father said he lost someone he loved."

"Was she in the fire?" Calla shuddered at the thought.

"Your uncle thought she was and he was trying to save her. It turned out she wasn't in the barn that burned."

"Then what happened to her?"

"Your father said nobody knew. They never saw her again. Her father wasn't in favor of her marrying your uncle. Perhaps he sent her away."

"Couldn't she have come back?" Sienna looked sad.

"Perhaps not." Mama sighed. "Sometimes things happen that we can't change, but whatever happened to Anneliese has forever been a mystery."

"Anneliese. That's a pretty name." Calla frowned a little. "But looks like somebody would know what happened. Where she went."

Mama gave Calla a stern look. "Now, don't you go worrying

your head over whatever happened twenty years ago. I know how you like figuring things out, but some things are better left alone. Your uncle doesn't need to be pulled back into his sad memories by your curiosity." She pointed her finger at Calla and then Sienna. "That goes for both of you."

"I just want to ask him about owls and frogs and mice," Sienna said.

Mama smiled. "I'm sure if he has time he won't mind answering those questions."

"Can I go look for a mouse in the meadow now?" Sienna pushed away from the table.

"May you," Mama corrected her. "Yes, after you help Calla clean up the kitchen and make the beds."

Sienna sighed and looked longingly at the door. "Yes, ma'am."

"The day is just beginning. You'll have time to hunt that mouse," Calla said. "If you wash the dishes, I'll go make the beds. And Uncle Dirk says you can feed the chickens this afternoon. He left a note."

"Calla, go into my room and change into one of my dresses. I see the one you're wearing is torn. I'll mend it for Sienna. And hem it." Her eyes went to the hem that Calla had ripped out before she left the home. "Perhaps your uncle has a catalog where I can order some things for you two. Until then, you'll have to wash your underthings out in the sink at night."

"I don't care if I'm dirty," Sienna said as she carried the dishes to the sink. "A mouse might like me better if I stink."

"But we would not like that at all." Mama's laugh turned into a cough. She had to hold on to the table as she stood up.

"I'll take care of things. You go sit on the porch." Calla

went over to let her mother lean on her. "Isn't that what you did at the sanitarium? I'll carry a chair out for you."

But when they went out on the porch, a padded lounging chair was already situated in the morning sun with a pillow and cotton blanket on it. Magazines and a book were on the table beside it. A note peeked out from under the book.

Mama picked it up. "It appears your uncle wants to communicate in writing."

"He doesn't really want to get to know us, does he?"

"Perhaps not, but since he is being kind, we can be grateful." She eased down onto the chair and unfolded the note. "He just says to feel free to use whatever is in the house if we need it. So, see if you can find a sewing basket. I'm sure Mrs. Meadows would have had one. Bring it out with your dress after you change."

When Calla started back inside, her mother added, "And tell Sienna not to go out of sight of the house unless you are with her. A river runs around the farm and who knows what other dangers Sienna might ignore if she saw that mouse or whatever to chase."

By the time Calla straightened the beds and found a dress in her mother's suitcase that almost fit, Sienna was sitting out in the middle of the field in front of the house. Calla saw her through the upstairs window and had to smile before she started searching for sewing supplies.

The room across from where she'd slept was empty except for some boxes of books and magazines. She knelt down by one of the boxes and pulled out *The Adventures of Huckleberry Finn*. She leafed through a few pages and thought about her father reading this when he was a boy. She felt rich as she looked at more titles. Sienna was sure to love *The*

Jungle Book, and Calla had wanted to read *Little Women* forever.

Down in the box, she found a Bible. She thought it might be her father's, but when she opened it, *Dirk Samuel Meadows* was written on the front page along with his birth date, *July 25, 1884.* Below that was a line saying the Bible had been given to him by his mother on his birthday in 1900. The cover was worn as if it had once been well used before being hidden away among these books. She let the Bible fall open where it willed.

She whispered aloud the first verse she saw, Psalm 34:4. "I sought the Lord, and he heard me, and delivered me from all my fears."

If Calla could remember that and repeat it the next time she had to go down the cellar steps, maybe the Lord would deliver her from her fears of the dark.

She started to put the Bible back, but it fell open again to where a photograph was stuck among the pages. A young woman stared up at Calla with eyes that practically sparkled with life. The barest hint of a smile turned up her lips. Her pompadour hairstyle made a dark puff around her face. A locket decorated with what looked like roses lay against her skin just above the low neckline of her dress. She was beautiful.

Love forever, Anneliese was penned on the bottom left corner of the photo. Her uncle's lost love. But why wasn't her picture in his room? For that matter, why wasn't the Bible in his room?

Calla laid her hand softly on top of the woman's face, as if some truth from the picture might transfer through her palm to let her know what happened. Her mother was right.

She couldn't ask Uncle Dirk about his Anneliese, but that didn't keep her from being curious.

She carefully put the picture back in the Bible exactly where she had found it in the book of Ecclesiastes. *A time to love, and a time to hate.* A couple of verses down from that, her eyes caught on a line she read twice. *He hath made every thing beautiful in his time.* Was that why her uncle had placed the picture here? To remember her beauty?

"Anneliese." Her name almost sounded like music when Calla whispered it.

She gently closed the Bible and replaced it in the box before piling the other books back on top of it. She felt a little as though she had peered into a forbidden place.

20

Calla found a sewing basket beside a rocker in the sitting room, as if her Grandmother Meadows might have been mending something there just the day before. Something else to wonder about. What had her grandmother been like? At least she might be able to ask Uncle Dirk about his mother if she got the chance. And Mama had met her once and said she was eager to have a grandchild. But she'd died a few months before Calla was born.

Memories floated all through this house. She didn't know what they were, but she wanted to. Her father had lived here. He'd heard the clock on the mantel chime out the hours. He'd eaten at the table in the kitchen and no doubt shared in big family gatherings in the dining room. He might have even had to carry things down to the cellar and run back up the steps to escape the dark. She shook her head at that idea. Her father wouldn't have been afraid of the dark.

She had been so young when he'd gone to the army that her memories of him had faded like a picture left in the sun. She remembered him coming in tired and dusty from working on roads. She could still almost taste the bitterness of his coffee she begged to sip from a spoon because it always made him laugh.

She also remembered the disappointment on his face when the doctor told him he had another daughter when Sienna was born. She hadn't been able to keep from wondering if he had been disappointed when she was born too.

What she wished she could forget were the angry words in the night and the sound of his boots stomping down the steps to the street after the door slammed behind him. The night always got blacker then when she heard her mother's quiet weeping.

Here, perhaps she could put those memories behind her and find out about her father when he was her age. He was surely happy in this house with windows to let in light and so much room to be free on Meadowland.

She shut her eyes and imagined him in this very room hearing the clock ticking. He could have talked with his father about their work that day or run back to the kitchen to see what his mother was cooking. In the evenings, he might have stretched out in front of the fireplace to read one of those books upstairs. Maybe he and Dirk played checkers. He could have known Anneliese and teased Dirk about being in love.

This very room might have been where Mama first met his mother and Dirk. When Mama felt better, she would get her to tell about that time and about the woman who had once slept in the bedroom her mother was using now. While in there looking for a dress to wear, Calla had opened a dresser drawer full of scarves and handkerchiefs that must have belonged to her. On the dresser, hatpins stuck up out of a holder like porcupine quills. A glass perfume holder still held a scent of roses. The wardrobe was empty, but a couple of boxes in the corner of the room were packed with clothes and hats.

Calla shook away her meandering thoughts about the past and headed outside with the sewing basket.

"Oh good." Her mother took the basket and then gave Calla the once-over. "You look good in blue, and the dress fits you fairly well. I still have trouble seeing you as such a young lady. When we can get some material, we'll make you a new dress. Did you do any sewing at the home?"

"We hemmed skirts and sewed on buttons. But all the dresses were the same, so it wasn't much fun."

"But necessary if needed." She pulled a spool of thread out of the basket and broke off a piece, but her hands shook when she tried to thread the needle. She sighed. "I hate being so weak. Would you do it for me?" She handed the needle and thread to Calla.

"Will that get better? The trembling." Calla moistened the end of the thread in her mouth before she pushed it through the eye of the needle.

"Thank you." Mama took the needle and stuck it in a pin-cushion. "I think I will get stronger, but the doctor warned me that doing too much could set me back a little. Yesterday was a very long day for all of us. I'm sure you need some extra rest today too after . . ." She paused. "Well, after what happened."

"I'm fine now that we're here." Calla started to ask Mama about the picture she found and about her grandmother, but talking might tire her out even more. "I can mend the dress and you can just relax in the sunshine."

"No, no. I can sew. But it is warm, isn't it?" Mama lifted

her face toward the sun. "A day like this is a gift. You should enjoy it. Weather in April can be fickle and tomorrow it might be cloudy and cool."

"But I need to fix lunch and take care of things here. I promised Uncle Dirk I'd keep the house clean if he let us come."

"That wasn't why he agreed to take us in." Mama smiled and put her hand on Calla's arm. "Not that it won't be good for you to do that. But you can start tomorrow and we can have bread and butter for lunch. Today, my dear Calla, rejoice in your freedom. Go chase after joy the way Sienna is doing out there in the field."

"She's just waiting for a mouse to show up."

Mama laughed. "And if it does, she'll be happy. But what about you, Calla? What do you want to show up?"

"You." She looked straight at Mama. "Ever since you left us at the home."

"That was a constant hope for me too. But now that we're together in this lovely place, you can think of new things to want to do or see."

"I don't know what to want, Mama."

Mama squeezed Calla's arm. "You will. You can pray about it, and I can't imagine a better place to pray than walking in the sunshine across a newly green spring field. Do you see those trees blooming over there?" She pointed across the field. "The purplish red ones?"

When Calla nodded, she went on. "Redbud trees. And soon the dogwoods will bloom, and already dandelions are dotting the field like sunspots. We are going to heal here, Calla. All of us. Perhaps even your uncle."

"But he's been here the whole time."

"Alone though. So very alone for many years. Even when

we were apart, you and Sienna and I, we knew that love still bound us together and we kept alive the hope of being a family again."

"Do you think Uncle will ever want us to be his family?"

Mama dropped her hand away from Calla's arm and looked out toward the trees again. "You know, I think he already does, but he's afraid to admit that."

"Why would he be afraid?"

Mama's gaze came back to Calla. "Why are you afraid of the dark?"

Calla frowned. What did her fear of the dark have to do with Uncle Dirk? "I don't know. I guess I'm afraid of something lurking in the dark to hurt me."

Mama smiled slightly. "That's your uncle too. He's afraid of being hurt. When we love, when we care, we can be hurt, but trust me, Calla, giving and receiving love is worth more than whatever hurt might come."

"Did you feel that way about Papa?"

"I did." Mama studied her face a few seconds before she went on. "I know you sometimes heard us when we had disagreements, but I loved your father. And he loved us, even though he was often unhappy with his life. But it wasn't because of you and Sienna or even me. He had things he needed to change, and he thought going to the army would make that happen." Mama looked down at the dress in her lap and began folding up the hem. "Perhaps it would have except for the influenza."

"Why are there diseases like that? Like tuberculosis?"

"Some questions don't have answers we can understand. We have to keep trusting in the Lord whatever happens. You haven't fallen away from believing, have you?"

"I never stopped praying you would get well and come for us."

"Prayer answered for both of us. Now enough of all this serious talk." Mama began pinning up the hem of the skirt. "Bring me a glass of water and then you and your sister should go exploring. It's not far to the river. Just make sure Sienna knows to never go alone."

"Do you think that's where Uncle Dirk is?"

"I have no idea. He didn't say in his note." She nodded toward the piece of paper tucked under one of the books on the table. "If you see him, just go a different direction. When he's studying something, he doesn't like to be disturbed. I learned that when I was here years ago."

After Calla brought her mother a glass of water, she headed across the field toward Sienna. A gentle breeze lifted the curls away from her face, and she was glad to be out under the blue sky dotted with fluffy white clouds. Yesterday she was walking along a city sidewalk with every step a worry. Today, all of that seemed to be no more than a bad dream. Or perhaps it was now she was dreaming. But no, the sun warming her shoulders was real. Very real.

A crow flew up in front of Sienna when Calla got closer to her.

Sienna looked over her shoulder. "You scared it away."

"What?" Calla knelt down beside Sienna. "Your mouse?"

"No. I'm sorry to say mice are very shy."

"Oh? And who told you that? Uncle?"

"Nobody had to tell me. I figured it out for myself. But I still hope a mouse will decide to make friends with me someday." Sienna scooted around to face Calla. "Since no mouse wanted the bread I saved from breakfast, I was feeding birds." She opened her hand to show a few crumbs of bread.

"What birds? That crow?"

Sienna nodded. "Two of them. They liked the crumbs I threw out. I thought they would be too shy like the mouse, but then they weren't shy at all. At least until they saw you."

Calla looked around. The crows were no longer in sight, but cawing came from the trees along the edge of the field. "How come they were afraid of me and not of you?"

Sienna shrugged. "Maybe because you were moving. I sat very still here for a long time before they decided to fly down and see what I was doing. Crows are very curious birds, you know."

"No, I didn't know. How do you know?"

"I've always liked birds. You knew that, didn't you? I used to want birds to fly down to light on me when we went to the park before Mama got sick. Even at the home, I listened for the birds whenever I was close to a window."

"I thought it was mice you liked."

"Oh, I do. And butterflies and bugs and earthworms."

"You do know birds eat worms and bugs." Calla lifted her brows as she pushed some truth at Sienna.

"I know." For a second, Sienna looked sad. Then her face brightened. "But Miss Wilma told me that was how the Lord planned it all. So we wouldn't have too many bugs. She told me about crows being curious too. She liked birds. She said a crow sometimes came to visit her and she always left corn out for it. I wish I had some corn."

"I didn't know Miss Wilma liked birds." Calla frowned a little. She couldn't remember Miss Wilma talking about birds.

"It was our secret time together while you and Mama cleaned her house. Miss Wilma hated to dust. She liked being outside with the birds and flowers."

Calla did know that she had taken Sienna outside while they cleaned to repay her kindness. Calla dusted her shelves of whatnots and books in her parlor, and there had been several bird figurines. No crows that Calla could recall, but she had been more interested in the books on the shelves. She had so missed those books after Miss Wilma died.

Of course, she missed Miss Wilma more. So many bad things had happened, one right after another. Miss Wilma dying suddenly while digging weeds out of her flower garden. Then Mama getting sick, and last, the orphanage.

Calla shook away her sad thoughts. "I'm surprised you remember Miss Wilma that well. You weren't but five."

"Almost six. I loved it when she showed me birds and what they were named. She gave me a book with bird pictures. Miss Agnes took it away from me when she saw me reading it at the home. She thought I stole it." Sienna sounded sad.

"I'm sorry."

"It's okay. Maybe other girls who like birds can read it, and I have real birds to see now."

"Come on." Calla stood up and brushed off her skirt. "Mama says we can walk to the river. Maybe we'll see more birds there."

"Where is the river?" Sienna shook the crumbs off her hand and jumped up.

"I'm not sure, but Mama says we can find it."

"I don't think I've ever seen a river. Not for real." Sienna skipped ahead a few steps and spun around to Calla. "It's so good to see things for real, isn't it?"

"It is."

"Do you think Uncle will be at the river?"

"I don't know, but if he is, we have to go the other way. Mama says he doesn't like to be disturbed when he's studying something."

"I didn't care if you disturbed me a while ago, but the crows did." She laughed. "Hear them. They're still fussing at you."

They went past the redbud trees and found a dirt road going downhill and through an opening in a fence made of rocks. Each new thing seemed a special treat. They walked across a wide field toward a line of trees.

"Another meadow." Sienna sounded excited.

"But you can't come here by yourself. Mama says you have to stay where you can see the house."

"Now, but she might let me go farther when we have been here longer." Sienna looked up at Calla. "We will be here longer, won't we?"

"I do hope so."

"So do I." She stopped and turned her head to listen. "I think I hear water. Can I run ahead to see?"

"I'll run too, but I know you'll be fastest." Calla laughed as Sienna took off across the field.

She let her get a head start and then lifted her skirt and ran after her. Some birds flew up out of the spring grass with a complaint at being disturbed. She thought Sienna might stop to watch them, but she looked over her shoulder at Calla and kept going. Joy bubbled up in Calla. It was so good to be far from the Home for Girls where freedom to run and laugh was practically forbidden.

Sun glanced off water visible between the trees along the river. Calla ran faster just in case Sienna forgot about not getting too close to the river. Sienna stopped abruptly when a man stepped out from behind the trees in front of her.

It wasn't Uncle Dirk.

21

"What are you doing here?" The man confronted Sienna.

Calla ran faster to catch up with Sienna. She breathed easier when she saw the person wasn't a man at all but a boy who didn't look much older than her. Her heart slowed down a little, but he didn't sound very friendly. And he was still bigger than her. The same as that man had been yesterday.

But he wasn't that man. Probably only a neighbor here along the river. She stepped in front of Sienna. She could face down a boy her age. "We could ask that of you." Her voice only had the slightest tremble. "You're the one on our uncle's property."

"Your uncle?" He frowned. "Dirk Meadows doesn't have any family."

"That's not true." Sienna peeked out from behind Calla. "He's our uncle and he won't like you saying we aren't his family."

"Shh, Sienna. This must be a misunderstanding."

She gave the boy a tentative smile. He was kind of cute, with dark brown hair falling over his forehead and eyes almost as brown. If he smiled, he might be really cute. He certainly didn't look like anyone she or Sienna had to fear.

"I'm Calla Meadows and this is my sister, Sienna. Uncle Dirk is letting us stay with him for a while. Our father was his brother."

His frown disappeared as he gave her a considering look. "Then I guess I should say I'm sorry, but Mr. Dirk didn't tell me anything about having a brother."

"Our father died years ago. So maybe that's why he never told you about him," Calla said. "Besides, I don't think Uncle Dirk tells many people much about anything."

"I can't argue with that. But I've never known him to have visitors. Well, other than me."

Calla waited for him to say who he was, but when he didn't, she asked, "You know who we are. Who are you?"

"Yeah, who?" Sienna stepped up beside Calla and put her hands on her hips to glare at him.

"Sorry," he said. "I'm Lincoln Rainsley. I live down the river a ways. Mr. Dirk lets me fish here and I help him out on the farm. I guess going to get you must have been why he asked me to see to Maisy and his stock this week. He didn't tell me where he was going, but he never does when he has to make a trip to the big town. Is that where you live? In Louisville?"

"We did," Calla said quickly before Sienna could say anything. This boy didn't need to know they'd been in an orphanage.

"Were you fishing now?" Sienna seemed to forget being angry as she eyed the boy.

"I was before I saw you," Lincoln said.

"Did you catch anything?"

"A few."

"Can I see them? I've never seen fish from a river." She looked out toward the water flowing past them a few yards away. "Is that the river? I thought rivers were bigger."

"Well, some are. Like the Mississippi or the Ohio or the Kentucky," the boy said.

"Have you seen all those rivers?" Calla asked.

"No," he admitted with a shrug. "Just the Kentucky. What makes a river be a river and not just a creek is not how wide it is but how long it is and how many other creeks run into it. At least I think that's what Mr. Dirk told me. Salt River is long enough and wider in places. Deep in places too, but other places it's shallow enough to wade all the way across. If it rains a lot, it can jump its banks sometimes."

Sienna giggled. "Does it jump like a frog?"

That made the boy smile. Calla was right. He was even cuter when a smile lit up his brown eyes. She was beginning to be glad they had run up on him today, even if it had given her a jolt when he first stepped out in front of Sienna. It would be nice to make a friend here, and he was obviously already friends with Uncle Dirk. She liked the way he looked at Sienna, as though he thought her questions were worth answering.

"Nope. Not like a frog." He turned toward the river and pointed. "But when the river floods, it overflows here in the field. Sometimes all the way to where we're standing and on over into the fields. If the rain comes down fast, it can roar, but other times the river just gradually pushes out over its banks. Sometimes pools of water with fish in it get left in the field. A fellow can catch fish easy then. Sometimes big ones."

"What do you do with them?" Sienna asked.

His brow wrinkled as though he wondered why she had to ask that. "Eat them for supper."

"Oh." Sienna looked so surprised that Calla had to laugh.

"Remember the bugs and birds." Calla told Sienna before she looked back at Lincoln. "We've never fished for our supper."

"Then you've missed out on some fun," Lincoln said.

"Can I look at them before you eat them?" Sienna asked.

"If you want to." The boy laughed and led them past a couple of trees to where he'd left his fishing pole and a can of dirt with worms trying to crawl out of it. He stepped to the very edge of the river and pulled a line out of the water that had a few small fish threaded on it somehow. A couple of the fish flapped their tails while others were still. He held the line out toward Sienna.

She reached to touch their wet fins. She wrinkled her nose. "They don't smell good."

"They smell like fish." The boy dropped the line back down in the water and shoved the stake at the end of it back into the ground. "They probably think we stink."

"Especially if they know we want to eat them."

"Birds and bugs," Calla reminded her again. "It's how nature is."

"I know." Sienna sighed. She looked at his fishing pole. "Are you going to catch more?"

"Maybe. Maybe not," Lincoln said. "What are you two thinking about doing?"

"We're just looking around to see what Meadowland is like," Calla said. "And to see the river."

"What do you think of it then?" he asked.

"It's nice." Calla moved closer to the brownish green water that whispered past them. Out in the middle, ripples made patterns on top of the water. "It makes me wish it wasn't too cold to take off my shoes and wade in to see how deep it is."

"A little too deep for wading here, but up the way it's usually not over waist high. This summer, I'll show you some good swimming holes where you can jump in." He gave Calla a considering look. "Can you swim?"

"I don't know."

"Are you saying you've never been swimming?"

"Not yet," Calla said. "No swimming holes where we lived."

"Never fished. Never swam." Lincoln shook his head. "I'll bet you've never caught a frog or ever even climbed a tree."

"Ladies don't climb trees," Calla said. "Or play with frogs."

"I think I'd like to climb a tree," Sienna said. "And catch a frog. I'd really like that. Can you show me one?"

"Maybe," Lincoln said. "We'll have to look for it. Tell you what, since you two city girls don't know beans about the country, I'll show you around and let you know where Mr. Dirk's land ends so you won't be trespassing on somebody else's fields." He peeked over at Calla. "Might even find some wildflowers. Surely a lady can pick flowers."

A blush climbed up in Calla's cheeks as her heart started beating a little faster. She did like flowers, after all. When he stepped past her to start down the river, his arm brushed against hers. When he shot a grin over at her, she knew that wasn't entirely accidental. Could be he thought she was as easy on the eyes as she thought he was. Even with her messy hair and freckles.

Sienna ran ahead watching the ground for a frog. Lincoln waited for Calla to catch up to him. She hadn't talked to a boy for almost two years. She felt tongue-tied as she tried to think of something to say that wouldn't sound stupid.

He spoke first. "Your sister is cute," he said, but he wasn't looking at Sienna. He was looking at her.

"Yeah, she is. I hope she sees a frog. At least that's better than the mouse she's been wanting to see since forever."

"A mouse? That's funny. Most girls don't like mice."

"Sienna isn't most girls." Calla wanted to add that neither was she, but she bit back the words. He might not like girls that were different. And even though she'd just met him, she sort of hoped he would like her.

"Is she clumsy?" He glanced back at Sienna.

"What makes you say that?" Calla frowned a little.

"I don't know. Just looks like she has a lot of bruises on her arms."

Bruises from that horrid Miss Agnes or Miss Warfield. "She had a mean teacher."

Calla was glad the dress she'd borrowed from her mother had sleeves down to her elbows to hide the bruises on Calla's arms from where the man had grabbed her yesterday. She definitely didn't want to talk about that. All that was yesterday. She wanted to think about today.

"Wow!" Lincoln blew out a breath. "She must have. I guess old Mr. Higgins wasn't so bad after all."

"That your teacher?" When he nodded, Calla went on. "Do you go to school now?" She had no idea if she and Sienna should be going to a school here or not.

"No. I'm through with school unless Mr. Dirk talks me into going to college. He's trying, but I don't know what would happen to Ma if I wasn't around to help her. She was proud and all that I went to high school, but she's not keen on me going off to the city to school."

"Is there a school around here? I mean, should we, Sienna and me, be in school now?"

"School let out a couple of weeks ago. Won't start back up until July. Most of the kids live on farms and need to help get the crops out this time of the year."

"Do you live on a farm?"

"Ma says we used to, but I was too little to remember." He pointed across the river. "It was right over there. Nice land, but Pa sold it when his mother died. He just kept us a little corner down that way where he built a house."

"So what does he do if he doesn't farm?"

"Pa died back when I was twelve." He blinked a few times as if talking about it still made him tearful.

"I'm sorry."

"You said your pa was dead too. What took him?"

"Influenza. When I was eight."

"That means your sister must have still been a baby."

"Nearly two. She doesn't remember him." Calla looked at Sienna, still crisscrossing the ground in front of them, intently watching for something in the grass.

"That's rough. I'd hate it if I couldn't remember anything about my father."

"I hadn't ever thought about that." Calla turned back to Lincoln. "But I guess so would I. Was your father sick?"

"No. He shot himself."

"Oh." Calla didn't know what to say.

"Ma is always telling me it was an accident, but I know better. Pa got the gloomies every spring about this time. He'd go off and not come home for days sometimes. But he built barns for people, and Ma always said he had to be working somewhere too far away to come home at night. Maybe that was so, but that year he must have decided he didn't want to ever come home." He stared off in the distance for a few seconds before he went on. "Mr. Dirk heard the shot and found him. He was on this side of the river down where there used to be a barn."

Calla reached over and touched his hand. "That had to be really hard for you."

"Yeah." He curled his fingers around hers. "I guess that's more than I should have told you, seeing as how you never even knew my pa and only just met me."

"That's okay. Sometimes a person needs to talk about things."

He stopped walking and turned toward her, still holding her hand. "You're a good listener. I can be a good listener too if you want to tell me about those mean teachers."

Calla's knees went weak as she looked into his brown eyes. She was still searching for what to say when Sienna yelled, "I found a frog, but he won't let me catch him. He keeps jumping away."

Lincoln laughed. "Sounds like we need to go catch us a frog."

Calla laughed too. "I guess so."

The next minute they were running after Sienna, still laughing and still holding hands.

22

*D*irk put his hand on Maisy's head so she wouldn't bark when he caught sight of Lincoln walking along the river with the girls. Lincoln was a good boy. The girls would be safe with him. Dirk had to smile when he saw Lincoln holding Calla's hand. The boy moved fast. Something Anneliese said he never did.

The sound of laughter drifted back to him from where he watched from the high rock above the little creek that made a waterfall into the river. All three youngsters chased back and forth across the field, stopping now and again to pounce on something in the grass. He pulled out his field glasses and focused in on them. With a cry of victory, Lincoln held up a frog, but it slipped away from him and the chase was on again.

They must have tired the poor frog out. Sienna captured it and held it gently against her middle. It wouldn't be one of the spring peepers he'd promised to show her. But she looked happy as she stroked the frog that must have been mesmerized since it didn't leap out of her hand. The child seemed to have a special feel for the natural world. Earlier he'd seen her sitting still as a statue in the middle of the front field.

For a minute that morning, he'd been tempted to go ask

what she hoped to see, maybe even sit with her, but he'd kept walking. It was best to keep his distance.

This time he knew what she wanted to see. He put the field glasses back in the case and sat down on the rock. Maisy settled beside him with a huff of breath, perhaps of disappointment that they didn't walk down to see Lincoln. But she stayed by Dirk's side. He doubted the children would see him there among the trees. Besides, they were wrapped up in their own world. Just as he and Anneliese had once been when they walked along the river and she had accused him of being slow to make his intentions known.

That April day had been something the same as this one when she looked at him with that teasing smile he loved and said, "Aren't you ever going to ask me to marry you?"

As the sound of her voice played through his head, the scene in front of him faded and he was back walking hand in hand with Anneliese. The water, up a little from a week of rain, sang its river song as it rippled past them. A mockingbird ran through its repertoire in a tree over their heads.

He had fetched her across in the rowboat he hid in the bushes last fall after the water got too cold for wading. Through the winter, whenever she could slip away to meet him, they took shelter in the barn near the river.

They didn't need shelter from the cold this day. The spring sun warmed their shoulders, and before she had surprised him with her question, he had picked a bunch of violets for her.

She stuck one of the blooms behind her ear and threaded a few more into her dark hair before she demanded an answer to her question. "Has the thought of marriage rendered you speechless, college boy?"

She did have a way of knocking him off-kilter with the way she was forever one step ahead of him. She was again, even though she had no way of knowing about the ring box in his pocket. Only the jeweler in Louisville knew about that. Dirk had been saving for months and finally had enough when he sold an article about barn owls.

Nobody knew about the article either, except his professor who had encouraged him to submit it. Dirk didn't tell his mother because he feared she would want him to use the money for something they needed on the farm. But the article pay felt like found money. He was prepared to work the summer for his mother.

And for Anneliese if she answered yes when he offered her the ring. But there were problems. Her father. And maybe his mother, but he felt sure once Ma met Anneliese, she would be won over.

So far, he'd kept his wooing of Anneliese a secret. Frank knew, just as Anneliese's brother, Jerome, knew. It was hard to keep secrets from brothers, but both brothers were keeping secrets for them. Frank, at fourteen, griped about having to take care of whatever needed doing on the farm during the week while Dirk was at school, but Dirk let him have the weekends free. Mostly to get in trouble. But Dirk covered for him in exchange for Frank's silence about Anneliese. Not that Dirk intended to stay silent forever. He wanted his mother to meet her when the time was right.

He wanted everything to be right. Especially giving Anneliese this ring. But maybe he was too hesitant. Too concerned with what everybody might think, when the only person he really needed to worry about was this beautiful girl beside him.

"Are you proposing to me?" he said.

She flashed him a wide-eyed look of fake shock. "Never. That would not be proper at all. But a girl can do some wondering if a fellow doesn't make his intentions known."

"Never fear, fair lady. I do have some fine intentions."

"Is that so?" She stopped beside a huge oak tree and leaned back against the trunk as she eyed him. "Do they have anything to do with me?"

He put his hand on either side of her against the tree to keep her captive there. "They have everything to do with you." He looked deep into her eyes. "I love you, Anneliese Rainsley."

She started to say something, but he moved his hand to cover her lips with his fingers. "Shh. I'm not through yet with my intentions. I intend to love you forever and ever. You are the sun and moon and stars to me. I intend to devote my life to making you happy."

"Oh?" she whispered through his fingers.

"Oh yes. I intend to make you mine if you will have me." He took his fingers away from her lips, reached in his pocket for the ring box, and went down on one knee in front of her. "Will you marry me, Anneliese Rainsley?"

She leaped away from the tree into his arms. He tried to keep his balance and catch her, but they tumbled to the ground. He did manage to click the ring box shut before he fell. They were both laughing as he gathered her into his arms in a bed of last fall's leaves. Then their eyes met, and silence fell like a blanket over them. The whole world seemed to hold its breath as she melted into his embrace, and the joy of their love blocked away all doubts and fears as his lips met hers.

He was dizzy with desire before she pulled away from the kiss to lay her head on his shoulder. Her breath tickled his chin. He picked a leaf out of her hair even as he smiled at the violets still tangled in her curls.

After a moment, she said, "You know I haven't answered you."

"I thought your answer was in your kiss," he said.

"How I wish it could be that easy."

And just like that the world rushed back at them.

She pushed away from him and sat up. He sat up too, found the ring box, and held it out toward her. "Why can't it be that easy?"

She stared at the box for a moment before she took it from him and pushed it open. The small diamond flashed in the sunlight that filtered down through the oak branches just beginning to bud.

"I wasn't expecting this." She studied the ring.

"You just asked when I was going to propose."

"True." She shot him a smile before she looked down at the ring again. "But I didn't think a college boy like you would be able to actually buy a ring."

"College boys in love find a way." He ducked his head down to peer into her eyes. "Don't you like it?"

"Oh yes. It's lovely." She stroked the top of the ring.

"Then slip it on your finger and say yes."

"I do love you, Dirk Meadows." But she still didn't lift the ring out of the box.

"And I love you more than life itself. So, why are you torturing me by not saying yes?"

She sighed. "You know why. I think my father would rather see me dead than married to a Meadows." She looked up with tears spilling from her eyes. "Your mother might feel the same."

"No. She will love you once she meets you."

"I can't say the same about my father."

"I'll go talk to him." He took out his handkerchief and gently wiped away the tears on her cheeks. "I'll get my mother to agree to give him the field he thinks is his." For Anneliese he'd give away any field he wanted.

"I fear it's gone beyond a field. Gone beyond understanding. Or healing." She didn't look away from him. "That first day when you saw me in the river, I should have told you to go away, and then I should have run back to my house and never come hunting you again."

"That couldn't be." He traced her cheek with his finger. "Our love was meant to be. Our meeting that day was planned by angels."

She smiled. "You do have a way with words, college boy."

"Then let me go see your father. Convince him with my words."

She shook her head a little. "No, not yet. Better for me to find a way to tell him."

"So you are saying yes?" He took the ring out of the box. She held her hand up to let him slip it on her finger. It was a perfect fit.

"My heart has no other answer. Yes, I will marry you." When she held out her hand to admire the ring on her finger, her smile came back.

He stood and pulled her to her feet. They waltzed around the tree to the sweet music of the river. He rested his cheek against her hair. "You've made me the happiest man in the world. Thank you."

"Aren't you going to ask me when?" She leaned away from him to peer up at his face.

"Anytime is good. Tomorrow? Next week?"

She laughed. "You won't be home from college until May."

"You could go to Louisville with me."

"I wouldn't know what to do in a big town like that. I belong here."

"Then so do I." He kissed her forehead. "Don't make me wait too long."

"This summer. When the flowers bloom in the meadows."

"Perfect. When the meadow blooms." This very summer she would be his wife.

She lifted her face up toward his, and once more, he covered her lips with his. Truly she was a gift from angels.

She stepped back from his embrace and touched her neck with a sudden look of panic. "My locket. It's gone." She sounded frantic as she looked down at the ground. "I can't lose my grandmother's locket."

He had never seen her without the gold filigree locket around her neck. "Don't worry. We'll find it." And he did. In the leaves under the oak tree. "Here it is. The catch just came undone."

She ran over to let him fasten the chain back around her neck. She covered the locket with her hand. "Thank you, thank you. I couldn't have borne losing it. Grandmother said my grandfather gave her the locket after their first child died while still a baby. Ma named me Anneliese after that sister she never knew."

"Is there a picture in the locket?" She'd never opened the locket for him to see.

"No. Only a snippet of the baby's hair and something

my grandmother wrote on a scrap of paper she placed in the locket."

"What does it say?"

She stroked the oval locket before she answered. "Love never dies."

Now he shut his eyes and bent his head as the memory of those words stabbed him. Maisy sat up, whined, and licked his face.

"I'm all right, girl." He fondled the dog's ears. "Just walking down too many memory lanes when I need to keep my feet in the here and now."

The children were gone from the river bottom. From the looks of the shadows, it was well past noon. The girls had no doubt gone back to the house to find something to eat, and Lincoln might have gone home or found a better spot to fish.

"Come on, Maisy. Time to do something besides woolgather." Dirk stood up to head back to the house. The day was right for readying the garden plot for the plow. With more mouths to feed now, he'd best make it bigger.

He hoped they had found food enough today. He should have written more in his note to Calla so she'd know what to cook. After all, she was just a girl. Rose could guide her, but she had hardly looked able to stand the night before when they got to Meadowland. He should have put a pot of beans on the stove that morning before he left the house.

He pushed aside his concerns. The girls were old enough to take care of themselves, and Rose could advise them from her chair in the sun. But the worries sneaked back to poke at him as he walked across the fields toward the house.

Purple violets bloomed among the grass in the bottom. Dirk tried not to think about how the field might look when the daisies and Queen Anne's lace bloomed. Maybe he'd hitch up his horse and plow the meadow under to plant corn instead of letting it grow for hay. Right now, he didn't want to see flowers in the meadow. Not with the way memories of Anneliese were plaguing him.

Later that afternoon, he paused from clearing vines out of the garden fence when he saw the girls head out to feed the chickens. They had to see him in the garden, but they seemed to intentionally look the other way. That was best and what he wanted, he told himself, even as he continued to watch them. Sienna's giggles when the hens, eager for the corn, ran toward her made him smile.

Whining, Maisy looked from them to him. He waved his hand to let her go. He expected Sienna to pet Maisy but was surprised when Calla dropped to her knees to bury her face in the dog's fur. Maisy's tail flapped back and forth.

At sundown, after he milked the cow, he carried the bucket back to the house, thinking they might be in the kitchen, but the room was empty. And spotless, with dishes washed and dried. The stove was warm and a pan of potato soup was pushed to the back. A note stuck under a spoon by a plate and bowl said they'd left enough for him. Calla's writing. He remembered from her letter.

They were figuring things out with no need of his help. That was good. He strained the milk and set it out on the back porch with a plate covering the top. The night was cool. The milk would be fine until morning and then he'd skim off the cream to make butter. After he found some meat scraps for Maisy, he didn't bother sitting at the table but ate the soup standing by the stove. He could hear voices from the sitting room, but with the dining room doors closed between

230

them, he couldn't make out words. Even so, the sound was soothing. Peaceful somehow.

He could go sit with them. After all, it was his house, but instead, he went back outside to walk through the barn lot while stars popped out in the sky. Maisy ran out ahead of him, barking at some unseen varmint.

Dirk tried not to think. To just be there in the gathering darkness with the sound of the spring peepers chirring in the air. The air smelled of spring. A green scent mixed with that of mud and cow pies. Maisy came back to him and he turned toward the house again. The girls would be abed by now and he needed to be the same.

But when he went back in the kitchen, Calla was at the sink. She started when he came in the back door. "Oh, Uncle Dirk. I thought you had already gone in your room."

"I was just checking things out." He peered at the clothes in the sink. "What are you doing?"

"Washing our clothes."

"Why not wait until morning?"

"I needed to wash out some things so that they could dry tonight for us to wear tomorrow. Mama didn't think you'd mind me using the sink."

"No, that's fine, but there's a gasoline-powered machine in the washhouse out back. I can show you how to use it."

"Thank you. That would be wonderful. I can wash your clothes too." Calla pulled a dress out of the water to wring out.

"You don't have to earn your place here, Calla."

"But I want to help."

"If you take care of your mother and Sienna, that will be help enough." He watched as she pulled more things out of the water. "Don't you have anything else to wear?"

231

"Mama has some things I can wear, but her clothes would swallow Sienna. She says if you have a catalog, maybe she can order what we need when she gets the pension check from the army."

He should have thought about them leaving the orphanage with no baggage. "Do you have anything for sleeping?"

She blushed and turned away from him. "We can make do."

He supposed this wasn't a conversation he should be having with a young girl, but that didn't keep it from being necessary. He went into his room and found a couple of old undershirts. He carried them back out to her. "Here. These might help you make do."

He didn't wait for her to thank him before turning back to his room. Maisy scooted in behind him and he shut the door. Somehow they were all going to have to make do.

23

*I*f only she had some knitting needles and yarn. At least that would make Rose feel more useful as she lounged in her chair on the porch. She had never felt guilty sitting in the sun at the sanitarium, but there, maids did the various housekeeping chores. Not her daughter.

Calla hadn't made the first complaint. She was so happy to be away from the orphanage, she would have cheerfully hauled rocks off the fields or cleaned stalls in the barn, were Dirk to ask her to. Rose was glad she'd convinced her to explore the farm the day before. She'd come back with pretty, flushed cheeks and news of meeting a young man at the river. That had obviously been an exciting discovery.

Sienna had been as happy telling Rose about catching a frog, the fish she'd touched, and the crows she'd fed. The bruises from her mistreatment at the orphanage might still darken her arms and legs, but her joy at being here at Meadowland obviously overpowered those sorrowful memories.

Now the sweet child was in the spot she appeared to have claimed out in the middle of the meadow. Again, ready to feed the crows that obliged by flying down in front of her.

At least she had something clean to wear after Rose had remade Calla's dress yesterday. That had kept Rose busy for a while, but now her hands were restless. Frank's mother surely knitted shawls and such. Perhaps Calla could search out knitting needles the same as she'd found the sewing basket.

If not, Rose could fetch writing supplies from her suitcase. Dr. Bess claimed it helped to cleanse the mind of troublesome concerns by spilling them out on paper. But Rose shouldn't even have any such thoughts here in this beautiful place with her girls within the sound of her voice. Frank had always told her she worried too much, that most of the things she fretted over never came to pass. But then some of them did.

Those should have been reason for prayer, not worries. Dear Miss Wilma had told her that so many times, and Rose knew it was true. Yet she had kept her worries clasped tight even when she did pray about them. She never seemed able to release them to the Lord's care or to totally believe Miss Wilma when she said the Lord would supply. And yet, with or without her belief, the Lord had supplied Miss Wilma when Rose so needed a friend, and now Frank's brother had taken them in.

Poor Dirk. While he had answered their pleas for help and done what he must consider his duty, he didn't appear ready to give up his reclusive ways. Writing them notes and staying off to himself. She smiled, thinking about his offer of marriage to save her reputation. That had taken courage. No doubt he was relieved when she had been unworried about gossip. If she fetched that writing paper, she would write him a note to ask about a way to get the things the girls needed. But first she needed to rest.

She closed her eyes, pulled in a deep breath, and relaxed. It did no good to fight against her weakness. Dr. Bess had told her time and time again she had to accept that her condition would not allow her to do things she once had. She needed to count her blessings and be thankful as she rejoiced in sunshine on her face and birdsong in her ears. She could rest and continue to gain strength without the struggle of finding a way to pay rent and buy food.

She didn't think she dozed off, but she must have because when she opened her eyes, Dirk sat in the chair alongside of her. She couldn't keep from pulling in a surprised breath.

"Forgive me," he said. "I didn't intend to startle you."

"No, no. I guess I was in another world. I didn't hear you coming."

She looked straight at him and wondered how many times people had shrunken away from meeting his eyes because of his scarred face. Perhaps she had herself when she first met him years ago. She hoped not, but she had been so young. Only a few years older than Calla now. Since then, experience had taught her that not all scars showed, and those that did might be the least bothersome. Whether that was true of Dirk, she couldn't be sure, since he had avoided contact with people for most of his adult life.

"At least I kept Maisy from licking your face," he said.

His smile was a bit crooked with the scars pulling down the left side of his face, but it lit up his blue eyes that looked so like Calla's. Their red hair was the same too. Frank had always said Calla looked more like his brother than him.

She laughed. "I do thank you for that. I might have been very startled in that case." She reached a hand out to the dog that came over and laid her head on her lap. "She seems a very nice dog. What did you say her name is?"

"Maisy. Don't ask where I came up with it, for I have no idea."

"Did you get her when she was a pup?"

Satisfied with the attention Rose gave her, the dog went back to sit near Dirk. He rested his hand on the white blaze on her head.

"No. She simply showed up one day when I was out in the field, and nothing I did could dissuade her from following me home. I expected someone to show up to claim her, but they never did."

"Did you name her right away, even though you thought she might belong somewhere else?"

"How did you guess?" He looked down at the dog. "I suppose I shouldn't have, but I had to call her something, and the name Maisy popped into my head at first sight of her."

"Then perhaps she told you her name."

"Perhaps she did." The thought seemed to please him.

"How long have you had her? Or has she had you?"

"That could be true both ways," he said. "She will have been here four years in May." A shadow of a frown crossed his face and he quickly looked down at the dog. When he looked back up, it was gone. "I guessed her about a year old at the time. Someone probably dropped her on the road. People have been known do that at times to get rid of a dog they don't want."

"How sad."

"I suppose it does seem so, but it worked out for Maisy," he said. "And for me."

"Yes." It appeared to have been a boon for both man and dog.

"Here comes another stray that decided the farm was her home." He pointed toward a small gray cat coming up on the porch. "That's Cricket. She's friendly to the point of pushiness, so I hope you like cats."

Before she could answer, the cat jumped up in her lap and started purring. Rose laughed as she stroked the cat. "I think anyone might like this cat."

"There are a couple more around that aren't as demanding of attention. Gabby and Jake. Jake has a way of venturing off now and again, but so far, he has always found his way back, and Gabby stays out at the barn most of the time. So they won't bother you. Just Cricket here."

"She's no bother." The cat's purr was comforting. "It's been forever since I've had a cat in my lap. Not since I was a girl."

"Did you live on a farm?"

"No, we lived in a nice little house on the edge of town. My father worked for the railroad. He was killed in an accident when I was twelve. My mother died of a lung ailment not long after that."

"That must have been very sad for you," Dirk said.

"Yes." Rose stroked the cat head to tail. "I had to go live with my aunt until I was old enough to find a position as a housemaid." She didn't see any reason to tell him she'd run away from her aunt's house. That was long past importance now, but he picked up on her choice of words.

"Had to?"

Rose kept her eyes on the cat in her lap. "My aunt wasn't happy about taking me in." She sighed. "But she made sure everyone knew she did her duty."

"Is that why you didn't contact me when you got sick?"

"I simply didn't consider it." Rose looked up at him. "It had been so long since I had met you that one time, and Frank always said you didn't want to be bothered." She didn't go on to say that Frank refused to even mention Dirk's name after their mother died. More old history that no longer mattered.

"I see," he said.

"As it turned out, perhaps I should have contacted you, but I did believe the girls would be safe at the orphanage until I recovered. I thought it would be no more than a few weeks before I could go back for them. Dr. Bess at the sanitarium said it wasn't uncommon for patients to be misguided about their conditions and recovery time. Of course, I knew after I was there, but I still thought the girls were all right. Calla wrote that they had school, enough to eat, and were fine. She didn't tell me about Sienna's troubles since she didn't want to worry me. But this year, I did guess that something was wrong."

"Something was always wrong with that woman in charge." Dirk's voice was almost a growl.

"She seemed very pleasant when I left the girls there." Rose sighed. "My heart hurts every time I see those bruises on Sienna." She looked out at Sienna still in the same spot in the field. "She's always been a bit different. Entranced by nature but uninterested in the more common pursuits for a child her age."

"Like now." Dirk gazed out toward the field too. "It appears she has made friends with a couple of crows."

"She slipped her bread from breakfast into her pocket to feed them." Rose smiled and shook her head. "I let her think I didn't see. The crows won't hurt her, will they?"

"No. They will enjoy the free meal."

"She is so happy to be here at Meadowland." Rose looked at Dirk again. "Thank you for taking in three more strays."

"Not strays. Family." He stared at her with no smile now. "Please, remember that."

She nodded slightly, and he went on. "I want you to have

whatever you or the girls need. If you make a list, I'll get Lincoln to take Calla into town. There's a store that has clothing and yard goods and such as that. Whatever ladies and girls need."

"That is kind of you, Dirk. I do get a small pension from the army for Frank's service that I can use for our necessities."

"I'll let you know if that is needed." He stood up. "And you don't have to worry about Lincoln. Calla met him yesterday down at the river."

"I know. She told me. How old is he?"

Dirk frowned. "I'm not sure. Maybe seventeen. I've never thought to ask him. But he's a good boy. Calla will be safe with him."

"That's good to know."

He started away and then turned back to her. "Mother never put on much weight as some older women do. She wasn't as tall as you and Calla, but I think she might have been near your size otherwise. Why don't you have Calla look through the boxes of her clothes in your bedroom? You might be able to make over some of her dresses or use the material for something different. I know Mother would be glad for her granddaughters to get the good out of her things. There might even be nightgowns the girls can wear."

"All right. Thank you, Dirk. And thank you for talking to me today. I'd like to get to know you better."

He looked surprised or maybe discomfited by her words, but she was still glad she had spoken them. She leaned back and lifted her face to the sun while she kept her hand softly on the cat's back. From the blush on Calla's face when she talked about meeting Lincoln the day before, she would be more than happy with Dirk's plan for her shopping trip. And if Dirk said he was a good boy, then that was good enough for her.

———

Why had she thanked him for talking to her? Dirk frowned as he walked away from the porch. That sounded odd to him. As though he had done something unusual. People talked to one another all the time. At least, other people did. He did most of his talking through letters. It was easier to make sure he said what he intended to say then, without wrong words slipping out.

Had wrong words slipped out? He thought back through their conversation. He'd said nothing that a man wouldn't say to any acquaintance or relative. She was a relative. By marriage. Even if Frank had been dead these many years. How many years? 1918. And now it was 1925. Seven years. It didn't seem that long to Dirk, but he supposed it would to Rose. And Calla. She would have been eight when he died, and he would have been in the army and away from his family even longer.

The army. Why in the world had Frank left his wife and daughters to fight in a war when he could have surely avoided service with the need to support his family? But that was Frank. Always thinking the next thing would be better than the last thing. He'd been an idiot to leave a beautiful woman like Rose and the same as desert his daughters. Sienna wouldn't even remember him. Perhaps that was why she was, as Rose said, different.

He was so deep in thought that he hadn't paid mind to where he was walking. Now, at the thought of Sienna, he looked up to find he was only a few yards away from where she sat. A crow took flight as Sienna slipped something under the edge of her skirt.

He frowned. "What are you hiding, Sienna?" When she visibly shrank back from him, he was sorry he hadn't softened his voice. The child had faced too much anger from adults in her young life.

"Nothing, Uncle." She hurried out her words.

He looked at her without saying anything more. He didn't want her to be afraid of him, but he couldn't let her lie to him.

She let out a shaky breath. "I'm sorry, Uncle." She pulled an ear of corn out from under the hem of her dress and held it out to him. Some kernels were gone from the cob. The crows' breakfast, no doubt. "I stole some of the hens' corn. I thought my crows would like that better than bread."

"I see." He squatted down beside her. Maisy, sensing her worry, moved over to lean against the child's arm. "And did they? Your crows. Did they like it better?"

"They did." She stared down at the ear of corn. "But I shouldn't have taken it. Are you going to punish me?"

His heart clenched at her words. How easily just the hint of a tear in the child's eyes broke through the barriers he had thought to put up against any feeling for her. When he reached to touch her arm, she flinched but didn't jerk away from him. She kept her eyes cast down, ready to accept whatever punishment she imagined he might mete out just as she had surely done at the orphanage.

"Look at me, Sienna." This time he gentled his voice to not much louder than a soft whisper.

Slowly her eyes came up to his. Unique eyes, more gray than blue, with a depth of feeling that had to be unusual in a child.

"I would never intentionally hurt you. You are safe here at Meadowland, and if you want to feed your crows corn, that will be fine. The hens have plenty."

"Oh, thank you, Uncle." She clapped her hands. "Stanley and Josephine will be so happy." She jumped up to grab him in a hug that knocked him off balance.

"Whoa." His hat flew off and he ended up on his backside. Maisy barked and danced around them.

Sienna's eyes got bigger for a second before she put her hand over her mouth to try to hide her giggle. Nothing for it but to laugh along with her. He couldn't remember the last time he had laughed out loud so freely. It felt good. Maisy wagged her tail and licked his face.

"I'm glad you're not mad." Sienna picked up his hat and handed it to him.

Dirk put his hat on. "I'm not mad." He was serious now. "But I don't want you to ever try to hide anything from me or tell me a lie."

Sienna put her hands behind her back and hunched her shoulders up. "I won't. I promise."

"Good." Dirk stood up and brushed off his pants. "So exactly who are Stanley and Josephine?"

"My crows." Sienna's smile came back.

"Stanley and Josephine? Those are fancy names for crows."

Sienna shrugged a little. "They like them." She looked toward the trees before she picked up the ear of corn she'd dropped and put it in her pocket. "I'll save this for in the morning. Stanley and Josephine have other things to do now."

"What things?"

"Crow stuff. They fly around looking for things and fuss-ing."

"Why do they fuss?"

"I don't know. I think they just have to. Maybe God made them that way. Miss Wilma told me that God made all birds know what they need to do. Like where to build their nests and what to feed their baby birds." Sienna looked up at Dirk. "Don't you think that's wonderful?"

"I do." He didn't know who Miss Wilma was, but he was glad Sienna had once had her in her life.

"I should go see if Mama needs something." She looked over her shoulder toward the house.

"I just left her. She's resting. Why don't you go with Maisy and me to see what we can find?" His own words surprised him, but he didn't wish them back.

"Do you think we can find a mouse?" Sienna looked ex-cited. "I do so very much want to meet a mouse."

"I'm not sure I know where a mouse lives, but I do know where a chipmunk lives. That's something like a mouse with a stripe down its back."

"Oh, that would be wonderful." Sienna jumped up and down. Then her face fell as she looked back toward the house. "But Mama says I can't get out of sight of the house unless Calla is with me."

"That's a good rule. Tell you what. You run ask her if you can go for a walk with me. Maisy and I will wait here for you."

As he watched her race across the field, he assured himself that one day of mice and chipmunks and toad frogs wouldn't mean he'd let down all his barriers. He'd make sure to keep a shield around his heart. But when she ran back toward him with a smile that could light up a dark room and put her hand in his, he didn't pull away from her.

For just a moment he thought of Anneliese and how she'd talked about the children they would have one day. A girl first for her, then boys for him. He pushed the thought away and looked down at this child, here and now, and began to tell her about chipmunks.

24

Calla tried to compose herself as Lincoln pulled Uncle Dirk's car through Meadowland's gate out onto the road, but she felt like bouncing up and down like a little kid. She was that excited. In a motorcar with a boy—a good-looking boy—driving. But she didn't want Lincoln to know she was so inexperienced in what to him would be commonplace. He said he ran errands for Uncle Dirk all the time.

She'd only ridden in a car twice before. Once when her mother hired someone to drive them to the orphanage and her on to the sanitarium and then again coming to Meadowland with Uncle Dirk. For a second, an image of the car the man had tried to force her into popped up in her mind, but she pushed it aside. That was a nightmare to be forgotten. This was a dream to enjoy. It was almost like they were on a date. Just thinking that made her cheeks feel hot. Maybe Lincoln would keep his eyes on the road and not notice.

His cheeks looked a little red too, but he'd probably been out in the sun somewhere the day before. Fishing again or who knew what. She had been at the house all day as she and her mother went through her grandmother's clothes. The boxes were a treasure trove of things they could use.

That's where she'd found the hat now perched on her head. She'd felt a little funny putting it on since she hadn't worn one after she went to the orphanage. But a lady needed a hat, her mother said that morning when she told Calla to wear proper clothes to go to the town. Calla wasn't sure what proper town clothes might be, but she picked out a yellow-and-white-striped skirt and pinned the waist to fit. She looked longingly at a lacy blouse they'd found, but picked a plain long-sleeve white blouse instead. Best to be sensible. People didn't wear lace to go shopping or at least she didn't think they did.

Lincoln looked over at her as they tooled along a straight stretch of road. "Nice hat."

"Thank you." She could feel her cheeks heating up again. "It was my grandmother's."

"I'll bet it never looked as pretty on her as it does you."

Now her cheeks were burning. Her freckles would be on fire. She looked down at her hands and had no idea what to say.

"Aww, I didn't mean to make you blush," he said. "I figured lots of boys had told you that you were pretty."

"Actually, no." Calla looked over at him, relieved he was watching the road again. She waved a little air toward her too warm face.

"You've got to be joshing me." He glanced at her before looking back at the road as they came up on a curve. "Weren't there any boys with eyes in their heads where you lived?"

That made Calla laugh as she thought how quickly things could change. Last week she'd been wearing an apron and peeling buckets of potatoes or scrubbing pans. This week a boy was driving her to town while she wore a hat with roses and had a pocketful of money Uncle Dirk had given her to buy the things on his and Mama's lists.

"No boys where I lived," she said.

"That had to be a strange place. Without any boys. Where'd you live? In a convent?"

"Sienna and I were in a home for girls while our mother was being treated at a sanitarium." She had avoided telling him that when they met, but there was no shame in being in an orphanage.

"A home for girls?" He frowned a little. "You mean an orphanage?"

"Yes."

He glanced over at her again, this time with a look of sympathy. "That had to be rough for you."

"It was worse for Sienna than for me. She didn't handle all the regimentation well."

"Regimentation?"

"The rules. Everything had to be done at certain times in an orderly way. I was okay with that, but Sienna can get distracted by almost anything. Well, things like birds and bugs."

"And fish and frogs?"

"Those too." Calla smiled, remembering how happy Sienna had been after she caught the frog.

He was silent a moment before he said, "After my father died, I used to worry about having to go somewhere like that if something happened to Ma."

"Was she sick?"

"No, but neither was my father. Things can happen a person doesn't expect. My grandparents were all gone, and Ma said her brothers went out west, but she didn't know where.

Pa had a sister, but I didn't even know about her until after Pa died. Ma said nobody knew where she was. So I didn't have anybody but Ma, but after I started working for Mr. Dirk, he told me I could live with him if I ever needed to."

"That was nice." If only Mama had asked Uncle Dirk to take them in when she got sick. "Have you always known Uncle Dirk?"

"Nope. Never knew him at all until Pa died. Pa told me I'd better not step foot on Meadowland. He said that Mr. Dirk was apt to shoot trespassers."

"Why would he say that?" Calla shook her head. "I only met Uncle Dirk this week, but I don't think he would shoot anybody just for getting on his land."

"I don't think so either now, but I was scared of him back then. Besides what my pa said, I had seen Mr. Dirk, and you have to admit those scars make him look a little off." His grip tightened on the steering wheel. "But now I don't pay any mind at all to how he looks. Ma and me couldn't have made out after Pa died without his help. So, once back a while, I asked Ma about why Pa said that about Mr. Dirk. She told me I shouldn't worry over it, that there were things I just couldn't understand. That the Meadows and the Rainsleys had been on contrary terms with one another for a long time."

"I'm glad things aren't like that now," Calla said.

"Yeah, me too. Else I wouldn't get to drive a pretty Meadows girl to the store."

"You like to drive, don't you?" She decided to ignore the pretty girl part.

"Driving is the best. I've been saving the money I make working for Mr. Dirk to get a car of my own. Well, what Ma doesn't need to keep us going."

"Your mother is lucky to have you to help her out."

"I guess." He shrugged a little. "But Ma says where we're really lucky is having Mr. Dirk letting us work for him."

"What do you do for him? Besides taking his niece to town."

"I'd have done this for nothing. What with getting to drive the car and all." He grinned over at her. "Not to mention the company."

"It does look fun to drive," Calla said.

"You can give it a try on the way home if you want."

"I don't know about that." Calla held her hand palm out toward him and shook away that idea.

"Don't say no so fast. Driving is easy as pie. Well, the guiding part. Not always easy to get the engine started or to change the tires when you have a blowout. But driving is just a matter of turning the wheel the way you want to go." He twisted the wheel to jerk it left, then right, and laughed when Calla gasped.

"Don't do that!" she said. "You're scaring me."

"It was okay. Nobody was coming."

"Uncle Dirk almost hit a truck the other night when he was bringing us to Meadowland."

"He did?" Lincoln sounded surprised.

"He must have dozed off."

"I don't see how. Not while wrestling the wheel on this old girl and the way she bounces over bumps. He probably just let his mind wander." Lincoln nodded as though he had figured it out. "Yeah, that had to be it. I've been around him when he gets to studying on something and it seems like he goes off in another world. You ever see him do that?"

"No, not unless that was what happened while he was driving. Since we got to Meadowland, he's been busy. We haven't seen him much." Calla thought a minute. "But Sienna does something like that when she's watching a bug or bird or whatever."

"She was pretty intent on that toad frog the other day. Didn't bother her at all when I told her she might get warts." He laughed a little. "But I think it's different for Mr. Dirk. First couple of times it happened, I was afraid he was having some kind of spell or something, but Ma told me not to let it bother me. That Mr. Dirk had some hard times. Bad memories, you know, what with the fire and then that about Anneliese."

"Anneliese?" The name on the picture she'd found in Uncle Dirk's Bible. "What do you know about Anneliese?"

"She was Pa's sister. The one that just sort of disappeared. So my aunt, I reckon, even if I never knew her. She was gone before Pa married Ma. Like I said, Pa never talked about her, but Ma told me some things after I started working for Mr. Dirk. She knew her from church, although Ma was some younger than her. She said Anneliese was a girl that just grabbed your eyes and kept them. She was that pretty."

The girl in the picture was beautiful. "Was she in love with Uncle Dirk?"

"Ma said everybody thought that might be the case. According to Ma, folks were all talking about how Anneliese was going against her father to marry Mr. Dirk. That was before all the bad stuff happened that summer."

"You mean the fire?"

"I suppose that's what Ma meant. It had to be bad. Getting burned like that." Lincoln gave the car a little more gas. "Anyway, Ma thought it best I know some about what happened in case he ever said anything about her."

"Has he?"

"Nope. Not once. He hasn't ever even said the first thing about the fire where he almost died. Leastways, nobody around gave him much chance of making it. Ma said every church in the county was praying for him."

"Where was Anneliese? Was she praying for him too?" Calla thought of the words the girl had written on the picture in the Bible. *Love forever.*

"Ma said that was the part she never understood. Anneliese was gone. At first, they thought she might have been killed in the fire, but they decided she wasn't. They said they'd have found something in the ashes to prove that if it was true. But nobody saw her after the fire. Some figured her father wouldn't let her leave the house to go see Mr. Dirk. He was dead set against them marrying, or so the rumor went around. Then there was other wild talk too. That Mr. Dirk had done something to her because she backed out of marrying him."

"That's crazy," Calla said.

"Yeah, that's what Ma said too, but the sheriff even came out and looked all over the farm. Didn't find anything. Since nobody thought Mr. Dirk was going to live, or if he did, he might not be right in the head again, they figured nobody would ever know for sure. But then, according to Ma, people started thinking straighter. Most folks ended up deciding Anneliese just ran away. Maybe because of her father or that she thought Mr. Dirk was going to die. Some wondered if after she heard how bad Mr. Dirk was burned, she couldn't face being married to a man who was all scarred the way he would be."

"She couldn't have loved him very much if that was true." A surge of anger at the girl swept through Calla.

"Well, that was just people talking." Lincoln shrugged. "Nobody ever knew for sure."

"Do you think Uncle Dirk knows? That he might have tried to find her?"

"I don't know, but I'm sure not going to be the one to ask him." Lincoln looked over at her. "Some things are better left be."

"But don't you want to know?"

"I know all I need to know. I know Mr. Dirk and I know he didn't do anything wrong." He frowned as he stared back out at the road again. They were passing more houses now. "My ma says there isn't any use in stirring in the swampy mess of the past. That if you do, things you don't want to see are liable to rise up out of the murky depths."

"I guess you're right." Calla tamped down on her curiosity. At least she knew more about Anneliese now. She smiled. "Just think. If Uncle Dirk had married her, we would share the same aunt."

"Yeah. We'd be practically cousins. Maybe kissing cousins."

When he looked over at her with a wink, her face bloomed red again. That made him laugh before he pointed out through the windshield. "There's town. Mr. Dirk said you'd need to go to Sanderson's first."

"Wherever they sell clothes and shoes."

"Right. Sanderson's. While you're shopping, I'll get some gasoline and make sure the tires are aired up proper." He stopped in front of a store with dresses draped over some sort of form in the big picture window. "I'll come back to help you carry your packages out to the car. Then we'll go to Brown's Grocery before we head back. I need to get a couple of things for Ma too."

She stood on the sidewalk in front of the store and watched Lincoln drive away. She felt unaccountably nervous. What if she didn't know what to get or spent too much of Uncle Dirk's money and then didn't have enough for the groceries? What if she did everything wrong? At least at the orphanage, somebody had always told her what to do. She didn't have to decide on anything.

Pulling in a deep breath, she squared her shoulders and headed toward the store's door. She was fifteen. Plenty old enough to go shopping by herself. It was time to be part of the world again.

25

The April days passed with sunshine and rain. And peace. The redbud blooms began to fade as leaves pushed out around them, while the dogwood tree in the front yard became a cloud of white. Rose had enjoyed watching the buds open up and the petals grow until fully bloomed. The cat came every morning now to jump into her lap and purr as she stroked her gray fur. Sweet Cricket.

She always hated to make the cat move when she picked up her knitting or sewing. Sometimes the cat stayed in her lap under the fabric or yarn. The girls had several dresses now and no longer looked like ragamuffins. Sienna's bruises on her arms had disappeared to be replaced by shin bumps from climbing trees and chasing after butterflies.

Calla no longer looked haunted by the worry she needed to do more to ensure their place at Meadowland. She kept the house straight and was getting better at cooking on the woodstove in the kitchen. She still panicked whenever she had to go to the cellar, but she did it.

At least she had until Dirk somehow found out about her fear. Now he brought things up for her to cook before she or the girls were up. Well, except for Sienna who was up before sunrise every morning, as if she had to grab every minute in the day after her time at the orphanage.

Rose tried to get Sienna to talk about that. She thought she might need to share the bad things she'd experienced there, but when Rose asked her about the Home for Girls, Sienna would shrug and say she didn't remember. Then she'd start talking about her crows, Stanley and Josephine, or whatever new animal or bug Dirk had shown her lately.

Dirk still wasn't taking his meals with them. She didn't know when he ate, but he was either off in the fields or secluded in his room for most of the day. Writing his articles, she supposed. He no longer left her notes about what she or the girls might need or could do. Instead, he came to sit and talk with her early every day while the sun was still full on the porch. She had come to so look forward to their morning conversations.

While his stated lack of faith did worry her, he was such a good man and so ready to help not only her and the girls but Lincoln and his mother too. Sometimes she wondered how it would have been if she had taken him up on his offer of marriage. A marriage of convenience only, of course. She wasn't sure it would be proper to marry her husband's brother, for convenience or otherwise, but she did believe some woman would be fortunate to be Mrs. Dirk Meadows.

So she was glad to see him coming for their morning talk on this beautiful first day of May. In the house, Calla was singing as she swept the floors, and out in the field, Sienna was in her spot feeding her crows. Cricket was curled in Rose's lap, content under the folds of the skirt Rose was hemming.

She didn't look up until after she heard Dirk settle in the

chair beside her. He would have his hand on Maisy's head to keep the dog from poking her nose against Rose's arm. He appeared to like the idea of surprising her the way he had that first day he'd sought her out on the porch. She played along and continued to ply her needle.

What might they talk about today? While in the beginning their conversations had focused on the needs of the household, now they had lively discussions of books they'd read, news events, or sometimes his nature studies for his scientific articles.

After she did a couple more stitches, she looked up with a smile. "Good morning, Mr. Meadows." At the sound of her voice, the dog came over to get her ears fondled before she settled down practically on top of Dirk's feet.

"The same to you, Mrs. Meadows, but I thought we had long ago gone from being so formal to first names." He returned her smile.

She paid little mind to his scars any longer. He was simply Dirk, a man she was glad to have sitting in the chair next to hers. "So we did. Have you plans for your day?"

She always asked. Sometimes he told her. Other times he scooted around an answer by saying he'd see what the day brought.

But today he answered. "Plowing more of the river bottom. It's almost time to plant corn. I'll need to plant a few extra rows for Stanley and Josephine." He looked out toward Sienna.

"If you want, I can make her stop feeding them," Rose said.

He whipped his gaze back to her face. "No need for that. The child enjoys her friends."

"But it might be better if she made friends with your hens or one of the cats instead."

"I think you have Cricket cornered."

At the sound of her name, the cat stuck her head out from under the skirt. That made Dirk laugh and Rose felt as if she'd been given a gift. She did so wish Dirk could embrace happiness. Rose pinned her needle into the hem and scooted the skirt aside to stroke the cat. "But I do worry about Sienna. She's so different from most little girls. Out there feeding crows instead of begging for a kitten or a puppy."

"She is a unique child, but nothing wrong with being different." He touched his cheek as though thinking about how different he was. At least in looks. "We're all different."

"I guess so. The Lord made us that way. Each for a purpose."

"What's your purpose, Rose?"

"To be mother to my two girls."

"You need a purpose other than what you are to someone else."

"Why?" She frowned as she looked at him.

He stared down at his hands spread out on his knees. "People can disappoint us." He looked up at her. "I daresay Frank disappointed you at times."

"Perhaps not as much as I disappointed him."

"I can't imagine you being a disappointment to anyone."

"I'm a disappointment to myself now with my weakness." She sighed. "It seems wrong for my children to have to do everything for me. To forever have to depend on the kindness of others."

"If the housework is too much for Calla, I can have Lincoln's mother come help her."

"No, no. She's fine."

"She certainly sounds fine." Dirk looked over his shoulder toward the open window that let Calla's voice drift out to them. "Is that a hymn?"

"It is. 'Come, thou fount of every blessing.'" Rose sang the first line of the song, then had to pause to catch her breath. "Sadly, I don't have enough air to sing anymore, but before I got sick, I sang to the girls to help them fall asleep."

"My mother often sang hymns while she worked around the house, but I don't remember that one."

"It has beautiful words." She hesitated, remembering his desire not to talk religious matters with her, but surely he wouldn't mind the poetry of a hymn. She spoke the next words. "'Tune my heart to sing thy grace. Streams of mercy never ceasing call for songs of loudest praise.'"

"Her heart sounds nicely tuned."

"True," Rose smiled. "But I think she's feeling more than the joy of the song. It appears love is in the air."

"Love?" He frowned as though the word puzzled him.

Rose dipped her chin and raised her eyebrows as she peered over at him. "She's taken with your young friend, Lincoln."

"Is that a problem?" Dirk looked worried.

"Not at all. Young love is to be treasured." Rose reached over and touched his hand.

He tensed and then surprised her by turning his hand over to clasp hers for a second before he pulled away. She stroked the cat in her lap as an awkward silence fell between them.

The warmth of his hand in hers was unexpected but not unpleasant. In fact, she rather wished he had held her hand a bit longer. For that brief moment, she had felt she truly belonged here at Meadowland. Maybe forever.

Why in the world had he done that? She would surely think he was crazy, but then she hadn't pulled her hand away. He had pulled his away instead. Maisy got to her feet and laid her chin on his knee. The dog always knew when he was agitated. He stroked her head, glad to have something to do with his hands while he tried to forget the tingle that had swept through him at her touch.

That talk of young romance must be to blame, or perhaps nothing more than the novelty of an affectionate touch from a woman. He couldn't remember the last time he'd felt that. No, that wasn't true. He could remember it all too well. The last time he'd said "until tomorrow" to Anneliese and tomorrow never came for them. That last day he had held her hand until her fingers slid away from his before she ran across the field to her house. Their last touch.

He couldn't think about that now. He wouldn't think about that now. Nor would he think about how nice Rose's hand had felt in his. He needed to keep up the walls he erected around his heart. He didn't want to care. Rose and her girls wouldn't be here at Meadowland forever. She would get better. They would go back to the city and he would be alone again. Best to stay alone to begin with.

But they kept knocking holes in his walls. Calla singing while she cleaned house or did the laundry. Sienna listening with rapt attention when he told her about the creatures of the fields. Those holes he could patch, but Rose's hand touching his had blasted through the wall to leave nothing but rubble.

When had he begun to see her as a beautiful woman instead

of simply his duty as his brother's widow? He did enjoy the time he spent with her each day. They were easy with one another. At least they had been before now.

She was stroking Cricket, perhaps as astounded by his welcome of her touch as he was. He didn't know if he should apologize or get up and walk away without a word.

Before he could decide which to do, she spoke as if nothing at all had happened between them. Perhaps it hadn't set off alarms for her. Only for him.

"Has Sienna showed you the things her crows have been bringing her?" She nodded toward the girl. She was there in that spot feeding her crows every morning, rain or shine.

He shook his head and managed to speak in what he hoped was a normal tone, even if his insides were still in an upheaval. "I've been holed up in my room finishing an article and haven't talked to her for a few days." Another wall he had to continually keep bracing up. The child did tug at his heartstrings.

"I hope we didn't bother you while you were working. We can try to be quieter when we are in the kitchen."

"A little noise doesn't bother me." That wasn't entirely true. More than once when he heard them in the kitchen, he'd wanted to put down his pen and go join them. But he had managed to keep that wall up and intact. At least at those times.

"That's good. We don't want to disturb you."

"You haven't." Nor was that true. Just looking at her now was disturbing him. Was he falling in love with his brother's wife? Widow, he corrected. Frank had been dead for seven years. But no one could take the place of Anneliese in his heart no matter how many years passed.

"What are you writing about now? Or would you rather not say?" she asked.

"It's not a secret. Mourning doves."

"That sounds interesting." She looked out toward the trees at the edge of the yard. "I've been hearing them every morning. Are they nesting now?"

"A pair has a nest in that apple tree over there." He pointed to the first in a line of fruit trees at the side of the yard. "They returned to the same nest they had last year. Doves raise several broods during the summer."

"Really? I always thought birds had babies in the spring and that was it." She looked out toward the tree.

"Most people don't know much about birds. Oh, they know what they look like and they enjoy their songs, but few know their habits." He was relieved their conversation had shifted to birds. He knew about birds.

"Do they mate for life?" She turned her gaze back to Dirk.

He wasn't expecting that question, but they were talking about birds, not people. "Oftentimes, yes, as do many birds." He looked toward the tree he'd pointed out. No doves were in sight. "Of course, while some birds live longer, mourning doves don't have long lives in the wild. Two or three years on average. Longer in captivity."

"Not long at all, but what happens if their mate dies? Do they find new mates then?"

"They do grieve." Birds, he reminded himself again. They were talking about birds. It had nothing to do with their personal losses. "Sometimes they stay close to the dead bird for a while, but yes, they eventually find new mates."

"I see." She lowered her eyes to the cat again. "I suppose that's as nature intends it to be."

"Why didn't you remarry, Rose?"

She looked up, surprised by his question. A question he probably shouldn't have asked, but the words were there between them now. When she didn't answer right away, he added more words. "After all, Frank has been gone a long time. Seven years. You were a young woman when he passed. You're still a young woman."

That made her laugh and eased some of the tension his question had settled between them. "Not so young now." She kept her eyes on the cat as the smile lingered on her lips. "But yes, I was hardly past the age of marrying again when I lost Frank. I suppose I needed time to grieve. I never expected Frank to die. I thought it more likely he would end up a widower than me a widow."

Now he was the one surprised. "Why would you have thought that?"

"I had difficulties giving birth to both the girls." She looked out toward the field as if needing to see one of her children. She sighed and looked back at Dirk. "You knew Frank. He was a man to take risks and live a bit on the edge."

"Yes."

"So, reasonably I might have worried about him having an untimely death, but I never did. Even after he went to the army, something I begged him not to do, I didn't think he would be killed. That seems foolish when he was going off to war."

"But the war didn't kill him."

"Guns didn't kill him, but he might not have come down with influenza had he stayed home."

"You can't know that. People everywhere died in that epidemic."

"True. I did worry about the girls so much then. I wouldn't let Calla go to school even before the schools closed down."

"That was probably wise of you," Dirk said.

"I didn't feel wise. I was panicked. I wrote Frank, begging him to find a way to leave the army and come home." She paused and pulled in a deep breath. "But then I got the telegram. That's when I contacted you. I did so appreciate your help."

"It only seemed right to bring him home to Meadowland."

He thought of the sad ceremony at the graveyard with only his mother's preacher and him in attendance. He should have found a way to bring Rose and Frank's daughters to the farm then.

At least now he thought that. To his shame, he had done what he'd done for Frank out of duty and not love. Frank and he had been on bad terms for so long, but the words the preacher had spoken at the gravesite had touched his heart and made him remember the good in Frank. By then, it was too late to think about whether his widow would have wanted to be there.

"I'm sure that would have pleased your mother," she said.

"Frank was my mother's favorite."

Rose smiled. "He always thought you were."

"He was wrong," Dirk said flatly. "But you haven't answered my question." He didn't know why he pushed her for an answer.

"About why I didn't remarry?" She twisted her mouth to the side in thought.

He waited for her to say more.

"As I said, at first I was too sad to consider courtship. Then the girls and I lived a cloistered life. They went to school and we did attend church, but I spent most of my time fashioning hats for the society ladies. I had little time for personal activities, and I was satisfied with the life the girls and I had. We did struggle to make ends meet, but there were good times too." She paused as her face changed. "Before I got sick. That changed everything."

"Why didn't you contact me then?"

"As I told you when we first came, it never occurred to me," she said. "I had only met you that one time shortly after I married Frank, and I have to say you didn't seem especially happy to have a sister-in-law."

"I suppose not."

She stroked the cat head to tail before she said more. "Besides, I didn't think I would take so long to get well enough to claim the girls again, but tuberculosis is much harder to conquer than I thought. Even now, I have little strength for anything but a bit of sewing. Just those few words I sang earlier stole my breath."

"And now I've had you talking too long." He looked at the dress in her lap. "I can hire someone to do the sewing for you too."

"That's kind of you, but I like having something to do with my hands while I sit in the sun."

"Do you feel you're getting stronger?"

"I do think I may be, but Dr. Bess warned that relapses can happen."

"And did she think you would need to go back to the sanitarium if that happened?"

"She thought it possible, but I'm praying fervently that I can remain with my girls." She looked straight at him.

"However, we won't impose on your hospitality forever if you wish us to find other accommodations."

"Only if that is what you desire." His heart sank at the thought of them leaving. Obviously, no wall had been thick enough or tall enough to keep them from winning his affection.

"Oh no, we don't want to leave. The girls are very happy here."

A whisper of relief swept through him at her words. "They deserve happiness after their time in that place."

"How about you, Dirk? Don't you deserve some happiness?"

Maisy had settled back at his feet, so he rubbed his hands up and down his thighs. "I've been content here at Meadowland these years."

"Did you never think of marriage? Of having children?" Then as if she had remembered what Frank had probably told her about Anneliese, her cheeks reddened a bit. "I'm sorry. Frank did tell me that you planned to marry once before the fire."

"Yes." He had to push out the word.

"But as you said about Frank, that was some time ago. Much longer even than for me."

He turned his head purposely to make his scars more visible to her. "No woman would be interested in a man who looks like me."

She didn't flinch and look away but kept her eyes on his face. "Your face is scarred, but what's inside a person matters much more than how the outside looks."

"I suppose the same as you, I needed time to grieve."

He was relieved when she didn't count up the years and

push that number at him. "Then I will pray that your grief will lighten as mine has."

He didn't bother reminding her that he lacked faith in prayers. In fact, he had to bite back the words in answer that he would pray for her to continue growing stronger. Where had that come from? The morning was taking him in some new directions, for whether he told her that or not, he felt prayer words in his heart. Maybe it would be better if he did give her money to find accommodations in town.

The very thought made his heart clench. His gaze went from her face out to the child in the field. Whether it would be best or not, he did not want to send them away. However, he could get up and walk away from this woman whose very presence was disturbing his soul.

"Thank you," he mumbled as he stood up. "You're kind to spend your prayers on me."

"The Lord doesn't charge for prayer. Nor does he limit the ones we want to offer."

When he looked down at her without a smile, she hurried on. "Forgive me. I did promise I wouldn't preach at you. If you come sit with me again, we'll talk of birds and books and the treasures Sienna's crows bring to her."

"That might be better," he agreed. "But no need to apologize. I was the one to ask you a question I shouldn't have."

"You mean about why I didn't remarry?"

"Yes."

"Well, the question has been asked and answered. So we can continue our friendship from there, or at least that's my hope."

"And prayer?" He raised his eyebrows in question.

"And prayer." She smiled. "But it would make Sienna

happy if you would ask her about her crow gifts. Did you know they would bring things to her?"

It was easier talking about birds again. "I have heard ravens or crows do that sometimes, but no crow has ever been so friendly with me. Then again, I never got up and fed them every morning." He looked out toward the child. "Where does she keep the things they bring her?"

"I don't know, but I would be surprised if she didn't have at least some of them in her pocket and ever with her."

"What are they?"

"She has shown me something new nearly every day, so she has quite a collection now. Buttons. Green glass. Shiny rocks."

"No gold coins?"

"Not yet." Rose laughed. "But it's all gold to Sienna."

"Then I best go see what spell she's put on these birds to have them bring her treasures." He laughed too, glad to have these easy words between them before he left her.

He had surely imagined that jolt her touch had given his heart. And it was beyond ridiculous to think any woman would look on him with favor. Not now. Besides, Anneliese, wherever she was, still owned his heart.

With loud, cawing complaints, the crows flew away as he walked across the field toward Sienna. He liked nearly all birds, but crows always seemed entirely too bossy and noisy. He did once get a hummingbird to light on his finger after many days of patience. But Sienna had seemingly had these crows eating out of her hand from the first day she was here.

The child was a wonder. Perhaps today, instead of him teaching her something, she could teach him about crows.

Her eyes lit up when he stopped beside her, and she

practically glowed when he asked about the crow's gifts. She pulled the treasures from her dress pocket one at a time—a pebble, a bit of broken crockery, two buttons. She had no gold coin, but she did have a penny.

She started to run to the house to get more things to show him, but he stopped her with a promise to look at them later. Then he sat down beside her to talk about crows.

26

Calla couldn't remember ever being so happy. Thoughts of their time at the orphanage were like the last vestiges of a bad dream that evaporated in the warmth of Meadowland's spring sunshine.

Spring here was different from any she'd ever known. In the city the bright colors of tulips and daffodils at the park signaled the end of winter. But here, spring wrapped around them day and night from the sweet scent of the lilacs to the moonlight slipping in their bedroom window accompanied by the music of the spring peepers and the whip-poor-wills.

Not that every day was sunshine filled, but even on chilly or rainy days, Calla was ready to dance as she cooked and cleaned while making sure her mother had whatever she needed. No matter the weather, her mother sat on the porch in the mornings, sometimes wrapped in a quilt, and every morning Sienna fed her crows.

Who would have thought you could make friends with crows? To Calla, they sounded noisy and anything but friendly, but Sienna said they were merely talking to their friend crows.

"I hope they don't tell all their friends to come have breakfast with them," Calla had said.

Sienna looked very serious as she said, "I told them not to. That Uncle Dirk's hens need the corn and I just had enough for them."

Maybe they did listen. Only the two came each day, often bearing those gifts for Sienna. At first, Calla was sure it had to be coincidence. The birds merely had a pretty rock in their beak they dropped in order to eat Sienna's corn, but most days Sienna brought in something new from the crows. Sienna was thrilled when Uncle Dirk made her a wooden box to store her treasures.

Uncle Dirk. He was the one cloud in Calla's sky of happiness. While he had been nothing but kind in supplying for their needs, his every sideways glance, closed door, or frown stabbed her with the worry he might wish them gone. Calla kept the house clean as she'd promised in her letter to him. She even offered to do the garden planting, but Uncle Dirk said she'd have plenty of garden time later on when the beans and tomatoes were ready to pick. She could help Mrs. Rainsley with the canning and preserving she did for him every year.

That should have calmed Calla's fears. He expected her to still be at Meadowland into the summer, but she couldn't shed her worries. Or her curiosity about his past. Especially his love for Anneliese. The questions ran around and around in Calla's head, but they found no answers.

Sometimes after she made her bed, she'd slip into the room with the boxes of books. The picture drew Calla. She stared at the beautiful young woman and wondered about her. About Uncle Dirk too. Had he given Anneliese a photo of himself with *Love forever* written in its corner? Was it yet hidden away in her Bible somewhere?

270

Calla had searched through the Bible for love notes that might be hidden among the pages, but all she found was a violet pressed between two tissue-thin pieces of paper.

The story had so many unknowns. Calla tried to tamp down her curiosity, but the questions kept poking at her. Why was Anneliese's father so against them loving one another? If only she could ask Uncle Dirk, but her mother made sure she knew she shouldn't do that. "Some stories are best left untold," Mama had told her.

"Why?" Calla had sat down in the chair beside her mother's lounger.

As usual her mother's hands were busy. This time with knitting. The same as every day, Cricket was settled in Mama's lap. When the cat raised her head and mewed, Calla leaned over to stroke down her back and start up her rumbling purr.

"You're still very young, Calla. What you will discover as you get older is that having all the answers doesn't necessarily make things better. Sometimes those answers only bring pain." She kept her eyes on her knitting needles as she counted stitches.

"But wouldn't it be better to talk about it with others so they could help?"

Mama rested the sweater she was knitting in her lap and looked at Calla. "Not everything can be helped. I have noticed that neither you nor Sienna want to share your bad experiences at the home."

"That's different." Calla sat back in her chair.

"Oh?" Mama tilted her head a bit as she looked at Calla. "Why is that?"

"It's over and done and better forgotten. Especially for

271

Sienna. She wants to fill her thoughts with new things that make her smile." Calla shivered as the one thing she especially wanted to forget pushed into her mind. That man trying to force her into his car. "So do I."

Her mother must have guessed her thoughts. She reached to put her hand on Calla's arm. "See, there are things that trouble us when we think about what happened or could have happened. Those are the kind of memories that if we dwell on them can bring on nightmares."

"I have had nightmares about that man, but then I wake up and remember I'm here at Meadowland with you and Sienna."

"Yes, thank the Lord for that and for your uncle being there at the right time. But your uncle's nightmares might not have good endings."

"Papa saved him from the fire."

"True, but it left your uncle scarred. Both physically and emotionally."

"Because of whatever happened with Anneliese?" Calla dared ask.

"I think so, but whatever happened between him and the girl he loved can't be changed. And now your uncle deserves his privacy." She pointed her knitting needles at Calla. "And you are to respect that."

"Yes, ma'am," Calla had said.

Even as she kept that promise, she couldn't stop wondering about his lost love. Maybe because she was curious about what being in love, really in love, might feel like. And that was because of how her heart felt lighter whenever she saw Lincoln coming across the field toward the house. Sometimes just thinking about him made her hug herself and spin in circles. Could she be in love?

In the middle of May, Calla was doing the laundry the way she did every Monday it wasn't raining. As she hung towels on the line, she peeked over them at Lincoln, working in the garden patch.

He had waved at her as he passed by the washhouse going to the garden earlier. She had hoped he might stop to talk, but he was diligent about doing whatever tasks Uncle Dirk gave him. Maybe it was just as well, since working in the washhouse was hot and she definitely didn't look her best.

That didn't mean she couldn't tidy up after she hung out the last load of clothes and dumped the wash water. Before she poured the rinse water on some raspberry vines, she splashed some of the water on her face to cool her cheeks. Then she went back to the washhouse to smooth down her red curls and hang her apron on a nail by the door. She looked up at the sun. She had time before fixing the sandwiches they always had for lunch on washday.

They still had peanut butter from Lincoln's last trip to town. Calla hadn't been able to come up with a reason to ride along. She supposed she could have simply asked. Funny how things a person wanted the most were sometimes hardest to speak aloud.

She flounced out the skirt of her faded blue dress. The top fit snugly while the skirt swirled out full to draw attention to her narrow waist. She wanted Lincoln to notice she wasn't a little kid. She was pretty sure he had noticed, but she didn't want him to stop noticing.

27

t the garden gate, she slipped off her shoes and went barefoot on the soft dirt. "Hi, there. What are you planting?"

Lincoln looked up with a smile. "Beans." He held out a paper sack. "Want to help?"

"Sure. I've got a little time before I have to fix Mama and Sienna something to eat." She took the sack of small white beans.

"How about me?" He picked up the hoe. "I'm about starved."

"You too, if you want a peanut butter and jam sandwich. That's our washday menu."

"Sounds good to me." He leaned on his hoe and watched her.

She looked down at the slight trench in the dirt. "What do I do?"

"Haven't you ever planted beans before?"

"Nope."

"City people." He shook his head. "I don't know how you keep from going hungry."

"We weren't far from it at times." Calla stirred through

the beans with her fingers. "But then Mama would sell a hat and we could buy some food."

"Gee, I guess I shouldn't have said that. I'm sorry. Ma tells me I should listen more than I talk sometimes."

"That's okay. Mama used to say the Lord would provide, and he did. At least until we went to the orphanage, and I guess we still had food there, even if not many smiles." She dug down in the loose dirt with her toes.

He stepped over closer to her and reached to lift her chin up. "I like your smiles now."

Calla did smile as her heart banged around in her chest. "And I have reason to smile. The Lord outdid himself bringing us here to Meadowland." Then the old worries sneaked in to make it hard to keep her smile sincere.

"What's the matter?" he asked.

"Oh, nothing." She stepped back from him.

"It doesn't look like nothing."

Calla shrugged and dug her hand down into the beans. The slick-feeling bean seeds slid off her fingers back into the bag with a little rattle. "I just worry that it won't last. That Uncle Dirk will want us to leave."

"Why would he do that?" Lincoln frowned. "You're family."

"I don't know. It's just so great here with the flowers and trees and plenty."

"Plenty?"

"Plenty to eat. Plenty of space to live. Plenty of everything."

"I hadn't ever thought about it like that, but yeah, I guess I have always had plenty of those kinds of things. Trees and the river and such." He looked off across the field toward where the river would be flowing past. "Ma and me don't have a lot but we get by." He turned his gaze back to Calla. "Thanks to Mr. Dirk letting us work for him, and how he found places for Ma to sell her quilts. She sent one off to New York last week."

"That's amazing."

"You're what's amazing."

She met his eyes fully, even though it was probably brazen to look at a boy the way she was doing. She should ask her mother, but then maybe she wouldn't. This felt like a moment to treasure just between Lincoln and her.

He put his hand on her cheek and leaned toward her. She didn't think her heart could beat any faster, but she was wrong. He was going to kiss her. Right here in the middle of the garden in full daylight. What if Uncle Dirk saw them? She ought to move away from him, but her feet felt stuck to the dirt.

A rooster crowed just outside the garden fence to break the spell between them. Lincoln jerked back, his face as red as hers felt.

"I better get these beans in the ground before Mr. Dirk comes around to check to see if I'm done," he muttered as he scraped the trench a little deeper with the hoe.

"Right. So what do you want me to do?" She sort of hoped his answer would be to kiss him.

"Just drop the seeds in the row and I'll cover them up." She dropped a few seeds and he pulled the dirt over them before he grinned at her. "Guess you'll be the one picking beans this year. Maybe Mr. Dirk will find jobs for me that aren't women's work."

"Is gardening women's work?"

"Definitely."

"But you're doing it now." She pulled a few more of the bean seeds out of the sack.

"Sometimes there aren't any women around to do the work, like here on Mr. Dirk's farm. At least until you all came."

"It doesn't seem all that hard. At least with us working together." She dropped two bean seeds instead of one and leaned to pick one up.

"A heap better than me working out here by myself."

"How about working with Uncle Dirk?"

"You're prettier."

"You probably tell all the girls that." Calla concentrated on placing the seed just so in the row.

"Every one that helps me plant a garden." He laughed a little. "That's you and Ma."

"Is your mother pretty?"

"I guess pretty enough. I never thought that much about it. She's just Ma, and meaning no disrespect to Mr. Dirk, but it doesn't take much to be prettier than him."

Calla had to laugh at that. "Mama says I look like him. Curly red hair and freckles." She put a seed in the last spot in the row.

"They look some better on you."

"I'm glad the Meadows and the Rainsleys aren't still having a feud."

"A feud?" He finished covering the beans and then tamped down with the flat bottom of the hoe. "I guess maybe that was sort of what was going on between them back when."

"Do you know why?"

"Ma says it had to do with a field they both claimed. And then Mr. Dirk wanting to marry my pa's sister."

"Anneliese." Each time she said her name she thought of the picture and how pretty she was. No red hair and freckles for her. "Didn't she want to marry him?"

"Ma says she thought so, but then she went away. I guess nobody can know what she was really thinking."

"I wish I did."

"Why?" He gave her a curious look.

"I don't know." Calla shrugged a little. "Maybe because it's like a love story without an ending."

"You like knowing the endings?"

"I do. Don't you?"

"It could be a sad ending. Almost has to be since she ran away." He blew out a breath as they walked back up the row toward the gate. "Sad endings poke at you and never give you any peace. Like Pa shooting himself."

"I'm sorry. That did have to be awful."

"No matter now. What's done can't be changed." Lincoln shook his head as if to get rid of his sad thoughts. "You want to help plant the sweet corn?"

Calla looked up at the sun. It was overhead, which meant it was noon. But it wouldn't hurt them to eat a few minutes late. After dropping some corn seed for Lincoln.

They planted one row and were almost to the end of planting another row back when Sienna rushed toward them. "Calla!"

Calla froze, fearing something was wrong with their mother while she was here in the garden where she couldn't hear her. But no, Sienna looked excited.

Calla went to the garden gate to meet her. "Whatever is wrong?"

"The crows." Sienna had to catch her breath. "Look what Josephine brought me."

She opened her hand to show a gold ring with a stone encrusted with dirt.

Calla took it and rubbed the dirt off with a corner of her skirt. The stone sparkled like a diamond.

"Hey, Sienna. What you doing?" Lincoln came up behind her. "Catch a frog?"

"Show him, Calla," Sienna said.

Calla held up the ring. The diamond caught a glimmer of sunlight.

"Wow," Lincoln said. "Where'd you find that?"

"The crows brought it to me," Sienna said.

"Crows?" Lincoln gave Sienna a blank look.

"They bring me something every day."

He looked back at Calla. "What's she talking about?"

"The crows she feeds. They bring her stuff," Calla said.

"You have got to be kidding."

"I wouldn't kid about Stanley and Josephine," Sienna said.

"Who are Stanley and Josephine?"

"My crows."

Lincoln looked like he might have fallen down a rabbit hole into Wonderland with Alice. Calla couldn't keep from laughing as she shrugged a little. "I know it sounds crazy and I didn't believe it at first either. But Sienna feeds these two crows and I guess they appreciate getting corn. So they bring her stuff." She looked down at the ring. "But never anything like this."

"They brought me a glass button last week," Sienna said.

"Right, but this is a diamond ring. We better go show Mama." Calla tried to slip on the ring, but it wouldn't go past the knuckle on her ring finger. She slid it on her pinkie finger instead and held it out to look at her hand. She'd never had a ring.

"That diamond looks real." Lincoln took her hand and held it while he studied the ring. "Wonder who lost it."

"I don't know, but whoever it was, she must have had slender fingers." Calla reluctantly pulled her hand away from his to take off the ring and hand it back to Sienna.

"It's too big for me." Sienna put it on her middle finger. "But it's really pretty, isn't it?"

"It is." Calla thought of Anneliese then. Probably because they had been talking about her while they planted the seed. Could the ring have been hers?

28

*T*he crows brought you this?"

Rose looked from the ring in her hand to Sienna. The girl's cheeks were rosy with excitement. Behind her, Calla looked just as excited, with a blush warming her face, but that could have more to do with Lincoln beside her. She definitely was entertaining the idea of young love. And so was he, if the way he let his eyes slide over to watch Calla was any indication.

It was hard to think about Calla ready for love. But Calla was fifteen. She'd grown up while Rose wasn't with her. Rose hadn't been much older when she fell in love with Frank.

Sienna nodded as she bounced up on her toes and down again. "It's pretty, isn't it?"

"Very." Rose ran her finger around the inside of the gold band and then peered at it. Something looked etched there, but if it was initials, they were too faint to make out. "But it must have been lost a long time ago."

"Can I put it in my box with the other things the crows have brought me?" Sienna asked.

"No, dear. This is different from the other things you have. This may have been treasured by someone and they surely grieved its loss." Rose hooked the ring over the tip of her finger. The owner must have had a slim hand. She tried to remember Frank's mother's hands. She had been a small woman. She might have lost the ring working out in the field. "This could have been your grandmother's ring."

"Or Anneliese's," Calla spoke up, then looked sorry she had.

Oddly enough, the mention of the name seemed to make Lincoln uneasy too as he shuffled his feet.

"I suppose that could be," Rose said.

Lincoln stared at the ring then. "If you think it's hers, you ought to hide it away somewhere before Mr. Dirk sees it."

Rose looked at him. "Why's that, Lincoln?"

Lincoln glanced behind him as if to make sure Dirk wasn't there to hear him. "Because Mr. Dirk will get all bothered if he has to think about her."

"What makes you think that?" The boy wasn't much older than Calla. He couldn't have known Anneliese.

When he hesitated to answer, Calla said, "She was his aunt."

"Does that mean you know where she is now?" Rose asked.

"Oh no, ma'am. I don't know nothing about her other than what Ma has told me. She knew her back when she was in school. Anneliese was my aunt the way Calla says since she was Pa's sister, but she was gone long before I was born."

"I see." Rose took the ring off her finger and closed it in her palm.

"I'm not aiming to be smart-alecky or anything, but I think you probably don't," Lincoln said. "There was always something wrong about everything with Anneliese."

"Wrong? How?"

"I don't know, but Pa never talked about her at all. I didn't even know he had a sister until after he died. He wouldn't talk about any of his family other than his ma now and again. My ma said he had too many sad memories. I always figured it was losing the family farm."

"How did he lose it?" Rose asked, although she wondered if she should just stay silent and let the troubles, whatever they were, stay back in the past. Still, the boy looked so upset.

"Ma said he didn't want anything to do with the farm after his mother died. So he sold it and just kept a little plot of land to build our house and a barn. He aimed to start training horses, but Ma said that never worked out. He got talked into some bad investments."

"I'm sorry," Rose said.

Lincoln looked straight at her then. "Ma claims some of it was your husband's fault. That he talked Pa into gambling away what we needed to live on."

Rose sighed. She didn't doubt it true, but it did little good to place blame now. She was sorry she'd encouraged him to talk in front of the girls. They didn't need to know bad things about Frank. "There's nothing I can do to make up for that now," she said.

"I know that. Mr. Dirk, he more than made up for it to us after Pa died. He's a good man." He pointed toward her hand. "That's why you oughta just throw that ring in the pond."

"I understand you're trying to protect him, but hiding things isn't the answer. Secrets nearly always surface eventually and bring with them troubles." Rose looked at her girls. Perhaps she had kept too much from them, as both looked stricken now. Calla might be remembering arguments in the night that had left her trembling. Sienna, on the other hand, might merely want possession of the crow's gift to her.

"Like snakes up out of murky pools of river water," Lincoln said.

Rose clutched the ring tighter in her hand, suddenly wishing she could do as Lincoln said and hide the ring away. Let the crows take it back to wherever they found it. But instead, she took a breath and looked directly at the boy. "We are not going to hide this from Mr. Dirk."

"Hide what from me?" Dirk came around the side of the house.

Lincoln jerked around to stare at him and Calla let out a startled breath. Rose's heart did a funny jump inside her chest when she looked at Dirk's face. He looked bothered already, as Lincoln had warned. She had grown so fond of him as they'd shared morning talks that now the thought of causing him grief made her chest heavy, the way it felt so often at the sanitarium but for a different cause.

Sienna didn't seem aware of the tension between them all as she ran to grab Dirk's hand and pull him toward them. "They're afraid you won't like what my crows brought me this morning." She did look a bit apprehensive then as she peered up at Dirk.

"Why wouldn't I like it?" Dirk looked down at Sienna and then at Rose.

"Lincoln fears this might bring back sad memories." Rose lifted her hand up and opened her fingers to reveal the ring on her palm.

———

Pain stabbed Dirk as he stared at the ring. The one he'd

given Anneliese so many years ago. The one she'd put on her finger before twirling around with such a happy smile that he imagined shimmers of joy flying off her.

"Where'd you get this?" His voice sounded gruff to his own ears.

Sienna backed away from him and answered in a small voice. "I told you. My crows brought it to me this morning."

"Your crows?!" He couldn't make sense of it.

"They bring me things." She almost looked scared as she eased farther from him to lean against Calla. "You know. I told you about them and you made me a box to hold everything."

He shut his eyes, remembering the things she'd shown him that the crows had brought her. The bit of green glass. A red button. A penny. But where would they have found this ring?

He reached and took the ring out of Rose's hand. The circle of gold was so small. Something shattered inside him. Anneliese had to have thrown it away.

In what almost seemed an echo of his thought, Calla said, "Was it Anneliese's?"

He spun toward her. "How do you know about Anneliese?" The anger rising in him threatened to explode. Maisy whined and hunkered down at his feet.

Calla shrank away from him, a frightened look on her face. "I . . . I . . ."

Rose sat up straighter in her chair. The cat jumped out of her lap and ran away. "Frank told me about her. Calla must have heard the name from me."

Dirk didn't even glance over at Rose. She was covering for the girl. He stared at Calla.

Lincoln stepped in front of her. "We were just worried about you."

"Go home, Lincoln." When Lincoln hesitated, Dirk pointed toward the field in the direction of Lincoln's house. "Go."

When he still didn't make a move to leave, Dirk said, "I told you to leave."

"It's okay, Lincoln." Calla's voice was barely above a whisper.

Lincoln looked from her to Dirk and took a few slow steps away. After another look back at Calla, he started running as if he couldn't get away fast enough.

Dirk continued to stare at Calla as he waited for her to tell him the truth. She lifted her chin and met his look even as she wrapped an arm around Sienna's shoulders as though to protect her. Sienna's eyes widened with surprise or maybe fright as she stared at Dirk. A sliver of shame poked him, but his anger pushed it away.

"Well," he said. When Rose started saying something again, he held a hand out toward her. The ring clutched in his other hand seemed to burn into his skin. "Let the girl answer for herself."

"I'm not afraid to answer him, Mama." Calla glanced toward her mother and then back at Dirk. "I did wonder about why you were so sad, Uncle Dirk. And then after I found her picture, I guess I let my curiosity get out of control."

"What picture?" He narrowed his eyes on the girl.

"The one in your Bible."

"My Bible?" He couldn't think straight now, as anger consumed him. He had managed to keep his temper tamped down for years, but this was too much. "I told you never to go in my room."

She looked puzzled. "I didn't."

"You're lying. You had to be in my room if you found my Bible."

Her eyes widened as she shook her head. "No—"

"Don't add more untruths on top of your lies." He almost shouted. He took a breath to try to keep from exploding. "Did you leave the Bible there or did you steal it?"

"I wasn't in your room." Her voice trembled. "The Bible was in the box of books upstairs."

Rose was on her feet, moving faster than he thought she could to stand between him and Calla. "Stop this right now. My daughter doesn't lie and she doesn't steal." Behind her, Calla started weeping. "You need to leave until you can control your temper."

"I think you have forgotten, madam. This is my house." Where had those words come from?

"I have forgotten nothing." Rose's voice was soft. "You are right. We will leave, but we beg you the grace of another day to pack, and then you can drive us back to the city."

Sienna let out a wounded sound. "No, Mama. Please."

"Shh." Rose gave her a look and the child said no more as silent tears streamed down her cheeks.

"I'm so sorry." Calla's words were choked out between sobs.

Maisy was on her feet, licking Dirk's hand. Dirk didn't know what to do. Everything was crumbling around him. He couldn't stand their tears, but the girl shouldn't have lied to him. She had to have been in his room to find Anneliese's picture.

He had to get away from them. He needed time to think. He turned on his heel and started across the yard. Before he went through the yard gate, he looked back at Rose. Her shoulders drooped as Calla helped her to her chair. She seemed barely able to move one foot in front of the other. He wanted to go back and plead for forgiveness, but instead he clutched the ring so tightly in his hand that the stone cut into his skin and he kept walking.

Perhaps this was for the best. They had broken down all his walls and were endangering his heart. He couldn't let love in again. That would lead to nothing but pain.

29

irk watched the river flowing past him without really seeing it. He was on his perch above the little waterfall where usually the sound of the rushing water and birds singing could bring him peace. Not today. Maisy had her head in his lap as he sat on the cold rock. That's how he felt. Hard. Cold. Broken.

He stared at the ring in his hand. Anneliese had to have thrown it away. How else could it have been anywhere those crows could have found it? He shut his eyes and could see her slinging it away, trying to rid herself of even the thought of him.

She had been upset with him that last time they met after he'd disregarded her wishes and had gone to talk to her father. He had known how torn she felt defying her father to marry him and thought he could change things. His mother had agreed to give Rainsley the field he thought was his. Frank had been against it. Accused Dirk of being besotted by Anneliese.

He was right about that, but for once their mother had given in to Dirk instead of Frank. At fourteen, Frank wasn't old enough to make demands on Dirk or their mother.

Dirk planned to work to pay his mother for the field. Frank wouldn't lose anything.

Once Rainsley had ownership of the field, he'd have no reason not to accept Dirk into the family. At least that was what Dirk had thought. Perhaps if his father had still been alive, Dirk would have had a better understanding of how deep the hard feelings went between the two families. He wanted to believe his father would have been ready to forgive and forget. That he would gladly exchange the field for Dirk's happiness.

Whether that might have been true or not, Anneliese's father wasn't ready to make peace at any price. He met Dirk in the yard, carrying a rifle pointed at Dirk's chest.

"I don't know what you want here, but I'm advising you to hightail it back over the river if you're fond of breathing."

Dirk held his hands up in the air but didn't run. "I just want to talk to you, Mr. Rainsley. About the land you want. About Anneliese."

"You been messing around with my girl?" His eyes narrowed on Dirk.

"Not messing around. No sir. I want to marry her."

"What are you talking about? Is that your way of trying to steal my farm the way your grandpa stole our field?"

"No sir." Things weren't going at all the way Dirk had hoped. He looked over Mr. Rainsley's shoulder toward the house where Anneliese was hanging on to the porch post as if that was all that kept her standing. "I came to make things right between us. To give you the field you say is yours."

"I don't just say it's mine. It is mine. It's always been ours. It ain't the first bit of matterance what those books down at the courthouse say." The man appeared to be getting angrier by the second, even with Dirk trying to make peace between them.

"Yes sir. It's however you say."

Rainsley had let the gun barrel sink a little, but now he pulled it back up to point directly at Dirk again. "You trying to buy my daughter with a measly field?"

"No sir. I love your daughter."

He acted as though he didn't hear Dirk's words. "She ain't for sale. You couldn't buy her were you to offer your whole farm, kit and caboodle. I'd druther see her dead than married to a Meadows. Now get on out of here before I put a hole right through you." He jerked the gun up and shot into the air.

Dirk couldn't keep from jumping, and that made the man laugh. His son ran from the house toward his father, but he stopped short of grabbing his arm as Rainsley leveled the gun on Dirk again. This time Dirk wasn't at all sure he wouldn't pull the trigger.

"Pa, leave him be," Jerome said. "He won't come around bothering us anymore. Not after you've given him a scare." The boy, who didn't look much older than Frank, gave Dirk a pleading look. "That's right, isn't it, Meadows?"

"I'll go." What else could he do? He couldn't fight a man with a gun. A half-crazy man with a gun. He looked back toward the porch, but Anneliese was nowhere to be seen.

Dirk turned and walked back across the field toward the river. He did not run but walked steady. Even when a shot whistled past him, he didn't run. If Rainsley wanted to shoot him, he wouldn't be able to outrun a bullet.

At the river, Anneliese stepped out from behind a tree in front of him. She had her fists planted on her hips and her eyes flashed with anger. "What do you think you were doing? I told you that you couldn't talk to Pa."

His legs had been trembling all the way across the pasture to the trees, but now in the face of her fury, he trembled all over. Not afraid for his life, but afraid for his heart. He'd never seen her so angry.

"I'm sorry." He reached to touch her, but she spun away from him. "I thought if I gave him the land, he would be ready to make peace."

"Ready to welcome you as a son, I reckon." She gave him a withering look. "For a college boy, you can be pretty dumb."

Anger surged up in him to match hers. He took a deep breath and mashed it down. He didn't want to fight her. He wanted to hold her in his arms and tell her how much he loved her. "I was doing it for you. For us. I wanted to make things easier for you when we marry."

"If we marry." She spat the words toward him.

His heart sank. She couldn't mean that. She couldn't. "Please, Anneliese. I love you."

"I know." She burst into tears and moved into his embrace.

He held her and stroked her hair while whispering, "Shh, don't cry. It'll be all right. We'll make it all right." He wiped away her tears with his fingertips.

"It's just that you don't know Pa. When he gets his mind set, there's no reasoning with him."

"I should have listened to you, but I thought I could make it better."

"But you can't." She took the handkerchief he offered and mopped up the rest of her tears.

"You didn't mean it when you said 'if we marry,' did you?" His heart stopped beating as he waited for her answer.

"Of course not." She poked her finger into his chest. "I can't live without you, you silly college boy."

"And I don't want to live without you." Dirk kissed her forehead.

"You won't have to." She blinked away the last of her tears. "No matter what my father says, I'm still marrying you when the meadow blooms."

"I think I saw some blooms when I came across it today."

That made her laugh. "I want it all to be in joyous bloom."

He held her close for a long moment before he said, "Come with me now. Ma will let you stay in my bedroom if I sleep in the washhouse until we marry." He didn't like to think about her going back to face her father.

"He won't hurt me." She looked down and fingered her grandmother's locket, something she did when she was upset.

He put his fingers under her chin and lifted up her face to look at him. "Are you sure?"

He thought he caught a flash of doubt in her eyes, but she said, "I am. I'll stay out of sight until he calms down."

"And if he doesn't calm down?"

"Then I'll pray for the meadow to bloom overnight, and I can start a new life as Mrs. Dirk Meadows." Her smile was a little shaky, but he saw love in her eyes.

"Come with me now," Dirk begged.

She put her hands on his cheeks. "I'll meet you at the barn tomorrow. We can go count the flowers in the meadow."

She'd kissed him then and left him standing bereft on the riverbank. He wanted to follow her, to be sure she was all right, but he'd already made a shambles of things. He had to trust her.

That was the last time he saw her. The next day the barn

was on fire when he got there. He had run into the flames, fearing she was trapped inside. He would have died if Frank hadn't picked that day to follow him across the field for whatever reason. Dirk never knew why.

Dirk stared down at the ring in his hand. Such a small thing to hold such promise and now such despair. *I can't live without you.* She'd said the words, but had she meant them? He'd said the same thing back to her, and here he sat on their riverbank without her. He'd been without her for over twenty years. But had he really been living? Hiding here at Meadowland, afraid to love again.

His last day with Anneliese had been a fiasco. He hung his head. And now he'd ruined things with Rose and her daughters. How could he have said the things he did to her? To Calla. They would go away. Chased off by his words. By his fear of opening his heart to hurt again. In truth, the hurt penetrated no matter the barriers a man put up.

Maisy whined and licked his face.

"I've made a mess of things, Maisy. I don't know what to do."

The dog looked at him as if she understood his every word before she leaned against him.

Dirk tightened his fingers around the ring. If Anneliese had thrown it away, changed her mind about him, he should throw it in the river. Be done with it. Be done with his memories. He raised his arm to sling it away, but then he stopped. The ring was not at fault. If the crows had found it and brought it to Sienna, then with the child the ring should stay.

He stood up and slipped it into his pocket. "Goodbye, Anneliese," he whispered as he turned to walk back to the house. He wanted his words to at last be final.

The sun had gone down and light was fading. The cow would be bawling, in need of being milked. That was the thing about living here on Meadowland. No matter what happened, how he might be feeling, the farm animals still needed tending. If he hadn't sent Lincoln home, the boy could have milked the cow.

Another stab of guilt. Would the boy think he meant for him not to come back? As if Lincoln hadn't already suffered enough with his father's death and the hardscrabble life he and his mother had to keep the wolf from the door, now Dirk's anger could have driven a wedge between the boy and him. Lincoln was obviously attracted to Calla. He might not forgive Dirk's anger that threatened to chase her and her mother away.

The very thought of them leaving was worse than a stab of guilt. He didn't want them to leave. Ever. The thought of being alone again was like a band tightening around his heart as he walked across the fields with Maisy stepping along beside him. She didn't leave his side to investigate any late day scents, as if the dog, the same as he, felt things crumbling around them.

When he got to the house, the clothes were off the line, the hens gone to roost, and the night bugs chirping. Clouds were gathering in the west when he got the milk bucket off the back porch and went to the barn without going inside. While he was milking, he could think of the best way to apologize and ask them to stay.

By the time he brought the milk back to the house, thunder sounded in the distance. It seemed only right that a storm was coming, since he carried a storm within him.

The house was dark. No lamplight showed in the windows

and until then, he hadn't realized how good seeing a light in his house felt.

No one was in the kitchen. Not uncommon since he often came in late, but even on those days, he could generally hear the muffled sounds of voices from the parlor. Sometimes if he stood absolutely still, he could make out that they were reading one of books from those he had stored away in the upstairs room. He must have been wrong about the Bible. In spite of his angry words, he really didn't think Calla had lied to him.

He lit a lamp and strained the milk. There, covered with a domed pan lid, was a plate of food Calla had left for him, as she did every day. A basket with his clothes neatly folded sat in front of the door to his room. On top of the clothes was the Bible.

He turned from the sight of it and lifted the lid from the plate. Potatoes, boiled eggs, beans. He took a bite of the potatoes, but his stomach was churning too much for him to eat. Still, he couldn't leave the plate full for Calla to find in the morning and think he had rejected her food. He scraped it out for Maisy, who looked at him as if to be sure he knew what he was doing. When he nodded, she finished off every bite.

For years he had embraced the silence of solitude, but tonight it mocked him. He picked up the lamp and pushed the basket of clothes through the door into his room with his foot. Maisy found the rug where she slept and lay down with a huff of breath as if the dog was ready for this day to be over. As was he. Better would have been the chance to start the day over, but days couldn't be done over. A man had to live with whatever had happened, whether that was caused by him or not.

He took the Bible off the stack of clothes and sat down beside the lamp. It fell open to where Anneliese's picture was stuck between the pages. He let the Bible close after he picked up the photograph. She was so beautiful. He stroked her face and traced her words with his finger. *Love forever.*

He had loved forever. Would love her forever, but one love didn't rule out more loves. And he did love those girls sleeping in his upstairs rooms and the woman, his brother's widow, in his mother's bedroom. Rose's pale face hovered in his mind. She needed him, but even more, he needed her. Her gentleness. Her kindness. The way she looked directly at him without shrinking from his scarred face. Her prayers.

Prayers. Why had he thought that? Must be because he was holding the Bible his mother gave him. His mother had prayed ceaselessly for him, but he'd told Rose not to pray for him. Not to bother trying to soften his heart toward the Lord. Prayers were empty words thrown out into a void. Too many bad things had happened to him to believe in a loving God. But he was wrong. So very wrong.

He shut his eyes, thinking of the bad things Rose had endured. Her parents dying when she was young. Losing Frank. Entering a sanitarium. Even worse, leaving her daughters at an orphanage.

And now, he'd added to her bad things. Making her think she had to leave. Where would she go? How would they have enough to live on? He could give her money, but that wasn't what he wanted to give her. He wanted to give her his love.

How much he wanted that surprised him. He had thought he didn't have any love to give. A prayer without words swelled up inside him. After a moment, he whispered, "Help me, Lord."

When he opened the Bible to stick the picture back between the pages, it fell open to the Old Testament book of Ezekiel. He started to flip back to Ecclesiastes where he'd left the photograph years ago, but something stopped him. As if guided by the Lord, his eyes fell on verse 26 of chapter 36.

A new heart also will I give you, and a new spirit will I put within you: and I will take away the stony heart out of your flesh, and I will give you an heart of flesh.

A stony heart. That was what he'd had these many years. Loving Anneliese but unable to forgive her desertion. Unable to shed his sorrow. Rose and her daughters had given his heart a chance to come back to life. Had given him that new heart.

After he extinguished the lamp, he sat unmoving in the dark. No stars showed in the sky he could see out the windows. Lightning flashed as thunder sounded closer. Wind with the promise of rain pushed in through his open windows.

First thing in the morning he would apologize. More than apologize. Beg Rose to stay. It was time to find love somewhere besides in his memories of Anneliese at the river.

30

*U*ncle Dirk was still gone as the afternoon wore on. Calla somehow got through the rest of the day. Her mother said they should keep doing what had to be done the same as usual. Carry in the clothes from the line when they were dry. Feed the chickens. Cook supper. Fold their clothes and leave them ready to pack.

Pack. The word cut a hole in her heart. They couldn't leave Meadowland. Even if they'd only been here for a couple of months, it was home. But Mama didn't look as if she would change her mind when she said they would have to leave.

She made Sienna stay beside her whenever she wasn't helping Calla. With a woeful look, Sienna did as she was told. Poor girl, she didn't even try to pet the hen she'd named Brunhilda when she pitched the corn out to the chickens. She didn't talk except to answer Calla if she asked her something and then in as few words as possible.

Tears didn't edge out of Sienna's eyes the way they continually did Calla's. And Mama's. Mama dabbed at her eyes more than once. But Sienna was crying inside. Calla knew.

It was all Calla's fault. She'd let her curiosity, her need to know all the answers, mess everything up. Lincoln had warned her not to stir up the past. He'd told her she might not be happy with what rose to the surface. He was right. She did very much regret making Uncle Dirk so angry.

If only he had believed her about the Bible and realized she hadn't meant any harm looking at Anneliese's picture and wondering about her. About the two of them. But she had caused harm. The hurt on Uncle Dirk's face was easy to see when he looked at the ring.

Not that the ring had anything to do with her. Sienna's crows had brought the ring. She wished her mother had hidden it the way Lincoln said. He knew Uncle Dirk better than they did. He knew things were going to be bad if the ring belonged to Anneliese.

Uncle Dirk must have given it to her. An engagement ring. But Mama said hiding things just made everything worse. She told Calla that might be why Uncle Dirk had lost his temper. He'd hidden too much of his hurt over the years.

That night after they ate the supper none of them wanted, Mama said it sounded as if a storm was coming up and they should go to bed without their nightly reading time in the parlor. None of them felt like reading anyway. She did have Calla read the eighth chapter of Romans.

"'For I am persuaded, that neither death, nor life, nor angels, nor principalities, nor powers, nor things present, nor things to come, nor height, nor depth, nor any other creature, shall be able to separate us from the love of God, which is in Christ Jesus our Lord.'"

Her mother held up a hand to stop Calla after she read those verses. "Dwell on that tonight, girls. And don't worry. Pray instead. The Lord will provide."

Calla tried to do as her mother said as she changed into

her nightgown, but she couldn't keep from thinking the Lord had provided. She had spoiled his provision.

In bed, she held Sienna close, more for herself than for Sienna. The storm clouds moved in with thunder and lightning. She wasn't afraid of storms, but in between the flashes of lightning, the night was very black. With the unknown facing them, the dark seemed to press down on Calla and make it hard to breathe.

The clouds burst open and rain crashed against the tin roof. On other nights, the sound of the rain had been soothing, but not this night. It pounded against the roof with such fury that Calla had to scoot down in the bed to put her face next to Sienna's to hear her.

"Are you afraid, Calla?"

"Not of the storm." Calla tightened her arms around Sienna.

"But of the dark?" Sienna asked.

"A little. Are you afraid?"

"No."

Calla pushed Sienna's hair back from her face. "You've always been braver than me."

"How do you know if you are brave?"

In a lightning flash she saw the puzzlement on Sienna's face. "I don't know for sure." Calla thought a minute. "Maybe when you do whatever you have to do even if you're scared."

"Then you're the one that's brave. Taking care of me when you're scared." Sienna's breath tickled Calla's cheek. "Like the way you came through the dark to be with me at the home when we were first there. Do you remember?"

"Yes."

"I hated being there."

"I know."

Sienna was quiet for so long Calla thought she might have gone to sleep, but then she said, "I love being here."

"I know that too," Calla said.

"I don't want to leave."

"We have to do what Mama thinks is best."

"But what if she's wrong?"

"Then, we have to be with her anyway. To take care of her wherever we are."

"She's still sick, isn't she?" Sienna didn't wait for Calla to answer. "Her hands shook so much, she had to quit knitting."

"She was upset. That made her tired. She'll be better tomorrow. But don't worry. I told you I can take care of you now. I'm old enough."

"I know." A little hope trickled into Sienna's voice. "If you marry Lincoln, we could go live with him."

Calla had to smile, a sad smile. "That might be nice, but I don't think it can happen that fast. We're just friends right now."

"But you could ask him."

"No, I couldn't." A heavy feeling settled in Calla's chest. She might never see Lincoln again. "But we'll be all right. Now we need to go to sleep." She kissed Sienna's forehead. "So we can be brave tomorrow for whatever happens."

Sienna sighed, but she didn't say any more as she settled her head down on her pillow. In a few minutes her breathing let Calla know she was sleeping. Calla kept her arm around her and shut her own eyes to block out the dark night.

The rain kept pounding down. She gave herself over to the

sound. Another thing she might never hear again. Rain on this roof. She pictured the water sliding off the tin to sweep free and hit the ground. Somehow that soothed her enough to fall asleep.

When she woke the next morning, light struggled to seep through the window. It was no longer raining, but clouds ruled in the sky. Sienna wasn't in the bed. Nor was she sitting in the chair waiting impatiently for Calla to wake.

Calla felt a moment of panic but then took a deep breath. Sienna might have run to the outhouse. She might have gone to sit in Mama's room. She often did that in the mornings, and with all that had happened, she might need to be close to Mama. Calla had no reason to think the worst.

She sighed. Worst was already going to happen unless her mother had a change of heart. Unless Uncle Dirk forgave Calla. She found a sheet of paper and pencil. She'd written him a letter once and he had rescued them. Truly rescued her from that man trying to steal her away.

Calla cringed at the thought of the word *steal*. How could he have thought she would steal anything from him? She pushed aside her hurt feelings. It wasn't a time to dwell on how she might have been wronged. Better to think how she had wronged him with her overreaching curiosity.

> *Dear Uncle Dirk,*
> *I am so sorry that I let my curiosity about Anneliese cause you to be angry. Mama says we have to leave but we don't have anywhere to go and I don't think she's able to move right now. After she got upset yesterday, she was very weak.*
> *But I understand if you don't want me to stay. I can*

leave and find a job somewhere, but I'm begging you to let Mama and Sienna stay here. Sienna does love being here at Meadowland so much. It is breaking her heart to have to leave.

So, please just take me back to the city. Mrs. Jenkins told me about a friend of hers who ran a boardinghouse and how I might be able to work for her. I'll be fine. If I make any money, I will send some back to you to help pay for whatever Mama and Sienna might need.

Again, I am very, very sorry, but I really didn't go into your room. I wouldn't have done that.

> *Your loving niece,*
> *Calla Harte Meadows*

She folded the paper and wrote "Uncle Dirk" on the outside. Then she got dressed and quietly slipped down the stairs to prop the note against the milk bucket. It must be even earlier than she'd thought since he hadn't gone to milk as yet. She looked toward his closed door, but she didn't dare knock on it.

Instead she went to find Sienna.

Mama's bedroom door was open a crack. Calla peeked in. Her mother was still sleeping, but Sienna wasn't in the room. She wasn't in the outhouse or the chicken yard. It was so early only a few of the hens had ventured out of the roosting room, but the rooster was crowing to announce morning, even if the light was only that grainy gray of dawn.

When she went back inside, she checked the clock on the parlor mantel, but it had run down. The hands were stuck on twelve thirty. Uncle Dirk must have forgotten to wind it.

Outside the wind had picked up. Dark clouds swept toward them, stealing even more of the early morning light. But Calla could see out in the meadow to the spot where Sienna fed her crows. She wasn't there either. She wasn't anywhere.

Calla stood very still and listened. The rooster crowed again. Then a rumble of thunder rolled across the sky. She ran out to the yard gate and called Sienna's name. The wind snatched the sound and whirled it away. No crows could fly in this weather. Then a crow flapped past, riding with the wind to prove her wrong. Whether it was one of Sienna's crows, she had no idea. But she had the feeling Sienna had gone looking for them. To tell them goodbye or more likely to hide with them.

Calla moved across the meadow toward the river. She had to find Sienna before her mother woke up. Mama didn't need any more upsets.

31

The storm had crashed around Dirk all night. Not only the storm that whipped rain against the wall of windows in the sunroom he'd turned into his bedroom but inside his mind as he thought about his anger pushing Rose away. And hurting the girls. He could still see Calla's wounded look when he accused her of lying. Finally he did doze off, only to dream of running into the flames to save Anneliese over and over. That he couldn't find her haunted his sleep.

As the first hints of daylight crept through his windows, the storm outside seemed to be abating. The clouds were still heavy in the sky, but the lightning and thunder had moved off to the east. He did his best to tamp down the storm in his thoughts. He would talk to Rose, beg forgiveness from her and from Calla. He thought Calla would forgive him. He wasn't as sure about Rose.

He was putting on his shoes when he heard someone in the kitchen. It was early for Calla to start breakfast, but perhaps her night had been as bad as his. Another fault to lay at his feet. He considered going out to see her, but he should talk to Rose first. So he stayed quiet until he heard her go outside. That surprised him, but she might be making a trip to the outhouse.

His gaze fell on the Bible he'd left on his desk, still open to the verse in Ezekiel about the Lord giving his people a new heart. Could he count himself in the Lord's people after the years he had turned away from him?

He flipped back through the pages, not really looking for anything but stopping here and there to read a verse in Psalms. So many of them written by David, a king who in verse after verse humbled himself before the Lord and begged forgiveness for his sins. The Lord had listened to David, and now these many years later, David's words were in front of countless eyes with the same need for forgiveness.

Dirk's eyes stopped on verse eight of Psalm 103. *The Lord is merciful and gracious, slow to anger, and plenteous in mercy.* That surely meant Dirk could be forgiven even as David was, but could he forgive himself?

He read on through the verses. *As far as the east is from the west, so far hath he removed our transgressions from us.*

His mother had quoted that verse to him many times in hopes that he would be able to leave his guilt behind. She said if he gave it to the Lord, then he could be at peace with what had happened with Anneliese's father that might have led to Dirk losing her. He should have listened to his mother, but instead he hardened his heart against her, the Lord, and the world.

Now, reading the Scripture words and hearing the echo of his mother's voice, he remembered how much she loved him. While she might have spoiled Frank more, she had loved Dirk no less. She had nursed him through the pain of his burns. Kept him alive with her care. She had never turned her back on him, even when at times he had turned his back on her. More reason now to ask forgiveness. Were she still here with him, she would give it as freely as David said the Lord would in this psalm.

Dirk felt the need to do something more, but he didn't know what. He shut the Bible. If the Lord was giving him a new heart, he would know what Dirk was feeling in that heart.

Maisy had been sitting patiently as Dirk held the Bible, but now she went to the door and whined.

"All right, Maisy. I've made you wait long enough. It's time to face the day."

After he milked the cow, he would search out Rose to ask her forgiveness. Rose first. Then Calla.

With the clouds still heavy outside, light was dim in the kitchen. He let Maisy outside and then started a fire in the cookstove to make things easier for Calla when she came to start their breakfast. He let Maisy back in to feed her some meat scraps. When he went to pick up the milk bucket he'd rinsed the night before and left by the sink, he saw the folded paper with his name written on it. Calla's writing.

Dear Uncle Dirk.

Each word he read made his heart heavier. He should have believed her. He did believe her. Now.

Your loving niece.

What had he done? He sat down at the table. Her willingness to leave and be separated from her mother and sister to appease him stabbed his heart. Tears slid out of his eyes and down his cheeks as he read through her words again. Maisy whined and leaned against his leg, but he didn't have the heart to rub her head.

He didn't realize Rose had come into the kitchen until she spoke.

"Are you all right, Dirk?"

"No." He looked up at her without trying to hide his tears.

"What's wrong?" She looked concerned as she came to the table. "Are you ill?"

Dirk swiped his tears away on his sleeve. Then without a word, he held the letter out toward her. His hand shook.

She looked at him for a moment before she sat down across from him and took the paper. After she read Calla's words, she shut her eyes without looking up. Her lips trembled and her breath sounded shaky.

Dirk wanted to reach across the table and take her hand, but he wasn't sure she would accept his touch. "Can you forgive me, Rose? I shouldn't have let my temper explode against Calla the way I did. I should have believed her."

Rose pulled in another breath and let it out slowly before she did finally look at him. "Yes, you should have. Calla would not lie. She's always faced whatever consequences came of her actions."

"I'm ready to do the same," Dirk said. "But the sight of the ring I gave Anneliese had me reeling."

"That's understandable." Rose lay the letter down on the table. She looked very pale and tired.

"But not an excuse for lashing out at Calla. I so regret hurting her. Making her think she needed to write this letter." He let his gaze rest on Rose. "I love you and the girls being here at Meadowland. I don't want you to leave."

Her eyes narrowed a bit as if she weren't sure she could believe him. "You haven't always acted as if that is true."

"What do you mean?"

"You seem afraid to be near us at times."

"Afraid." He echoed her word. "That's the right word. I was afraid to open my heart to hurt again. I tried to build barriers against having feelings for you, but instead I kept seeking you out to talk every morning."

"At times I wondered if you only did so out of duty."

"No, no." He shook his head. "But I can see why you might have thought so. I even tried to tell myself I was simply doing my duty for my brother's children, but from the first time I saw them in that dragon woman's office, I wanted to protect them. And then when I found Sienna locked in a closet and that man grabbing Calla, I had such a burst of feeling, it frightened me. It had been so long since I had let myself love anything. Except Maisy here." He looked down at the dog that had settled at his feet before he raised his gaze back to Rose's face. "I didn't want to admit how much I loved them. How I was falling in love with you."

She seemed at a loss for words.

He did then dare to reach across the table to touch her hand. "Do you think you could ever feel any affection for me? Any at all?" He hesitated and then added, "Please don't say as a brother."

Rose eased her hand away from his, but she didn't look away. "You are my husband's brother."

"Yes, but never your brother. Until now, we only had that one brief meeting years ago."

⁓

He was right. She had never known him as a brother. "I don't know what to say."

"Say you will forgive me and stay here at Meadowland. Give me a chance to earn your affections."

She didn't doubt the sincerity of his words, and her heart was not untouched. Seeing him in such a state of despair when she'd come into the kitchen had made her insides clench. She did care for him. While it wasn't the kind of love she'd once felt for Frank, this gentle tug at her heart was sweet and endearing. She felt so at home with Dirk here at Meadowland, or she had before yesterday when he had been so angry.

She moistened her lips, trying to come up with what to say. She needed to find words that were right for both of them and for the girls. A flicker of worry went through her at the thought of the girls. She'd expected to find them in the kitchen, but it was early. They must still be upstairs. She'd have to go wake them, but first she had to answer Dirk.

"I do feel affection for you already, Dirk, but I can't live where I have to fight for my girls." She kept her gaze steady on his face as she went on. "I loved Frank and I know he loved the girls and me. At least as much as he was able. He never wanted to settle down. He was always hunting something more, hoping to strike it rich somehow. We were often at odds. When we fought, the peace of our home was destroyed. Frank would storm out of the house, and I wasn't strong enough to hide my unhappiness from Calla. She would hear me crying in the night and come crawl in bed with me to do her best to comfort me."

Dirk frowned. "He didn't hit you, did he?"

"No, but hard words can be painful too."

He reached across the table to put his hand over hers again. This time she didn't pull away.

She sighed and went on. "I was so very young. I felt like such a failure as a wife and mother. I hated having to beg for money to buy food for our children before he gambled his pay away." She looked away from Dirk toward the kitchen window. It was raining again. "I wanted him to be someone he couldn't be."

"I'm sorry." He sounded sincere. "That wasn't your failure, but Frank's."

"Blame hardly matters now. But I can't live like that again. Fearing confrontations. Having to fight for my children."

"I understand."

"Do you?" She turned her eyes back to Dirk's face.

"Maybe not completely." This time he pulled his hand away from hers and sat back, silent for a moment, as if measuring his words before he went on. "But I am not Frank. I am more than willing to supply whatever you and the girls might need if it's within my means. Plus, I can assure you I want peace in my life every bit as much as you do."

When she started to speak, he held up a hand to stop her. "I know. I didn't prove that yesterday. The sight of the ring and thinking how Anneliese must have thrown it away, thrown away my love, made me lose control. While I can't promise that will never happen again, I will do my best to see that it doesn't. And I do promise to never again lash out at you or the girls. That I can control."

"Can you?"

"Yes. If I ever lose my temper like that again, I'll walk away. Wait to talk about whatever has upset me until I can do so with a cool head." He smoothed his hand across Calla's letter. "Please let me apologize to Calla. To Sienna too. And please change your mind about leaving. If you can't stay here with me also in the house, let me be the one to leave. I can sleep in the barn or build another house. But let this be your home and the girls' home."

"I don't want you to sleep in the barn. This is your house."

"I want it to be our house." He leaned toward her. "I asked you to marry me once and you turned me down."

"I hardly knew you."

"I know. And my offer then wasn't spurred by love. It is now, Rose. I love you. I know I have a monstrous face and a hermit's ways, but I can change. Well, not my face but my ways. Do you think you could ever consider my offer of marriage?"

His words softened her heart and brought tears to her eyes.

"Please, don't cry," he said. "I never want to make you cry."

"Some tears are good tears." Rose blinked back her tears as she let out a slow breath. "But what will people say if I marry my husband's brother?"

"You said you didn't care what people said the first time I offered marriage."

"And I don't. But what would Frank think?"

"Frank, the same as Anneliese, is gone from our lives. But I think Frank would understand. Maybe even be glad you came home to Meadowland. I have no idea about Anneliese. I was so sure our love could conquer any obstacles, but it must not have been as strong as I thought." He looked down at Calla's letter under his hand. "It's been over twenty years. I should have moved on years ago and sometimes thought I had."

"But you hadn't?" It really wasn't a question.

"Not completely. I kept thinking she might come back. Explain why she left."

"Why do you think she did leave?"

"I don't know. My burns perhaps, but she hadn't even seen me. She didn't know how scarred I was or even if I would live. Nobody ever saw her after the fire." He looked toward the window, and she wondered if the storm inside him matched the storm outside. "Her father didn't want her to marry me. He would have disowned her. Maybe she couldn't face that, but then, her mother told me after Anneliese's father died that Anneliese never came back to the farm. She claimed to have no idea where she was. And I believed her. Her brother had said the same when I cornered him once to ask about Anneliese."

"You mean Lincoln's father? Calla told me he shot himself. That Lincoln's mother said it was an accident, but Lincoln didn't believe that."

"Mrs. Rainsley only said that for Lincoln's sake. She knew. Said some demons from the past bedeviled him." Dirk took a breath and let it out. "The odd thing is that he came over on my side of the river to do it. I had rarely seen him since the fire except in the distance. Didn't see him that day until it was too late. I heard the shot and found him where the barn had been."

"The one that burned?" she asked.

"Yes. The barn stood close to the river, so Anneliese and I met there when the weather was bad. Jerome probably knew that, but why he would pick that place to kill himself, I don't know." He looked toward the window again as though he needed a minute to get his thoughts in order before he went on. "I took the poor man's body home and helped Lincoln dig his father's grave. That was all I could do."

"Calla says you help them now by letting them work for you."

"I need their help as much as they need mine." Dirk looked down at the letter again. "I have to apologize to Lincoln too. But I haven't told you the oddest part. Jerome shot himself on the exact date the barn burned years before. I could never fathom why, unless he felt guilty because he set the fire instead of lightning being the cause the way everybody assumed. There had been a storm that night, so nobody considered arson. I don't know if I would have seen anything amiss if I'd been the one clearing away the rubble instead of Frank."

"But you were fighting to live then."

"The doctor didn't think I would, but my mother never gave up. She had the whole county praying for me."

"But you wouldn't pray yourself," Rose said.

"I did then. Only later after I knew Anneliese was gone did I turn away from the Lord."

"That might have been when you needed the Lord the most."

"I wasn't ready to see that then." Dirk shifted uneasily in his chair.

Rose studied him a moment before she asked, "And now?"

"And now." He bent his head and rubbed his forehead. "Now I think my mother's prayers for me are finally being answered." He looked up at her. "Calla put my Bible with the clothes she folded yesterday, and I found it last night when I came to the house. When I opened the Bible, the first verse I saw was about the Lord replacing a stone heart with a new one. My heart has been stone for years, but I want that new heart now. I want to give it to you."

His face showed such raw feeling, she had to shut her eyes a moment as an echo of the love he was offering filled her heart. Could she truly love this man? That seemed to need more thought. She opened her eyes and met his gaze directly. "I can see that you're sincere, but this is too sudden for me. I need time. I think we both need time to be sure of our feelings."

He started to smile, but then looked as if he didn't know if he should. "Does that mean you'll stay? To give us that time?"

She did smile as she reached across the table to lay her hand on his cheek. Not on his smooth cheek, but the other one so he would know she wasn't bothered by those scars. "Yes. As long as the girls want to stay, and I'm sure they do. Calla tried to talk me out of leaving all day yesterday, and dear Sienna wouldn't talk at all, she was so sad."

He put his hand over hers once more. "Where are the girls?"

"I thought they might be in here getting breakfast." She looked back toward the front of the house. "With the clouds making the morning so dark, they may still be asleep."

"I don't think so. I heard Calla in the kitchen before I came out of my room to go milk. I didn't hear her come back in, but I assumed she came in the side door. And then I found her letter."

Her heart gave a lurch. Why hadn't she realized something was wrong at once when Sienna didn't come into her room as she so often did? "If they aren't in the house, they must be out in the storm."

He suddenly looked as worried as she felt. "Do you think Calla might have tried to go to Lincoln's to get him to take her to the city?"

"No. Not Calla. She wouldn't run away." She felt sick as she looked back at the window where the rain was coming down harder. "But Sienna might. To keep from leaving. Calla is probably looking for her."

Dirk stood up so quickly his chair fell over. Maisy jumped up and started barking. "Easy, girl," he said. The dog hushed at once and sat down to watch while Dirk came around the table to put his hand on Rose's shoulder. "Don't worry. They won't have gone far. I'll bring them back to you."

"What about your milking?" She looked at the milk bucket on the cabinet.

"The cow can wait." He squeezed her shoulder gently. "You rest. I'll find them."

"How? You won't know which way they went."

"If I don't miss my guess, Sienna will be looking for her crows. I told her once where they might roost overnight. That's where she'll be."

He was simply trying to reassure her. He couldn't really know where the girls might be, but Rose still clung to the confidence in his words as she watched him go out the door with Maisy trailing him.

32

alla had headed across the pasture toward the river. She didn't know why, but she had a feeling Sienna would have gone that way. Rain started falling again, but she paid it little mind. Getting wet didn't matter. She had to find Sienna.

As she hurried around the edge of a plowed field to keep from sinking in the mud, Calla didn't know which she was readier to do—yell at Sienna or grab her in a hug if she found her. Not if. When. She pushed "if" out of her thoughts.

The farther she got from the house, the more she wished she'd awakened her mother so she'd know where she was. She could have knocked on Uncle Dirk's door too. She should have. To ask him to help her look. But she'd thought she would find Sienna before anybody knew they were missing. If not for the rain, Sienna might have heard her calling. She would answer if she heard Calla. But the rain and the wind deadened the sound of Calla's voice.

A few kernels of corn were on the ground where Sienna fed her crows. That gave Calla hope she was headed in the right direction. But where was Sienna going? She couldn't hide out here in the fields and woods for long. Surely she didn't think the crows would feed her the way the ravens brought food to the prophet Elijah in that Bible story.

Calla blew out a breath and walked faster. Who knew what Sienna was thinking? Except that she didn't want to leave Meadowland. That had to be why Sienna had run away. Her faulty reasoning didn't matter. Calla simply wanted to find her so they could go home.

Home. What a beautiful word. They had moved around a lot before her mother went to the sanitarium. They continually needed to find a place with lower rent. That's how they ended up in the dark apartment over the butcher shop. She hated the place and never thought of it as home. At least not until her mother got sick and she and Sienna had to go to the Home for Girls. That was no home at all. One day there had been all it took for her to realize four walls and a roof didn't make a home. People she loved made a home. Those dreary rooms over the butcher shop seemed filled with light in her memory because her mother was there. Sienna was there.

Now they did have a home actually filled with light and fresh air where they could be together as a family. Or they did before Calla spoiled it with her questioning nature, but she had done what she could to fix that for Mama and Sienna.

If Uncle Dirk had read her letter by now, he might be ready to take her back to the city. Calla's heart was heavy at the thought of leaving Meadowland, but she would do whatever had to be done to give her mother and Sienna the chance to stay. She did hope she saw Lincoln one more time before she had to leave.

She heard the river before she could see it. A crashing roar. Nothing like its gentle flowing sound on the other days she'd been there. The rain dashed down harder and thunder rumbled overhead. She bent her head and pushed into the wind as it whipped her hair and skirt sideways. The air grew dark, as if night were falling instead of morning beginning.

Lightning flashed and thunder boomed with barely a pause between them. The ground seemed to shake, but maybe it was only her legs trembling. She had never been afraid of storms, but that was when she was inside somewhere safe. Out in the middle of the wind and lightning was different and scary.

She hoped Sienna found shelter somewhere. It could be that she hadn't run away but was even now safe back at the house and Calla was on a fool's errand. She wished that were true, but she didn't believe it. Sienna was somewhere out here in the storm.

Lightning flashed again, and almost as if Calla had summoned him with her earlier thoughts, Lincoln, wearing a yellow slicker, came out of the trees along the river. He stopped and stared at her as she ran toward him.

"What are you doing out here?" he yelled when she got closer. "Don't you know it's storming?"

He sounded angry. To keep from dissolving in tears, she yelled back at him. "Of course I do. Don't you?"

A streak of lightning slashed through the air and struck a tree along the river. The tree exploded in a blast of sparks as the branches and trunk splintered and pieces flew through the air. Lincoln grabbed Calla and pushed her to the ground before he covered her with his body. This time there was no doubt the ground was shaking, but then so was Calla. The boom of thunder seemed to go on and on.

When at last the sound faded, Lincoln lifted himself away from her. "Are you all right?"

She sat up and pulled in a shaky breath. "I think so. Are

you?" She jumped when lightning flashed again, followed by a clap of thunder, but this time no trees exploded. Rain started pounding down harder, as if the lightning had split open the clouds.

"I am now that you are." He gently pushed her wet hair back from her face. His fingers were trembling. "Why are you out here? Are you running away?"

That surprised Calla. "I wouldn't run away." Then she blinked as tears filled her eyes and spilled out to join the raindrops on her face. "But I think Sienna has." She tried to dry off her cheeks with the edge of her sweater, but it was useless. She was soaked through and through.

Lincoln pulled her closer to him under his slicker. "Run away?"

Calla leaned against him. "Mama said we'd have to leave after Uncle Dirk got mad at me. Then this morning I couldn't find Sienna at the house, and I had the feeling she might have come this way to look for her crows."

"Why would she do that?"

"I don't know." She sniffed and wiped at her face again. She felt safe, cuddled next to Lincoln with the rain sliding off his slicker, but she couldn't stay there while Sienna might be alone out in the storm. She pushed away from him to stand up. "I have to find her."

He got up too. "Don't worry. She can't have gone far." He slipped off his raincoat and handed it to her. "Here, put this on."

She pushed it back toward him. "You keep it. I'm already soaked."

"No." He wrapped the slicker around her shoulders. "The rain is letting up. I'll be fine."

She gave in and slipped her arms through the sleeves. "Why are you out here? I know you're not running away. Are you?"

Water sprayed off his hair when he shook his head. "I wouldn't ever do that to Ma. But I told her about the ring and Mr. Dirk getting so mad at you. At me. At everybody. She said she couldn't sleep thinking about it. So, this morning she gave me a letter for him and said I had to take it to him right away, even if it was raining. That she should have given it to him after my pa died, but she didn't think it would matter if she kept it hid. She thought it might cause more sorrow if she gave it to him."

"What's it say?"

"I don't know. She told me not to read it. To just give it to Mr. Dirk, and if he wanted to tell me what it said, he could. But that she wouldn't."

"Didn't you want to read it?"

"I am some curious," he said. "And a little worried about what Mr. Dirk will do, but Ma told me not to read it. So I won't."

"Of course you shouldn't read it." Calla shut her eyes and shook her head. "I'm sorry. Me thinking I have to know everything is why Sienna might be out here in this storm. What if she was close to that tree?"

"We won't think that." Lincoln looked toward the trees and then started walking that way. "The storm is moving off. If you think she went this way, we will probably be safe enough checking it out now. But the river is jumping out of its banks."

"Did you wade across?" She followed him.

"No, Mr. Dirk gave me a rowboat to cross the river. I'd

have been swept away if I'd tried walking across, with how fast the water's running."

New fears awoke for her. "What if Sienna has been swept away?"

"Don't think that either." He frowned over at her. "She wouldn't have any reason to get in the water. She might not know to stay away from trees when it's storming, but she's smart enough to stay out of the water."

He was right. Sienna wouldn't get in the river. Her crows wouldn't be in the water. But she might be near the trees. Calla sent up a silent prayer. *Please, Lord. Keep her safe.*

The rain slowed to a gentle shower. Calla pushed off the hood of the slicker so she could hear better. Then she called Sienna's name. Lincoln cupped his hands around his mouth and yelled for her too.

They could see the river now as it spilled out of its banks and rushed past. After walking a little bit farther, they stopped and called again. Then they stayed still to listen for an answer over the sound of the water and the rain on the leaves overhead.

After several more times, Lincoln said, "Maybe we should go back to the house to see if she went home."

"Not yet," Calla said. "Let's go a little bit farther first."

He seemed reluctant to move on.

"Is something wrong?"

He stopped walking as he looked on up the river. "No." He pulled in a breath. "Yes."

"What is it?"

"There used to be a barn up there."

"Then that's where Sienna might be to get out of the rain." Calla started to walk on, but Lincoln grabbed her arm.

"The barn's gone. It burned down a long time ago." His face looked tragic.

"Is that where Uncle Dirk got hurt?"

"Yes. Last time I was there years ago, nothing was left except the rocks from the foundation and some iron scraps from old farming equipment that must have been in the barn." His face was stiff. "I can't go up there."

"Why? Has Uncle Dirk told you not to?"

"No, it's not that." He moistened his lips and seemed to have to push out his words as he went on. "That's where Pa shot himself."

"Oh." She reached over and touched his arm. "I'm sorry."

"She won't be there. She must be back at the house. She would have answered us by now if she was out here."

"I guess you're right." Calla turned to follow Lincoln, but then a crow cawed and was answered by another one. She whirled around and called Sienna's name as loud as she could.

Lincoln stopped and watched her. After a minute, he yelled Sienna's name too and Calla echoed him. Calla held her breath as silence fell around them except for the sound of the river and the crows cawing again. She had no idea if they were Sienna's crows. All crows sounded alike to her, but she wanted them to be telling her something about Sienna.

"She's not here." Lincoln sounded sad as he turned away. "Nobody's here."

Calla sighed and started to follow Lincoln. Then she heard something. Not a crow but something that sounded like a sob. A bird couldn't make that sound.

"Wait." She glanced at him. "Listen."

She could tell he was trying to hear whatever she'd heard, but then he shook his head.

"I don't hear it now either, but I did a minute ago. I have to make sure it wasn't her. You go on. If it's nothing, I'll catch up." She started following a trace of a path. The river was only feet away here as it flowed past. She didn't look back at Lincoln again, since she didn't want him to think he had to come with her. She couldn't blame him for wanting to avoid the place where his father had died.

Still, her heart lifted when she heard him running after her. "You didn't have to come," she told him when he caught up.

"I know. But it's just a place. Pa isn't here now."

They were both quiet then. Calla took shallow breaths as she listened for the sound she'd heard.

Beside her, Lincoln must have been shuffling through memories because he said, "I loved my pa. He was a good man, even if he did do what he did. He couldn't have been thinking about how hard it would be on Ma."

"And on you," Calla said.

"Yeah. On me too. Ma wouldn't ever talk about it. Said it was better to just remember the good times we'd had. And we did have good times. But Pa always had those sad spells too. Dark times, Ma called them. She said we just had to leave him alone then to make his way through it. He always did. Until he didn't."

She took his hand without saying anything.

"I always thought I ought to have been with him. That he wouldn't have done it if I'd been with him," Lincoln said.

"But you couldn't be with him all the time." She squeezed his hand a little. She truly did understand. If anything happened to Sienna now, she would feel blame for not waking up and stopping her from running away.

They were quiet then as they saw the rock piles ahead.

Calla was listening with every fiber of her being. "Sienna." She didn't yell but spoke her name firmly the way her mother did when she didn't want Sienna to ignore her.

She heard the same choked sob. And then she saw her huddled beside some tumbled-down rocks. Her dress looked soaked and her almost-white hair was plastered against her head. She didn't look up even when Calla stooped down beside her.

"Sienna." This time Calla kept her voice gentle. "Are you all right?"

The girl pulled in a ragged breath and finally looked at Calla. "I don't want to go back. I want to stay here."

"All right." Calla sat down on a rock beside her. "I'll stay here with you. Lincoln will too."

"Lincoln?" She looked up at him. "Did you ask him to marry you?"

"Not yet." She peeked up at Lincoln with a shy smile and then back at Sienna. "But maybe someday."

"He won't stay here." Her face scrunched up. "You won't either. Not forever."

"Forever is a really long time. Mama would worry about us."

"I know my ma would. Then she'd come after me with a switch." Lincoln tried to smile, but Calla could see it took effort. He shifted uneasily on his feet, perhaps worried he might be standing on the very spot his father had died.

"You're too big for that," Sienna said.

"I'll let you tell my ma that." He looked behind him as if expecting someone to be sneaking up on him right then.

"Are you scared?" Sienna cocked her head to the side and stared up at him. "You look scared."

"I guess I am. A little," he admitted. "Not of Ma. But of other things."

"What things?" Sienna asked.

"The river flooding." He pointed toward the water creeping ever nearer to them. "The storm." He looked up at the sky and then back at Sienna. "What about you, kid? Are you scared? Is that why you ran away?"

"The storm scared me," she said. "But that wasn't why I came here."

"Then why did you?" Calla thought she knew already, but Sienna might need to talk about it.

"I wasn't planning to. I just wanted to go out and feed Stanley and Josephine before Mama made us leave. I wanted to tell them I was sorry I wouldn't be feeding them again. It wasn't raining when I went outside."

"You must have gone out in the dark," Calla said.

"It wasn't dark dark. Sort of gray dark. I thought maybe they'd be watching for me or I could watch for them."

Lincoln gave the river another look and finally squatted down in front of them. "Did they come?"

Sienna gave him an exasperated look. "Of course they did. They always come."

"I didn't know you could make friends with crows," he said.

"Not everybody can," Calla said. "But Sienna knows the key."

"I'm guessing corn," Lincoln said.

That brought an angry glare from Sienna. "You don't know anything about crows."

Lincoln held up his hands. "Simmer down. I know enough. Like how crows mess up a corn crop."

"Mine won't." Sienna lifted her chin and set her mouth. "I'll tell them not to."

"We'll worry about the corn crop later." Even to her ears, Calla sounded cross. "But if you weren't planning to run away, why are you here? Why are we all here, half drowned and practically tinged by that lightning blast a while ago?"

"I'm sorry. But I was afraid to come back to the house. I was afraid to see Uncle Dirk."

"Why? He wasn't upset with you. Only with me."

"It wasn't you. It was the ring. That's what made him mad," Sienna said.

"She's right." Lincoln nodded. "I told your mother to hide it."

"But how did you know it was Anneliese's?" She looked at Lincoln. Even with all that had happened, with how her curiosity had ruined things for them, she still couldn't keep from wanting answers.

"I didn't really know. I just had a bad feeling it might bring on one of Mr. Dirk's dark moods." He paused and looked around before he went on. "The same kind Pa used to have."

"Okay." Calla tried to work it out in her head. "I can understand that and I can understand why Uncle Dirk got upset when I said Anneliese's name." She looked at Sienna. "But I don't know what any of that has to do with you running away in the middle of a storm if that wasn't what you were intending to do all along."

Sienna blinked and looked up at the trees still dripping from the rain. Then she pulled in a breath and held out her fist. "My crows brought me something else this morning." She slowly opened her fingers to reveal a locket. "I was afraid it might be hers. I didn't want Uncle Dirk to get so mad again, so I came to the river to throw it away. But when I was getting ready to drop it in the water, there was all this thunder. Like it was telling me not to." She looked up at Calla. "I don't know what to do now."

Calla stared at the locket. Lincoln leaned closer to stare at it too. It did look like the locket Anneliese wore in her photograph. Maybe it would be better to throw it in the water. But no, Mama would say they shouldn't have secrets from Uncle Dirk.

"We can't hide it," she said.

"Hide what?"

Calla gasped at the sound of Uncle Dirk's voice behind them. Lincoln jumped up to face him, and Sienna tightened her fist around the locket and buried her face against Calla's chest.

33

*D*irk hated how the children flinched at the sight of him. He'd startled them. They had been so intent on whatever they were talking about they hadn't noticed him coming up through the trees.

Maisy had led him here. He'd followed her in case she was leading him to the girls, even though he had wanted to turn and go the other way. He hated being anywhere near where the barn had once stood. Without thinking, he touched his scars.

Lincoln looked uneasy, but Dirk wasn't sure whether it was because of him or from being where his father had chosen to die. The place was one of sorrow.

Sienna's fear as she hid whatever was in her hand wounded Dirk the most. He had no idea what she was afraid for him to see. After his burst of anger the day before, he would have to earn back her trust.

Calla held Sienna close against her but met his gaze without shrinking away. "Uncle Dirk," she said and then seemed not to know what else to say.

Your loving niece. The words from her letter jumped into his thoughts. He needed to assure her she had a forever home here at Meadowland with her mother and sister.

Beside him, Maisy whined. The dog was trembling with eagerness as she waited for Dirk's permission to run to the children. Dirk released her with a wave of his hand. She didn't go to Lincoln as she usually did when the boy was around but instead went straight to nuzzle Sienna's ear. Sienna peeked around at the dog, and Maisy licked her cheek. Two days ago that would have made her giggle, but today she ducked away from the dog to press her face back against Calla.

"I didn't mean to startle you." He did his best to soften his voice. A crow cawed as it flew overhead.

"We weren't doing anything wrong," Lincoln spoke up.

"All right," Dirk said. "But what are you doing here?"

Calla spoke up first. "We were looking for Sienna. Well, I was, and then I met Lincoln on the way to your house."

"In the storm?" He looked at Lincoln. "Were you coming to see me or Calla?"

"You." The boy reached in his pocket and pulled out an envelope to hand him. "Ma told me to bring you this. Said she wanted it out of her hands and into yours before she changed her mind about giving it to you."

"That's odd." He looked down at his name scribbled across the envelope and had the feeling he was staring at another letter he'd rather not read. One she'd sent Lincoln out in a storm to deliver couldn't be good. "She's not sick, is she?"

Lincoln shook his head. "She just said it was something you needed to know." He seemed to have to pull up his courage to go on. "I told her about what happened yesterday."

"You mean the ring?" When Calla's eyes widened on Dirk as though afraid he might explode at them the way he had the day before, he went on. "Don't worry, Calla. I won't let my temper get away from me again."

"It's okay. You had reason to be upset." Calla's voice sounded a little shaky.

He wanted to step closer to her, but he stayed where he was. "I'm sorry I yelled at you and accused you of lying. Even worse, stealing. That was wrong of me, but I wasn't thinking straight. Can you forgive me?"

Calla pushed Sienna away from her and stood up. He wasn't sure if it was to face him or to get ready to run. "I'm the one who's sorry, Uncle Dirk. I shouldn't have been so nosy."

Sienna got to her feet too, but she kept her head bent, staring at Maisy as she stroked the dog's head with one hand. She kept the other hand hidden in the folds of her wet skirt.

He shoved the envelope in his pocket. Whatever Mrs. Rainsley had written could wait.

Calla was still talking. "Did you see my letter?"

"I did."

She squared her shoulders. "I can be ready to leave whenever you want."

"No, Calla." He shook his head at her. "You can't leave. Your sister and mother need you here. I want this to be their home. Your home too. Forever."

She looked surprised by his words and then she was crying. Deep sobs. Dirk stepped toward her, but Lincoln was there first to wrap his arms around her.

"Don't cry." Dirk couldn't stand her tears. "I thought you'd be happy."

"I am happy." She choked back her sobs and reached for Sienna's hand. "We can stay at Meadowland, Sienna."

A strange look, almost of horror, flashed across the child's face. She jerked away from Calla and ran toward the rushing river water.

"Sienna!" Calla seemed too surprised to move.

Dirk raced past Calla and Lincoln after Sienna. She still might have gotten to the river before he could catch her if Maisy hadn't grabbed her skirt and pulled her down. Sienna didn't fight Dirk when he helped her up. Instead, she slumped against him, defeated.

"I thought you'd want to stay at Meadowland, Sienna." He tipped up her face until she had to look at him.

"I do, but this is going to ruin everything." She held her hand out, still clutched in a fist. "My crows gave it to me today. I wanted to throw it away, but I couldn't."

"What is it?"

She tightened her fingers and looked past Dirk at Calla.

"You have to give it to him." Calla's voice was firm. "If it's hers, he needs to see it."

Dirk looked over his shoulder at Calla. *Hers.* She had to mean Anneliese. He turned back to Sienna, who had opened her fingers to reveal what she held. Anneliese's locket.

Almost as if he were in one of his nightmares, he carefully lifted the necklace out of Sienna's hand. But this was no dream. He'd never seen Anneliese without her grandmother's locket around her neck.

His legs gave way and he dropped down on the ground. Anneliese might have thrown away his ring, but she would have never given this up. She hadn't left him. She was still here somewhere. Had been all along.

Her father had said he'd rather see her dead than married to a Meadows, but Dirk hadn't believed he was serious. Even now, he couldn't believe the man was that cruel. Could she have been in the fire and he hadn't found her? Nobody had found her?

"She didn't leave me." Tears welled up in his eyes and spilled over to stream down his cheeks. He looked up toward the sky and whispered, "I am so sorry, Anneliese."

He hadn't realized until this moment how much bitterness had built up inside him through the years. Now it seemed to roll out of him with his tears. She hadn't deserted their love. He was the one who had deserted hers.

Maisy whined, danced around him, and licked his face. Sienna pushed the dog to the side to throw her arms around Dirk's neck. "Please, don't cry, Uncle Dirk. We love you."

The child's embrace was so pure, her declaration of love so sincere, that even more of the hardness that had calcified around his heart broke away. He put his arms around her and looked up at Calla, who had tears streaming down her face to match his. Lincoln stood behind her, not sure what to do. Dirk wasn't sure what to do either.

"Are you all right, Uncle Dirk?" Calla asked.

"I will be," he managed to say. It was time he made that true. He swiped away his tears. "Lincoln, help me up."

Calla hugged Sienna back against her and Lincoln took his hand to pull him to his feet. He stared down at the locket he still held while the children seemed almost afraid to breathe as they waited for whatever might happen next.

He looked at Sienna. "You say the crows brought you this?" When she nodded, he went on. "But where did they get it?"

"I don't know." She gave a tiny shrug. "They don't tell me that. They just bring me things."

"I see." The locket felt warm in his hand. If only it could talk.

He looked around. The river was still rising and already covered the lower part of where the barn once stood. Again, a crow cawed as it flew overhead, but it had no answers he could fathom. He tightened his fingers around the locket. Whatever had happened was long lost to him just as Anneliese had been lost to him all these years. He pulled in a breath and let it out slowly.

Lincoln spoke up. "Maybe you should read Ma's letter. She said it had answers."

"Answers?" Dirk stared at the boy. "What kind of answers?"

"I don't know. That's just what she said."

As Dirk considered his words, a gust of wind swept through the trees and shook down a spatter of raindrops on them. Calla took off the rain slicker Lincoln must have given her and wrapped it around Sienna, whose teeth were chattering. The morning air was cool and they were all soaked.

The envelope crinkled in his pocket, but he didn't pull it out. Back at the house, Rose had to be worrying about her girls. Whatever Lincoln's mother had written could wait until they were dry. It could be he shouldn't read it in front of the children in case those answers Mrs. Rainsley sent him might knock him down the way sight of the locket had.

"Come here, Sienna."

She came to him with no hesitation. He lifted her up. She was all legs and arms and hardly weighed more than a sack of corn.

"She can walk," Calla said.

"I can, Uncle Dirk," Sienna said.

"I know." Dirk didn't put the girl down. "You can walk after you warm up."

Sienna sighed happily and laid her head on his shoulder.

"Let's go home," he said.

"Home." Sienna's breath tickled his neck.

"Yes, home," Calla echoed.

Dirk headed away from the river. Calla started to follow him but then stopped to look back at Lincoln, who hadn't moved. "Aren't you coming, Lincoln?"

"I don't know. Can I come, Mr. Dirk?"

Dirk smiled over his shoulder at him. "I think you should. The cow needs milking, and once you do that, Calla can make us some hot cocoa."

All the way back around the plowed field and then through the pasture, the envelope crackled against his leg with every step. He didn't know what answers Lincoln's mother could have written to him, but they would surely deal with the past. Here now, in this present, he had his answers walking with him back to where another answer awaited. They would help him leave the past behind and begin anew.

Rose must have been watching for them, because she came down off the porch and along the rock walkway to meet them. When he saw her, he put Sienna down so she could run to her mother. Calla followed her. Dirk stopped at the edge of the yard. Maisy sat down beside him to wait too.

Lincoln said, "Poor Blondie. I hear her bawling. I'd better go get the bucket." He ran toward the kitchen door.

Before she got to her mother, Calla hesitated and looked at Dirk. Without a word, she came back to take his hand and pull him on up the walk and into the circle of their family.

His family. Whatever was in the letter in his pocket couldn't change that.

34

Rose felt faint with relief when she saw Dirk coming across the field with the girls. Her girls. She feared Sienna was hurt since Dirk was carrying her, wrapped in a yellow slicker. But then he put her down, and she ran toward Rose. The coattails flapped against the ground and she tripped. She was up in a second, shrugging off the slicker to run faster.

"I'm sorry, Mama." She threw her arms around Rose and buried her face against Rose's chest.

"My sweet child." Rose stroked her head and paid no attention to how wet she was as she held her close.

Calla wasn't quite running, but almost as she started through the yard toward them. Then she turned and went back to get Dirk, who had stopped at the yard gate. Lincoln was with them too, but he took off around the house.

"I don't want to get you wet," Calla said when Rose held out an arm to her.

"I'll dry." Rose drew her into their embrace and looked over the girls' heads at Dirk. "Thank you," she whispered.

"I didn't run away." Sienna pushed back from her to say. "I didn't. Really. My crows brought me something I was afraid for Uncle Dirk to see. I wanted to throw it in the river, but when I got to the river, I couldn't. I don't know why except it thundered really loud and that scared me like it was telling me not to. And then Calla and Lincoln found me and Calla said I couldn't hide it and Uncle Dirk came and I tried to throw it in the river again but Maisy grabbed my skirt and kept me from getting to the water and Uncle Dirk saw the necklace and fell down. I thought he was sick but he was sad instead, I think."

"Whoa." Rose held up her hand. "Slow down." She looked over Sienna's and Calla's heads at Dirk. "Are you all right?"

"I will be," he said.

She blinked, trying to take it in. "I'm not sure I understand."

"I'll explain things to you, but the girls are soaked. Maybe they should find some dry clothes," he said. "Then we can get breakfast. I promised them hot cocoa after Lincoln brings the milk to the house."

"Yes, that sounds good." Rose pushed them away and shooed them toward the door. "Go. Change."

Calla looked back, obviously reluctant to miss out on whatever Dirk was ready to explain, but she shook her head slightly and followed Sienna inside.

A tremble ran through Rose and she looked for something to catch to steady herself. Dirk stepped closer to offer his arm. She took it gratefully and let him help her to the lounger on the porch. Once she was seated, he tucked the blanket around her.

When Cricket appeared out of nowhere to jump into her lap with a meow of complaint, they both laughed a little. That broke the tension building between them.

Rose stroked the cat and looked up at Dirk. "So, what did Sienna's crows find this time?"

He reached in his pocket and pulled out a necklace. "Anneliese's grandmother's locket. I never saw Anneliese when she wasn't wearing it."

Rose took the necklace from him. She looked from the dirt-encrusted gold filigrees on the locket to Dirk's face. "I'm not sure what I read in your eyes. Sorrow? Relief? Joy? Or none of those."

"Maybe some of all. I don't know if I can explain." He pulled in a breath and let it out slowly. "I did love Anneliese more than life. All these years I've thought she ran away, rejected me after the fire. Now I know she didn't."

"Why does finding this change your thoughts?" She held up the locket.

"Anneliese treasured that gift from her grandmother. She would have never thrown it away or stopped looking for it had she lost it."

"So?" Rose frowned.

"That locket means she didn't give up on our love. She must have died in the fire after all." He was silent for a moment before he went on. "Maybe it seems wrong, but knowing she didn't leave me is a kind of relief, even if I do feel guilty for doubting her love. I should have searched for the truth and not waited until some crows brought it to me."

"Through a child." Rose rubbed the locket between her fingers. Something about it bothered her. "Do you think this would have come through so undamaged in a fire that left no trace of Anneliese? You did say that was true, didn't you?"

His face changed and she worried he was going to be angry at her words. Then he reached to take the necklace back. Even part of the chain was still intact.

She reached to touch his arm. "I'm sorry. I shouldn't have questioned that."

"No. You're right. I don't need to accept more untruths about Anneliese." He sighed and reached into his pocket to pull out an envelope. "Lincoln's mother sent me this. Lincoln says she told him it has answers." He fingered the envelope. "I'm not sure I'm brave enough to open it."

"Would you rather read it when you're by yourself?" Rose moved to get up, even though the cat protested.

"No need disturbing Cricket. If I want to be alone, I can go, but I don't want to be alone, Rose. Ever again." He held the letter out toward her. "Would you read it to me? Help me figure out the truth?"

She hesitated to take it. "Are you sure? It could be personal."

"I'm sure. Please."

She couldn't turn him down. Her fingers shook a little as she pulled the letter free of the envelope. There were three sheets folded together. The two inner sheets were yellowed with age. She unfolded the outer one.

"Dear Mr. Dirk," she read. "I should have given you this a long time back but I worried what it might do to Lincoln. I didn't want him to be hurt more than he was already by his pa dying and how he died. I wanted Lincoln to think it wasn't on purpose but I guess it was wrong trying to lie to him even if I did have noble intentions. And you never seemed worried that much about it all. But I reckon sometimes a person doesn't show his worry. I hope you can find it in your heart to forgive me after you read Jerome's last note."

Rose looked up at Dirk. "This must be his suicide note."

"I think so."

She picked up the yellowed sheets. "Do you want me to keep reading now that we know what it is?"

"If it won't upset you, I'd like for us to both hear it at the same time."

"All right." She unfolded the letter and scanned the first few words before she started reading aloud. "I'm sorry, Mary. I love you and our boy, but I can't live with what happened with Anneliese any longer. It's haunting me, tearing my heart out."

Rose had to swallow back the sadness of those words before she could go on. "You knew Anneliese. How pretty she was. How good she was. I should have found a way to protect her or found a way to keep her from sneaking off to meet Dirk Meadows instead of keeping her secret. But she was so in love and I hadn't ever heard anything all that bad about Dirk. Later I reckon I should of stayed away from Frank but how I let him talk me into gambling away our money didn't have anything to do with Dirk and Anneliese."

Rose dropped her hand holding the letter down in her lap as she remembered Lincoln's accusations from the day before. "Did Frank cause this?"

"I'm sorry." Dirk reached over and took the letter from her. "I wouldn't have asked you to read it if I'd thought about him writing something about Frank."

"What did Frank do to this poor man? To his family?" she insisted.

Dirk seemed to consider what to say before he answered. "You know how Frank was. Always trying to get something for nothing."

"Yes, go on." Rose had never hidden from that truth.

Dirk sighed. "Frank and Jerome got to know one another after the fire. I didn't pay it much notice. Like I told you, Jerome did his best to avoid me. But I was closing off everybody back then, even Frank. It was the only way I could keep living. I didn't know until after Jerome died that Frank talked him into some bad investments. He lost almost all the money he got from selling the family farm."

"I see." She reached toward the letter he held. "You want me to finish reading it?"

"Maybe I should just read it myself. I don't want you to be troubled by what he wrote about Frank." He looked down at the letter. As he read, his expression went from anger to despair. His head and shoulders drooped over and he stared at the ground without saying anything. The letter fell from his hands.

She reached to pick it up. "Do you mind if I read the rest?"

"You can. If you want." His voice was muffled since he didn't look up. "There's nothing else about Frank."

She looked down at the letter again. The poor man's handwriting was shaky as it continued.

Pa didn't aim to kill her. I know he didn't. It was an accident, but he feared what the sheriff might think. And Ma. She never knew until I told her when she was on her deathbed. I don't think she ever had a true happy day thinking Anneliese just left her without a word. But Pa made me promise to keep it secret. Anneliese was running away to marry Dirk. Pa had locked her in her room, saying he'd keep her there forever before he let her marry a Meadows. But Anneliese was as bull-headed as him. She tied some sheets

*together and climbed out her window just as it was
getting daylight. I was down on the ground to catch
her if she fell. She aimed to sneak off, but Pa saw
her and went after her. I took off after them hoping I
could do something. Pa was a terror when he got mad
like that. He didn't catch her until she got to the river
along beside that high cliff area. She had a path where
she climbed down through the rocks. I'd watched her
do it plenty while holding my breath thinking she'd
slip, but she was surefooted and claimed it was the best
place to wade across down at the bottom. Pa grabbed
her before she could go over the edge. She fought him
like a crazed wildcat, and he slapped her so hard her
head had to be spinning. He went to hit her again and
I grabbed his arm. He turned loose of her to slug me.
She might have got away then if she hadn't leaned
down to make sure I was okay.*

Rose shut her eyes a moment, imagining too well the desperate scene on the river cliff. One that wasn't going to end
well. Dirk paced back and forth, with the words no doubt
burning into his mind. His dog paced with him, watching
his every movement.

She took a breath and started reading again.

*Pa jerked her up from me and slung her aside. The
wrong direction. The direction toward the cliff. She
stumbled and couldn't catch herself. Her scream as she
fell haunts me. That and the sound of her hitting those
rocks. There was a splash and then nothing. Pa sank
down on the ground like he'd been shot. I scrambled*

up and somehow made it down to the river. I don't remember much about that. She was under the water. I pulled her out, but it was too late. She was gone. There was blood on her head where she'd hit the rocks. I stood there holding her up out of the water and cried like a baby until Pa came down where we were and smacked me. Told me weren't nothing to do now but hide her somehow so's he wouldn't go to prison. I told him it was an accident, but he said those Meadows would see that the sheriff thought it was murder. And I reckon in a way it was. He said we'd take her on across the river so that if anybody found her body they'd blame it on Meadows. Faulty thinking when I consider it now, but I wasn't thinking good at the time. Pa wasn't either. We took her to the barn where I knew she met up with Dirk. Pa said we'd put her under the hay and then set the barn on fire. It'd stormed in the night and folks would think lightning caused it. But then when we got to the barn, Pa saw a couple of shovels. We both felt better about burying her instead of burning her. If there was any way to feel better. We dug as fast as we could, not knowing when Meadows might show up. Once we got it done, I prayed over her, but I think it was me and Pa I should've been praying for. Pa found a coal oil lantern and he had matches for lighting his pipe. So we set the barn on fire and went on home.

Pa told me to put it behind me. What was done was done. And somehow I did, may the Lord forgive me. At least for a spell. You helped with that, Mary. And little Lincoln. But lately what he did, what we did has tore me up. I just can't bear up under the guilt anymore. I pray the Lord and you can forgive me. I know you'll raise our boy to be a good man.

She folded the note.

"Tear it up," Dirk said.

"No. Lincoln needs to take it back to his mother. It's hers to keep or destroy."

His face crumpled.

"Come here, Dirk." She lifted the cat out of her lap and reached toward Dirk, who knelt beside her chair and laid his head in her lap as he sobbed. She stroked his hair. "Dear Dirk. I'm so sorry."

"I should have known she wouldn't leave me." He raised his head to look at her. Maisy pushed in beside him.

She ignored the dog and put her hands on Dirk's cheeks. "I think you did know. You just couldn't understand how that could be true."

"But don't you see? Instead of her betraying me, I betrayed her." His tears were gone, but the sorrow in his eyes went deeper than tears. "I don't know how I can live with that. With how I failed her."

"We all fall short, Dirk. In the last two years I have felt such a failure as a mother with my girls in an orphanage."

"But you couldn't help that."

She gentled her eyes on him. She hated seeing him so upset. "And you couldn't help this."

"But—"

"Shh." She held up a hand to stop him. "There are so many times we wish we could go back and do things over, but we can't. We can only ask forgiveness."

345

"You mean from the Lord?" He didn't wait for her to answer. "I do believe the Lord will forgive me, but would Anneliese? If I could even ask her for such."

"If she truly loved you, and from the little I know of your story, I think she surely did, she would." She looked at him for a long moment before she went on. "But the person you need to ask for forgiveness, the person you need most to forgive, is yourself."

"Me?" That silenced him for a moment before he said, "I'm not sure I can."

"I think you must. You see what happened to this poor man who could not forgive himself for something he couldn't change." She held up the letter. "And what that did to his family."

"Family." Something in his face changed. "For so many years, I have had no family. But now . . ." He let his words slide away.

"But now you have us."

"Do I, Rose?" Again he hesitated. "Will you still consider being my family?"

"I already am."

"Even more than you are now." His eyes burned into hers. "Be my family as my wife?"

"You need to give me time. Give yourself time." She smiled to soften her words. "You need to grieve for Anneliese first."

"And you need to grieve for Frank?"

"No." She shook her head. "I grieved for Frank after he died, but then life continued on."

"Anneliese has been gone longer than Frank. Many years longer."

"Gone, but until now you were never sure if she was truly

gone. Right now your heart is divided between the past and the present." She kept her eyes locked on his.

"I can't lose you both on the same day."

"You haven't lost me. I'm not leaving. I'll be right here with the girls."

"So you will marry me?"

He looked so in need of hope that she couldn't deny him. She didn't want to deny him. "When the time is right."

"When will that be?"

"I can't say for sure. But if I'm well enough, we can marry when the maple here in the yard turns golden." She looked up at the tree with its fresh green leaves. "If you are still sure that is what you want when fall comes."

"I'll be sure."

"Then Lord willing, I think so shall I."

Maisy seemed reassured enough by their voices now that she lay down beside the chair.

Dirk said, "Should we tell the girls?"

Rose smiled. "I wouldn't be surprised to find Calla listening at the door." She gave him her hand. "Help me up and we'll go see."

But Calla wasn't at the door. Instead, Sienna met them there. "Come on. Calla says the pancakes are going to get cold and Lincoln says he's going to starve."

"Pancakes?" Dirk said. "My mother always made pancakes for special occasions."

"It is a special occasion." Sienna grabbed Dirk's hand and then Rose's to tug them through the dining room to the kitchen.

"Oh?" Rose had to wonder if Sienna had been eavesdropping instead of Calla.

Sienna's face lit up as she looked up at Rose. "Uncle Dirk says we can live here at Meadowland forever. Forever is a long, long time."

"So it is," Rose said.

"A perfect time." Dirk smiled over at Rose.

"Yes, I think it will be." Rose smiled back at Dirk and was suddenly very sure that was true.

35

*T*he next week on the first day of June, Dirk stood in the family graveyard as they laid Anneliese to rest. He'd found her and would have months ago if he hadn't avoided the site of the barn. Over the years, floodwaters had washed away the ground to reveal where Anneliese's father and brother had buried her.

The sheriff and coroner came out. He had considered not involving the authorities with so many years gone by, but Rose said he had to go for them.

"Too many secrets have been kept for too many years," she had argued.

"But it means Lincoln will have to know."

"Lincoln already knows the part most painful for him. While his mother tried to shield him from the truth, he knew that his father committed suicide. He didn't know why. This might actually help him. There's no blame for his father in Anneliese's death. No blame for anyone really. At least not now."

"Only mine," he said.

"No, not yours either." She had taken his hand in hers.

"But if I hadn't gone to confront her father. If—"

She put her fingers over his lips to stop him saying more. "Remember the need for forgiveness. There are always ifs," she said. "But when we can't change those things, we have to give ourselves grace even when we do wonder if we could have done this or that differently. You may have made mistakes with Anneliese. But then who among us hasn't made mistakes? Her death was a tragic accident."

That was what the sheriff and coroner decided after they read Jerome's letter and talked to Mary Rainsley. Even if there was fault to place on Anneliese's father, he was beyond earthly punishment now.

But it wasn't right to leave Anneliese there on the riverbank. She deserved a proper burial. Dirk hired the undertaker to come collect her remains in a proper coffin for burial in the Meadows family graveyard. She would have been family with a Meadows name had things turned out the way they had hoped. Reverend Moore from Glenville came out to say words at her graveside. Rose managed the walk to the family cemetery. She and the girls stood with him, along with Lincoln and his mother. And Maisy. Dirk had no more tears. The time for tears seemed past now.

Calla brought roses from the yard to lay on her grave and on her father's grave as well. Sienna brought an armload of daisies from the meadow to scatter with the roses. That only seemed right when he thought of his and Anneliese's plans to marry when the meadow bloomed.

After the preacher finished, Rose turned the girls back to the house. Lincoln and his mother followed to leave Dirk alone to say his final goodbyes.

Beautiful Anneliese. His love for her would ever live in his heart, but thinking of her no longer brought a piercing pain. Instead, her memory settled into a treasured place in his mind. They had loved each other so desperately, and it could be, if she'd come away with him that day after he talked to her father, they could have had a good life together. One without the scars both physically and emotionally he'd carried with him through the years. But their chance for happiness had been lost in tragedy.

Now he was ready for a different sort of love. This joining with Rose would accept the sorrows and joys of the past while building a new future for them as a family.

In time. Rose was right. He did need time to grieve this final chapter of his love for Anneliese.

He put his hand in his pocket and pulled out the locket. He had thought to bury it with Anneliese, but instead he remembered Sienna clutching the locket and not being able to throw it in the river. He would return to her what her crows had given her. She could embrace the love in the locket now.

While the paper Anneliese's grandmother had enclosed in the locket all those years ago had disintegrated, the words lived on in his memory. *Love never dies*. He would share them with Sienna and with Calla too. Share some of Anneliese's story and her love.

"Goodbye, Anneliese." He recalled all the many times he'd said those words on the riverbank and had never been able to completely let her go. But now the words freed him to move forward, and he felt her smile in his heart.

He could almost hear her saying, "It's about time you figured things out, college boy."

He smiled as he turned toward the house. Maisy looked back at him to be sure he was coming before she ran ahead to where Sienna waited at the yard gate. Then, as if Sienna couldn't wait another minute, the child came up the path toward him. As natural as breathing, he let her take his hand. Love felt good.

36

$\mathscr{S}$ummer passed in a whirl of gardening for Calla. Miss Mary, Lincoln's mother, came to help her can the produce and make jams. Calla didn't mind the work. The sight of jars of beans, tomatoes, and blackberry jam lined on the cabinet gave her a feeling of security. This was going to last. Sienna did her part to help too, even though she would have rather been finding new friends in the meadow. Mama was okay with the toads and tortoises but told her she had to leave the snakes in the field. Uncle Dirk laughed and made sure Sienna knew which snakes to not bother. How very good it was to hear his laughter joining theirs in the house.

The time at the Home for Girls hardly entered Calla's mind or Sienna's either. They'd shed that time the same as Sienna's snakes shed their skins or the land tortoises shook loose their shells when new ones pushed the old ones away.

They were home.

This felt even more sure when Calla stood with Mama, and Lincoln with Uncle Dirk, under the maple tree in the yard after its leaves turned golden in the fall. Their voices were strong and sure as they vowed their love for richer and poorer, in sickness and health.

Sienna giggled when they said "I do," and Calla wanted to burst into song. Even Maisy must have felt the joy as she barked her approval.

The preacher pronounced them man and wife, and Uncle Dirk embraced Mama. Then everybody was smiling and Calla couldn't stop herself. She did start singing. "Praise God from whom all blessings flow."

Mama joined in and then Uncle Dirk did too. "Praise him, all creatures here below."

Sienna and Miss Mary added their voices. Reverend Moore looked more than a little surprised, but he shrugged and started singing with them too. "Praise him above, ye heavenly host."

And then so did Lincoln on the last line. "Praise Father, Son, and Holy Ghost. Amen."

Amen and amen and amen. The Lord had answered her prayers and made them a family with a forever home.

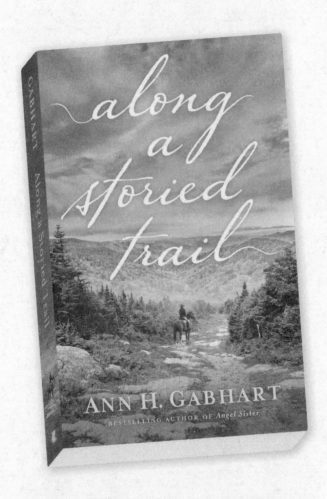

1

*E*verybody thought Tansy Calhoun was heartbroken after Jeremy Simpson threw her over for Jolene Hoskins. Or that she should be. She had to admit her pride was bruised, but the whole thing was simply a shin bump in life. In fact, after pondering it some, she decided she'd gotten the best of things.

Of course, that had been some while back. Three years, when she counted it up. Jolene had a baby now, with another on the way. That could have been Tansy if she'd gone down the path folks thought she was ready to take. Married at seventeen. A mother at eighteen. Worn out by thirty, with more children than she had chairs around her kitchen table. A poor man's riches, some said. That was about the only riches a man was apt to see here in the mountains in 1937.

Family did matter. Tansy wasn't against marrying and having her fair share of children, but she was glad enough to put it off a while. Longer than most around here thought sensible. Marrying young and for forever was the way of life in these Eastern Kentucky hills. A person should marry with the intention of staying married forever, but that could still be a long time even if you waited a while for forever to start.

Her own mother had been eighteen when Tansy was born and

she wasn't the firstborn. Her sister Hilda was nigh on two when Tansy came along. Hilda married young too, but that wasn't because she was following in Ma's footsteps. She had in mind to escape mountain life by marrying the schoolteacher and happily going off with him to live up in Ohio somewhere. Hilda sent a letter now and again and sometimes a book for Tansy, but no word of any babies on the way. Ma worried some about that.

She worried about Tansy even more. Ma was glad enough to still have her home to help with things. She needed the help. Giving birth to Livvy, the least one who was only four, had stolen her health. Did something to her hip so that moving was ever painful. She said Livvy might need to be her last and sounded sad about that, although Tansy thought five a fine number. Well, six. She couldn't forget her little brother Robbie, who got the fever and died when he was seven. He did count. Dear little Robbie. The sweetest of the bunch. Way sweeter than Tansy. But Livvy was turned sweet too.

Took that after their ma. Not their pa. Might be a blessing Pa took off on them last September. Him being gone would be a sure way to save her mother from the ordeal of carrying another baby.

Looking for work, Pa told Ma. No work was to be had here in the mountains. Coal mines had mostly shut down, with nobody having money to buy anything since what they called Black Tuesday happened off in New York City. Tansy still hadn't quite gotten her mind around how rich people losing their money through something they called a ticker tape had leaked down to close mines and bring such hard times to Robins Ridge. Didn't people still need coal to keep the fires in their grates burning? At least those who didn't have trees to cut for firewood.

But Pa never liked the mines anyway. Said working down under the ground stole his breath. Sometimes at night he did seem to do more coughing than breathing.

Ma hadn't wanted him to go. Tansy heard them talking the night before he left. Her bed in the loft was right over theirs, and she often covered her ears with her pillow to keep from hearing more than she should. But this time she'd done the opposite and leaned off the side of the bed to catch every word when she heard the pleading in her mother's voice.

"Joshua, looks to me it would be best you stayin' here. Little Josh can help you do the farming. We can get by."

Pa's voice rumbled in return. "Unless another dry spell comes along. Corn don't grow without rain, Eugenia. You saw that this year, what with the beans drying up in your sass patch and some of the corn ears no more than nubbins."

"We had enough sass to get by." Ma didn't like admitting her vegetable garden didn't supply food enough for their table. "I made pickles. We got some of the early planting for shucky beans. They're hung up all over the attic."

Her father didn't say anything for so long that Tansy about decided he'd let Ma have the last word and gone to sleep. But then he said, "It ain't your fault, Eugenia. Ain't mine either. The Lord just didn't send us no rain."

"The Lord supplies our needs."

Tansy heard the absolute certainty in Ma's voice. She refused to hear complaints against the Lord. Even when Robbie died. She had sat by Robbie's bed night and day, praying fervently for him to get well. But once the boy's breaths stopped, she folded his little hands together, kissed his forehead, and accepted it as the Lord's will. She didn't war against that, like Tansy wanted to. Or like Pa did. He'd gone off and not come back until after the neighbors dug a grave and helped lay Robbie to rest. Ma said that was the only way Pa could take losing a son.

"At times better than other times." Pa sounded worn out. "Lately he must not be paying much mind to what folks is needin' down here."

That went too far for Ma. "I'm thinking you best offer up a prayer for the Lord to open your eyes to the blessings he sends down to us."

"Maybe so." Pa's voice gentled. "Be that as it may, I see how you never put much on your plate at suppertime. If I head out to find work somewheres, that'll be one less mouth at the table. Tansy and Josh are old enough to take care of things around here."

"Tansy might find a feller and get married."

Tansy couldn't decide if Ma sounded worried or hopeful about that. Maybe resigned to their fates, whatever they were.

Pa made a sound of disgust. "She had a good enough feller and let him get away. That's been over two years back and I haven't seen no boys making paths to our door. The girl turned twenty in July. She ain't liable to find a suitor less'n a widower comes along. Maybe not then if she don't get her head out of them books. Hilda hasn't done us no favors sending storybooks that's got Tansy thinking above herself."

Thinking above herself. Those words had made her want to get up and climb down the steps to tell her father a few things. Like she had a right to think. To read. She didn't slack off helping Ma, but in stolen moments, books took her beyond the mountains. Let her fly like an eagle to take in the view of other places and ways.

That didn't mean she didn't want to roost right where she was. She loved the mountains. Time and again she did let a little daydream tickle her mind. That maybe a prince on a white stallion might ride into her life the way it happened sometimes in fairy tales. Not really a prince, but a man with aplomb. She'd discovered that word a while back and studied out what it might mean. A man who was handsome. Self-confident. Capable. Like the men in the stories she read.

She had lain stiff in her bed while the words she wanted to throw at her father boiled in her head. She never got the chance to say any of them. The next morning he was gone.

Books had always been a bone of contention between them. Once he'd even jerked a book from her to sling into the fire. She had a scar on her hand from yanking the book out of the flames. The page edges were charred, but the words were saved. After that, Tansy hid out to read. In the hayloft. In a tree during the summer. In the loft, crouched beside her bed near the half window as soon as light dawned.

Her pa might change his mind about books if he could see her now. Her love of reading had opened up a way for her to be a packhorse librarian, since it turned out she wasn't alone in thinking books mattered. The government did too and had established a work program to get books to people in these Eastern Kentucky mountains where roads a truck could travel were few and far between. Women like Tansy on mules and horses took books to the people.

Sometimes Tansy thought every prayer she'd ever thought to pray and some she hadn't thought up had been answered the day she got one of the book routes here in Owsley County. Then on top of the pure pleasure of working with books, to get paid for it. Let people feel sorry for her because they thought she was on an old maid's path. She wasn't ready for a rocking chair on a relative's front porch yet. She had time to find a man to love.

But now, she had a horse, access to more books than she had time to read, and money to keep food on her mother's table. She'd felt practically rich the first time she collected her monthly wages. Twenty-eight dollars.

Not that she didn't earn every penny. Her route was over some rough ground, up and down steep hills, through creeks and woods. And she couldn't let the weather stop her. Rain, sleet, or snow, she had promised Madeline Weston to faithfully ride her routes.

Mrs. Weston, the head librarian, had found a room in the back of an old store building in Booneville for their central location. She talked some local men into building shelves along the walls and then sent out a plea for book donations. Tansy had carried the few she had down to the library even before she was hired. Without books, a library was nothing more than a quiet room. Others had brought in books and magazines too, and the headquarters of the women's work programs in London, Kentucky, sent them a few boxes of books. Little by little, the place was beginning to look like a real library.

"We have to make this work," Mrs. Weston told Tansy when she traced out her route. Three other women had routes in other parts of the county. "The people who live in your area will depend on you making your rounds on a regular schedule. Winter coming on doesn't make things easy, but when was anything ever easy for us up here in the hills?"

November had gifted them with some fine fall weather. Riding her route had been a pleasure. Then December was nothing to complain about. But January came in cold and mean.

Rain had poured down all night, and now ice pellets stung Tansy's face as she rode away from the barn to start her route. She was relieved to see snowflakes mixing with the rain, even if that did mean the temperature had dropped. Snow made for better footing for her horse than ice.

Easy or not, Tansy was glad to head down the hill with her saddlebags loaded with books on this first Monday in the new year. She reined in her horse at the edge of Mad Dog Creek. Well named, she thought every time she crossed it. The creek could be a sweet, flowing stream, or it could turn evil when rains brought the tides. Flatlanders thought it odd to call floods *tides*, but that might be because they'd never seen tides of creek water sweeping down the mountains after a downpour.

Tansy stroked her horse's neck. She leased Shadrach, a Morgan gelding, from Preacher Rowlett, who lived at the bottom of Robins Ridge. Their mule was so old he'd give out if she tried to ride him on the miles of her rounds each week. Preacher Rowlett promised Shadrach would be sure-footed on the rough trails, and a person could depend on what Preacher said. Not that he was really a preacher. At least not one with a church pulpit and all, but he did know his Bible and could be counted on to say words at a funeral whenever no bona fide preachers were around.

He was right about Shadrach. The white stockings on his front legs were the only thing fancy about the horse, but Tansy didn't need fancy. She needed willing. Shadrach was that. If she pointed him up the side of a hill, he did his best to climb it, although sometimes Tansy got off and walked to make it easier for him.

"What do you think, boy?" she asked now as the water churned past them. She weighed her options. Heading down the creek for what might be a better crossing place would put her off schedule. Crossing here would be cold and wet.

When she flicked the reins, she wasn't sure if Shadrach was game to give the creek a try or simply resigned. He shook his head slightly and stepped into the water. Tansy gasped as the water sloshed over her boot tops and soaked the wool pants she'd borrowed from her brother. She twisted around to grab her saddlebags of books and lift them above the water.

She let the reins hang loose to give Shadrach his head. The gelding would get through the creek. All she had to do was not fall off. And keep those books dry. Books were hard to come by, and she wasn't about to ruin her allotment.

Her feet were soaked by the time they climbed out of the creek, but the books were dry. After she settled the saddlebags back down on Shadrach's flanks, she stopped the horse to dump water out of her boots. Then nothing for it but to stick her wet feet back in those boots and head up the hill. Her pant legs stiffened and froze in the frigid wind.

She could warm up at her next stop, Jenny Sue Barton's house. Poor woman had lost her husband a few months back when a tree fell on him. A dark cloud had settled down over her house after that, what with her son, Reuben Jr., falling sick with an ailment nobody had exactly figured out. They'd fetched in a doctor from the next county who didn't have any more answers than the granny healer, Geraldine Abrams, who'd concocted a tonic for the boy. The doctor said to feed him eggs to build up his strength and time would heal him. A boy of six should shake off whatever was ailing him.

Reuben Jr.'s grandmother claimed that was the first town

doctor with sense. While he hadn't come right out and said it, he'd tiptoed all around how losing his pa had bruised the boy's heart. Until that healed some, they simply needed to be patient and do what they could to give him something to think about besides missing his pa.

Tansy was glad to help with that. She always stayed long enough at their house to read some from *The Life and Adventures of Robinson Crusoe*. A while reading aloud to bring cheer to the Bartons' worried cabin seemed little enough to do, and as a book woman, she was supposed to find ways to awaken people to the joy of books.

Today, she could dry out her boots while she read more of Crusoe's adventures and taught young Reuben some new words. Learning to read did seem to lift some of the sorrow off the boy. *Snow* might be a good word for him to learn this day.

2

The weather was mean. Worse than mean. Wicked. Rain, sleet, snow. All at once. Caleb Barton shivered. He tried to fasten his mind on how hot he'd been last summer down in Tennessee working with the Civilian Conservation Corps to make trails up into the Smoky Mountains. He'd been glad enough to do the work and thankful he'd been sent down south to the mountains instead of stuck in a city hauling rocks for bridge abutments, digging ditches, or whatever. He was happiest with his feet on a mountain.

After being in the Smokies, the Kentucky mountains here in Owsley County didn't seem near as big as they had when he was a boy. The Appalachian Mountains were old, worn down from centuries of standing in this place. He straightened up from the tree he was working up for firewood and peered across the hill. Couldn't see much with the snow clouds hanging low. But he didn't need to see the hills to know what they looked like. Worn down or not, they were home, and he was glad to be standing here on one of them even with the cold seeping through him.

He looked back at the tree he'd felled. He needed to trim off the branches and then saw a piece of the trunk into a size his mule could pull back to the house. Ebenezer, hunched up over to the side, looked longingly in the direction of his barn. The animal was more than ready to be out of the weather, but a work mule knew to wait.

"All right, Ebenezer. I'll quit woolgathering and get this done." Caleb spoke aloud as though the mule would know what he was saying. Ebenezer. He couldn't imagine what had possessed his brother to name his mule Ebenezer. A mule needed a name you could yell. Like Joe or Bud.

But Reuben always did have a fanciful streak. Caleb smiled, thinking about the brother only a couple of years older than him. At the same time, his heart clenched with grief. He did miss Reuben. It didn't seem right him being taken while Caleb was away working with the Corps. Made it not seem real, like Reuben might just come out of the trees and ask Caleb why he didn't bring the two-man saw.

But in November, Reuben had cut his last tree. Nobody for sure knew what happened. Whether Reuben didn't notch the tree right or maybe the tree had a weak side he didn't notice, but something had gone wrong. Tragically wrong.

Caleb's ma said Jenny Sue didn't get worried at first when Reuben didn't come in for supper. But then Ebenezer had come back to the barn. By himself. With night falling. Ma said Jenny Sue was beside herself when she came across the field to Ma's house.

Ma shook her head as she told Caleb about it when he came home after his enlistment time with the Civilian Conservation Corps was up in December.

"That Jenny Sue is a sweet child and pretty as a spring flower," she said, "but fortitude ain't never been her strong suit. Jest as well I was the one to go huntin' for Reuben 'stead of her." Ma swallowed hard but didn't let any tears fall. "'Twas a wonder I come up on him at all in the dark. Figured the Lord must have led me to him. Poor boy. That tree had him pinned tight to the ground. The day had turned cold the way it can once we edge toward winter. Gone to raining some, the kind of rain that ain't exactly sleet but don't feel far from it. So he was chilled to the bone. Didn't hardly know where he was at when I first knelt down beside him. He shook that off and come back to his senses when I put my hand on his cheek. It was cold as death."

Caleb had reached over and taken her hand that felt cold to his touch the way Reuben's cheek must have felt to her that night. "You don't have to tell me everything about it if it's too hard."

"No." She shook her head. "A man should know about his brother dying. The two of you was always nigh on close as twins."

She was right. In fact, he'd felt a strange uneasiness about home even before the letter reached him down there in the Smokies.

"All right then," he said. She needed to say the words. To put him down there with her on the ground by his brother.

They'd been in front of the fireplace, her in the grapevine rocker Reuben made her some years before. He'd always had a way about him, ready to try anything. The rockers had been the hard part and he'd finally given over that job to Caleb. He knew Caleb would figure it out and make it work. Caleb had watched his mother rocking back and forth and felt a flare of anger at Reuben for whatever he'd done to get himself killed.

Then sorrow drowned that out as he waited for her to

say more. She stared at the flames leaping up around the wood he'd just laid on the fire. The cabin he and Reuben built for her was small. Just two rooms, but the fireplace was big. Spread halfway across the back wall. It had taken them days to gather enough rocks for the chimney. When he made it home last week, Caleb had been happy to see smoke drifting up out of their chimney, still standing strong on the side of the cabin.

For a bit, Ma had rocked back and forth as if letting the words build in her. "He'd been trapped there for a good spell, but he could still talk a little. Weren't easy for him and I had to lean down close to hear." She paused again. "I can still feel his breath on my ear."

Caleb didn't say anything, but he wanted to be anywhere but sitting in that straight-back chair with the fire heating up his face while he heard how his brother died. Not that shutting out the words would make them any less true. Reuben would still be gone.

Her voice was soft when she started talking again. "I didn't tell Jenny Sue ever'thing he said. Just about how much he cared for her and the children. Having to leave his young'uns was a pain worse than any he was feeling from the tree on him. I hurt for him and tried to get him to hush. Told him we'd pray and the good Lord might lift the tree and he'd find out he weren't hurt so bad after all. I was already prayin' underneath my words, but there is times prayers don't move mountains. Or trees."

"Did he say what happened?"

"I never asked him that. Didn't seem to matter none then with whatever it was havin' done happened."

"I guess not." She was right. Knowing what happened

wouldn't bring his brother back, but for some reason it seemed something he needed to know.

"Don't let it trouble you, son. I know how you like to put reasons behind things. That's where you and Reuben were always different. You reasoned it out and he . . ." She paused as a little smile slipped across her face. "And he, he just ran after whatever he saw out ahead."

Caleb didn't say anything to that. He knew Reuben was their mother's favorite. That never bothered Caleb all that much. Reuben was Caleb's favorite too. Everybody's favorite. He said he hadn't ever seen the need to make an enemy. And when he had now and again got on somebody's wrong side through some unintended, often careless cause, he let Caleb take care of settling things down.

Caleb had thought it would be good for him to be gone for a while. That would make Reuben step up and figure ways to take care of his own messes, but Caleb hadn't thought he'd die from one of those times. Caleb was glad when his mother started talking again so he could push away the feeling that if he'd been there, he could have kept his brother from being taken down by a tree. Caleb liked trees. Felt a kinship with the woods on their place, and now one of them had stolen his brother from him.

"Like I said, I didn't tell Jenny Sue Reuben's every last word. At the time I was hopin' with ever'thing in me that there'd be plenty more words for him to share with her. But I reckon you need to hear them."

"Not if they were for Jenny Sue."

"I didn't say they were for her. They was about her. And you." His mother looked straight at Caleb then. "I ain't sure you'll be wantin' to hear them, but I can't not pass them along."

Caleb wanted to shut his ears, but that wouldn't stop his mother's words.

"He said he always thought you were some sweet on Jenny Sue and that he'd take it as a favor if you'd see to her and his young'uns. That maybe you could take his place. Be a daddy to them." She rocked back and forth twice before she went on. "A husband to her."

Caleb held his breath a few seconds and then blew it out slowly. "I'll do what I can for his family, Ma. You know I will. See they have what they need." He looked straight at his mother. "But I'm not marrying my brother's widow. Reuben was deluded thinking I was ever sweet on Jenny Sue. Or that she'd ever be sweet on me."

"That's how Bible people used to do things," his mother said. "When a brother died, another brother took the man's widow as wife."

"But they weren't worried about how many wives they might have and it was just a way of giving them a roof. Besides, this isn't Bible times. It's the 1930s. Things aren't the same as when Jesus walked on the earth."

"No, I reckon not." His ma looked over at Caleb. "I ain't saying it's something you oughta do, but that don't keep you from needin' to know your brother's last words to you."

"Reuben didn't always think before he spoke."

"True enough, but he had time to think things out that day." She stared down at her lap and folded her apron in pleats. "I told him not to talk nonsense. That he'd be all right as soon as I got some men to carry him back to the house. That me and Jenny Sue would nurse him back to health. Then I had to leave him there in the dark. By hisself. I did leave the lantern. 'Twas the least I could do, but by the time

371

I got back with Frank Sims and his boy from down the way, my Reuben was past nursing. Preacher Rowlett said he'd been healed. Just not the healing we was wanting."

Caleb shook his head now to get the memory of his mother's words out of his thoughts. He needed to get finished with his own tree cutting and not think about his brother pinned to the ground, offering his wife to him. That wasn't something he wanted to even consider.

Not that he had any other woman in mind to marry. He was in love once. If he was honest, he had to admit he still carried feelings for her, but the girl he fell for had fallen for someone else. That's why he'd gone off the mountain to find work. Best thing for all of them. He didn't have to see the girl he loved married to another man, and once he went to work for the Corps, he had money to send home.

He bent back to the task at hand to get firewood for his mother and his brother's wife and children. He hadn't picked one of the big trees to cut. Those needed two men working a crosscut saw. He'd chosen a smaller one. Second growth. Most of the trees were second growth now. Settlers early on had cut the trees for cabins and to clear ground for corn, even if the hills were more suited for woods than crops. Then loggers had come in to cut the big trees and float them down the river to a sawmill. They left the hillsides scarred, but they brought jobs to the area. Back then before the market collapse, America had been building everywhere. Lumber was at a premium. Especially the American chestnuts growing across these hills and all through the eastern states.

Then a fungus rode in on the wind to take down the mighty trees. He'd heard it started in New York. That seemed too far away to be a worry, but the fungus had blown south to find more trees to kill.

Caleb wanted to straighten up and look around again to let his eyes rest on one of the rare chestnuts still standing. You couldn't tell the trees were dying in the winter. But they were. Some dead ones were gray trunks that served as signposts these days. But most everywhere, folks had come into the woods and taken down the chestnut giants. In the Smokies too. No reason to leave them standing to fall down. Might as well get the good out of the trees. But that left a mighty hole in the forests. There. And here.

Caleb sighed and kept working his axe. He might be foolish to mourn a tree. But it wasn't just one of them. It was thousands. He prayed the Lord would leave a few standing. That man would too. The mountains needed the chestnuts, but needs weren't always answered. Prayers either.

Or Reuben would be the one out here cutting wood for his family.

Acknowledgments

I have been blessed to have so many of my stories become novels for readers like you. Each story has its own path from the initial idea to finally being wrapped up in an attractive cover to catch your eyes so my words can come to life in your imaginations. I thank you, my readers, for trailing along with me down some varied story roads through small towns, Shaker villages, the big town of Louisville, the Appalachian Mountains, and now out to a farm called Meadowland for this story. I appreciate you choosing to read my books.

I am also blessed to work with all the people at Revell Books and Baker Publishing Company. My editor, Rachel McRae, gives every story her full attention to make it the best it can be. I thank Barb Barnes for her careful editing that has helped me be a better writer. I appreciate all Karen Steele and Michele Misiak do to get my books in readers' hands and for knowing the answers when I have questions. The art department wraps my books in great covers that are admired wherever they are on display. I know many more have a part in getting a book from writer to reader, and I'm grateful to each and every one of them.

My agent, Wendy Lawton, is always ready with encouragement, which I often need, as do most writers. However, I admit she has been known to laugh when I tell her, in the midst of writing, that my story is going nowhere before she reminds me to just keep writing. And so I do and another story gets told.

I can't thank my family enough for putting up with me disappearing along those story roads through my many years of writing. They have been unfailingly supportive.

Last and never least, I am forever thankful the Lord granted me the desires of my heart and gave me stories to share with you.

Ann H. Gabhart is the bestselling author of several Shaker novels—*The Refuge, The Outsider, The Believer, The Seeker, The Blessed,* and *The Gifted*—as well as other historical novels, including *These Healing Hills, River to Redemption, An Appalachian Summer,* and *Along a Storied Trail.* She and her husband live on a farm a mile from where she was born in rural Kentucky. Ann enjoys discovering the everyday wonders of nature while hiking in her farm's fields and woods with her grandchildren and her dogs, Frankie and Marley. Learn more at www.annhgabhart.com.

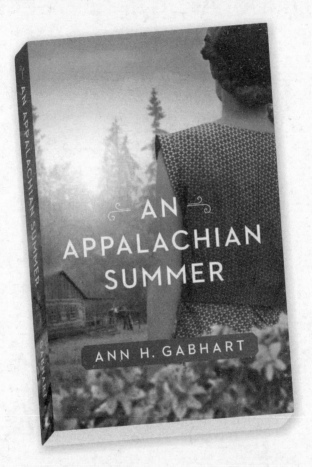

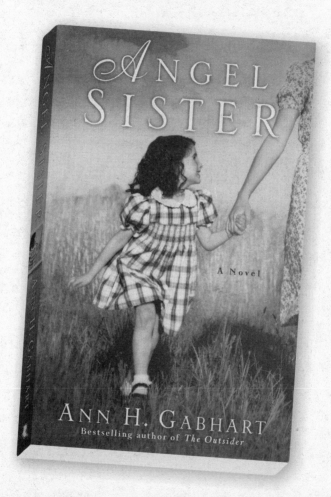

Meet
Ann H. Gabhart

Find out more about Ann's newest releases, read blog posts, and follow her on social media at

AnnHGabhart.com